EDEN'S ORE

SECRETS

Pat,

B. V. BAYLY

Welcome to
my world.

B.V.B.

PROMONTORY
P R E S S

EDEN'S ORE SECRETS
www.edens-ore.com

Copyright © 2014 by B. V. Bayly

Promontory Press
www.promontorypress.com

First Edition: May 2014

ISBN: 978-1-927559-45-1

Typeset in *Celestia* with *Felix Titling* display at SpicaBookDesign

Printed in Canada

ACKNOWLEDGMENTS

First, I would like to thank Bennett R. Coles and his team at Promontory Press for working so hard, and in such a short amount of time, to prepare my novel for the world. I will always be grateful for the opportunity and blessed by working with you all.

To Mary Rosenblum, my editor – you helped to clear away the fog and expose what I had worked so hard to show my readers. My mentor, Kathy Tyers – teaching someone to write and teaching someone to write a book are two very different things. I want to thank you for showing me the difference.

To my wife, who lovingly pushed me to pursue my dream and share my story with the world – you stayed beside me every step of the journey and didn't let me stray. This book is as much yours as it is mine. To my boys – without knowing it, you both took care of me on my rough days with a simple smile and snuggle. To my parents – thank you for never giving up on what you saw in my writing even when I didn't see it myself. To my father-in-law – I would not have walked down this road if you had not gently pointed out the way first. To my brother – our adventures are fuel for my stories. I hope they never stop. And to the many others who have all played a part in making this novel what it is, I thank you.

Above all else I want to praise God for giving me a creative spirit and opening the many doors needed for having my novel published.

CHAPTER ONE

AN EERIE SCREECH TORE THROUGH GABRIEL'S MIND, WAKING HIM FROM A PEACEFUL SLEEP. His eyes opened to darkness, the screech continuing to annoy him. He followed the sound to its source – his bedroom window. There, struggling under the force of a strong wind, a single branch from a nearby tree clawed the glass. *Seriously?*

Unwilling to endure the sound any longer, he sprang from his bed and marched to the window. He slid the stiff sash up, popping goose bumps all over his body. He shivered in the outside air as he snapped the branch off with a twist of his wrist, flinging it down to the ground. He shut the window firmly, looking forward to retreating back to his bed, when a flash from outside grabbed his attention. Another burst of light forked across the black sky, while thunder rolled in the distance.

They hadn't said there was going to be a storm tonight.

He stared across the northwest fields of the ranch, trying to decipher the dark clouds. Storms typically meant more work on the ranch for him in the morning. He glanced towards his nightstand.

The red glow of his clock flickered, as another minute ticked by. 3:38 am. He turned back towards the window and surveyed the yard. Something didn't feel right to him.

Hearing the livestock begin to stir, he glanced towards the barn. If there was a problem, Nate – a soldier-turned-ranch-hand and best friend to his father – would find it and fix it, regardless of the hour. The loft above the large barn doors was still dark. Where was Nate? *Probably asleep like every other sane person.* He shrugged off the ominous feeling and climbed back into his lukewarm bed. He squished his pillow into a ball as he rolled onto his side. 3:48 am.

Past the clock was a clear case that protected a mysterious glowing crystal. It was a memento from his father who had died when he was a boy. He lifted the case off the side table and balanced it on his chest. He knew every line and angle on the glowing shard as well as he knew his own face. It was the last thing his father had given him and was worth more to him than anything else he owned. He stared at it, watching its faded flow of light pulse across its sharp corners.

Lightning cracked just outside his window, followed instantly by an ear-splitting drum of thunder. The house rattled as more lightning struck nearby. He abandoned the crystal and scrambled out of bed, returning to his lookout at the window. Staring back at him in the weak morning light was a menacing black wall of clouds. Lightning streaked across its surface, cutting through the dark clouds as it connected wildly with the ground around it. The wall of black stretched up to the moon as it rolled towards the ranch, blanketing the fields in darkness. As the storm moved closer to the ranch, its surface began to distort and twist. Dirt and debris was scooped from the fields and hurled into the air by an invisible force. It twisted and spun around in a huge column, giving shape to a massive tornado.

My God.

His jaw dropped.

The black tornado sucked everything up in its path as it rolled across the fields towards the ranch. Gale force winds approached the yard, and terrified livestock cried out as the tornado shifted towards the barn and corrals. A loud bang echoed on the roof, his vision jerked upwards as the sound rapidly multiplied. With another bang, a golf-ball-sized hailstone slammed into his window. His muscles jolted at the sudden noise. He scrambled across his room, through the hallway and burst into his mother's bedroom.

"Mom!" He rushed to her side. She was already sitting up in bed, looking upwards at the ceiling. "We've got to go! Come on! We gotta lock down the house and get in the basement."

"Gabriel! Stop! What is happening?" She climbed out of bed, glancing from him to the ceiling and back.

"We've got a tornado coming across the plain, heading straight for us!" Gabriel grabbed his mother's dressing gown and threw it at her.

He ran back to his room. Pulling on the first pair of jeans he saw, he kicked at the other clothes sprawled across the floor, searching for a pair of shoes. A thump rolled across the floor as he uncovered them and crammed his feet into them. He whipped a T-shirt off his bedpost and pulled it over his head, fighting to get his arms through. Out his window, he could see the black wall of terror moving closer to the house. His mother shuffled into his room in her lime-green housecoat, still looking up at thumps of the hail bombarding their house.

"If there was a storm why haven't the sirens ..." She gasped and stared out the window. He grabbed her as a howl blasted in the distance, warning all to take cover and hide.

"Oh my God ..." His mother's mouth hung open. She seemed frozen where she stood. Gabriel twisted her away from the window and pushed her towards her room.

"Get the blinds down!" He pointed to her windows. Nate had drilled him on how to lock down the house since he was a boy. He sprinted back to his own window and pulled down on a steel chain. A series of metal blinds cascaded down over the windows, covering them inside and out. He finished locking the blinds in his own room then raced to another bedroom – his brother Adin's old room. He pushed through the stacks of boxes stored in the abandoned room, blindly tossing the boxes out of his way, until he finally reached the steel blinds in the room. As he raced out of the room he slammed into his mother, nearly knocking her to the ground.

"My room is done and your father's office is too," she told him as he steadied her from falling.

"Okay, downstairs now!" He pulled her towards the stairs and out into the kitchen. "Get the windows!" Gabriel yelled as he ran for their front door. He heaved on a large steel panel to slide it over the door as the heavy winds blew against it.

"Help me!" His sweaty hands slipped on the steel handles as he pulled. He repositioned his shoulder against the side of the steel panel and, with the help of his mother, pushed back against the force of the wind.

The sound of broken glass filled the room as the windows shattered around them, the metal blinds failing to hold back the storm. Protecting his face with his hand, he abandoned the steel panel and staggered back towards the kitchen, holding onto his mother. Pieces of the living room wall exploded, punched in by a broken fence posts. Gabriel dropped to the floor with his mother, shielding her from the splinters as more unknown objects slammed through the wall.

He stared through the broken walls. Lightning flashed in the yard – striking so close to the house he could feel the electricity in the air. The tornado battered everything in the yard, tossing steel feed containers like paper cups. Pieces of wood tore off the barn, disappearing into the black emptiness of the storm. The old tractor flipped onto its side and was dragged across the yard. A painful grip dug into his forearm. He turned to find his mother's hand latched onto him. He planted his feet and stood, pulling her up with him as he stared at the barn. The huge old building was being torn apart piece by piece like someone had placed it in a giant blender. NATE!

"Nate!" His mother echoed his thought. She went limp in

his arms, sobbing. He jerked her back up and, with all his might, dragged her towards the basement door in the kitchen.

"What about Nate?" she cried.

"I don't know!" He gritted his teeth and continued his struggle to get her to the basement door. He couldn't think about Nate now.

Gabriel reached the door and had barely opened it when the wind ripped it from his grip, swinging it off its hinges. He hurried down the steps into the storm shelter below, his mother close behind him. As he entered the room, his mother ran straight past him to the back wall of the shelter, sobbing as she slid down the wall. He turned away from her to secure the metal door at the bottom of the stairs. Just as he was sliding the final bolts into place, he stopped. *The shard … Dad's crystal!*

The thought of losing the white crystal was too much and he began to slide the bolts back to unlock the huge door. His mother mumbled something behind him then yelled, "What are you doing? Shut that door, Gabriel. Nothing else matters. We are safe here!"

"Just stay here. Don't leave no matter what!" He didn't have time to explain.

Ignoring her cries, Gabriel opened the door just enough to slide through and leaped up the staircase. He burst onto the main floor and raced through the broken kitchen then stopped at the bottom of the stairs leading up to their bedrooms. A loud snap began to repeat itself above his head, like the crack of a whip. Holding onto the unsteady railing, Gabriel looked up to the disappearing ceiling at the top of the stairs. Pockets of blackened sky showed through as the tornado torn apart the roof. A blast of howling wind gusted down the staircase, spitting rain and dirt into his face, temporarily blinding him.

He focused past the roof being torn off the house, past the cold pellets of hail stinging his chest, past the distant cries of his mother in the kitchen. He pictured the pure white soft glow of the piece of ore his father had given him. Ignoring his surroundings, he bolted up the staircase, his muscles pumping faster than he'd ever run, his heart thundering in his ears, blocking out every other sound. He barrelled down the hallway. The roof was nearly gone, raining pieces of itself all over his path. As he reached his bedroom he was knocked back by a gust of wind. A searing pain sliced down the back of his left shoulder as a board fell from the broken roof. His skin felt on fire, and warmth rolled down his back. *Almost there.* He gritted his teeth and pushed himself into his bedroom. One of the outer walls was completely missing; his bed had been flipped and pinned against a remaining wall. He crawled to where his bed should have been, not able to stand anymore in the raging winds. He scrambled on the floor for what seemed like an eternity, wildly searching for the plastic container. Then he saw it.

The crystal was lying in the far corner of his room, broken free from its container, gently rolled around by the random gusts of wind. *Don't touch it!* His father's voice screamed out in his head. Quickly grabbing a shirt that was wadded against the wall, Gabriel bellied along the floor towards his goal.

He scooped up the shard in his shirt and carefully wrapped the cloth around it, making sure the shard didn't touch his skin. He pressed the bundle to his chest and staggered to his feet. Defying the winds and debris, he made it out of his room and down the hall. As he struggled to stay standing, he looked down the stairs towards the kitchen.

There, at the bottom of the stairs, was his mother. His stomach wrenched. She was clutching what was left of the outside wall of the kitchen.

"Go back! Get downstairs!" His voice was overpowered by the storm, stealing any sound he could push from his lungs.

He slid down two steps on his back, trying not to get sucked out into the open rage of the storm. His eyes met hers. She reached out a hand towards him, barely hanging onto the broken wall with the other. Her lime green dressing gown blew in all directions as she held on for her life. Gabriel continued towards her, gripping the

6

stairs with his free hand. His shirt began to unravel around the shard, the wind pulling the fabric free from his grip. His hand burned, as if dipped in fire. His back scraped down the metal edges of another two steps as he pushed towards her. The storm raged above his head. Pain erupted in his head from the immense pressure. The crystal came free from its cloth covering. Gabriel clutched it with his bare hand. *Hold on.* He had made it halfway down the staircase. She was still trying to reach to him. He needed to get to her faster. He needed to leap the rest of the way. Grabbing firmly onto the hand rail, he pulled himself up but it collapsed under his weight. He plunged off the stairs through the weak outer wall of the house. Unable to stop his free fall, he smashed through the old cellar doors outside the house.

The roughly cut wooden steps broke his fall as he tumbled into the dark pit. Reflexively tucking into a ball, he rolled down the stairs. As he landed face down on the hard earth floor, he felt a sharp blast of pain in his chest. Something warm oozed between his fingers. Dazed, he tried to stand but was pelted from above by nail-studded boards. He collapsed in agony under the bombardment, rolling onto his back. His hands shook. He felt pressure, a sharp point rising out of his chest, covered in warm blood. He tried to pull it free, but it refused to leave. It sank deeper into his ribcage. *Mom ... Help.* Praying against death, he felt sick and dizzy as a white light flooded his vision. More pieces of the house fell down towards him. The outer wall collapsed above him. Then all was black; the suffering and the storm were no more.

CHAPTER TWO

A REPETITIVE LOW THUD ECHOED IN GABRIEL'S HEAD. His heart thumped, each beat sending a pulse of pain through his skull. Something crashed in the distance, and his eyes jerked open. He stared, through several broken beams, at the calm sky above him – white clouds drifting by in a light breeze. Slowly looking around, he found himself lying in a pile of rubble. Carefully he pushed himself up into a sitting position, ducking his head under the broken beams. His last conscious memory was of the handrail failing to hold him, sending him down into darkness through the old wooden doors of the cellar. He surveyed the scene around him. Several beams had caved through from the floor above him. The structural supports should have crushed him but here he was still alive.

After carefully crawling out from under the tepee of broken wood, he rose to his feet. He felt sore, but nothing appeared to be broken. He surveyed the loose wood around him and ducked under several other large beams as he groped along the cellar wall, searching for something that could hold his weight. At last he found some compacted chunks of wall strong enough and cautiously crawled up from the cellar onto solid ground.

He turned slowly, not recognizing anything he saw – the scene was like a war zone. The tornado had focused its fury on the small ranch and left nothing standing. The barn had completely collapsed onto one side, leaving the livestock pinned under the wreckage, bodies crushed and still. Farm equipment had been picked up and thrown all over by the storm. Even the heavy water tank was tipped over on its side, water still draining from it.

He walked over to a small metal water trough strapped to one of the few fence posts left standing. His reflection bobbed in the still water, his face covered in a thick paste of bloody dirt. Breaking the image into ripples, he dipped up the cool water and splashed his face. He continued to wash until the prickles of his day-old beard scratched at his finger tips. As he scrubbed his hands clean from the dirt and blood clinging to them, he remembered the searing pain he had felt in his chest. He placed his right hand over his chest and breathed deeply. He felt no pain as he inhaled and exhaled. *Thank God.* Still, when he took his hand off his chest, a smear of blood remained on his palm. *What?* Down past his hand was the source – a large red stain around a rough tear in his t-shirt.

After gingerly tugging the t-shirt over his head, he breathed deeply and gently pressed the area where blood had caked onto his chest. It didn't hurt. He pressed deeper and found something hard under the tips of his fingers. He tucked his chin towards his chest for a closer look. A glint of light caught his eye. Puzzled by the flicker, he leaned over the trough, splashing his whole front with water. He washed the area clean of dirt and clots of dried blood. Satisfied, he stopped and stared at his reflection in the ripples of the disturbed water. And froze. His lungs struggled to suck in air as he stared at the reflection, every muscle in his body locked in fear.

The glowing white crystal was embedded in the centre of his chest.

What the hell! He tried to remain calm, scratching at the sides of the ore to free it from his skin, desperate to get it out of his chest.

This can't be happening. He stared at his blurry image in the water trough. What was going to happen to him?

His father had told him that the ore – all colors of it – had proven to be deadly to anyone who came in direct contact with it. But here he stood, clearly not dead. He wasn't even feeling ill. He looked down at his chest and noticed his skin had completely healed around the ore – like it belonged there – like it had merged with his body. How?

His pulse quickened as he recalled the series of events. The branch. The storm. The shelter. The stairs. The fall. Something wasn't right. He was missing something. He was missing ... someone.

Oh my God. He spun on his heel, searching.

"Mom!" Only empty silence answered him back. Nothing in the broken landscape moved. He pulled his shirt back over his head and sprinted towards the ruins of the house, hurdling over any debris in his path.

"Mom! Where are you?" He yelled so loud it hurt.

Despite Nate's training, he felt panicked. His breathing was erratic and his stomach cramped in pain. Spinning around on the spot, he surveyed the destruction, searching for any sign of her. He ran towards where the kitchen should have been. Broken cupboards, chairs, dishes, and sodden drywall littered the area. He threw them in every direction until finally he found the stairs leading to the shelter. The door, broken into pieces, partially covered the top of the stairs.

Thank God! His heart leaped with joy. "Mom, I'm coming down!"

He pushed the final things out of his way and climbed down to reach the bottom of the stairs. He saw the grey of the steel door of the shelter and banged on it with his fist as he leaned against its heavy frame with his shoulder. The third hard shove on the steel door moved it open. He looked inside the thin gap.

"Mom?" He pushed the large door completely open. His eyes met a blanket of darkness, but as his pupils dilated, items appeared out of the dark: an empty cot, a shelf full of supplies, and a small table with two empty chairs. "Mom?" Why wasn't she in here?

He turned and climbed out of the empty shelter. He reached the sunlight and sat down on a pile of debris, numb. *Where is she?* He began to shake, and his mind filled with confused emotions of hope and loss.

Taking several deep breaths, he calmed himself then carefully navigated through the broken house, passing by shattered pieces of his life – a picture he liked, a vase he made at camp that was still holding yesterday's flowers, bits of furniture, shattered dishes. He didn't stop to pick up anything. He continued towards the front of the house, where several of the largest walls had come crashing down, piling high atop of one another, forming an impassable mountain of rubble.

It rocked under his feet as he stepped onto it. Better go back the way he came. As he turned, something caught his eye. Sticking out from under a wall, speckled with blood , was a piece of lime green material. It was the same colour as his mother's housecoat. He remembered it whipping in the wind as his mother held onto the section of broken wall in the kitchen.

Mom! Then he saw the hand, the smooth skin white with death. He lunged towards it but fell to his knees, suddenly dizzy. He swallowed hard as he reached out to touch the lifeless fingers. The cold skin shocked him. *No!* His jaw quivered. Tears burned his eyes, and he couldn't catch his breath.

He clung to her hand. "No … No … Please God, no!"

He had experienced death many times on the ranch but this holding his dead mother's hand, he felt the world around him suddenly go darker. He stared at the enormous wall that had come crashing down, killing her. *Why? Why didn't you go back to the shelter?*

He threw his head back and screamed. Rage surged through his body, like when his father died. He shook his head, desperate to wake up from another nightmare. He stood, grasped the wall lying on his mother, and tried with all his might to lift it off of her body.

The wall didn't move. His hands dug into the jagged edge of the broken wall. Blood dripped out from between his fingers as he continued to struggle.

Finally he burst into tears and let go. He pounded at the metal siding of the fallen wall with his fists, leaving dents and blood all over its flat surface, until his hands hurt too much to continue. He dropped to his knees as a rush of heat exploded inside him. It crawled across his chest, spreading a fiery sensation down his arms and up his neck. Pure white light rolled down his arms like a liquid until it covered his hands. The light spread, covering every inch of skin on his arms. It slowly crept up his neck towards his chin. There was nothing he could do to stop it. The light surged with power – his skin felt like it was burning. Only hotter. Stronger. Fierce. His body was being consumed with intense pain. He screamed at the heavens as his tear-blurred vision filled with the strange white light.

CHAPTER THREE

Nate Reinhart's pickup truck barrelled down the abandoned road leading to the ranch. The main road to the house was littered with debris or he would have come in that way. But time was of the essence. And, despite its roughness, this old road hadn't been touched by the storm. The truck struck potholes, bouncing violently all over the road as he struggled to control it. He didn't have much time. The truck skidded sideways as he slammed on the brakes to avoid hitting a smashed gardening shed. *Damn it.* Turning off the ignition, he kicked the door open. He snatched up the duffel bag resting on the passenger seat and sprinted up the hillside. As he reached the top, the levelled buildings came into view. The barn had fallen over onto one side – the wall underneath it completely collapsed. Farm equipment was turned over everywhere, their steel frames bent and beaten by the storm. The house was a pile of shredded wood, littered around the foundation. His home was destroyed. It hit him like a punch in the stomach.

"Gabriel! Jess!" He fumbled his way down the hill, nearly falling.

He reached the level ground of the yard and he sprinted towards the house shouting their names. *Let them be alive. Please.* Nothing in the shattered house moved. His military training told him not to panic, but his heart sank. It was his job to keep them safe. He had promised Calvin. It couldn't end like this. He scaled the side of the flipped over tractor and stood on the huge tire.

"Jessica! Gabriel! Where are you?" The strain of his scream left him coughing as he tried to catch his breath.

He felt torn. Time was against him. Dr. Cymru would send a team here soon, hoping the storm might have uncovered his best friend's hidden laboratory. He'd spent the last ten years protecting it – he wasn't about to stop now. He jumped off the tall tractor, absorbing the shock of landing with his legs as he dropped to one knee, surveying the area around him, looking for any sign of them, as he sprinted towards the barn. He focused on the fallen structure, searching for a way to enter. *Everything needs to be locked down.* He circled the building and found the entry he needed. Kneeling down, he carefully reached through the broken wall. His fingers brushed away the broken bits of wood covering the floor.

Gently removing his arm, he dug into his bag and pulled out a small flat metallic plate no bigger than the palm of his hand. The cover slid open at his touch, revealing a keypad. He punched in a ten-digit code and slid the cover closed. Manoeuvring his arm back through the broken wall, he carefully laid it against the flat wooden floor and waited. A high pitched buzz filled the air around him, and the ground trembled below him. A minute later it stopped. He picked the plate back up and placed it in his pocket. He needed both keys to unlock it – but the second one was in his strongbox in the loft. He scanned the wreckage for the one-and-a-half foot by two-and-a-half foot silver box. The loft should have been right on top of the broken barn but nothing in the ruin looked familiar. He'd have to dig through the rubble. As he climbed up on the wreckage, the empty air was broken by the hum of an engine and a stranger's voice. He ducked back down behind the rubble of the barn, keeping silent as he moved to get a view of the main road. *Shit.*

"Carl, just move the debris off the road so we can get the truck closer." The driver yelled out the window.

A thin man hurried along the road in front of the truck, dragging wreckage off to the side. Nate watched them silently. They were not who he had expected, but it was too dangerous for him to stay now. He slipped away quietly, moving back up the hill without being spotted. As he crested the top, he dropped to his belly and crawled towards some tall grass for cover. He fumbled the high-tech binoculars from his bag. Resting his chin on the dirt he lifted the binoculars to his eyes.

The black screen quickly illuminated as it rested against his forehead. Holding his vision steady on the strangers, he opened the bottom of the binoculars. A tripod dropped out automatically, positioning itself in the dirt. An earpiece also dangled underneath. He stretched out the cord and hung it over his right ear. The two men's voices came in crystal clear.

"– be the worst one." The voice was deep and couldn't belong to the skinny one.

"I dunno, the last house was pretty bad, Brett. That whole family was dead." The high pitched tone was a better match.

"Let's hope it ain't the same here."

Nate zoomed in on the heavier man – Brett. The man ran his fingers through his thick red hair and then scratched at his full beard. Hair and beard made a mane around his face, hiding his mouth. He was a mountain of a man. His chest and arms were thick, and he was a solid foot taller than the other one. He put on his protective overalls, his hands moving routinely to each button and strap, as he stared at the levelled buildings.

Thieves? Nate wondered. Or did they work for those he wanted to avoid? His concentration broke as Brett shouted, "Carl! Get your ass over here and put your gear on *before* you go checking things out!"

Nate zoomed out to see the small bean-pole of a man hurry back to the truck and start suiting up. The two men were opposites. Carl was short and thin all the way from his feet to his hair line. He wore thick-rimmed glasses that bubbled his eyes, like a big-eyed goldfish.

Nate switched back to Brett, following him back to the cab of the truck. He grabbed a handset and spoke, "This is unit 619 on Range Road L19. We are going to need some heavy equipment here and a medical team on standby. I am turning on the GPS unit." He took his finger off the handset and waited.

They're rescue workers! They must be searching the area for survivors. Nate resisted the urge to rush down and help them. He needed to keep watch. Even if these two weren't with T.E.R.A., they would be showing up shortly.

"Roger, we copy. On our way to your location." The speaker finally buzzed back after several minutes.

Brett got out of the cab and reached for the toolbox resting in the large truck bed. He handed two laz-saws to Carl who had finally gotten his overalls on right.

"Why'd you call in a medical team? I doubt anyone is alive." Carl's voice sounded plaintive.

"Because that's the procedure!" Brett barked. "It don't matter if no one's left alive, it's part of the protocol."

"None of the other teams has found anyone alive in the path of that storm," Carl pointed out. "Seems like a waste of fuel if you ask me."

Brett grabbed the handle of the three foot laz-saw and swung it up on to his shoulder with ease. "Well, no one is asking you, Carl! Now let's go check this out!" He marched towards the farm house, slowly looking around the area. Carl clopped up behind him, tripping over his own feet as he tried to keep up with Brett's large strides.

Brett pointed. "You go check out the barn. I'll go through the house."

Good, send the stupid one to the barn. Nate followed Carl, zooming the screen out to see the wreckage. Everything should be safe but, if not, he'd have to deal with these two.

Carl fired up the small high-pitched saw, a red glow forming around the spinning blades. He sliced up a poorly chosen piece of the barn and the rubble shifted. Part of the barn collapsed around the dim-witted man, narrowly missing him. Nate smiled grimly. He might just bury the whole thing – which would be helpful.

Brett stormed over. "You call out for survivors first, you idiot! How many times do I have to –" His focus shifted back towards the road.

"Who's that?" Carl pointed.

Nate quickly shifted and watched as a black cube van rolled down the lane towards the house, every window tinted to hide who was inside.

"We better talk to them before they rush the wreckage. It's probably the family." Brett grunted. "You stay here."

It was definitely not family. It was Dr. Cymru – his best friend's old research partner. No doubt he had sent his men down to see if the storm had uncovered the hidden laboratory. Nate reached into his bag, pulled out a pistol and rested it beside him. He watched as two men in black suits stepped out of the van and were promptly met by Brett.

"Gentlemen, I cannot let you approach the wreckage. I realize you might have family here but you need to let us look for them. I must ask that you get back in your vehicle and we will contact you as soon as we find something. " Brett crossed his arms in front of his large chest.

"I understand you completely." The driver of the van spoke. "However, we are not with the family – we are representatives of T.E.R.A: The Energy and Resource Acquisition-"

"I know what it means." Brett didn't move, blocking them from walking any further.

"Of course, you do." The driver smiled. "This location is of interest to us. Have you found anyone yet?"

"We were just getting started as you arrived. Once you gentle-men leave, we will continue." Brett just stared at them.

"There could be sensitive material on the site here, we are just asking to do a quick sweep of the area. We won't get in your way. The faster we can do that, the faster we will be out of your way." The stranger attempted to hand Brett a card.

"Can you do it from where you're standing right now?" Brett kept his arms crossed.

"No, I'm afraid not." The stranger shook his head.

"Then, I'm afraid you're going to have to wait. Now, I have to clear the area before the rest of our team arrives." Brett turned to walk away.

"You don't understand. T.E.R.A. needs to scan the area now!" The stranger followed after Brett.

He pivoted on the spot and stepped up to the stranger, tower-ing over him. "Either bring me a court order, or get lost. This is me being nice."

Nate chuckled as the two men got back in their van and slowly backed down the lane. He knew they would be back – and with the court order too, no doubt – but by then the lab should be invisible to any scan.

"Let's do this Carl!" Brett shouted, drawing Nate's attention back.

Carl gave a thumbs up and Brett called out, "Hello, anyone in there? If you are, please do not move! I will be clearing some safe paths around the house to reach you!" After a few moments, he sighed loudly. "Just like all the rest."

Nate felt his heart sink as he watched them work.

Brett made quick work of the house, despite Carl's cries of dis-gust from over at the barn. Carl's running commentary of what he was finding let Nate keep an eye on Brett's progress in the house. The large man had made several paths into different areas of the house, and he now stood in the direct centre of the rubble calling out once again for anyone to respond. Silence.

Nate watched his movements, hoping he would see some-thing. Willing him to see something. *Please let them have made it to the shelter.* He thought Brett had tripped when he saw the man take a few steps then drop quickly to the ground. Nate's heart quickened. Brett was cleaning debris – same as before – but something was dif-ferent. His movements were faster, not as careful. He zoomed the binoculars in on the wreckage. What was Brett looking at?

"Carl! Get some med-packs and some blankets!" Brett com-manded from his knees.

"Why?" Carl's voice yelled back.

"Because I got someone here. Now stop asking stupid ques-tions and get me what I need!" Brett roared.

Nate nearly charged down into the wreckage. His hands dug into the dirt as he watched, his breathing shallow and his heart pounding. Brett didn't move, and the wreckage blocked Nate from seeing who was lying at his feet.

CHAPTER FOUR

GABRIEL FELT A LARGE, HEAVY HAND RESTING ON HIS CHEST. The sensation sent goose bumps popping all over his skin. His muscles twitched as he awakened, his eyes struggling to open against the bright light of the day. The face of a stranger with a huge red beard and matching fluffy red hair filled his field of vision. Instinctively, Gabriel smacked the hand off his chest and rolled over onto his hands and feet, crouching like a cat. The huge man stumbled backwards, his face full of shock. A yelp echoed out from behind him as a small man behind him fell over the rubble.

He stared at the strangers. "Who are you?"

"Relax. My name is Brett O'Connor and this Carl Ellis. We work for the state, as part of the disaster rescue team. We are sent in to give assistance to anyone in need after a severe storm happens in an area. We are here to help." The big man spoke as though he was reading from a piece of paper. "Are you okay, son? That was an awful big storm that hit your farm."

"The clouds … I watched it come towards us across the plain. I tried –" Gabriel stared down at his hands, drifting away from the conversation. *My hands – that light.*

"The storm hit a pretty big area." The little man – Carl – leaned against Brett's side as if he was stuck in his back pocket.

Brett handed Gabriel a blanket. "Here, son. Wrap yourself up. You might be in shock."

Gabriel pulled the blanket tight around himself and let it drape down like a cocoon as he rose to his feet. Still unsure of the two strangers, he eyed Brett suspiciously. The large man towered over both Gabriel and Carl.

"Son, who else is out here? What family might still be around?"

Gabriel froze as Brett's question pierced his heart. *Family? Mom.* His eyes stung. His vision blurred with tears. Unable to speak, he turned slowly around and pointed at the thin white hand reaching out from under the huge wall.

"My … my mom." He felt dizzy.

A large hand gently came to rest on his shoulder, holding him steady.

"Come on son, we will get her out of there … I promise. Come on." Brett gave him a gentle push and guided him out of the house, away from the rubble.

Carl rushed ahead of them and pulled a pile of plastic out of a box in the truck. It expanded, unassisted, into a small tent.

Brett stepped away from him and nodded to Carl in approval. "I want that medical team and the heavy equipment here now. I don't care what HQ says! You get them here now!" Brett's shout echoed in Gabriel's ears. The tent finished expanding, and Brett motioned for him to enter. Obeying, he sat on an inflated cot. Brett knelt before him, putting them eye to eye.

"Is there anyone else out there?"

"In the barn. I didn't see him before the storm … Nate might … I … I dunno. He's our ranch hand."

"Alright son, you stay here and we will do the rest. Just lie down. You've had one hell of a day." Brett gently patted him on the back. "I know it doesn't mean much right now, but you're lucky to be alive." With that he left Gabriel alone in the tent.

Gabriel wasn't sure how much time passed, but the ranch became a hive of activity. Several different rescue teams arrived, including heavy equipment that filled the air with annoying beeps as they backed off the trailers. He stayed alone in the tent with only Brett coming in to occasionally check on him. Brett had asked him to lie down as he waited for the medical team to arrive, so he lay quietly with his hand resting against the shard, its cool surface giving off a small pulse of heat with each beat of his heart.

Why am I alive? The ore kills people.

He breathed in deeply, feeling the weight of the crystal rise and fall safely in his chest.

Wait. That light. My hands and arms – my skin felt like I was burning alive. Was that the ore? Is that how it starts – is that what it feels like as it kills you? I need help – a doctor.

A terrifying future played in his mind. Him strapped to a table, a bright operating light burning into his eyes. The heads of scientists moving between him and the light as they prepared to examine him. Tools readied to dissect him and take the crystal. It would be more valuable to them than he was. No doctors, he decided.

The front of the tent opened, startling him. Brett squeezed through the doorway. "Well, son." He breathed out loudly and cleared his throat. "I'm sorry to have to tell you this, but no one on the team has found anything alive. None of the animals in the barn survived. I'm not sure about your friend. I doubt anyone could have lived through it. I'm sorry."

Gabriel felt numb – if numbness even was a feeling. He thought about Nate. Gabriel was still young when Nate had moved into the barn. He remembered first seeing him standing at the front door with a silver chest, handing Gabriel's mother an envelope. She wept as she read the letter and allowed him to move into the barn. Gabriel never really knew why Nate was there but as the years passed, it didn't really matter. Nate was family. He was the one who had shown Gabriel how to punch properly, shoot a gun, drive a tractor, fix machinery. Every skill he had was because Nate took the time to teach him but now he was gone.

"Also, with all the livestock and mess in there, we need to spray the barn area down with some pretty nasty chemicals. It's just gonna become a big bio hazard if we leave it. Was there anything you wanted out of there?" The large man waited.

He ran his fingers through his dark hair, pulling out some chips of wood. "You guys find a steel strongbox? A silver trunk?"

Gabriel had asked many times over the years what was in the chest but Nate always gave the same answer. A smile and a 'don't worry about it'. It was important, something Nate had guarded all these years. He didn't know why but he wanted it with him.

"Don't think so, but I'll have the boys take another look." The big man nodded and left the tent. Eventually he returned, carrying a one-and-a-half foot by two-and-a-half foot grey alloy strongbox.

Relief surged through Gabriel as Brett set the chest at the end of his cot. "Want anything else, son? We're about to start spraying."

He shook his head and sat up on the cot to look at the metal box. *Locked.* Gabriel eyed the mechanism on the lid; Nate had taught him how to pick simple electronic locks. This looked a little more complex.

"Well? Anything?" Brett stared at him waiting for a response.

"Sorry ... I didn't know where to begin ..." Gabriel shrugged.

"Don't worry. We'll put aside anything salvageable and make sure it goes in the container." Brett nodded and left the tent.

He was mentally making a list of things that might have survived, when a new vehicle pulled into the long driveway. The blanket slid off his shoulders as he stretched his neck up over the tent wall to try and see what was coming. Unable to get a good look, he pulled the blanket back around him and stood to peer through the open entrance of the tent.

The sun reflected off the vehicle's windshield, stopping him from getting a good look at it until it neared the plastic tent and pulled to a stop. It was a white ambulance.

Shit.

CHAPTER FIVE

GABRIEL PANICKED, LOOKING AROUND FOR SOMEWHERE HE
COULD GO. He needed to leave.

Before he could run, Brett came barrelling through the plastic doorway. "Good! The medical team is here." Brett pointed to the
ambulance. "Now they can have a good look at you. Also, I got a little
something for you."

Gabriel opened the small duffel bag Brett handed him. Inside
were shiny silver envelopes that had "Financial Relief Aid Packages"
stamped on them in bold red letters. "What are these?"

"It's a little against procedure but I gave you three. These have
food cards and vouchers for free hotel stays. Also, some government
cash cards for buying new clothes and things. Typically, you only get
one per person but I figured you could use a little bit of extra help."
Brett smiled so big Gabriel could see a couple of missing molars in
his giant yellowish grin.

He felt a smile form on his face. "Thanks – For everything."

"I was happy as a pig in mud to find you breathing!" Brett gave
Gabriel a gentle pat on the shoulder. "I'm off to the next site. You take
care of yourself."

Gabriel watched as Brett and his partner stripped off their gear and climbed into their truck. He gave them a final wave as they drove down the lane and suddenly felt very alone.

"Hello." A friendly female voice interrupted his thoughts. The voice's owner set down a medical bag on the ground in front of him and sat down on the other cot. She wore a pair of thin glasses that matched her round face and the small bun on the top of her head. "My name is Rita. And you are?"

"Gabriel." He shifted on the cot, uneasy about his new guest.

"Hi Gabriel. I just want to check some of your vitals. Is that okay?"

A male paramedic joined them, standing silently in the corner of the tent.

"I suppose." He tried to calm himself.

She smiled and reached for his right arm. He carefully slid his arm from beneath the blanket that was still wrapped around him and watched as she wrapped a metallic band around it, midway up his forearm. She then pulled a small set of goggles out of her kit. They looked a bit like binoculars.

"Alright, I want you to just look into these." She held the goggles up to his eyes. "And try not to blink."

Maybe they won't see anything. Gabriel took a deep breath and pressed his face into the goggles. A surge of red light flooded his eyes, blinding him. Blinking away the burst of light, he rubbed his eyes until his vision returned to normal.

Rita put the goggles away and looked at a small LCD screen attached to her uniform forearm. "Well, your retina scan looks good," she reported. "I see you've had some trauma to your chest though."

Not good. Gabriel tightened the blanket around himself, his throat suddenly dry.

"Let's see now." She smiled at him. "Here comes your medical history ... alright, that looks to be fine. You appear to be in good condition, but I want to take a look at your chest before we let you go.

Can you tell me about what happened?" She stared at him, eyebrows raised.

Clearing his throat, he breathed in deeply. "I don't remember," he lied. "I feel fine though."

She stood up and tapped the top of the cot while attempting to ease the blanket off his shoulders. "Lie down, please." She patted the cot.

Shaking his head, he pulled the blanket back around him tightly. He made a point of staring her in the eyes. "I feel fine, thank you."

She frowned and tilted her head at him. "I just want to take a look. Sometimes we feel fine but our bodies are in trouble."

"Your computer says I am fine, and I really don't feel like being poked at!"

"Sir, I need to look at your chest!" She used a stern tone.

The male medical officer stirred beside her, pushing his sleeves up to his elbows.

"I don't care what you want. I don't want to be looked at! Get it?" His voice rose as his fear quickly changed to anger.

The woman reached out and grabbed his arm. The man put a hand firmly on his shoulder. Jerking his arm out of her grip and shaking the hand off his shoulder, Gabriel raised his voice even louder. "I said NO!" He stood up, breathing hard. "Get the hell out!" He pointed to the door.

"Sir! There's lots of blood on your shirt. I just need to make sure you are okay!" Her eyes widened.

Gabriel glanced down and readjusted the blanket to cover up his blood-stained shirt. "NO! Get this through your head. You have no right –" His jaw tightened as he clenched his teeth.

"We have a right, and we will restrain you if we must!" The male paramedic pointed at Gabriel.

"Try it!" Gabriel glared into the paramedic's eyes. A flash of heat burned inside his chest.

"STOP!" A commanding voice rang out inside the small tent.

Startled, Gabriel glanced at the entrance of the tent. *Thank God.*

"Leave him be!" The familiar voice seemed louder than normal in the small tent. Gabriel felt the anger rush out of his body, overwhelmed with relief at seeing his brother. As he struggled to control his emotions, the two paramedics stood frozen in place, clearly unsure of what to do. Adin often had that affect on people. Even though it had been at least a year since they had seen each other, Adin looked exactly how Gabriel expected him to. An expensive-looking black suit matched his dark sunglasses. His black hair was short and gelled forward, every hair perfectly in place. Adin held their attention. He sauntered into the tent, moving to Gabriel's side without a glance at the paramedics.

Adin set his hand on Gabriel's shoulder. "If my brother doesn't want to be looked at, he doesn't have to be. And by no 'rights' can you force him to be examined." He turned to face them, his expression stern and his nostrils flared. "He is in my care now and I will see to it that he is looked after. Thank you for your time." Adin gestured towards the door of the tent. "Now get out."

The two paramedics silently packed up their equipment and left without a word.

When they were out of earshot, Adin turned to Gabriel, looking him up and down. He put his hand on Gabriel's face. "You alright?"

I am now. Relieved, Gabriel nodded as he took a deep breath to steady his emotions. "You were pretty menacing there." He gave a small crooked smile.

"Very funny." Adin grinned. "Gather your things, I don't want to be here any longer than we have to be."

Adin turned to leave the tent, but Gabriel reached for his arm. He tried to speak but nothing came out. His eyes welled with tears as he forced himself to meet the gaze behind the dark glasses. "Mom … she …"

"I know." Adin put his hand on top of his brother's. "They were moving her body when I drove in. I have to go see to some things.

Here are my keys – mine's the black SUV – take your stuff and wait there."

"What about Mom? Where are they taking her?"

Adin unexpectedly pulled him so close their noses almost touched. Adin removed his glasses with his free hand, while tightening his grip around Gabriel's arm with the other. Gabriel stared into Adin's deep blue eyes. They were blurred with tears, but they still managed to burn into him.

"Gabriel, please! I am barely holding it together. Stop arguing and just listen to me! Wait for me in the car."

Gabriel nodded in surrender.

Adin let go, put his glasses back on and trudged towards the black body bag that held their mother. Gabriel knew his brother's heart must be hurting as much as his own, but he was still surprised to see the depth of Adin's agony. He grabbed the chest and the duffel bag and headed over to the black SUV.

He loaded his things into the hatch and climbed into the passenger seat, all the while watching Adin just feet in front of the SUV. Adin was nodding his head to an individual who had opened the black body bag for him to see. Adin gently lowered the black plastic around her face, to stroke her cheek. Seeing her face made Gabriel's vision blur, and he let out a loud sob. Tears burned his eyes and another sob burst out as he tried to stay calm – his chest suddenly burning hot. *No – stop. Please.* It must be the ore, slowly taking its toll. He wiped his nose on the corner of the blanket and focused. He forced his lungs to take in as much air as they could hold, exhaling slowly. Again, he sucked as much air into his chest as he could and breathed out. The heat slowly subsided and he refocused on Adin, who gently pulled on something within the bag. He turned on the spot, walked swiftly towards the SUV, climbed in and shut the door loudly behind him. Gabriel sat silently and watched tears trickle from under Adin's dark sunglasses. A bloodied gold necklace was clenched in his fist.

CHAPTER SIX

Nate opened the glass door to the empty electronic repair shop on the east side of Burlington. It was important they know that Cymru would be coming for the hidden lab. They had found Gabriel safe, he could only hope Jessica was in the same condition. He had managed to slip away from the ranch unseen as more emergency crews arrived, but he still needed to be careful. He glanced around outside before shutting the door and locking it. A man stepped up beside him and flipped a switch, illuminating a hologram on the door that read "Closed for lunch."

"Thanks, Alex. We all set up?" Nate kept his eyes on the street.

"Encrypted line is all set in the back. Should be clean to call from." Alex leaned against the wall beside one of the front windows. "I'll keep watch, sir."

Nate nodded, turned around and marched to a door at the back of the shop. Inside was a large work table covered in electronic parts and small tools. In the centre was an old headset wired to an open box containing a complex mother circuit board. *He must be getting bored.* He chuckled. Alex rigged up something different every time, at least it kept him busy. The headset fit over his ear without too much discomfort – still, it was awkward.

He waited, tapping his fingers on the table until an English accent echoed in his ear. "The connection is secure Nathaniel."

"We've got problems. I don't know if you saw the news but a massive storm hit the ranch." Nate cleared his throat as emotion welled up. "I wasn't there but managed to get the lab locked down."

The voice's pace quickened. "Are Gabriel and Jessica alright?"

"I saw them move Gabriel out of the wreckage … Jessica – I don't know." He slammed his fist against the table. "I shouldn't have been out on mission! I should have been at home with them!"

"I'm sorry. If we had known this was coming, you would have been. Believe me."

Nate exhaled, rubbing his face with his hands. "Damn it."

"The storms are nearly impossible to predict in advance, with all the climate change. There is nothing you could have done differently. Let it go. God willing, Jessica is alright."

"It's my job to keep them safe!" His fingers clenched the table edge, twisting it upwards.

"Calvin's last request was that his family would be safe from any retaliation from Cymru or T.E.R.A. Not from a storm. Gabriel will be alright, your training over the years will kick in. He'll manage on his own for the time being. What about the lab?" The voice crackled in his ear.

He stood up and wandered the small room as he spoke. "It's locked down. Cymru sent a team in immediately – they showed up right after the first emergency team. Luckily, one of the emergency crew wouldn't let them on the property. The lab should be completely hidden by the time they get back, but that won't keep it hidden forever. The system will run out of power eventually without us maintaining it. Once the area is cleared by T.E.R.A. I'll need to get my chest to unseal the lab. It should still be in the wreckage."

"The chest shouldn't draw too much attention. Cymru is looking for the lab – he knows of its existence – but I don't know if he truly believes it is on the ranch. Once their scans come up empty, he should move on. Then we will deal with the lab."

"You sure he doesn't know where it is?" Nate didn't believe Cymru would give up that easily.

"Calvin said Cymru knew about his private lab when they were partners, but he never revealed its location. Regardless, we will need all of Calvin's research, if we want to stay ahead of T.E.R.A."

"Why Calvin ever partnered with that man is beyond me." He shook his head.

"They were both the top researchers in their respective fields. He was determined to find a new energy resource. With T.E.R.A.'s nearly unlimited resources, partnering seemed like the opportunity of a lifetime. If he'd known it would cost him his life, he would have never agreed to it." The voice sighed. "It doesn't matter."

The door in the room opened as Alex poked his head in, signalling Nate that the line would not be secure for much longer. "I don't have much time left."

"Ensure that the lab is safe. Then find your family – make sure Gabriel and Jessica are alright. We will need to track Cymru's movements for the time being. I will put some of our team on it. You'd better increase your contact. I will meet you in Denver in two days, the usual place."

An audible click ended the conversation. Nate set the headset down and walked out of the small room to join Alex.

Alex glanced at him from his lookout at the window. "What did he say?"

"The usual. Keep an eye on the ranch for me. I'll back in a couple of days." Nate knew he could trust Alex with anything.

"You got it." Alex walked over and unlocked the door. "Have a good day, sir."

CHAPTER SEVEN

GABRIEL DIDN'T SAY A WORD AS ADIN STARTED THE SUV AND DROVE DOWN THE LONG LANE AWAY FROM THE RANCH. He gazed into the side mirror at the work crews sifting through his home. *Everything's gone. Mom. Nate.* As the workers grew smaller and smaller in the distance, he leaned his heavy head against the cool glass of the window. The scenery drifted past, revealing the path of the storm. Fence posts and power poles, broken into scrap wood, littered the road and fields. His neighbours' houses and barns had been torn apart. More work crews were trying to pick up the pieces strewn across the fields. Ambulances sat quietly in front of the homes, not a single one rushing away. *Did anyone else live?* The scars left by the storm disappeared behind him as they finally reached the freeway and headed for Denver. An hour passed, filled only by the sound of the tires humming along the freeway. He stayed pressed against the window, his eyes closed, unsure, even, of what to feel.

Adin finally spoke. "What happened?"

Rubbing his eyes and sitting back up straight in the plush leather passenger seat, Gabriel cleared his throat. "I woke up in the night. A branch was scratching at my window." His lips tightened. "Stupid thing. I saw the lightning. It lit up the horizon but there was nothing behind it. Just a wall of black. It just moved towards the house. The tornado came so fast. We scrambled to try and lock down the house but … it was too strong. Nothing we did helped – the blinds, the doors – nothing held. The house just started to fall apart."

"So you didn't make it to the shelter?"

Gabriel's eyes burned. His throat felt dry as his voice trembled. "We … I don't remember … the storm hit the house and everything started to break apart." He covered his face with his hands, dragging his fingers down across his face, he breathed out. He felt sick, his stomach twisting with guilt. He turned to Adin. "Let's talk about something else."

"Of course. Sorry." Adin cleared his throat. "You decide on a school? I know Mom was hoping you would pick somewhere, starting this fall."

"I hadn't given it much thought." He stared down the freeway, his gaze aimlessly moving from one car to another.

"Well, its a good idea. You'll be living in Denver so you should go to one of the colleges there. "

"I'll be living in the city? Where?" His mind flashed with memories of the ranch.

Adin smiled at him, "You'll be living with me."

"What about your job? How do I fit into that?"

"What about it?" Adin furrowed his brow and stared blankly at him.

"Well it's … It's always been more important … than anything." Gabriel focused on Adin.

"It will be fine." Adin shrugged. "I spoke with Dr. Cymru, the details aren't important. What is important is moving forward. I'm technically your guardian now, and you will be 21 in a year. I thought it would be the best option for you."

"So, you suddenly want us to act like family?" He had always resented Adin's priorities, choosing to work rather than be with family even through the holidays.

"Look, Gabriel. I know I haven't been around much."

"Much? Adin, you're never around."

"The work I do with Dr. Cymru is important!"

"I don't care!" He wanted to whip Adin with his words. "Dad was never home, Adin! He died working. Not at home, not with any of us. And you – did it make you act differently?" He barely paused. "No, first you run off to university, and then you go work for the same company that killed Dad! Mom would have given anything to have you around more. Anything, Adin." He scowled. "But that just didn't work for your career. Did it?"

"T.E.R.A. didn't kill Dad! It was an accident!" Adin shook his head and breathed out, his voice returning to normal. "Sitting around pitying the dead isn't going to help anyone. It'll be best for you to focus on something like school."

"Mom just died!" Gabriel yelled the words at him.

"And wasting time sulking about it, isn't going to help you in life." Adin shrugged. "I was lucky Dr. Cymru pushed me into school after Dad died."

"Your precious doctor can make your decisions but he's not making mine!" Gabriel despised the man. He was the one who had taken Adin away from his family after their father died. The man was evil – Nate had given him enough reason to believe it but Adin seemed blind to the fact.

"This is not about him! Dr. Cymru has been nothing but supportive since Dad died. He was Dad's partner at T.E.R.A. for crying out loud! He has done nothing but help me along my path. You should be so lucky to have someone like him in your life." Adin gripped the steering wheel tightly, his knuckles turning white.

"You had Mom, Nate, Me. You didn't need him!"

"Really!" Adin glared at him, ignoring the road. "Who helped me through all my schooling? Mom? Nate – the washed up soldier living in the barn? You, my little brother who barely made it out of high school? None of you could, but he did! When I left for school, he was a lot more supportive than the rest of you. Hell, he even paid for it all – just like he plans on paying for your schooling."

"Your family needed you!" Gabriel was tired of having the same fight with Adin, every time they saw one another. "You know what! I don't care." He threw up his hands.

"Damn it, Gabriel. Why can't you just let me help you! You think Nate's survival training is going to help you in the real world? You need to face reality. When Dad died, I went to school – I focused. I graduated at the top of my class with honours. I got a great opportunity with T.E.R.A. and worked hard to get where I am today. You are going to need to do the same, if you want to make anything of yourself."

"What makes you think I want to be anything like you?" Gabriel was furious.

"I'm eight years older than you and I am more successful than most 40 year olds. You're an idiot if you don't want that kind of life." Adin shook his head. "You know, I'm your brother for crying out loud. You'd think you could trust me."

The air in the SUV suddenly felt thick. The whirl of the tires was the only noise in the uncomfortable silence. Gabriel didn't want to go with Adin but what choice did he have? At least there, he would have a chance to think. Decide what his life would look like for himself.

The tall towers of Denver crested the horizon. "The city's gotten bigger." Gabriel stared at the network of neighbourhoods, stretching out across the horizon.

"More and more people are moving inland as the coastal cities lose the fight against the rising ocean." Adin shrugged. "I guess it's a little crowded."

Driving towards the downtown core they passed through suburb after suburb. Gabriel gawked. All the houses looked the same – tightly packed along the streets below the freeway. The roofs had solar panels built into them, every one positioned for

35

optimal energy absorption. Not so different from the ranch. His father had designed their home to function on its own, off the grid. This meant some days were better than others for water and power. Very few rural homes were connected to city power and water grids anymore. A decade ago T.E.R.A. spent billions of dollars renewing all the city power lines with high efficiency materials to prevent energy loss. Unfortunately, the rural communities didn't get very many upgrades. The old lines were simply cut off over time, forcing people to create their own power. An idea that his father had been excited to embrace.

"We're almost there." Adin drummed the steering wheel as they turned off the freeway and approached their first traffic light. "Little different than Burlington, huh? You will get used to it. It's really all the same. Just a lot less elbow room."

"I'll work it out." He wasn't sure who he was trying to convince more.

"Look." Adin sighed. "I know what helped me when Dad died. I don't mean to push you, I just wanna help."

"I know. You're just shitty at showing it." Gabriel couldn't help but grin at him.

Adin chuckled. "Yea, well it was easier when you were little. You weren't so stubborn."

"I blame Nate."

"So do I." Adin reached and patted him on the shoulder. "I'm glad you're still here. We'll find a rhythm – you and I. It'll be nice not to have dinner alone all the time."

"Last time I checked, you didn't know how to cook." Gabriel let go of his anger.

"Still don't. Take out is so much easier." Adin winked at him, a simple grin on his face.

Gabriel couldn't help but laugh. This would be a new start for them, a chance to be brothers again.

As they travelled into the downtown core, he saw a huge sign for the city's new transit system. It read "Sometimes new problems are fixed with old ideas" and showed a steam engine from centuries past moving along the modern day streets.

"What's with the old train?" He pointed out the window.

"That's a project I worked on with Dr. Cymru. It uses the power of the red ore as a heat source, producing an almost infinite amount of heat to boil water. We found a way to amplify the output using super efficient heat shields, thereby focusing the heat on a water containment system ..." Adin went on for several minutes.

Gabriel blocked out Adin's science lesson and recalled his father's story about finding the ore and the different types they discovered. As the energy crisis peaked, the North American government had seized control of the area that used to be Iran. His father had gone hunting there for any remaining oil reserves. Seismic imaging had revealed an anomaly deep within the earth's crust, and they dug for months before finally reaching it – deep underground, the resting place of Eden. Apparently the ores had been one source of the garden's perfection. Each had a unique colour, depending on its actions. Blue ore purified water of any quality, even the most toxic, and could gather moisture from open air. Green ore promoted plant growth at exponential rates. It appeared to affect animals in a similar way, as well by making them completely docile. Red ore produced controllable heat for an apparently unlimited time.

These life-giving colours were found surrounded by crystals of a very different ore; a pitch black ore. It was like crystallized death, killing anything around it in minutes. The strange aura affected the other ores – cancelling their effects and polluting them until they turned black. Handled incorrectly, they could release an uncontrollable, destructive energy.

The white ores were discovered last. Their soft glow seemed void of any effect, nothing like the others. Gabriel's father had carried one of the largest shards everywhere he went. Gabriel touched his chest and for an instant, felt the crystal warm.

His arm stung as Adin punched him. .

"Ow! Jerk!" He rubbed the spot.

"You aren't even listening to me."

"I was, too." He rolled his eyes. "You use red ore to produce heat, creating steam. You collect all the steam using the blue ore, which changes it back to water so you can reuse it. And voila! We have underground trains!"

"Yes!" Adin pointed at him. "The whole system is virtually self-perpetuating. There are some minor moisture losses, but it's easy to top back up. But basically we have a free energy source for the transit system."

I wonder what else they use the ore for now? He was impressed; he had thought they only used ores in energy and food production.

"It's truly amazing what Dr. Cymru has invented. He's finally gotten approval for all his devices to go commercial over the next six months. We are going to be able to produce free energy for everyone in a year or two. Fix a lot of problems." Adin drummed his hands on the steering wheel as the traffic slowed.

"I highly doubt that T.E.R.A. will give anything away for free." Gabriel rolled his eyes again.

"Well, we have to recoup the funds spent on the development of the technology, by charging every user at first, but in the end we plan to make it free."

"I still have no idea what you actually do," Gabriel admitted.

"What?" Adin changed lanes gently. "Seriously? How do you not know what I do?"

"Adin, I saw you once last year, if that. I think I left when you arrived." Gabriel laughed.

"That's right. You did." Adin punched him lightly on the arm again.

He put up his hands in defence. "Hey! Hey! You're boring. That's not my fault."

"And life in Burlington was just full of excitement, huh?"

"Good point." Gabriel leaned his head against the window to stare up at the tall buildings passing by. After several minutes they turned and descended into an underground parking structure, coming to a stop at a small set of gates and a guard shack.

Adin rolled down his window. "George." He nodded at the guard.

"You're all set, Mr. Roberts. Welcome home."

The gates in front of them lowered into the ground with a loud beep. Adin manoeuvred through the parking structure quite quickly, and Gabriel lost his sense of direction. After they came to a stop in an unmarked stall, he exited the vehicle, careful not to catch the blanket. Adin pulled the chest out on the other side of the SUV and strolled to the wall in front of the vehicle.

Impatiently Gabriel waited for him, stretching his neck from side to side as he stood on the spot. A loud buzz filled the air, and something vibrated under his feet. Staring at the ground, he stepped back from the SUV, unsure of what was going on. Adin calmly walked up beside him and chuckled. "Relax, it's just the anti theft."

"Huh?"

"The vehicles parked here are lifted just enough that the tires don't touch. Basically, if you don't have the code – you can't move the vehicle."

"That's pretty damn smart."

"If you're impressed by that, wait till you see the rest."

CHAPTER EIGHT

GABRIEL WALKED WITH HIS BROTHER TO THE FAR SIDE OF THE HUGE PARKING GARAGE. They stopped at a single steel door that reflected warped images of them on its smooth surface. To the left of the door was a keypad and large flat red screen with lines running up and down it. Adin placed his hand on the screen and then typed in a code. The door unlocked silently and, to Gabriel's surprise, split in the middle and retracted into the wall. They passed through.

After taking an elevator up several floors, they stepped into a long corridor, with walls made of glass, high above the street below. It connected to a tall tower across the street. As the moving walkway carried them towards the structure, Gabriel almost lost his balance. He reached for the hand rail to steady himself and tapped the path with his foot. "Hmmm."

Adin set Nate's chest down on the floor between them and grinned. "Impressed?"

"A little." He looked towards the end of the clear glass tube. Four massive high-rises rose out of the base structure they were headed towards. He pointed. "You live in one of those?"

"Yes. These towers are for T.E.R.A. employees. I live in the far one on the right." Adin pointed.

Gabriel leaned forward, stretching his neck to see what the tower overlooked. Suddenly, his view was disrupted by an image on the glass wall. *What the hell?* He stepped back to view the full image.

"Mr. Roberts, I see you have a visitor with you today. Please stop by and clear him before going to your apartment." The enlarged, ugly face stared directly at him.

"Yes Anthony, we'll come see you right away." Adin jokingly saluted the digitized face.

"Excellent, sir." The floating head faded into the glass as quickly as it had appeared.

"Sorry about that. Security can be a pain because all of the big executives live here as well." Adin pointed to the top of the towers.

Gabriel nodded, feeling like a country bumpkin. They exited the walkway into a crowded lobby with a ceiling several stories above them.

It looked like a high-end hotel, complete with everything one might ever need. *Wow.* He marveled, trying not to lose Adin in the busy crowd. There was a lounge, several restaurants, a small grocery and even a telecom room, all surrounded by shops and boutiques. The wooden walls were decorated with strange abstract art in thick carved frames, the wood glimmering from the bright lights shining down on them. The floors looked almost like mirrors, the sheen of the black marble reflecting a muted image of the room. Chasing after Adin, he felt like he should remove his shoes or something. With each step he sank into plush, beautifully patterned rugs.

As they reached the front desk, he recognized the floating head and was stunned that the face belonged to an actual person and was not some image generated by a computer. The man was huge and built like a stone wall, his face and hands rough and scarred. Gabriel imagined the giant on a medieval battlefield, fighting off hordes of enemy warriors. This man would have thrived back in those times, but he looked out of place here in the middle of luxury.

"Anthony, this is my brother Gabriel. He's going to be living with me." Adin slapped Gabriel's back.

Anthony said nothing but turned to the computer screen and began typing.

"Dr. Cymru already cleared it in the system, I assure you. We just need to code him into the building." Adin pointed at the keypad resting beside the desk.

Anthony ignored the command and continued working on the computer screen. A minute later he looked at Adin. "Dr. Cymru cleared him for permanent residence in your suite. I need to code him in."

Gabriel chuckled lightly. *Not too smart, are you?*

"Right." Adin rolled his eyes and gestured for Gabriel to approach the desk. The keypad and screen beside the desk matched the one in the parking garage.

Anthony stared at Gabriel. "Put your hand there. Wait for the scan and then put in a code, seven digits minimum."

Seems easy enough. Gabriel placed his left hand on the screen. Red lines rolled across it, marking the patterns of his hand on the screen in green. He input a code he hoped he would remember and began to remove his hand. The large man seized it and shoved it back down. Caught off guard, Gabriel's other hand instantly formed a fist, ready to strike him. *Oh god. He could rip off my arm.* Rethinking the move, he let the giant have his way.

"Wait for the scan," Anthony growled. One of his front teeth was chipped.

A beep went off, and Anthony's death grip relaxed. Taking back his hand he escaped with Adin into the elevators. He checked to make sure his hand was still working, moving each finger individually then all together. As the elevator door closed Gabriel began to protest but was silenced by Adin's hand over his mouth. His heart pumped faster as he waited for Adin to push the button for their floor.

When they exited the elevator Adin burst out laughing. "Sorry. The beast was probably listening to us."

"Where did you guys find him? On a battlefield in the 1200s?" Gabriel kept the blanket tight around him as he followed Adin down the hall.

Adin laughed. "Yes, we developed a time machine to recruit security guards."

Gabriel ignored the smart ass comment. "So do they monitor everything that you do?" He wanted to shiver. "Will they be watching me?"

Adin laughed again, then put on a serious expression. "They monitor me to some degree but nothing too crazy. As for you, I am going to ask them for extra monitoring with reports coming to my office hourly so I know what you're up to when I go to work. Especially if you go near my SUV." He pointed sternly at Gabriel.

"Very funny." Gabriel eyed the security cameras on the walls.

They stopped at a door that numbered 871. "Well, this is it." Adin pressed his thumb into the lock and the lock popped. "Home, sweet home."

Adin opened the door to the apartment and strolled in. Gabriel followed. He felt his jaw drop as he gawked at the apartment. A woman's voice filled the room, "Phone call from Dr. Cymru." It had a soothing tone, although clearly artificial.

"Dr. Cymru, hello." Adin put a small silver device behind his ear and headed down the hall. "Thank you for the offer. Yes, my brother survived …" His voice disappeared as he entered a room.

Setting his things down gently on the black slate entryway, Gabriel leaned forward to get the full view without moving his feet. The apartment was so much like Adin that even the cut of his suit blended into the design of the room. Everything was either black or chrome and spotlessly polished to give off a perfect reflection. The entryway was clean and contained an empty chrome coat rack and a strategically placed floor plant that Gabriel could only assume was not real. To the right was a huge kitchen, looking perfectly clean and symmetrical, as if it was never used. He had heard his mother rave about the high-tech kitchen – everything hidden behind panels and revealed with the push of a button. An island topped with black marble defined the edge of the kitchen flanked by four tall chrome bar stools. The only items in the kitchen that had any colour were the bright lemons and limes and the single orange in the fruit basket on the island. The room's lighting felt natural, almost like he was outside. He twisted his head up at the ceiling. It glowed. Not from individual sources but rather the entire ceiling gave off light. As Adin roamed through the room, the ceiling above him increased in brightness, following him. It was mesmerizing.

To the left of the entryway the floor dropped down several steps into a sunken den. Gabriel was happy to see that it was decked out with creature comfort in mind: high back leather chairs that looked like they reclined, a glass table magnetically floating in the centre of the room and, finally, a huge realism projection television unit. Gabriel remembered begging his mother to buy one. RPTV's used thin fibre optic strings, hundreds of thousands of them, running from the floor to the ceiling in a tight rectangle that formed realistic 3D images.

"Come in, don't be shy." Adin encouraged him with a wave of his hand.

Gabriel followed Adin on a brief tour of the apartment, as his brother pointed out where to find food and how the high-tech kitchen worked. A bracelet gave control of all of the electronics in the house through simple hand gestures, and Gabriel was eager to try it on. They strolled down a short hallway between the kitchen and sunken den, pausing at the simple bathroom with a toilet and a pedestal sink.

"How do you shower?" Gabriel looked around the room.

"Buttons on the wall." Adin pointed to a set of six silver buttons in the corner of the room.

"Of course." He smiled and he gave Adin a thumbs up. He was going to have to figure that one out.

Adin then showed off his huge master bedroom, complete with floor to ceiling windows that overlooked a small park and several smaller apartment buildings. Finally, he opened the door to the last room and stepped aside.

Gabriel walked into the room. It was about the same size as his room back home on the ranch but windowless. It had many of the same elements: a small desk, a bookshelf, a closet, and a single bed pushed into one of the corners. The bed was kinda small.

"It's not much, but I hope it will do." Adin leaned against the door frame.

"It will be fine once I bring some colour into it." Gabriel ran his hand along the flat dark grey walls.

"Yeah, I guess this place could do with some colour but I don't have much time to decorate. The place still pretty much looks the same as when I first moved in." Adin glanced back down the hallway.

"It's sharp looking. For sure." He nodded at Adin.

"Anyhow, I have things to do, but we have laundry service here so have a shower and get cleaned up. I'll put out some of my clothes for you and we can do some shopping tomorrow." Adin turned towards the door then hesitated. "I'm glad I didn't lose you to the storm … I'm happy you're here Gabriel."

Gabriel smiled at him. *Me too.*

Doing as instructed, Gabriel headed into the bathroom. He chuckled at his reflection in the mirror as he unwrapped the big blanket that was still resting on his shoulders. *Anthony must have thought I was a homeless guy.* After he tossed the blanket into a laundry sack and his blood-stained clothing into the trash, he turned to face the mirror again. He stared at his chest, taking his first close look at it. *My God.* Light rippled out from the crystal in waves under his skin, each pulse trying to reach further than the last. *So this is how it ends – slowly eating away at me.* His calloused thumb outlined the crystal. It pulsed softly with each beat of his heart, his skin tightly holding it in place. Despite the danger, it somehow seemed to belong there.

Pushing the thought from his mind, he turned to the six buttons on the wall. It couldn't be that hard. As he stepped up to them, he heard a click on the floor. A drain appeared. He pushed the button at the top. It flashed green, then a cylindrical panel rotated out of the wall. It smoothly arced around him, finally meeting the other wall and locking into place. Gently warm water rained down, slowly increasing in temperature. The small space filled with a warm mist with a hint of eucalyptus.

He breathed it in deeply. His mind drifted back to the sight of his mother's limp hand splattered with blood. *Mom.* He leaned against the cool wall of the shower. Tears blended with the hot water as he sighed heavily, his heart still aching from the loss. The intense heat in his chest returned. The sound of sizzling filled the stall, the water evaporating as it touched the brightly glowing crystal. The heat disappeared quickly, and soon the water drifted across its sharp surface easily. Nothing felt real.

His thoughts were interrupted as the misty shape of Adin walked into the bathroom and started to relieve himself. Instinctively, he turned to face the wall, hiding the crystal. The cool air from the open door rolled across his skin. Goose bumps popped up all over his body.

"Hey! A little privacy here?" he cried out in protest.

"Get used to it!" Adin hollered over the noise of the flushing toilet. "And here are some clothes."

Adin moved Gabriel's few possessions carefully down the hall and into his spare room. He removed the duffel bag from on top of the chest and tossed it on the bed. He hesitated, staring at the silver chest – recognizing it. *Why would Gabriel have Nate's chest?* He hadn't even thought of what happened to the ranch hand but guessed the worst now that Gabriel held Nate's most cherished belonging. It was sad. Nate was a good man, taught him and Gabriel what he knew – 'shooting and punching' as Nate always put it, an activity Adin never saw a point too. Nate did the best he could with two boys that weren't his. Adin was sure Gabriel was missing him – their relationship had grown deep over the last ten years. It seemed to be the opposite for him. As soon as Adin began to spend more time with Dr. Cymru and T.E.R.A., Nate pulled back. Adin couldn't blame him. When your best friend dies, you build up a little hate.

He absentmindedly rubbed his chin, which was now feeling a little rough, and thought about the week to come. He hoped to set up the funeral for later that week, leaving enough time for extended family to arrive and for Gabriel to buy some new things. Dr. Cymru had called to let him know that the costs would be covered by T.E.R.A. *I'll go back to work on Monday, surprise him. Hopefully, I am not too far behind.*

Sitting on the bed, he pulled out the small gold locket that he had removed from around his mother's neck. It was flecked with dots of dried blood. Wiping the front clean with his thumb, he gently opened the locket. A picture of his father, Calvin, lay inside. *Of course. I almost forgot.* On the other side of the locket was a small folded piece of paper. With a delicate touch he unfolded the aging parchment and read the hand-written note. "I will always be with you no matter where I go." His eyes filled with tears as he recognized his father's scribbled writing.

Adin missed his father incredibly; his longing to be like him had become his strength to do well in school and ultimately had led him to work for T.E.R.A. With Dr. Cymru's help, he had begun to create a name for himself and was finally being rewarded handsomely for all his hard work. It hadn't come easy, working at a company with so many reminders of his father, but Adin had grown fond of the connection over the years. He was proud to be the son of Calvin Roberts, the great explorer who found Eden's Ore. This drive consumed him, rarely allowing any time for family or holidays. A choice he wasn't so sure of now.

A keen sense of regret gnawed at his heart. Adin wished he had spent more time with his mother over the last few years but his busy life never allowed for it. He pushed the tears out of his eyes, holding the locket tightly and stood up – eager to get back to his day.

CHAPTER NINE

"Mom! Go back!" Gabriel screamed over the howling wind.

He screamed again and again at her, but she refused to leave the bottom of the stairs. She just held on to the broken outer wall of the house, stretching her hand out towards him. He slid down the stairs. The metal edge of each riser dug into his skin. The pain didn't matter. He had to get to her. One step after another, he dragged himself faster and faster towards her but she stayed just out of reach. No matter how fast he pushed, her stretched-out hand was always just out of his grasp. The steps between them seemed to multiply, one after another like an escalator, keeping him away from her. He tried to stand against the wind, but invisible weights kept him pinned to the painful metal edges of the stairs.

"Just go! Get back to the shelter!" he pleaded as his strength faded.

The house swayed back and forth under the pounding wind. He continued to descend the endless stairs towards her. Sections of the roof landed around him like pieces of shattered glass, exploding into splinters of wood and rusty nails. He covered his face as shrapnel pierced his body. The walls broke apart and were carried away by the whirling wind. A black wall rose up behind her. It climbed higher and higher, casting its shadow over her. She didn't notice anything; she just kept trying to reach for him. The wall that would crush her fell slowly towards her.

"NO!" He screamed so loud he felt his chest break open.

He shot up in bed. Sweat and tears ran down his face. Burying his face in his hands, he breathed heavily, his chest expanding against his sweat-soaked shirt. He sprang out of bed and peeled off the sticky shirt, feeling sick to his stomach. An eerie glow filled the room as he stood there in only his shorts – the crystal shining intensely in the dark. A strange burnt smell lingered in the room. He lifted the sweat-soaked shirt up in front of him, and his jaw dropped. The shirt had a hole burned through it. *The crystal.* His upper body tingled as sweat evaporated rapidly. Lowering his chin, he stared into the source of the light. The crystal pulsed with the loud, hard beat of his heart. Waves of light rippled outwards, through his veins. He grabbed a new T-shirt off his dresser, but he hesitated as he put on the new dry shirt. What if the bed caught fire? *Relax.* He shook his head. He wasn't going to burn the place down. He hoped. He pulled the shirt on and looked at the digital clock. 3:38am.

He lay awake in his dark room for hours, until the familiar pat of Adin's feet moved from his room and down the hall. He swung his feet out of bed and waved his hand across the front of his new sound system, a purchase compliments of the disaster relief funds. Its holographic display came to life – three dimensional cubes slowly twisting in the air. A flick of his finger through one of the floating cubes started an entrancing beat thumping through his room. He sat in the darkness waiting for his courage to build, hoping it would be stronger than the sense of guilt haunting him. His mother's funeral was today and he needed to put her to rest. To tell her how much he loved her for the last time.

After putting a second shirt on, Gabriel felt safe enough to emerge from his room. He met Adin in the kitchen, drinking a tall glass of juice in the early morning light.

"You okay?" Adin sounded concerned.

"Just tough sleeping," he said quietly. "New bed and all."

Adin looked at the coffee maker. "Dark roast. Two cups." A panel below one of the cupboards opened and rolled out a small steel tray with steaming cups. "It's just time. Things always get better in time. If you want to talk, even in the middle of the night, you know you can, right? My door is open."

Gabriel leaned on the kitchen island, staring at Adin's empty glass. "Yeah, I ... just ... I dunno."

Adin topped off the glass with more juice from the dispenser in the fridge door and pushed it towards Gabriel.

Gabriel could feel his insides crying out to break the silence and reveal everything that happened in the storm, but fear gagged him. Wrapping his hands around the glass, he continued to stare down into it, struggling to decide whether to speak. He finally lifted it to his lips. The sour, sharp taste of grapefruit gave him confidence. He would speak – later. After finishing the juice, he gave the glass back to Adin and smiled. Then he noticed a gold pendant swinging across his brother's bare chest. He'd seen that pendant before.

"You're wearing Mom's locket."

"Yeah ... I feel like it's all I can do to say goodbye," Adin delicately followed the chain down with his fingers until he reached the locket and cupped it in the palm of his hand.

"Does it still have the note from Dad in it?"

"Yeah, I remember Mom would read it when she felt stressed." Adin played with the locket between his fingers.

Gabriel smiled and turned from him, gazing out the window. The morning sun had burned through the cloud cover. Its rays showered the city, awakening it from its slumber. The apartment's ceiling had not activated yet, leaving the orange hue of the morning sun to slowly spread around the dark walls. Carefully lifting the two cups of coffee, he set one down in front of Adin then moved to sit across from him on one of the tall stools.

"Well, I guess there's no avoiding it," he admitted. "Time for the funeral."

"It's best to get it over with and try to get back to normal."

Not with this in my chest. He rested his hand on the crystal hiding beneath his shirt. "I don't know what that means anymore. Did we ever have normal? First Dad, now Mom. Maybe that is normal for us."

Adin looked him in the eyes but stayed quiet for the moment. Several sips of coffee later, he finally spoke. "You will find something sooner or later to focus on, help you find some routine. I still think even one class at the college would be good for you. Something to keep you busy."

"That's what you did when Dad died. You're going to do that again? Dive into your work and forget about everything else?" Gabriel regretted his words instantly. "Sorry."

Adin sighed. "That was my choice at the time. Anyhow ..."

"I shouldn't have ..."

Adin set his coffee cup down loudly. "Leave it alone. We need to get ready." He walked back to his room and shut the door behind him, leaving Gabriel alone in the kitchen.

Gabriel hated the funeral. A sea of people packed into a small room after the outdoor procession. He watched each of their faces. Some he knew, some he didn't. The strangers wept openly and talked about how she would be missed. How was that even possible, when he had never seen her with any one of them? The whole event seemed staged – as if each had a part to play for the family. He stayed out of the way as best he could, moving from corner to corner, even avoiding his own friends. He knew what they were thinking. Their eyes said it all – a pitiful look in each of them, like he was cursed to never find happiness. Adin spent most of the time running interference, addressing family, and letting everyone know that things would be alright.

Gabriel felt empty, alone – despite the buzz of activity around him. Even the melody strummed in the background by the cute harpist did nothing to lift his spirits. *Would they even notice if I left?* Just as he was considering his escape through a side door, a man stepped into his path. He was old, with a balding head and grey hair, thick glasses resting on his nose. His smile seemed warm, like a grandfather's.

"Gabriel." The stranger was almost beaming.

He smiled and nodded. There was no way to step past the older man in the crowded room. He kept his arms crossed and tried not to continue the conversation.

"Excuse me. I had forgotten how much you look like your father. Adin took after your mother, but you are definitely Calvin's son." The stranger's comments shocked him.

"You knew my father?" Gabriel offered his hand. "I'm sorry, I don't recognize you?"

"I'm not surprised, I haven't seen you since you were a boy. I'm Allan Cymru." He gripped Gabriel's hand firmly.

Hearing the name, Gabriel jerked his hand back quickly. "You're Adin's boss."

"Boss? I'd prefer the term mentor, friend, confidant but I suppose 'boss' is an accurate enough description."

"Why are you here?" He glared at Cymru.

"To pay my respects. I knew your mother well. Your father and I were partners for a long time – you don't spend that much time with a man and not get to know his family. A tragic end for such a lovely woman."

Gabriel's gut twisted as Cymru spoke. "I am sorry that you and your brother must endure this. My heart goes out to you both." He dipped his balding head in a bow.

Gabriel remained silent, his teeth dragging across one another. He did not want to discuss his mother's death. Especially not with this man.

"Gabriel, I can see you're upset. I am sorry if meeting me has offended you. I want you to know something. My interest in you and your brother's well-being is honest. I never had the opportunity for family of my own, but I always thought of Calvin as a brother. I always treated Adin as my family and I feel no differently about you. Now, I don't know what you have heard about me but – believe me – I only want the best for you both."

"Was it best when you pushed Adin to go to school instead of being with his family?" Gabriel didn't try to soften his tone. "Dad had barely been gone a year."

"Ah …" Cymru pointed his finger at him. "I can see how that might have looked. Yes, I did encourage Adin to leave, but only so he would not forget about his dreams and not be crippled by Calvin's death. I don't know if Adin has ever told you how much he wanted to be like his father. Your father's death affected him much more deeply than anyone knows. My pushing him to get back on his path – it saved him. Stopped him from becoming something he was not."

Gabriel could see the seriousness in Cymru's brown eyes. He seemed to be telling the truth and seemed to earnestly care for Adin. Gabriel had never thought about what Adin needed at that time, he just knew his mother had needed him. And Adin chose to walk away – to leave with this man, despite her begging him to stay.

"Well, you forgot about the rest of us – what we needed. My mother needed her sons. Excuse me." He pushed past Cymru, bumping into him purposefully.

"Dr. Cymru!" Adin's voice called out from the busy room. "Thank you for coming. And all of this – it was a beautiful ceremony. Thank you for that." Gabriel twisted around to see Adin embrace the old man. Dr. Cymru smiled and patted him on the back, all the while staring at Gabriel.

"Gabriel!" Adin noticed him, gesturing him to come closer. "Come meet a very important man."

"Actually, I already had the pleasure of meeting him. It's good to see you two together – a blessing in all of this." Gabriel kept his distance, staring back at the older man.

"Oh. Well, great." Adin clasped his hands together. "I hope to be back to work soon, I will let you know."

"Adin, take all the time you need. You have a lifetime of research ahead of you, but now is the time to mourn. When you're ready, you let me know. Nothing will change. Now, I must ask for your forgiveness as I must leave to attend to some important items." Dr. Cymru gave Adin another hug and then held out his hand to Gabriel. "I hope to see you again soon."

Reluctantly, Gabriel walked forward and grasped the man's hand. "I doubt it."

"I hope so." Dr. Cymru turned to walk away, signalling two men in black suits to follow. "Oh." He stopped and turned back to them both. "Adin, why don't you bring Gabriel down to the labs one day. He might like to see for himself what his father was a part of building. And, Gabriel, when you do decide on your path, let me know. I would be honoured to help." He nodded and left the room with his escort.

Adin moved closer to Gabriel. "Amazing man. You're very lucky to be given an offer like that. Be smart and take it."

Gabriel kept quiet. He was torn. Cymru seemed to genuinely want to help them. Everything Nate had told him about Cymru seemed cruel and unwarranted. Why did Nate hate Cymru so much?

The hours dragged on until finally the two brothers crossed the glass conveyer belt and went back up to apartment number 871.

As Adin pressed his hand down onto the blue screen and the door clicked open, Gabriel strode past him, heading straight for his room. Finally in the sanctuary of his own space, he let out a breath and ran his hands through his hair. With a wave of his hand, he turned on the hypnotic music that seemed to soothe him and sprawled face down on his bed. He wanted to climb into the darkness and stay for awhile.

The door eased open and Adin stepped in, turning off the music. He sat down on the corner of the bed. "It wasn't easy for either of us today."

"It's my fault … it's my fault she's not here," Gabriel mumbled into his sheets.

"It's not your fault." Adin grabbed Gabriel's shoulder and rolled him on to his side. "There is no way you or anyone else could have prevented that storm!"

"No. You don't understand." He stood up in front of Adin and paced the room. "We had made it. We were in the shelter."

"What are you saying, Gabriel?"

"It is my fault! I left the shelter, and she followed me out. I told her stay! That I would be right back!"

"What are you saying? Why did you leave?"

Tears rolled out from his eyes. "I went back for the white crystal."

Adin rose from the bed, pointing at him. "You left for that stupid piece of rock! What were you thinking?"

"It's all I have of him! I don't remember him like you do!" he yelled. "I went back for it – I don't know why – we were in the shelter and I went back. She was supposed to stay there!" His voice trembled. "I told her to stay in the shelter but she didn't. She followed me out and I couldn't get back … I … couldn't reach her." He dropped to his knees and pounded the floor with his fist. "She was right there … I … I couldn't save her." Tears blurred his vision.

Adin grabbed his shoulder. "Stop, Gabriel. Stop! It doesn't matter. Mom did what she did because she wanted to protect you, nothing else!"

"She was so close … I told her to go …" He hung his head.

"Look, Gabriel, you have to let it go. It's no more your fault than mine for not being there."

He looked up at Adin, his face wet with tears. Undoing his tie and buttons, he opened his shirt to expose the ore imbedded in his chest. "I … I fell …"

"My God, Gabriel." Adin's jaw hung open. "Why didn't you tell me?"

Gabriel touched his chest. "I'm sorry. I don't know what to do."

Adin left him on his knees and walked out of the room. Minutes later he appeared in the doorway and tossed Gabriel his coat, motioning for him to put it on.

"Adin, what's going on?"

"Gabriel, I am so thankful you're alive … do you understand that?" Adin spoke rapidly. "But if I don't get that ore out of your chest you are going to die!"

"Adin, stop! It's been in me for six days."

"And six days is far too long to have that in your chest! Most humans die after two days of constant exposure to any of the crystals. I don't know of any subject, animals included, that can survive that long in contact with the crystal." He turned on his heel and strode out of the room.

"Adin, wait!" He chased after him.

"It has to be taken out. Your exposure may be reversible with some treatment, but I have to remove it!" Adin sounded frantic.

Gabriel recognized the blue light flashing from the small disc just behind Adin's ear.

"Who are you calling?" he yelled, afraid of anyone else knowing his secret. "Hang it up!"

"I'm not going to lose you!" Adin snapped back.

"I don't know what's happening to me but you can't tell anyone. They would just use me as a test rat. Please."

Adin let Gabriel pull the silver disc from behind his ear. His chest heaved. Gabriel wasn't sure whose heartbeat was louder.

"Adin, please. We can figure this out together." Gabriel willed Adin to look him in the eyes. "But just us. No one else can know about this." Gabriel peeled back Adin's grip on the silver disc and put it on his desk. He looked up at Adin, his chest rising and falling quickly. "No one can know, Adin. You can't tell anyone."

CHAPTER TEN

NATE STOOD ON THE OPPOSITE SIDE OF THE STREET, KEEPING WATCH ON DR. CYMRU'S DRIVER AS HE STROLLED BACK TO THE RESTAURANT AFTER PARKING THEIR VEHICLE. The pace at which the driver moved meant this meeting was going to take awhile, there was no need for Nate to rush. "Let's keep our distance. Looks like he's going to take his time here."

His team had spent the last week trailing all of Dr. Cymru's movements outside of T.E.R.A. The man spent very little time outside of the offices and he always kept his meetings short. They had been collecting information: who he knew, what he was doing and more importantly, his patterns. He had no significant other or family. He didn't socialize with others in power, rarely attending any events despite being invited to them all. The man was an enigma; however, his intentions for power and the ores were quite clear.

Dr. Cymru was systematically absorbing other energy and research companies into T.E.R.A. This wasn't accomplished by owning shares or stakes in any of the companies. T.E.R.A. – The Energy and Resource Acquisition – was a government organization designed to regulate the energy market and maintain prices. With this decree came the right to acquire any private resource deemed necessary to maintain energy production and keep the market stable. Sure, it required a lot of red tape, but in the end T.E.R.A. was like a spoiled kid, pointing at whatever he wanted and demanding it be his. The funny thing was that the government didn't seem to care. As long as the energy market was stable, nothing T.E.R.A. did had a consequence, even if it broke the law.

"Sir." A voice whispered from inside his ear – connecting him to the rest of his team.

"Go ahead." His eyes surveyed the area in preparation for a problem.

"Crossing your path in 20 seconds. Man in a green coat, black pants, glasses. This is his fourth time circling. He's using an alley down the street to loop around the restaurant."

Nate waited, counting each second until the described man strolled in front of him. "I see him." Nate whispered.

"We're detecting a signal from him. It's electronic. Too weak to be dangerous. He's scanning for something. He might pick up our signals, sir. Hold all communication." The voice went quiet.

Nate moved after the green coat. He lagged behind, keeping his eyes on the man and waiting for the right opportunity. As his men had predicted the man in green rounded the next corner and darted down the alley. Nate followed, trying to keep his feet light and not give himself away. Too late. The man sprinted, briefly glancing over his shoulder at Nate. The chase was short as he accelerated after the stranger, stretching his hand out for the green coat. He yanked the man backwards, slamming him to the ground.

Nate stood over him. "Who are you?"

"What's your problem! I'm not doing anything." The man in green struggled to his feet.

Nate grabbed his shoulder and kicked the man's feet from under him. "Stay on the ground, please."

The man rubbed at his knee. "What do you want?"

"Who are you?" Nate remained focused on his target.

"I'm – I'm George Clark. Who are you?" The man glared at him.

"There are four holographic ads at the end of this alley. Two of them have the word 'George' in them and one is for Clark and company. Let's try again – Who are you!"

The man glared at him, his mouth shut.

"Fine." Nate grabbed him by the front of his green coat and threw him against the alley wall. "We can do this the hard way."

The man's quick jab barely missed Nate's jaw, as he smacked the fist to the side. He could fight. Sort of. Another combination of punches drove Nate backwards as he dodged them.. He ducked under a final swing and drove his elbow into the man's nose. The stranger's eyes filled with tears as his nose popped, flooding blood down his green coat.

Nate grabbed him by the front of his jacket and pressed him hard against the wall. A flash of a white around his neck caught Nate's eye and he pealed back the coat, yanking the white collar off. He sighed and let go of the man. The stranger was shocked and dropped to the ground.

Nate handed the collar back to the stranger. "You're a priest."

The man nodded. He fumbled in his pockets, pulling out a handkerchief to wipe his face. His eyes pierced Nate.

"I'm not your enemy. What's the church want with Cymru?" Nate crossed his arms.

"I can't answer that."

"Call Riley." Nate insisted. "Tell him Nate Reinhart wants to know."

The priest pulled a silver disc from his pocket. He slid it behind his ear and spoke. "Bishop Riley. A man named Nate Reinhart is with me. He would – right … I understand … Of course, yes."

Nate was impatient. He knew Riley would be behind this. He and Nate had served together in the military. Riley was once a military intelligence agent who excelled working behind enemy lines but, too many missions had driven him over the edge. He was discharged and sought sanctuary with the Church. Nate wasn't surprised when they gave him a fancy title and put him back to work for their own benefit.

"The Bishop says to remind you that you are a sinner and have not been to confession in your whole life. Perhaps you should see him. He would like to pray for you."

"Funny. What else?" Nate crossed his arms.

"Dr. Cymru has taken an interest in the black ore. Which means we have taken an interest in him." The priest opened his jacket and pulled out a small electronic device. "We recorded everything from inside the building. Every sound. Every conversation. Up till when you attacked me. Once it is filtered, perhaps we will find some answers."

Nate smiled. "So, if I want to hear what's on it I have to get 'prayed' for."

"Bishop Riley said he will see you in two days." The priest wiped his nose a final time and, half smiling, walked out of the alley and disappeared.

Nate sighed. "Well, I guess I'm off to church."

One of his team members spoke in his ear. "Why's the Church of Humanity so interested in the black ore?"

Nate walked back to the street, keeping his voice low. "The Church wants the black ore destroyed. They believe it's pure evil. Anyone who has any affinity towards any ore is considered a threat. Especially an ore user. The Church considers them abominations and usually executes them."

CHAPTER ELEVEN

THE DOOR TO THE APARTMENT SHUT, AND THE CLUNK OF TWO SHOES ECHOED FROM THE SLATE ENTRANCE. The noise surprised Gabriel. He turned down the volume on the RPTV with a wave of his hand and poked his head out from around one of the comfy black arm chairs. "You didn't tell anyone, right? Not even a hint?" He stared at Adin.

"You know your little secret could skyrocket my career, probably set us up for life."

"Adin." Gabriel got out of his chair, pointing a stern finger at Adin.

"Seriously, this could be huge. It's the discovery of a lifetime. A whole new field of research."

"I am not becoming a test rat. End of story."

"Gabriel, you wouldn't become a test rat. We're scientists, not barbarians. You need to consider the future."

His temper rose. "I am not going to be someone's guinea pig!"

"Fine. We get one chance to set us up for life and you don't want to take it." Adin dropped his briefcase and a large red rectangle made up of Cubes onto the kitchen island, then walked towards his room.

"Did you talk to someone?" Gabriel's stomach clenched as he mindlessly pulled apart the red rectangle – separating it into individual data storage Cubes. He had imagined Adin returning with a group of white coats to haul him away to a secret lab inside the towers.

"I told you I wouldn't say anything, so trust me," Adin yelled from his room. "I don't want to come home to the same question from you for the rest of my career."

"Good! So, what's with all the Cubes?" He picked one up and played with it – tossing it into the air and catching it with the same hand.

"Hey!" Adin hustled out into the kitchen and snatched the Cube from his grasp. "Damn it Gabriel, I put those in a certain order."

"Sorry." Gabriel shrugged and stepped back from the island. "That's hundreds of files … you that far behind at work?"

"Of course not, I got caught up today. These are research files from the past decade. There has to be something in these to give me a clue as to why the ore isn't killing you."

"Well, I'm not going to play the part of the guinea pig for you either!"

"Gabriel, you have to let me do some tests."

"You tell me what to do and I'll do it." He crossed his arms, his jaw set. "Myself."

"You run the tests? There are words in here you can't even pronounce let alone understand. You are just going to have to trust me. Period. Besides it should be easy to hide your sample – every employee at T.E.R.A. is required to have the same testing done."

"Whatever." He sighed and returned his gaze to the RPTV, motioning for it to flip through the channels as he wandered back to his chair. "So what are the files about anyhow?"

"Animal experimentation." Adin jumped into the seat beside him with a bottle of water and set the Cube on the hovering table in front of them. A small button unlocked the device and it unfolded itself into a 3 by 3 square grid. The line separating each grid disappeared and the whole surface became fluid. A holographic radial menu appeared, floating above it, waiting for Adin's input. He spun it to the left and selected some files, the table projected several grotesque pictures of dead animals across its surface. Double tapping them, Gabriel expanded each image to match the size of the floating table.

"All of these animals were injected with nanograms of ore for prolonged periods, several weeks of injections, so we could study the physical effects of direct contact with the ore. Now," Adin scrolled to the next image with a wave of his hand over the table. "When put in close proximity to humans, here's what happens."

The images made Gabriel sick to his stomach.

"Yeah, it's brutal." Adin closed the images. "Our best guess is the energy emitted from the crystals is a new type of neutrino with completely unique properties."

Gabriel stared at Adin blankly. "You're losing me here ... a neutrino?"

"It's a kind of elementary particle that is created from nuclear reactions. Like those that take place on the Sun – trillions of solar neutrinos hit the earth every second but those neutrinos are non-ionizing so they pass right through without hurting anything."

"So ... the crystals' neutrinos are different how?" He was feeling completely lost.

"Well to start – they're ionizing when it comes to humans."

Gabriel leaned back into the leather chair. "And that means what exactly?"

Adin laughed at him. "Alright, too much science. Basically, the energy from the ore destroys our cellular structure – like acute radiation syndrome. But it passes through everything else without issue, even other living things – plants and some types of animals."

"But we can stop that right – like the case the crystal was in before?"

"Right. The polymer acts like an anti-neutrino, absorbing the energy into itself and neutralizing it. Without the polymer, the reaction makes people sick around the ore — why they instantly feel the drain on them. And the black ore is the worst, for some unknown reason the effect is accelerated by a hundred fold."

Gabriel wanted to know more. "What about the white, like I have?"

"The white ore doesn't seem to react to any test; it didn't emit anything. It's considered to be void. I mean to say, there's energy there, but we don't know how to release it." Adin shrugged.

"Try sticking it in your chest."

"I don't think anyone has gone that far with it. Anyhow, the other ores killed the test subjects as well, just slower than the black." Adin opened another red cube and scanned through it. "There's notes here somewhere."

"Is the damage treatable?" Gabriel's stomach twisted as he flipped through the pictures of the dying animals.

"The best way is to get away from it. Despite them being neutrinos, they act like beta particles and don't travel very far. Any amount in your body would eventually decay but the cellular damage would already be done," Adin replied.

"Brutal."

"Yea, you can understand why I wanted it out of you." Adin gently pulled the magnetic table towards himself. With a wave of his hand, he scrolled to a directory of all the information on the Cubes. "I still do, actually."

"What about human experiments?" He could guess the answer.

"No, Gabriel." Adin shook his head. "Human experimentation is outlawed nowadays. Computer simulations only. T.E.R.A. is no different. We have to follow the laws."

"Hah! T.E.R.A. makes up half the laws in this country."

"T.E.R.A. does have a strong lobby group that works for us, but this country is still a democracy."

Gabriel frowned at him. "Seriously, does T.E.R.A. give you a book to study for every answer?"

Adin looked up from his reading, nodding. "Actually they do."

An hour later Gabriel abandoned his TV show and headed into the kitchen. Adin had already moved to the kitchen island and was reading through more of the red cubes. Adin met Gabriel's gaze and shook his head. "There's just nothing."

"Really?" Gabriel pressed a button on the counter and a section dropped down, sliding out of the way to reveal the stove top with four different sized pots to choose from. Touching the edge of one, he commanded, "Water, boil." The empty pot began to fill from the bottom up. Another button opened the cupboard, and he pulled out a box of pasta. "So what does that mean, Adin?"

"I guess we're on our own."

"I think I prefer that anyhow. I don't need everyone thinking I'm some kind of freak." He dumped the noodles into the steaming water, instantly producing a thick starchy mess. "What the hell?"

Adin rolled his eyes, laughing at him. "Why aren't you using the hydrator? That's for the noodles."

"Damn it. Do you cook anything properly?" He felt stupid. The technology of the kitchen felt like more work than the simple bio-fuel stove they had at the ranch.

"Actually, I don't even think restaurants do anymore." Adin was still laughing at him.

"Where can I throw this out?" He poked at the starchy slurry.

"Just close the stove. It will clean itself."

"Okay. You want some?" He shook a fresh box of dried noodles and searched for the button for the hydrator.

"No, I think I'll order in."

"Well, why am I making this crap?"

"No idea." Adin laughed again and showed him a takeout menu, complete with pictures, displayed on the phone's small monitor. "Here's a good one."

Gabriel had never had Russian cuisine before. Picking out some items that looked appetizing, he shrugged. "Hope it's good."

"The food is great and the little family that runs the place is friendly." Adin smiled. "Anyhow, I was thinking I would like to take a sample of your blood and analyze it in the lab tomorrow."

"Will they know it came from me?"

"They shouldn't. I'll do the test myself so it should be fine." Adin shrugged unconvincingly.

"*Should* be fine? Or *will* be fine?"

"It will be. Relax." Adin rolled his eyes.

"I don't know if I will ever be relaxed about this, Adin. Maybe the day someone else shows up with a crystal from the ore in their chest."

"That person will be rewarded. Then you will whine about not getting your share for the rest of your life. Roll up your sleeve." Adin got some equipment from his briefcase. He picked up a glass vial and put a five-pronged top on it. "This might sting a bit." He pressed the vial into Gabriel's forearm, catching him by surprise.

"Hey!" It felt like something bit him. A rush of energy travelled down his arm and a bolt of light sparked against the glass vial, exploding it in Adin's hands. *What the hell?*

"What did you do?" Adin stared at him.

"What do you mean what did I do? I didn't do anything."

Adin pointed to a small cord of white light sliding down Gabriel's arm. The light pooled over the five holes where Adin had poked him. The glowing thread sank deep into the skin, then retreated back up under his sleeve.

Feeling the rush of energy dissipate, he rubbed his skin. The puncture marks were gone, like it never happened. "Okay ... that's not normal."

"No." Adin raised his eyebrows and reached for Gabriel's shirt. He paused. "Just don't move." Adin slowly lifted up the shirt then dropped it back down.

"What?" He felt panicked.

"It was as if that crystal reacted to me ... hurting you ..." Adin stepped back and thought for a moment. "You lived through that storm ... no one could live through that. Maybe it wasn't a miracle." He was frowning. "How did the ore get there?"

"I ... I don't know, I uh, well ... the stairs fell ... I landed hard on ..." The memory suddenly became clear. "I landed on the ore. I remember the pain ... in my chest. I remember trying to pull it out but ... the light." He shuddered, the roar of the storm loud in his ears. "All I saw was that bright white light. Then I woke up the next day. I was lying in the dirt, the house broken around me." He blinked away the memory and shuddered again.

"The ore must have protected you but ..." Adin looked puzzled. "It can't be possible. The ore is toxic. Why would it react that way?"

"I don't know, you're the smart one. And didn't you say that the white ore didn't react to any tests? How do you know it's toxic? "

"Let's take another sample of blood." Adin grabbed another vial from his case.

Gabriel stared as the five-pronged vial pierced his skin with a sting. This time he expected it and there was no flash of light. A smooth, red silky liquid filled the chamber. Adin pulled it away from his arm and pressed a kitchen towel against the mark it left.

"You feel anything from the crystal this time?" Adin put the vial away.

"No. Nothing." He reached into his shirt. The ore felt hard and cool under his fingertips.

"That's odd." Adin pursed his lips. "I figured it would react again to your body being damaged if it was aware. Like a symbiotic entity might protect its host."

"Am I supposed to understand that! But I was pretty scared last time – you freaked me out! Jabbing that thing into my arm!" He exaggerated Adin's actions.

Adin frowned. "I wonder if the ore reacts to your emotions?"

"How would it do that? It's not alive. Wait – the heat."

"What are you talking about?"

"The ore heats up, like it's on fire. It burned a hole in my shirt the other night after a nightmare." Gabriel demonstrated the size of the burn mark on his chest.

"And that didn't alarm you enough to tell me?" Adin's mouth hung open.

"I was trying to figure out if it was killing me, not what it could do."

"Well, it certainly can do something."

"Well, blasting the vial like a bolt of lightning is new. Happy? You saw it first."

"Settle down. If it can react to your emotions it might also be able to sense your conscious thoughts." Adin grabbed another one of the Cubes and scrolled through it.

"So?" He didn't fully understand Adin's train of thought.

"Let's see …" Adin stared at the small projected screen for a moment then looked around the room. "Ah, there we are." He rushed over to the counter and grabbed an empty glass, filling it with water. He handed it to Gabriel.

"What do you expect me to do with this?" He stared at the glass and then back to Adin.

"I am guessing that the white ore might contain some of the properties of all the other types of ore. See if you can heat up the glass and make water boil, the way red ore can."

"So, boil the water?" He blinked at Adin. "How?"

"No idea." Adin shrugged.

"Well, this is stupid."

"Focus on it, picture it in your mind."

"You're kidding, right?"

"No." Adin shook his head and stared at him.

"You've done something like this before?"

"No."

"Well, how do you know it's going to work?"

"I don't, but it is worth a try."

"For the record, this is stupid." He shook his head and rolled his eyes but still clasped his hands around the glass of water.

He closed his eyes and tried to figure out how to speak to the ore. *Okay. Heat. Hot. Bubbles.* He tried to quiet his mind but was aware of his grip as he tightened it around the cup. *Nothing.* He took a deep breath and focused on the glass. He tried again and again with no success for several minutes. He hoped to feel some sensation or spark. Still, nothing happened.

His concentration was broken by the buzzer at the apartment door. His eyes jumped towards the source Who was there? Adin opened the door, and Gabriel spotted a uniformed T.E.R.A. guard carrying their take-out order. Seeing the guard at the door, he promptly pushed the glass away from him. His mouth watered as the smell of dinner filled the air.

"Thanks, Mark." Adin took the silver take-out bag from the guard.

"No problem, sir. The amount has been billed to your account."

"Great." Adin smiled and handed the guard a tip for his troubles. "Have a good evening."

"You too, sir." The uniformed guard gave Adin a quick wave.

As the two ate, they tossed around different theories about the ore. At Adin's insistence, Gabriel repeated the story of his fall from the stairs and how the ore must have slammed into his chest as he landed; he left out any details about their mother, he didn't want to talk about it. Adin proposed multiple new theories about free electrons and other possible molecular oddities the ore might possess. Gabriel tried to follow Adin's train of thought but ended up just watching the RPTV, randomly glancing at Adin and nodding. Eventually Adin ceased his scientific ramble and insisted he try to boil the water again.

"I'm too full from dinner. Let's try later." Gabriel sighed.

Adin pointed at him. "That wasn't the deal."

"Fine. If it works, I'm going set your pants on fire." He nodded at Adin in all seriousness. He moved to the kitchen island and positioned his hands around the glass and stared into it. He thought of fires, explosions, and any other fiery destruction that came to mind.

Minutes passed on the clock. *45 minutes of this. Come on just boil. Do something.* Adin had long since given up standing next to him, had retreated to the comfort of one of the reclining chairs and was reading another Cube. Gabriel's mind began to lose focus and he stared around the room aimlessly. Spotting Adin's sock he smiled. *Alright, sock. Catch on fire.* He stared at the black piece of cloth, annoyed by the whole process. After several minutes he gave up on Adin's sock and fixed his eyes on the glass, resting his chin on the cool marble surface of the counter. "Boil, boil, boil!"

As the water seemed to mock him in its refusal to boil, his anger at the silly experiment began to grow. All of a sudden, a thread of white light shot down his arm like a vine twisting around a tree limb. The narrow tip of the beam struck the glass in his hand and expanded around it. The glass turned bright red. It exploded, spraying shards across the counter top and all over the nearby floor. He barely closed his eyes in time. Shocked by what he had just done, he stumbled back from the island. His vision filled with black as he fell. Footsteps echoed in his fuzzy head. A warm hand immediately checked his pulse and lifted his head carefully. His eyes snapped open and he shot up into a sitting position staring at Adin. He touched the back of his head and winced in pain at the developing lump.

"How are you feeling?" Adin helped him to his feet and back onto a stool at the kitchen island.

"Man, my head hurts!" He pulled his hand away from his head, checking for blood.

"That was incredible!" Adin smiled from ear to ear.

"Painful too." He rubbed the back of his head. What had he just done?

"Gabriel, look! This is huge! We need to tell Dr. Cyrmu."

"Adin! We're not telling anyone!" He struggled free of Adin's excited grip. "Anyhow, what good is it if I pass out?"

"It's unheard of! No one in the world is like you ... look what you just did!" Adin clearly didn't understand how he felt.

"Forget whatever idea you're thinking. Even if I am the only one, I don't care. I don't trust Cymru and neither should you!"

Gabriel needed some space. Adin clicked a button on the bottom of the wall. "I don't know what kind of bullshit Nate has fed you about Dr. Cymru but it's a lie." A piece of the floor rose, revealing the top of a hose. Stretching it out he sucked up the glass, glancing up at Gabriel. "Don't you trust me?"

He rolled his eyes. "Of course, I do."

"Then –" Adin stared at him.

"No! Me and you … no one else." He could see the frustration on Adin's face.

"Fine!" Adin focused back on cleaning the floor while he thought out loud. "Maybe it's a matter of control. The power that came out was so strong – most likely because you weren't overly calm – that it shattered the glass! Now you just need to do it without losing control or passing out."

"And how do you suppose we fix that little problem?" Gabriel's head pulsed with pain.

"Simple." Adin finished the clean up job by tapping the top of the raised piece of floor. It retracted the vacuum hose, and the floor lowered back into place. "Just like any new skill you must practice it over and over. Although this time, let's try using a steel pot. You can sit in the big chair!"

Adin collected a small steel pot from the cupboard and added a couple inches of water. After setting down the pot, Adin grabbed one of the tall leather chairs and spun it around to face the kitchen. He motioned for Gabriel to come over and sit. This was crazy. Still feeling dizzy, he shook his sore head and walked slowly over. Adin pushed him down into the chair and set the pot into his hands. "Alright! Do it again!"

"I hate you."

CHAPTER TWELVE

ADIN WAS ALREADY TUGGING AT HIS TIE BEFORE THE DOOR TO HIS APARTMENT HAD FINISHED OPENING. As he stepped across the threshold, he let out a long sigh. He had found the monotony of his usual routine trying – he felt like more of a secretary than a scientist lately. Dr. Cymru daily praised him for his brilliant mind and elite schooling but in reality, he rarely allowed him the chance to use it. Now, he could change that. He could only dream about what they might discover about the white ore next. He looked around – Gabriel must be in his bedroom. He pushed down a twinge of guilt. Oh, he'd keep his promise for now – but one day he would publicly reveal his discovery, and share his triumph.

Kicking off his shoes, he commanded, "Image up." The RPTV instantly generated a 3-D image of the last channel it had shown.

A man in a suit continued the news, "… the attack on a T.E.R.A. facility in the Republic of China. That and other top stories from around globe in just a few minutes."

Interesting. He ambled around the kitchen, leaving the channel on to catch the full story. He always got a kick out of what

T.E.R.A. allowed the general public to know and what they didn't. He grabbed a bottle of water from the fridge, as the theme of the news network rang loudly through the room. He leaned on the counter to watch, sipping at the water. Gabriel's head poked out from one of the arm chairs, surprising him. He rubbed his sleepy eyes and nodded a lazy hello.

"Find out anything new?" Gabriel asked between big yawns.

"Thought you were in your room. Hold on a sec." He pointed at the news. He had heard some of the rumours around the office earlier and was eager to compare them to the news story. A slender brunette woman appeared on the RPTV, against the backdrop of a large map of China. "Late last night a small group of militants attacked a government resource storage facility in the Ming district as well as two of T.E.R.A.'s research facilities based in China. Damage was extensive at both facilities." An image appeared on the screen, flames erupting from each of the facilities. The camera zoomed in on a sign that read "T.E.R.A." and the flames crawling up the side of the structure. "T.E.R.A. spokesperson Andy Clarkson assured the public that nothing of value was taken, nor were any personnel hurt during the attack. The Republic of China did not release a statement about the sudden attack. These militants are allegedly linked to 'The Horsemen' – an elite organized crime syndicate based out of New Hong Kong ..."

Sheep, they believe anything we say. Adin lowered the volume, twisting an imaginary dial to the left in front of him until her voice trailed away.

"I saw that earlier today. What's the deal?" Gabriel pointed at the 3-D image.

"The deal is that T.E.R.A. isn't telling the whole story," Adin laughed. "I think they're embarrassed. You know the two research facilities in China that they showed pictures of?"

Gabriel climbed out of the overstuffed chair. He sat down on one of the island's stools across from Adin, giving him his full attention. He looked intrigued. Well, time to start letting him see the whole picture. "We only have one research facility in China. The second one they are calling a mobile research convoy but it isn't."

"What was it then?"

"It was a security task force T.E.R.A. hired to transport some things to the facility. Things that were secretly brought in two days earlier, through the New Hong Kong ports." Gabriel's eyes widened. Adin smiled at his brother. He was sharp all right.

Gabriel banged the counter top with his hand. "I knew it! Something didn't add up."

"Losing the task force wasn't the big deal. It was what they were carrying that has the company going crazy." He paused and took a swallow of water.

"Come on! What were they carrying?"

He smiled and laughed. "Well, I shouldn't be discussing this, but they had a load of ore."

"Seriously?"

"The worst part is that most of it was black ore." He shook his head.

Gabriel frowned. "I thought black ore just stole energy from the other ores."

"It does. But it also stores vast amounts of energy, tightly packed inside itself. That makes it extremely unstable. If they could find a way to weaponize it, they would have something extremely powerful. Something with enough bang to put any nuclear weapon to shame." Another discovery that would set me up for life, if I could figure it out.

"Wow, that's crazy!" Gabriel rose up out of his seat.

"Not to worry though. From what I've heard, it sounds like they've already deployed several teams to retrieve the shipment. We'll get it back." Adin searched for a snack, waving his hand in front of each cupboard to send it rising silently into the ceiling. "No one steals from T.E.R.A."

"You're acting like this is pretty normal."

"I suppose it is. T.E.R.A. has killed for ore before, that's no secret. The ore has been fought over, stolen, and traded on black markets for a long time. When Dad was working for T.E.R.A. they weren't prepared for his discovery. No one even knew exactly what the ore was, just that it was something brand new we'd never found before. Mistakenly, T.E.R.A. sold some. People stole some, and some just disappeared. It wasn't until Dr. Cymru took control of the company that T.E.R.A. became so strong." Adin spotted some cookies on an upper shelf and reached for them.

"Doesn't T.E.R.A. have all the ore?" Gabriel headed for the cookies.

"Hardly." He took two cookies out before Gabriel seized the package. "T.E.R.A. originally held almost seventy-five percent of the world's ore. But ... some of it was traded for resources and power ... some just disappeared. T.E.R.A. has spent the last couple of years reclaiming ore stocks around the world, through technology trading or simply by force."

"So, who else has ore?" Gabriel stuffed his face with two cookies at once.

"Next to us, the Church of Humanity probably holds the most. They claim it's their God-given right to govern the ore. Dr. Cymru finds that ridiculous and I agree. About fifteen percent is lost. Black market, private investors, who knows really? It's no different from diamonds or any other valuable resource. And people with power will always want more."

"Yeah, but diamonds don't kill you. Well, not generally." Gabriel tapped his chest.

"Speaking of that, I still can't find any information on the white ore, leaving us with not much to go on. "

"Well, Adin. You're the scientist, not me. Figure it out." Gabriel turned the volume back on the RPTV and returned to his chair in the den.

Yes. Adin was. He reached for another cookie. If he could only find the relationship – the reason behind why Gabriel was special.

It would be priceless, T.E.R.A. would have to give him anything he wanted.

"You know it sure would help our findings, if you let me get some extra help. Someone we can trust. Like Dr. Cymru." He needed to push Gabriel, get him to let go of the nonsense Nate had fed him all these years.

"Adin! No. You just said they would kill for a piece of it – what would they do for a piece that is in me!"

"I didn't say telling all of T.E.R.A. Dr. Cymru would make sure you had the best medical team and I bet, anything you wanted would be taken care of." His brother was so darn stubborn and annoying.

"No! I don't trust him." Gabriel turned away.

"Gabriel, you're throwing away the opportunity of a lifetime. Don't be stupid."

He had to convince him. This was the opportunity of a lifetime for his career.

"Stupid!" Gabriel whipped around. "They wouldn't be cutting *you* up for experiments, would they? No. It would be me."

"You think I would let that happen?" Adin shook his head. "Dr. Cymru wouldn't hurt you, he thinks of us as family."

"I don't care what he thinks. We're done with this conversation." Gabriel folded his arms and glared.

"You should at least take his offer to come see him at T.E.R.A., meet the man. He's great. Sit down with him, talk to him – you might be surprised at how much you have in common with him." If Adin could just Gabriel him to see that Cymru was not a monster then maybe ...

"Why?"

"Because he can help us. You can't hide in here forever with this thing in your chest. One day you're going to want to have a life. Having the right people on your side is going to make that a hell of a lot easier."

Gabriel stayed quiet, grinding his jaw. "Fine." Gabriel crossed his arms, his jaw still tight.

"You won't regret it. He's an amazing man." Adin clapped. "Don't worry about a thing; I will take care of it all."

"You better." Gabriel went back to the RPTV, plopping down loudly into the leather chair.

"Do any practice today?" Time to change the subject. "Try boiling water again?"

"Look in the sink."

"Alright ..." Down at the bottom lay what looked like a clump of metallic modelling clay. He picked it up and was shocked at the weight of it. It was a nugget of steel. He looked to Gabriel for an explanation but he didn't turn around. "Um? What –"

"It used to be a spoon."

"A spoon?" He stared at the formless lump.

"I melted it in my hands."

"On purpose?"

"Sort of got bored. Water isn't as entertaining as you might think."

"That's amazing! In a single night your brain is making new connections with the ore." He *could control it.* Adin felt his heart rate picking up. Wow.

"Yeah ... got a little crazy at one point. Thought I might melt the kitchen down, but I think I got it now." Gabriel gave him a thumbs up over the top of the chair.

Adin had never fully considered that the ore could be linked to Gabriel's brain. Maybe the white ore needed commands to function. Nothing in the research came even close to anything like this. He had to tell Dr. Cymru about this whether Gabriel like it or not.

He eyed the back of Gabriel's head. If he was going to move up the corporate ladder, Gabriel would be the key. He hoped their trip to see Dr. Cymru would convince Gabriel that this was worth too much to keep a secret.

CHAPTER THIRTEEN

GABRIEL AWOKE FROM THE FIRST DECENT SLEEP IN WEEKS AND RAN HIS HAND THROUGH HIS MATTED HAIR, TUGGING AT SMALL KNOTS AND SCRATCHING AT HIS SCALP. Still sleepy, he wandered towards the bathroom, almost bouncing off Adin, who had somehow mysteriously appeared in front of him.

"You still asleep or what?" Adin steadied him.

"Sorry. Just -" Gabriel yawned mid sentence. "Still trying to wake up. I actually slept well last night."

"Glad to hear it."

Yawning loudly in Adin's face for a second time, he smiled then continued his slow pace to the bathroom. As he shut the door, Adin knocked.

"Let's eat on the way. I don't want to cook anything here."

"Sounds good to me. You don't cook anything here anyhow. You just push buttons."

After removing his shorts and T-shirt, he stepped into the corner and hit the top button of the shower. The sliding glass wall smoothly encircled him, the instant hot water misting over its surface. Lowering his chin to his chest, he stared at the glimmering ore. The pulsing light radiating from the ore seemed calmer, not so erratic. He felt more in control and less afraid of the ore since he'd starting trying to use it. Closing his eyes, he breathed the warm air deep into his lungs and focused on a single thought – fire. Slowly he raised his right hand and waited. The sensation of a hot liquid bursting out of his chest happened immediately. It spread and grew across his shoulder, cascading down his right arm, around his bicep and down the elbow. It moved like liquid vines, twisting its own path around his forearm, finally reaching his fingertips.

Dozens of small sizzles filled his ears. Opening his eyes, he saw his hand and arm glowing like fresh snow on a bright sunny day. Droplets of water danced across his skin, evaporating into the mist of the shower. He grinned. *Incredible.* The ore was his new obsession. His control over it was growing daily, and he was making fewer destructive mistakes. Willing the ore's energy to return, he watched it retreat towards his shoulder and pool back into the shard in his chest. He let the water rain across his face. *What more is there? What else can it do?* He hoped the trip to the laboratories might produce a clue. When he finally emerged from the bathroom Adin waited by the door, tapping his foot on the marble floor.

"Are these clothes alright?" Gabriel held out the clothes he'd worn to his mother's funeral. "Nate never cared what I wore to work." They were the closest thing he had to business attire. Hopefully he'd look like he belonged there.

Adin nodded. "You're fine. There's an entertaining 1950s diner we can stop at to eat." Adin activated the door lock.

"Sounds good. I'm starving." Gabriel walked down the hall and pushed the glowing button for the elevator.

"You're always hungry." Adin followed.

He *was* always hungry lately. Maybe the ore was hungry, not him.

After the filling breakfast, Gabriel was eager to get to T.E.R.A.

despite feeling like he was walking into the lion's den. He could barely keep his hands still, cracking his knuckles repeatedly and drumming on his legs as Adin drove towards the facility.

Adin finally glared at him. "You're being annoying."

"Sorry." He sat on his hands.

"Relax. Let me do the talking and just act normal. We aren't doing anything wrong." Adin pushed a button on his visor and an oddly shaped polygon projected onto the window.

"What's that?"

"My parking pass. Pretty ingenious actually. Everyone has a different shape, and the gate scans the image as we drive up." The black SUV stopped at the gate, and a uniformed guard stepped up to the driver's window.

"Mr. Roberts, how can we help you today?" The guard tipped his hat at Adin then glanced suspiciously at Gabriel.

"Hey Edward, how's your morning going so far?" Adin gave a wave to the other guard in the shack.

"Doing alright. It's pretty quiet here today, being the weekend and all." Edward shrugged.

"Dr. Cymru is waiting for us." Adin leaned back for the guard to see Gabriel. "The clearance should already be in the system."

Gabriel saluted and smiled at Edward. Why didn't he wave? He felt a moment of embarrassment. Who salutes people?

"I remember seeing it in the system this morning. I'll get his pass for you, Mr. Roberts." Edward removed his hat, scratching at his balding grey hairline.

"Thanks, Edward." Adin gave him a quick pat on the shoulder as the older guard headed back to the steel shack. "What was with the salute?"

"I don't know. I blame Nate." Gabriel shrugged. *Had they ever found his body?*

The guard returned within minutes, handing Adin a level 4 clearance badge with VISITOR marked in bold red letters. Adin thanked him again and drove into the facility. As soon as they parked the SUV, Gabriel stepped out into the empty parking area and looked over at Adin.

"This way." Adin pointed. "I'm glad you decided to do this. You won't regret it."

I *hope so*. His nerves were still on edge. This place, these people, would want to know his secret more than anyone else. And here he was about to walk in, voluntarily.

After they swiped their badges on the door's security panel, the door automatically opened. They entered a small concrete corridor and continued walking through several other doors. All the while electronic eyes followed their movements through the building. After a series of twists and turns, they emerged into a large lobby.

Its appearance shocked Gabriel. This was T.E.R.A. – the biggest, wealthiest company in the world. He had expected something flashy – a giant fish tank built into the wall, marble floors, floating furniture – but not this. The area was primarily made of ugly shades of grey concrete. Two gigantic pillars of concrete held up the massive room. Behind them was a clear protective panel, and two security staff who looked like bored fish in a giant grey aquarium.

A loud voice projected into the huge, empty lobby. "Check your ID's and clearance at the front desk."

Following Adin, he approached the fish bowl. They scanned their badges into the computer console on the side. Adin smiled and nodded at the guards. When the scan was complete, a 3-D image of both their faces projected onto the clear panel for the guards to inspect.

How did they get that? Gabriel felt alarmed that they had a picture of him in their system.

"Working on the weekend, Mr. Roberts?" One guard spoke, while the other looked as if his face was set in stone.

"Hah!" Adin's voice echoed in the empty space. "You and I both know they work us hard enough during the week in this place." A long pause filled the air. "Umm. Dr. Cymru is waiting for us."

The stone-faced guard hit a button on the keypad in front

of him. "Your clearance checks out. If you remove any property of T.E.R.A., have it scanned out before you leave the building."

Nodding, Adin motioned towards the elevator behind the guards' glass box. Gabriel chased after him. The silver doors slid open and a large, red downward arrow appeared above the doors.

"Down?" Gabriel quickly stepped in.

"Yes, most of the facility's labs are underground. It makes it easier to maintain ideal environmental controls. It's also added protection." Adin pushed his hand against an illuminated blue panel.

"Is security always this tight when you come to work?" He pointed at the panel.

"This is normal, just a hand scan. Pretty simple. Although, I wonder how many people touch this every day." Adin made a disgusted face as he looked at the palm of his hand.

The elevator stopped an unknown distance under the earth, and the two emerged into a large open room filled with cubicles and whiteboards. Gabriel paused to take it all in while Adin continued on ahead of him. For being underground it sure felt bright. He could see four doors along the back walls, with plaques on each of them. It was too far away to read them, but he guessed Adin's office was behind one of them. Despite the two of them being the only ones in the large office area, he half expected someone to jump out and lock him away for what was in his chest. He zipped past the cubicles, following Adin and peering into each. Some had schematics all over the inner walls, with designs that he could only assume were current technologies being retrofitted to use the ore as a power source. Others were covered with statistical data that the poor soul in the cubicle must have to translate into something understandable.

As he neared the last line of cubicles, he noticed that they increased in size, giving their residents a little more space to work in. Sifting through the desk drawers of one of them, was Adin.

"Taking the chance to go through someone else's desk while no one is here, huh?" Gabriel rubbed his hands together, getting ready to snoop with him.

"Actually, this is mine." Adin sat down in the office chair and pointed to a small uncomfortable-looking chair against one of the side walls. As Gabriel sat down, he shook his head and felt himself grin. *A cubicle. A big one, but a cubicle. And I thought he had an office.* His amazingly successful brother, the prized son of the family, worked in a cubicle. The humour of it exploded in his head, and a giggle escaped him. Adin stopped what he was doing and threw a pen at him.

"Amused, are you?" He raised an eyebrow.

"I just figured you worked in your own office but this is so much better!" Unable to contain himself, he laughed aloud. "You work in a cubicle!"

"Yes, this is where I work. I fail to see why that is funny." Adin crossed his arms, leaning back on his chair. "Office or not. I've got more responsibility and authority than anyone on this floor!"

"It's true, Gabriel." Dr. Cymru appeared out of nowhere. Gabriel instantly stopped laughing. "Your brother is vital to our work. It's good he's down here in the 'pit' – lets him keep track of our teams. An upstairs office might be nice but you tend to lose touch with everything."

"Dr. Cymru!" Adin jumped to his feet.

"Good to see you, my boy. And you as well, Gabriel." Dr. Cymru smiled as he patted Adin on the back.

Gabriel frowned. Adin and Cymru shared a bond he didn't understand and their closeness annoyed him. "So, why did you invite us?"

Dr. Cymru chuckled at the pointed question. "I thought it would be good for you to see what your father helped build. Calvin was instrumental in everything we did. His knowledge of the ore was so extensive – losing him set us back years. Did you know when he first found the ore, it nearly killed him and most of his team. They all got radiation poisoning. We had to air lift most of the team out to get treatment, all except him. I begged him to leave the site but he refused – claiming he would be fine, that he 'needed' to be there. His drive for knowledge and thirst for the truth was incredible."

"Funny how he could live through that and then die from ore exposure in an accident?" Gabriel ignored Adin's glare and stared at Dr. Cymru.

Cymru held his gaze, refusing to look away. "I know it must have been hard growing up with no answer as to why it happened." He sighed. "I struggled with it myself. For months, we reviewed everything, searching through all the paperwork, video, all of it – trying to pinpoint the mistake. In the end, it was a faulty protective suit – accidents just happen. The reason wasn't good enough for your Mother or Nate and I am sure you feel much the same way. To be honest, I wanted you to come to here to understand this place. To put away any misconceptions of what took place here. Your father chose to be here for a reason. His ideals matched my own. Everyone at T.E.R.A., like Adin, are here to ensure a future for our children's children. To solve the energy crisis that is plaguing our world and stop it."

"Every day we get closer." Adin spoke up. "You should see some of the things Dr. Cymru is doing. It's amazing. I'm sure he would be willing to figure out any problem you might have." Adin's eyes carried a hidden message in them as he turn and focused on Gabriel.

Gabriel wanted to smack the look off Adin's face. "I'm sorry but I have a hard time believing that T.E.R.A. is a force for good."

"Gabriel!" Adin exploded at him. "Based on what? Nate's lies?"

"Adin, relax. I admire your honesty, Gabriel, but I think you will discover we are not the 'boogie man' that Nate paints us as." Dr. Cymru paused and Gabriel could see he was choosing his words carefully. "Nate hates us because of what happened to Calvin. I was very close to your father – we were partners in discovering the great mysteries of the universe. We argued and fought at times, but we were always on the same side in the end. When Nate arrived his ... attachment to Calvin was almost obsessive. He never let Calvin be separated from him, especially around me. My guess is something in Nate broke when Calvin died. I understand he moved onto the ranch. So, I can safely assume he's shared opinions with you?"

"He's family. I trust what he says." Gabriel glared at the Doctor.

"Then, let me show you the other side of the coin. You're an adult, decide for yourself." Dr. Cymru tapped the cubicle wall like a drum. "Why don't we all go down to the laboratories. Trying to understand something is so much easier, at its heart."

"Absolutely." Adin was grinning like a fool as he stood to follow Cymru towards the elevators. He pulled Gabriel from his chair, briefly holding him close for a moment. "Tell him."

"No." Gabriel's nostrils flared as he whispered. He took in a deep breath, his teeth clenched shut and shook off Adin's grip to follow after Cymru.

"Besides, look at all of this!" Dr. Cymru turned around as he walked towards the elevators to face him. "Words and numbers. Equations and symbols." He pointed at all the white boards. "Let's go see something real, something you can touch. Gabriel, let me show you how I plan to change the world."

The elevator dropped them deeper into the facility, Gabriel wondered how many people knew what was under their feet when they walked the streets of Denver. Dr. Cymru talked the whole way there, preaching about T.E.R.A.'s plans to harness the power of the ore for energy, for food production, clean water, manufacturing – everything humanity needed to prosper. A world without suffering. A chance to create a utopia. It all sounded like a fairy tale to Gabriel.

The elevator door finally opened, and Gabriel followed Dr. Cymru out onto a small platfom perched high above the laboratories below. He wandered over to one of the clear walls and stared out over the massive room. This was the laboratory? It was huge – the size of a football field, partitioned into smaller sections by 50-foot tall glass walls. He could only make out the first two sections of the dozens stretching out in the distance. Just below him was a massive chemical laboratory. Mechanical arms twisted and spun around the area.

They precisely snatched up vials and flasks in their fingers, taking them to their designated destinations. Beyond that the silver reflections of steel machines filled the next area.

"This is the biggest laboratory in the country. We built it big enough to suit our imaginations. This is where most of the technology for the ore was developed and tested. Almost every kind of technology the world uses can be replaced with more efficient models – new versions that utilize the endless supply of power from the ore." Dr. Cymru grinned. "We will have done the impossible and created a paradise of clean energy. Exactly what your father was hoping to create."

Gabriel couldn't deny that truth. As a child he had heard his father talk at the dinner table about a systematic world built on clean energy, a utopia.

A sinking sensation crept up his legs and into his stomach. The massive floor below was steadily getting closer. He placed his hand flat against the clear wall, feeling a vibration. The platform was descending. Less than a minute passed, and they came to a gentle stop on the lower floor. He turned to Adin, who motioned him to follow.

Adin walked over to a line of masks hanging on hooks along the wall. "You'll need one of these."

"Where's the rest of the protective gear?" Gabriel hesitated.

"Insightful observation." Dr. Cymru stepped over beside him. "Once you have your mask on you will exit by passing through one of the tubes." He pointed to the laboratory entrance at the bottom of the lift. "After what happened to your father, I was determined to never let it happen again. So, I invented a polymer that is sprayed onto your body inside the tube. You are then flashed with a specific wave length of light that hardens the liquid – creating a cocoon around your body. The mask allows you to breathe while every square inch of you is protected."

"What if it breaks?" Gabriel had to ask. Not that it mattered to him.

"Impossible. It has immense elasticity and strength to it, you can move freely in it and work as you would normally. The only drawback is its vulnerability to extreme heat – we're still working on building the polymer's resistance." Adin explained as he handed Gabriel a mask and a silver bracelet as they stepped off the lift.

"I will leave this tour up to Adin, he knows more about what happens in this lab than I do some days. I unfortunately have some problems that have been following me around for a bit. It is time I give them some attention." Dr. Cymru put a hand on each of their shoulders. "Adin, I will see you at work when you're ready. No rush. Gabriel, thank you for coming today, I hope to see you again now that you are here in the city. After you're done seeing the reality of our vision, I will answer any other questions you might have. I promise."

Gabriel smiled at him. "Thank you." This was a man who simply wanted to make a better future for everyone.

Dr. Cymru paused as he stepped back onto the lift. "Perhaps this might be a preview of your future, if you so chose. T.E.R.A. will always have a place for you." He nodded at them both and disappeared from sight.

Gabriel looked after him, frowning. The mass media praised T.E.R.A. for its desire to solve the energy crisis, promising free clean energy for everyone in the future. It was tough to know what to believe. His mother never spoke of T.E.R.A., avoiding the topic at all costs. Nate had a hate for them, constantly warning Gabriel about the dangers lurking in the shadows. Then there was Adin. He was proud of where he worked, he defended them religiously. They had given him a purpose in the midst of loss, a path, a place to stand.

Something Gabriel had never felt.

CHAPTER FOURTEEN

Once Dr. Cymru was out of earshot, Gabriel punched Adin in the arm. "What the hell was that crap upstairs."

Adin glared at him. "You need his help!"

"No. I don't."

"What do you see that is so evil? Does he have horns and a tail that I missed?" Adin waited for an answer.

"I don't know." Gabriel turned to Adin. "I didn't mean to be an ass but … it … he just doesn't match what I pictured."

"What you pictured or what Nate told you?"

Gabriel lifted his hands in defeat, sighing. "What Nate said."

"Then decide for yourself." Adin smiled at him and gave him a half hug. "Forget what Nate said, just tell Dr. Cymru – we can go together."

"I … I'll think about it." Gabriel shrugged. He didn't know what to think. Nate was the closest thing he'd had to a Dad, growing up. "I know you left after a couple of years with him but he's not a bad person, Adin."

"Neither is Dr. Cymru." Adin readied his own mask.

"Yea ... he seems to really care about you." Gabriel sighed, playing with the straps on the back of the mask.

"He does. We can trust him. Honest." Adin pulled his mask over his face.

Gabriel followed suit, putting on the mask – it fit snugly. "How the hell can you hear anything in these?"

He heard a faint response. "Put your bracelet on." Adin slid the thin metallic bracelet over his wrist. "Run your finger across the top of your bracelet, once we are done with the suits." Adin pointed to Gabriel's wrist.

The bracelet was loose on his wrist. Ignoring it he stood in front of the cylindrical tube to enter the lab. Adin nodded at him and stepped into his tube first. The clear tube instantly misted over and Adin disappeared into a white cloud of fog. The mist cleared and the tube was empty. It was Gabriel's turn now. He took a deep breath and stepped inside. The hiss from the sprayers blocked out every sound, even his own heart beat. The white fog felt heavy against his clothes and skin as it surrounded him. It hung around him for several minutes before a light began to pierce through the mist. It gathered and spun around the tube, moving from the top to the bottom and back up. The cycle continued several times before the mist had completely disappeared and he could see Adin waiting for him on the other side. Finally the whole structure spun, opening into the labs.

Adin pointed at his wrist, motioning for him to run his finger across it. Gabriel dragged his finger across the rubbery surface of the now snug bracelet. Numbers appeared to float on top of the metallic surface. They changed rapidly, spinning like a combination until a six digit code blinked back at him.

"Can you hear me clearly now?" Adin's voice rang out inside Gabriel's ear.

"Loud and clear." He gave Adin a thumbs up.

"Great. Let's head over to the system design area first and look at some of the prototypes. See if you can sense anything from the ore in the machines."

They walked towards a large sliding glass panel with a security pad on it. The door slid open at a wave of Adin's bracelet, and the two stepped inside. He followed Adin's bobbing head as they entered the first chamber, pulling at his suit. "Wow, this stuff sure stretches." he announced, lifting it several inches off of his skin.

Adin's voiced echoed slightly in his helmet. "Stop it ... Listen, I put our radios on an unlisted frequency, but let's not talk about you-know-what while we are here. Never know who might be scanning frequencies."

Gabriel let go of his thin rubber layer. "Fine by me."

They moved casually through the lab, side by side. Several oversized chemistry sets sat bubbling and brewing strange looking liquids, assisted by a large computerized arm that seemed to keep everything in balance as it zipped and turned automatically around the chemical lab.

"What is all that for?" He patted Adin's arm, stopping him from marching ahead.

"Most of the lab there is for material compound design and testing. We're always searching for new polymers to work with the ore. Shielding the ore's radiation is still a bit of a problem – nothing is 100 percent. There's always residual effects when working with the ore – it won't kill you, but we still don't know the long term effects of the radiation. Let's keep moving." Adin gently pulled Gabriel back along the path.

"Yeah, I'm –" Gabriel froze. In the distance the platform was rising back up to the elevator. That was odd.

"Gabriel? "

"How long does it take the platform to float back up to the elevator doors?" Gabriel's eyes darted around the base of the platform.

"A minute or two after we stepped off of it. Why?"

"I swear it just got there now." He pointed at it, keeping his eyes fixed on the platform.

"That can't be right, we're the only ones here. Hold on." Adin tapped his silver bracelet. A holographic screen expanded over it.

"Is someone else here?" Gabriel felt his muscles tighten across his body. "I can't see anyone. Can you see anything?" He stood on his tip-toes trying to look past everything in the room, searching for any movement.

"Relax. I scanned our radio channel. We are the only two on this frequency. You're just being paranoid." Adin pulled at his arm. "We are almost there. Put your imagination away and relax. Come on." Adin walked away.

Frustrated when he didn't see anything, Gabriel gave up and jogged after Adin, catching up quickly. The short walk ended at a towering clear wall. He followed Adin into one of the cube-shaped rooms at the base. As he entered, the door behind them sealed shut. The feeling that someone was watching him sent a chill down his spine. He turned quickly and studied the room behind them. The room remained still, only the mechanized equipment in the lab twisted around the space. That platform had been moving.

"Gabriel, this is pretty cool. Watch."

Gabriel turned around as Adin waved his bracelet at a steel pole sitting in the centre of the cube. The cubed room rose – he felt no lurch – and moved into the massive wall. He watched in amazement, as the tall thick walls separating the large lab slid smoothly along the cube's sides and roof as if they were made of thick liquid. The marvel of the room relaxed him, and he smiled as they glided to a stop. The room having completed its shift to the other side of the wall, opened to the next area.

"Very cool." He exited the room and watched as it reversed back through the wall. "That's amazing. How's it work?"

"The room is supported magnetically, like the table in my apartment, it just drifts along the floor and sets down on each side. I love these things." Adin patted Gabriel on the shoulder, turning him around to the machines in the room. "Alright, there are going to be samples of ore in different machines here. I want you to let me know if you feel anything as we look at them."

"Awesome!" Excited to see what might happen, he walked ahead of his brother.

Adin grabbed Gabriel's arm. "Slow down, you don't even know what to look at." He turned Gabriel sharply to the right and marched him towards a large machine that had dozens of silver tubes snaking around it. It made hissing sounds at one end and the sound of rushing water was audible at the other.

"What is this?" He stared up at the noisy silver octopus of tubing.

"This is the steam generator I told you about. We use it to power the rail system." Adin stepped out in front of him and traced his hand along the tubes as he spoke. "It's the prototype, anyway. Titanium piping makes it strong enough to hold high pressure. It has inner tubes and outer tubes that carry steam and water around the whole system, using each part as a natural heating and cooling system. Each tube has an insulating shell to prevent any heat loss."

Adin walked over to one side and motioned for him to follow. "This is the red ore side, which heats the entire system. Then the steam is recovered there." He pointed to a large blue piece of ore suspended in a holding tank. "That catches all the vapour produced and changes it back to water, and then recycles it back into the system."

Gabriel examined the machine closely, following the pathways of tubing to each area. "You helped design this?" He was impressed.

"Well, Dr. Cymru is the visionary who thinks of the ideas, but together we help bring it into reality. Now, can you feel anything on this side? We are right beside the red ore." Adin crouched down and traced the position of the ore with his hand.

"Don't think so." He shook his masked head and stared at the spot. "Can we open it?"

"Unfortunately no, the entire system must stay completely self-contained." Adin straightened up. "Let's move on, there are some other prototypes I want to show you."

They continued on and came to another contraption of silver pipes. Water slowly dripped out of the pipes into a bucket on the floor. Gabriel guessed it was an irrigation system. He stared up at a small shard of glowing blue crystal suspended above a silver drum.

Adin's voice filled his helmet as he stretched out his hand towards the crystal.

"This system is still in an experimental stage, but the idea is that moisture from surrounding air currents, from miles around, can be directed towards the crystal and be captured as purified water. Then we could redirect it into the ground, irrigating arid soils. We have other machines that use crystals from the green ore to amplify the growth rate of plants – which could one day help end starvation in the world."

He still felt nothing. What was supposed to happen? Was the suit blocking it?

They passed several greenhouse systems, each powered by green ore and with the same irrigation in place. As they kept pressing forward, Adin pointed out some of the heat shields developed to amplify the red ore's strength for use in manufacturing facilities or for smelting.

As they came towards the end of this section of the lab, Adin explained the goal of retrofitting all of the current technology in the world into safer ore-powered models. Gabriel was growing less and less interested with each prototype, despite Adin's genuine excitement about each of them.

"I don't feel anything from the ore."

Adin sighed. "It might not mean anything. Maybe the ore in the machines is not reacting any differently around you than it would anyone. I wasn't planning on any direct contact with the ore, but there are some smaller samples."

Adin walked over to a wall of large steel drawers, each with its own keypad. Gabriel stayed put and watched as Adin picked up a small clipboard, examining it. "A-12", he murmured as he walked over to the drawer matching that code. He waved his bracelet and punched in a key code. The drawer unlocked and slowly rolled out.

After removing a cubical black container, he shut the drawer halfway and put the cube down on a nearby work station. "Come here."

Gabriel stepped closer. *Finally!* Adin flipped down a latch on the side of the cube. It popped open, separating into two even pieces. Using a pair of steel tongs, he carefully removed the top of the case and plunged the tongs into the bottom half. He slowly lifted them, revealing a small piece of red ore. It glowed gently and was only a couple of inches on a side. He held it out toward Gabriel.

"Don't touch it. But get close and tell me how you feel."

Gabriel reached out his arms and put his gloved hands around the glowing red rock, being very careful not to touch it. The small shard glowed like a red Christmas tree light; he felt the heat from it through his rubberized skin. But the shard did nothing – it just sat in the tongs, glowing. .

"Nothing." He dropped his hands in defeat.

"What did you think would happen?" A female voice rang in Gabriel's ear.

CHAPTER FIFTEEN

GABRIEL JUMPED AND TURNED AROUND SO SWIFTLY HE NEARLY
FELL OVER. Over his shoulder, Adin's voice boomed: "Who are
you?"

"Thank god that didn't explode." She pointed.

Following her outstretched finger, Gabriel was surprised to
see the glowing red shard lying on the ground. Adin's tongs were
closed, shut tightly in his hand. He backed away from it, putting
some space between him and the shard.

Ignoring the ore, Adin demanded again "Who are you? This is
a restricted area!"

"I am sorry to have startled you, Mr. Roberts. I'm Susan
McCormick. I'm a lab tech from the research division of –"

"Ms. McCormick. You work on George's team in chemical
development and molecular composition." Adin put the tongs down
loudly on the table. He stepped between Gabriel and the stranger.

"That's correct, sir."

I knew someone was here. Gabriel tried to make out her face in
her mask, but the glare off the ceiling light was far too bright and he

couldn't make out any details. He shifted over to the table, hoping for a better angle. *How long was she watching? Or worse, listening?*

"What are you doing here, Ms. McCormick? I assumed we were the only ones in the lab today. I am sorry if my reaction seemed harsh." Adin crossed his arms as he stood in front of her.

"Yes, sir. I had just come in to check on one of our experiments, using the computerized arm to mix some new chemicals. You can't always trust the arm." Her red lips spread into a smile at the bottom of her mask. "I saw you two moving about and thought I would come over and say hello."

"You could have warned us and not snuck over here to spy on us!" Gabriel snapped.

"I'm sorry." She sounded frightened. "I didn't know what channel you were on. You certainly weren't using the standard channels, so I came close and scanned the frequencies. I wasn't spying on anyone Mr ... wait ... Who are you?" Her tone quickly changed.

"I'm –" Gabriel stalled, realizing he wasn't supposed to be in the lab either.

Adin stepped up beside him. "He's my younger brother, Gabriel. I was showing him around. An invited guest of Dr. Cymru."

Gabriel stared at his brother. "Right ... I wanted to see what this place is all about before I put my talents up for grabs."

"Another Roberts! How could the company refuse? Your family has done so much for T.E.R.A." She gave him a slight bow.

"Well, Ms. McCormick, thank you for saying hello but we are in a rush and should be going. Come on, Gabriel." Adin marched past her. "Sir, not to point out the obvious, but aren't you going to put the ore back in the drawer?" She motioned to the small shard still sitting on the ground.

"Of course! We're not idiots." Gabriel scooped up the ore with his right hand.

Heat instantly radiated through the thin rubber layer on his skin, burning him. His chest felt heavy under his clothes. He barely managed to take a breath as the ore awakened. The small red shard erupted with a blast of red light. Its intensity grew. His skin split and boiled, releasing an oozing liquid between his fingers. He cried out in pain – trying to let go of it – but failed. A shout from Adin rang out in his ears, but he felt frozen.

Then it all stopped.

The sensation of heat remained, but not scalding as before. He released his clenched fingers from around the ore. They moved freely, with no pain, as the shard rested in his palm. His glove had completely burned away, replaced by the familiar glow of protective white light. He breathed easy and stared at the power in his hand. *Amazing.*

Immediately Adin snatched the ore from Gabriel's hand with the steel tongs. The white light around his hand vanished, retreating back to his chest. He watched as Adin lowered the red ore slowly into the protective casing. It was still just as bright, and it warped the black steel as he set it inside. Adin rushed back to him, peeled off his own oversized protective gloves and covered Gabriel's hand with one of them. Gabriel felt unsteady as the rush of energy dissipated. His head clouded, and the room began to spin. He staggered on his feet, slumping back against Adin.

"Oh my god!" Susan's hands were at her mouth. "Is … is he okay?"

"He's burnt badly. I need to get him help right away. Please put the ore back in the drawer." Adin glared at Gabriel, jerking him by the arm.

Gabriel realized they had to cover up what really happened. He played his part, allowing Adin to support him as he staggered away.

Once out of Susan's vision, Gabriel picked up the pace under Adin's arm. They quickly passed through the giant clear wall and reached the entrance to the lab. Adin peeled off his suit then helped Gabriel out of his own suit and pushed him into the elevator before Susan could catch up to them. As the elevator began to climb, Gabriel stood on his own.

"Adin … I –"Adin cut him off with a jerk of his arm. "Keep quiet. We need to get out of here quickly. Keep your hand out of sight of the cameras." Adin pushed the elevator button.

"Adin. I'm okay. My hand is fine too. See? No burns at all." He spread out his fingers to show his brother.

Adin looked him right in the eyes, ignoring his hand. "You don't understand. This is technically an accident in the lab and it will need to be fully reported. I'm also positive that Ms. McCormick will say something to someone about what she saw. We need to play this out."

They exited the elevator onto a different floor than before, and Adin led Gabriel down a series of tight hallways and passages. They avoided any guards but still had to pass through several electronic security check points. They entered a medical room – it looked like a small hospital with med-bays separated by beds.

Adin quickly searched the drawers and cupboards. "Help me find a glove for your hand … I've seen them before on people who have burn injuries – they're silver with a big black pad on the palm."

Gabriel rushed to the opposite side of the room, whipping opening each cupboard around him. He checked the boxes in each, still unsure what exactly he was looking for. At the third cupboard, he called out. "Adin! Here … I think."

Adin rushed over and snatched the box out of his hands, opening it. "Which hand?"

Gabriel had to think. "Ah, right hand." He nodded. "Yeah, I grabbed it in my right hand."

"Shit." Adin threw the box aside and searched the cupboard again.

"What?" He grabbed the box.

"It's a left hand. Where the hell is a right hand one?" Adin pulled down two more boxes trying to see behind them.

Just then the beep of the security door to the room sounded. Adin reacted immediately grabbing a box and shoving Gabriel towards one of the medi-bays, pulling the curtain around them. "Put it on." He ordered.

Gabriel pulled it free from the box but hesitated "It's a left!" He tried to keep his voice down.

"I don't care!" Adin hissed quietly.

The curtains opened and two guards stepped into the space. "What is going on here!"

Adin faced them. "Just dealing with a burn from in the lab."

"Ms. McCormick notified us of the accident. We sent down a medical team but you left … why?" The guard seemed annoyed.

Adin got aggressive. "Excuse me? Why don't you scan my badge. You'll find I'm the personal assistant to Dr. Cymru. If I chose to leave the lab, what business is it of yours or Ms. McCormick?"

"Sir, there was a reported accident. Protocol has to be followed." The guard glared at Adin.

"This individual is a special guest of Dr. Cymru's. It is my job to ensure his safety while in the labs. I have the required medical knowledge to deal with his minor burn and do not need a medical team. If I did I would have called for one." Adin peeled off his badge and handed it to the guard. "Scan it."

Reluctantly, the guard waved the badge over an electronic armband. A hologram illuminated with a picture of Adin on it.

"Well?" Adin crossed his arms.

"I'm sorry to have bothered you, sir!" Still scowling, the guard stepped back from him and motioned to his partner to leave. "I hope Dr. Cymru's friend is alright. If you need us, please let us know."

"Have a good day, gentlemen." Adin smiled sarcastically. The door to the medical room shut and he twisted back to Gabriel. "Let's get out of here."

Gabriel was relieved to feel the fresh air when Adin opened a final door ahead of them. They climbed two flights of stairs and they walked towards Adin's SUV.

"When can I get this thing off? My hand is freezing." Gabriel had lost all feeling in his finger tips.

"When we're out of here." Adin pointed to the SUV. "Just don't think about it."

"Easy for you to say. You don't have this stupid glove on!" Gabriel waved it in Adin's face.

Adin shoved Gabriel. "I don't care, I have to fill out a bunch of phony reports now. You know what … no. We should tell Dr. Cymru the truth right now."

"No!"

"Why not?" Adin glared at him.

"I just need some more time. I don't know him like you do." Gabriel didn't really have an answer as to why not. Dr. Cymru might actually be able to help him.

"Why is she there?" Caught off guard by Adin's change in tone, Gabriel followed Adin's stare. There stood a porcelain-skinned woman with bright green eyes and long fiery red hair that matched her red full lips.

"Yes, Ms. McCormick? We are in a rush. I assume you understand." Adin walked around her.

"I know you need to go, but you left so quickly. I just wanted to make sure your brother's okay." She smiled at Gabriel.

Susan? He was dumbfounded. Under that mask had been a beautiful woman. *She can't be much older than me.*

"He will be just fine, but we do need to go to the hospital just to be sure. Sorry, but we should be leaving now." Adin typed in his code on the wall, releasing the anti-theft below the SUV.

"I'll be fine." Gabriel stopped beside her. "Just a little burn and some pain, but nothing I can't handle."

She cracked a smile and reached out, putting her hand on his shoulder. "Good. Labs can be dangerous."

He stared up into her green eyes and touched her wrist, giving it a quick squeeze. "I'll have to remember that in the future."

Her expression changed. She stared at his hand, taking it quickly into both of hers. "I thought you were burnt!" She gently rubbed his hand and inspected his skin.

Shit. He suddenly went numb, paralysed by his own stupidity. He quickly pulled away from her. His mind stuttered, barely forming a cohesive sentence. "No ... I ... ah ... I ... um, burnt this one." He lifted his left hand, the silver glove still freezing his hand.

She paused, shaking her head. "No, I am sure it was your right hand. You turned and picked up the ore with your –"

"Ms. McCormick!" Adin raised his voice. "You must have been mistaken and we do need to go now. Sorry but goodbye. Gabriel get in the car." Gabriel jogged away from her.

After backing out, Adin accelerated, pulling out of the parking stall at an alarming pace. "How could you be so stupid!"

Gabriel winced. He was right. "Give me a break!"

"All you had to do was get in the damn car!" Adin's fury showed in his driving. Gabriel tensed up as they tore around a sharp corner.

"Me? It was your idea to put on the left handed glove!" He peeled it off of his hand and threw it into the back seat.

"Just stop talking!" Adin glared at him.

CHAPTER SIXTEEN

THE PHONE ON DR. ALLAN JAMES CYMRU'S LARGE OAK DESK RANG, DISRUPTING THE PLEASURABLE SILENCE OF HIS HOME OFFICE. Dr. Cymru pushed a stack of Cubes aside and pressed a small button on the right side of his desk. A monitor rose up out of the wooden desk, reflecting his balding head and patchy, unshaven face in the dark glass. The screen remained black, barely giving form to a shadow.

"Allan, something has come to my attention and I wanted you to see it before I assume the worst," the deep voice croaked.

Clearing his throat, he replied calmly despite his heart thumping in his chest. "What is it that has you so concerned?"

The screen shifted to an image of three individuals, masks over their faces. He recognized T.E.R.A.'s main laboratory. They surrounded a small red shard lying on the ground.

"Is there no audio to go with this?" He leaned closer towards the monitor and adjusted his glasses.

The deep voice answered angrily, "It seems they were using private channels in the labs, but we will have the information soon enough."

The recorded video feed continued. An immense red light burst out of the small ore shard as one of the masked individuals picked it up.

Interesting. Dr. Cymru zoomed the camera in for a closer look then slowed the imagery down, replaying it several times, watching the small shard suddenly fill the room with red light. The surge stopped quickly, and two of the masked people hurried out of the lab, leaving one of them behind to put the ore away.

Dr. Cymru sat back to think for a moment. He had to choose his words when answering this man. "Well, it's interesting. It would seem that upon contact the ore reacted quite uniquely to that person's touch." He pulled his glasses off and played with the thin metal arm, spinning them around in his hand. *Stronger than I have seen before.* "When was this taken?"

"Today."

"Adin and Gabriel? Who is the third?" He put his glasses back on.

Three faces appeared on the side of the screen. The pictures were small and unrecognizable. He double tapped the screen to expand them. His eyes were immediately drawn to the beautiful face of a red-headed woman. Her credentials slowly scrolled on the bottom of the screen.

"The woman we have been watching. We will deal with her soon enough," the deep voice remarked.

"Why?" He dragged his fingers across the warm screen – flipping back to her picture.

"That is our concern, not yours. My people will bring them all in."

He felt the same frustration every time they contacted him. T.E.R.A. was his and what went on there was his business, not theirs. "No. There is no need for anyone to be harmed. I will have Adin and Gabriel come see me."

"Don't YOU dare tell me what to do! You work for us, remember? You came to us. We gave you everything you asked for. We did our part, now you are indebted to us."

It was true. Dr. Cymru clenched his teeth briefly. He hated it – but any obstacle to his research needed to be removed. They did his dirty work and T.E.R.A. prospered. Then, their demands started and he'd had to change the focus of his research.

"What happened in the lab?"

Dr. Cymru shrugged. "I am not entirely sure. It would appear that the ore's output was amplified upon contact with one of them." He flipped back to the screen and turned on an infrared setting. It revealed a huge spike in temperature around the ore.

"Which one?"

Dr. Cymru sighed. "My guess would be Gabriel. Adin would never hide something like this from me."

"Find them." The shadow lit a fat cigar and puffed its ember red hot. The faint light failed to reveal anything on the black screen but a mouth. "How are our other lab rats doing?"

Dr. Cymru took a deep breath, annoyed at the question. Their perpetual inquiries into the state of his research tried his patience. He would report when he had something to report. "My experiments are continuing as usual. The search continues though. We have found some excellent specimens over the last couple of weeks. Their immunity to the ore's affects is quite impressive. One individual seems to have an innate ability to detect the presence of the ore, signs of –"

"Unless their abilities are something we have never seen before, I don't care. How is the ore holding up?"

Dr. Cymru detested this man. "We are maintaining our stock at 97.4 percent – minimizing the losses as best we can and recharging it as quickly as possible."

"And our research. How close are we to testing its strength."

"Very close, once we solve a way to stabilize it effectively – we can begin testing on animal subjects."

"I want it tested on human subjects. The sooner we master the technology the better. I will leave you to deal with the brothers in the lab, but I want to know what happened with that ore. I want the one who touched the ore. Understand?"

"I am sure Adin will be more than helpful in explaining things once I speak with him. I am most certain of that. Adin believes in T.E.R.A., he won't disappoint us. Trust me." Dr. Cymru mentally decided to allow Adin until Tuesday morning to confess, but he doubted he would need that long. He had trained Adin better than that.

The monitor turned black, and a red "signal terminated" message flashed across the screen.

That man. Cyrmu stared at the screen. *Why did I ever asked for their help. If only I had the rest of Calvin's research, things would be so different. Damn him for hiding it from me.* He swallowed his anger and switched back to the laboratory footage. He watched the clip again, selecting different options on the side of the screen. The image changed to a deep blue hue, then exploded with shades of green. Slowing down the video, he tapped the screen moving it forward a frame at a time. He stopped. The image was still covered with the blue hue but showed two bright spots of green. *This one is the ore, but what is that? Its giving off the same energy field.* He reached out with his index finger and his thumb to expand the image. He repeated the action. And again. He stared at the green dot resting inside the chest of Adin or Gabriel. *One of them has been augmented by ore. It has to be Gabriel. He must have the same traits as his father.* He selected several other options, each showing a different array of colours exploding out of the ore but not the individual. The screen went back to the blue hue and the single green dot resting on the individual's chest. He was just going to have to wait on Adin. He must know something.

CHAPTER SEVENTEEN

Late Monday afternoon, Gabriel sat at the kitchen island eating leftover takeout from the night before. He had barely spoken to Adin since Saturday. Tensions in the apartment were high.

"Well, hopefully I dodged that bullet." Adin sighed loudly at him, shutting the door with a bang.

Gabriel looked up from his last forkful of chicken curry. "Huh?"

"I spent the last two days filling out paperwork to try and keep you out of trouble!" Adin tossed his briefcase into one of the leather chairs. "You could at least be a little more concerned about this."

Gabriel scowled and swallowed hard. "How is this my fault? You wanted to go see Dr. Cymru. Not me. Hell, if you had your way your boss would already know."

"And why not?" Adin circled around him towards the fridge. "He is one of the most brilliant men in the world. He would be able to tell us a lot more than we're finding out in our silly home experiments."

"Oh, so let them experiment on me. That's your solution? I'm your brother. I think you would be a little more concerned." He picked up his dishes and marched over to the sink.

"A little more concerned!" Adin slammed the fridge door. "I invite you into my house. You hide the facts about how mom died. I keep your secret even though it would skyrocket my career –"

"Your career! " Gabriel threw his dishes into the sink with a crash. "Your stupid career! Dr. Cymru and T.E.R.A. is all that matters to you, isn't it? You are never going to change." He stomped out of the kitchen, ignoring any remaining conversation from Adin. As he entered his room, he spun and kicked the door shut with a bang. *Damn him.*

He could still hear a mumbled rant from Adin in the kitchen. He spun around in the room unsure of what to do. On the desk rested his keys. They were useless, outdated and the door they once locked had been destroyed. But that didn't matter. He picked them up, running his thumb along each one in his hand. He missed his own room. The ranch. Nate. His mom. This wasn't his home. *It never was, it never will be. It's time to leave.* Quickly stuffing his backpack with clean clothes, he pulled open each dresser drawer, grabbing anything he might need. Double checking that the financial aid packages were zipped up tight in the front compartment he looked around to make sure he'd left nothing important. Calmly he slipped on his coat, pushed back his hair and pulled on a ball cap. This felt right. It was time to figure out his own future. He stepped out of his room and headed straight towards the door.

"Where are you going?" Adin glared at him from behind the kitchen island.

"I'm leaving."

"Gabriel, just stay put. It's been a stressful weekend and I don't need you running off into the streets just so you can avoid me."

Gabriel stopped his reach for the door. "Avoid you?" Furious, he turned to face Adin. "Adin, you were locked in your room for the last 24 hours! Then you skipped off to work extra early this morning.

You haven't spoken to me since the drive home two days ago and even then you told me to be quiet while you figured this out. If I wanted to avoid you, I would stay here!"

Adin slammed his fist against the island. "Well, sorry for trying to protect you! You know your little stunt in the lab could have cost me my job!"

"Your job! Always comes back to that doesn't it?"

"Well, why not?" Adin leaned forward. "I have worked for years to get where I am! I had to work twice as hard as the next guy because I was Calvin Roberts's son. I proved myself over and over to them. And finally, an amazing discovery happens right under my nose and I keep quiet!"

"It's not your discovery!" Anger was building up in his chest, pulsing throughout his body.

"No, you're wrong. It is!" Adin's eyes narrowed. "You listen up. T.E.R.A. kept the roof over our heads when Dad died. Dr. Cymru took care of our family. Then, when I wanted to go to school, he paid that bill. And he is going to pay for yours. He's done more for me than anyone ever has!"

Gabriel gritted his teeth. Nothing Adin said, truth or lie, mattered right now. He turned slowly and watched as Adin circled him.

"You don't know anything about the real world. You think sitting on the ranch, hiding from everyone with Mom and Nate, has prepared you for life? You failed at school. You sit around all day on your ass while your friends go off to college. You're twenty years old and have zero future. All because Dad died? People die every day! I pressed on! I made something of myself. You know why I didn't come to visit? Because that ranch is frozen in time, mourning Dad, accomplishing nothing. I thank God that Dr. Cymru got me out of there before it was too late." Adin's face had gone white. "It's time you grow up and face reality. That thing in your chest is your future. Like it or not. It's worth a hell of a lot more than you are. It's a chance to make something of yourself!" Adin walked to the door and locked it with a push of the button.

"And you know what else you need to do?" Adin looked him in the eye. "You need to ignore all that shit Nate told you about Dr. Cymru. He treats us like family. He's been more of a father than Dad ever was! The sooner you realize that and accept his help the better. In fact, we are going to talk to him tomorrow. We are going to tell him everything that is going on. He isn't the enemy. He will probably save your life and figure out what to do about that thing in your chest. "

A *father? How dare you?* Adin hadn't changed over the last couple of weeks. Serving Dr. Cymru was his first priority – not this talk of family. A thick silence hung in the room. Gabriel stood grinding his teeth. His rage continued to build.

Adin raised his hands in front of him, in a placating gesture. "Okay? Gabriel, trust me."

Gabriel looked around the apartment, mentally saying a final farewell. Adin's back was against the door. "No."

"What?" He could see Adin was taken aback by his answer.

"No, Adin. I am leaving. You're right! I do need to get to know the real world." He marched towards the door. He stared at Adin, unsure what he was thinking of or capable of.

Adin's face stiffened. He leaned harder against the door.

"Move." Gabriel said softly.

"No." Adin shook his head. "You're staying right here!"

"Move, Adin," Gabriel said calmly again.

"No!" Adin grabbed his biceps and pushed him backwards with a wild look in his eyes. "The only place you're going is to see Dr. Cymru."

Resisting, Gabriel put his hands against Adin's chest and pushed back. He gritted his teeth, determined to leave, to stop this charade of being a family. He tried to dig his feet into the floor but slid on the marble, losing ground to Adin.

"You going to see him!" Adin spit through his clenched teeth. "You're going to tell him everything!"

Adin's tight hold made Gabriel wince. He staggered back

another step, his mind filled with fear as he looked into Adin's eyes. *Who are you?*

"Stop!" Adin's grip tightened around his arms, pinching deeper, piercing his muscles. The pain increased. His balance was weakening, his feet sliding further back towards the hallway. He grabbed Adin's shirt in his fists. "Leave me alone!"

The heat building in his chest suddenly flared out across his body. His hands began to glow – deep beneath the skin. A web of light pulsed under his skin. He lifted Adin easily off the ground.

Fear flashed across Adin's face. He released his grip and clawed at Gabriel's hands. "What are you doing?"

Gabriel threw Adin forcefully to the right, sending him crashing into one of the recliners and breaking the chair in two. The noise thundered through the room. The top of the chair tumbled until it found a spot to stop.

Adin didn't move.

Gabriel stood still, heart pounding in his ears, hands shaking. His stomach turned as he realized what he had just done. Fighting the urge to vomit, he rushed to Adin and rolled him onto his back. Tears blurred his vision as he put his head down on Adin's chest.

A hollow thump-thump and the rasp of shallow breathing filled his ears.

Unspeakably relieved, he rushed to the bathroom and pulled two towels from the small closet. He waved his hand over the sink, and rushing water filled the basin. The sink stopped on its own as Gabriel dipped the corner of one of the towels into the icy water. He rushed back to Adin. Gently he lifted Adin's head onto the dry towel, using it as a makeshift pillow. Blood slowly trickled across the white towel, Gabriel leaned down and brushed at his brother's hair with the wet towel. Adin groaned as the towel dampened an open scalp wound.

"Damn it, Adin. Why couldn't you just let me leave?" Gabriel dabbed at the wound with the wet towel, but the blood kept coming. He ran back to the bathroom and dug through the closet, spilling its contents all over the floor. A small box tumbled out. He recognized the bright red cross on the front and snatched it up, rushing back to Adin. Inside the kit he saw what he needed, an aerosol spray that would help clot the blood, the same stuff he had used on animals at the farm. He sprayed the wound on Adin's head. The sharp smell of disinfectant filled the air as he used more than required, hoping to stop the bleeding immediately.

He succeeded. The can clattered on the marble, and he sat paralysed.

What now? I can't stay here ... but I can't leave him. Gabriel was torn, as he watched Adin's chest rise and fall. *What do I do?* He needed to decide.

CHAPTER EIGHTEEN

Gabriel exited T.E.R.A. towers into the gloomy night. Rain pounded the pavement and immediately soaked through his thin coat. His heart was still echoing in his chest, and tears half-filled his sight. *Where to now?* He needed a place to hide. A place to think. Blindly, he scampered across the wet street – too busy for such weather – and turned the corner without looking back. The rain bounced off the tables of a patio across the street. He ran towards them, avoiding the largest puddles along his route. He nearly slipped in the sloppy entrance as he opened the door. The shop smelled sweet, the air warm and soothing. He took a deep breath and looked around for a table. An open booth in the corner, out of the way, was exactly what he wanted. As soon as he sat down a young waitress appeared and began reciting the daily specials. The thought of food made him feel even more sick to his stomach.

"A tea, please." He didn't look at her.

"What kind of tea would you like? We have chai, green, earl grey, blueberry –" Her high-pitched voice began to work through the memorized list.

"Just a normal tea – plain – or you can pick one." Shrugging, she left with his order.

His mind replayed the fight with Adin. *What happened up there?* After everything they had gone through in the few weeks, how did it all fall apart? He had left after treating Adin's head wound, deciding it was for the best. It was too much of a risk to stay. Adin's loyalty to Dr. Cymru outweighed the loyalty to his own family.

The steam from the hot cup of tea brought him out of his reverie. After handing over a pay card and thumb printing the small pay-pad , he forced himself to take a deep breath. *Focus.* He remembered the packages Brett had given him and pulled them out of his backpack. Tearing them all open, he dumped the contents onto the table, careful not to drop anything in his drink. *Hotels. Where are they?* After flipping through the certificates, he placed the hotel stays to one side and counted up what he had left on the pay cards. Three hundred dollars. *Not much to work with.*

He noticed a large map on the wall of the cafe, pointing out tourist destinations across the downtown core. He walked over to it, carrying one of the hotel certificates; *Embassy Suites.* Locating the icon of a little red house with the word "Embassy" beside it, he zigzagged his finger across the smooth surface. The route seemed simple enough. It wasn't very far, either. He could take the subway.

Back at his table he returned the cards to his backpack and continued sipping his tea. The buzz of conversations between patrons at the other tables soothed him. They seemed happy with one another. He admired the strangers, knowing nothing about them, except that they weren't alone. They had each other and that was more than he had. He felt abandoned and betrayed. *How could my own brother not protect me? If it was Adin's secret, I would have kept it.* Thoughts swarmed in his head, each scenario playing out in his mind, what he could have done differently. He sat there thinking until his tea was lukewarm against his lips. Deciding to abandon the cafe, he stood up and studied the map one last time before plunging out into the rain. The small awning over the door provided some shelter as he looked up and down the street, getting his bearings.

A shadowed figure leaned against a brick wall across the street, watching him with eyes that bored into him and sent a chill down his spine. Even when Gabriel stared back, the stranger maintained his gaze. *Creepy.* Gabriel set off down the street at a quick pace. As he checked names on the street signs, he couldn't help but also glance over his shoulder at the green raincoat-clad stranger moving along the street in the same direction. *It's a coincidence,* he told himself. *Relax.* He had one more corner to turn before he could duck into the subway system for the remainder of the trip to the hotel. Hoping to lose his unwanted companion, he increased his stride and took the stairway entrance three steps at a time into the tunnel.

He hopped the electronic gate, ignored the subway fare, and entered the terminal. The train platform was hot and misty despite the moisture recapture system. It was obviously a hideaway for the city's undesirables during bad weather, and the platform was now filled with dozens of unfortunate souls asking for a hand-out. No train yet. He tucked himself around a large tiled pillar and, leaning against it closely, eyed the stairs to see if the green-coated stranger had followed.

Several minutes later, the loud hiss of an arriving train signalled it was almost time for his departure. A sleek train rolled to a stop. He darted for the train doors, cutting off several other passengers. He chose a seat hidden from the view of the platform and hunched down in it. *Is someone actually after me?* His heart beat wildly as the train pulled away. He scanned the faces of the other passengers, recognizing no one.

After counting eight stops he exited the train and sprinted up the steps to street level. He could see the hotel across the street and headed towards it, careful to dodge the busy traffic. As he reached the revolving doors, he allowed himself one last look down the street. *No one.* He chuckled slightly at how he had allowed his imagination to get the better of him. *I'm a stranger to everyone in this city but Adin. My friends don't even know I'm here. Who would follow me?* Probably just a thief, hoping to snatch his wallet. He shook his head as he entered the brightly lit lobby.

The front desk agent greeted Gabriel like an old friend. He handed her the aid certificate. "Now sir, I assume you are aware that this certificate will only cover you for a maximum three week stay with us?"

That long? He was impressed. "Um ... yeah. I'll have something worked out by then."

"Well then, enjoy your stay and sorry for your loss." The clerk gave him a sympathetic smile.

"Right. Thanks." He returned it awkwardly and took the key card from her along with an envelope of complimentary food vouchers for the hotel's restaurants. Stepping away from the desk, he promptly pulled out the vouchers. There were three choices: a coffee shop, a family-style restaurant and a bar. *At least I don't have to worry about food.* He looked up from the vouchers to see where the restaurant was. His appetite had returned.

As he wandered across the lobby, a shapely woman with vibrant red hair caught his attention. She was wrapping a white scarf around her neck and heading towards the revolving door of the lobby. *It's her.*

He reached out and touched her arm. She spun around to face him, tensing up as she pulled her arm back from his touch.

"Hi, sorry – Susan, right?" He smiled.

She stared at him for a moment. "Gabriel! You scared me."

"Um ... Sorry," he croaked. "I just wanted to say hi."

"I'm glad you did." Her eyes were flirty. "Your hand looks just fine!" She took it into both of hers and inspected it.

"Yeah. No major damage, really. Just some redness for a day or two." He smiled nervously as he pulled it back.

"That's good." She nodded, obviously waiting for him to continue the conversation.

He was at a complete loss for words.

"So, what are you doing here?" She gestured around the lobby and back at him.

"I'm staying here. Got a room for a couple of weeks."

"Weren't you staying with Mr. Roberts?"

"Adin? Yeah, but – it's time I get things sorted for myself."

"That's great!" She smiled. "My apartment is just around the corner. Maybe we could have dinner one night?"

His heart nearly skipped a beat. "You and me?"

"Well – yeah, I did ask you. If you're busy, I can give you my number." She began riffling through her small clutch purse.

"No, I mean, I'm not busy. That would be fantastic."

"Good!" She smiled widely. "How about the day after tomorrow? Here in the bar?"

"Sure!" His answer left his mouth before his brain could catch up. "The bar, great. I, ah, I'll be here. There."

To his surprise, she hugged him. "It was great to see you." She waved and turned to walk towards the revolving door. He studied her backside as she walked away and exhaled loudly, feeling terrified and excited all at the same time.

"The bar." He twisted around and stared at the entrance. The sign to the right of the entrance mocked him; 21 *and older* only. "Great."

CHAPTER NINETEEN

THE BACK OF ADIN'S HEAD SEARED IN PAIN. He pushed himself up, trying to ignore the dizziness. Carefully, he eased his fingers through the sticky tufts of his hair. The sharp pain in his head spiked, as the tips of his fingers touched a gash crusted with clotted blood. Nausea hit him and he crumpled. The room spun so fast, he threw up on the floor in front of him. His lungs heaved as he prayed for the feeling to pass, but it remained. Inch by inch, he slowly crawled towards the kitchen. The tight ball of his stomach seemed to bounce with each movement. He attempted to stand up again, gripping the sleek marble of the island, pulling himself up. The end of the cupboards was finally within reach and he pulled out a bottle of pills. After popping the top, he poured them across the black marble counter top. He put two into his mouth, grinding them with his teeth. The horrible taste sent shivers through his body and he fought back the urge to throw up again. A minute later, the medical marvels kicked in, the pain and nausea disappeared.

"Gabriel?" Nothing but silence answered him. *Damn*.

Now he remembered. The fight. The harsh words. He cursed

loudly and headed to the bathroom. He snatched a clean white towel from the cupboard, throwing it into the sink as he waved the tap on. The cold water sank into the dry towel as he leaned against the sink, his mind still replaying Gabriel's actions. *How dare he not help me?* The cold wet towel felt good on his face. Ringing out the extra water, he rubbed the back his head. Pleased to not feel any pain, he tossed the blood stained towel into the hamper and headed straight for his bedroom. *I should have told him right away.*

He spun his desk monitor towards himself and sat down in his chair. "Contact Dr. Cymru."

As he waited for his boss's image to appear, he focused his rage into one single thought. *Dr. Cymru needs to know. I need to fix things – for both us – even if he doesn't deserve it.*

The balding head and thin glasses of Dr. Cymru appeared on the screen. The mere sight of the man calmed Adin. This was the face of a mentor and a friend, someone he knew he could trust with anything.

Skipping the pleasantries of a hello, he dove right in. "Dr. Cymru, there's something I need to discuss with you."

"Adin. I've never seen you look so shaken up. You look like a ghost. What seems to be the problem, my boy?"

"Well, there's been an incident here at my apartment –"

"Incident? Did you send for security? I can send them over right away." Dr. Cymru sat up in his chair.

"No, no sir. Everything is fine. Please, just listen. There is a lot I need to tell you."

He did his best to describe the circumstances of the storm and how the shard had become implanted in Gabriel's chest. He described their experiments at home, as they tried to discover Gabriel's capabilities. Adin didn't leave out any detail; he even gave his own hypothesis as to what was going on. Finally, Adin described their trip to the lab and explained to Dr. Cymru how he had failed to follow proper procedure.

"– and so I just wanted to say that I am sorry. I've failed you.

I should have come to you right away, and I didn't." He felt ashamed of his actions.

"My dear, dear boy." Dr. Cymru smiled. "I forgive you for not telling me sooner. No doubt you were in a difficult position. Let's focus on what is going on now."

He nodded, feeling relieved. Dr. Cymru had always been pleasant to him, even in the worst of circumstances, always quick to forgive any wrongs.

"Adin, I have not only watched you grow at this company but I have watched you grow as a man."

Adin took a deep breath as he listened to the doctor's kind words.

"Now, before we go any further I need to ask you something of great importance, something that concerns your future with T.E.R.A."

"Of course." He held his breath. "What is it?"

Dr. Cymru leaned back in his chair, eyeing him. "First, how important is T.E.R.A to you?"

He thought for a moment. "I realize my actions over the last few weeks may not have reflected the best intentions but –" He was cut off by Dr. Cymru.

"Adin, that issue is done. There's no need to explain further. I do not want to hear about that anymore."

Nodding, he continued, "It's everything to me."

"Good. I trust you understand that everything we do at T.E.R.A. is to try and better the world."

"Yes, of course."

"Adin, for the good of mankind, and to help equip T.E.R.A with the best tools to help mankind, I need to know where your brother is."

"I – I don't know. We had a fight and he left. I am not sure where he might have gone."

"Adin, it's imperative you find your brother and bring him to me. While your brother still lives with that shard in his chest, he could be very dangerous. You need to find him."

"But what about his abilities and the way he can react with other shards? Don't you want my reports and findings on that?" Surely that was important!

"I already have several reports on those findings. In fact, I have two on my desk this very minute." Dr. Cymru said, boldly holding up a small blue cube.

"But – how?" His voice rose in anger.

The doctor laughed at him. "You thought you were the only one who knew about the ore's reaction to certain individuals? Come on now. I expect more from you, Adin. Our research into the ore is more extensive than anyone in the world. You didn't really think we would miss something so critical? You must have heard the rumours about human experimentation; you must have known some of them to be true." Dr Cymru shrugged. "While it is against company policy now, it wasn't always the case."

"That can't be true … It goes against what we stand for!" Adin leaned forward on his desk.

"Look at you – acting just like your father did! We sometimes must put aside what is right or wrong to discover truth. Your father failed to do so and wasted so much of his time looking for alternatives. Listen to me." Dr. Cymru's stare froze Adin in his place as he dropped back into his chair.

"What's done is done. Leave the past alone, only consider the future. You said T.E.R.A. is the most important thing to you? You want a future here? More than just a simpleton in a cubicle who has no idea about the wealth of information we have about the ore? Don't make the same mistakes your father did, Adin. I want you with us."

Dr. Cymru's speech hit home. This was what he wanted. The chance to prove his worth. "Of course." He nodded at his mentor.

"I have not always been the first to recognize your achievements and, I must say, you deserve better. For that I am sorry. I believe it is time for a new position, something specifically designed for your abilities. A position that allows you to help us find out more about the ore and how we can truly change this world. Is that something you can do?"

"Absolutely."

"Good. Then bring me your brother." Dr. Cymru didn't blink.

"What? Why?"

"He's family. We need to help him. He's a danger to everyone around him right now. We just need to know where he is. Let him cool off for a couple of days and then we will bring him home. We need to keep an eye on him in the mean time."

"The crystal has been in him for weeks, it's not hurting him. I –" He didn't understand.

Dr. Cymru slammed his hand down on his desk. "Adin. He's dangerous. Most ore users are extremely volatile, a simple emotion can trigger the ore. You need to trust me."

"Yes, of course." After what had happened in the apartment, he could see how Gabriel could be dangerous.

"Good. Now think ... where might he be. What did he leave with?" Dr. Cymru stared at him.

"Um ... he had a coat and a backpack ... the aid packages!" He jumped up at the thought.

"Packages?" Dr. Cymru leaned forward

"For disaster relief. We bought some new clothes with them. I'm sure he took them."

"Alright. We can track him from those. I will put some people on finding out where he used them. We'll find him and bring him home. I promise." Dr. Cymru rubbed his hands together.

"There's only a limited number of hotels where he can use them. I can go find him." Adin stood.

"Adin. Stop." Dr. Cymru sighed. "I want you to stay put. Let us find him and I will go speak to him myself. He's probably upset and seeing you might trigger the ore. Leave this with me."

"And what I am supposed to do? He's my brother, he took off because of me." He hated feeling helpless, it reminded too much of his youth.

"I have another project for you." Dr. Cymru held up the blue cube. "Perhaps it's time you become acquainted with some new research. I will have the cube sent down to you immediately by my driver. Keep it private and study it."

"What are they about?" He sat up straight.

Dr. Cymru smiled at him. "Ore users. I am hoping you can fill in some of the gaps that I cannot."

CHAPTER TWENTY

ADIN DIDN'T SLEEP VERY WELL THAT NIGHT — THE RESEARCH ON
THE CUBE WAS ADDICTIVE. His mind was filled with too many questions about the missing pieces and he was eager to talk to Dr. Cymru
about it privately. He woke up earlier than usual – shaved extra close,
donned his best suit, and even caught an early haircut before heading to work. It was good to get back to where he belonged. He pulled
up to the front gate at T.E.R.A. Laboratories and was greeted by the
familiar face of Edward.

"Morning, Edward." He smiled.

"I just need to switch your pass, Mr. Robert," the guard said,
scanning a small metallic strip in the corner of his windshield.

"Switch my pass?"

"Yes, sir. And congratulations." Edward activated the new polygon symbol. "There we go. You will now be parking on the executive
level, third floor. Have a good day." He waved Adin through the gate.

Adin didn't understand what was happening; Dr. Cymru
hadn't mentioned any of these changes. He needed to see him immediately. After parking his vehicle in his newly assigned stall – clearly

marked with his name on a plaque bolted into the concrete wall – he typed his pin into the anti-theft device. Another guard was waiting for him beside the silver elevator doors.

"Mr. Roberts, I just need a moment of your time." The guard promptly stood up as he approached.

"Sure, is everything alright?" He was completely confused.

The guard smiled and nodded. "Yes sir. We just need to prep you for use of the executive entrance way. It's a private security elevator that takes you directly to your office floor."

"I don't understand, why all the changes?"

The guard frowned at him. "I'm not sure I can answer that question. You are Adin Roberts?"

"Yes, of course." Adin showed the guard his badge.

"I'm not sure what to tell you. The order came directly from Dr. Cymru. Now, when you enter the elevator, the lights will dim while it scans your body." The guard punched a code into an electronic device that he set against the elevator door. "Typically this will only take seconds, but as this is your first time it will take a little longer. If you would please try to hold still during the process, it makes it a whole lot quicker."

"All right." Adin positioned himself in front of the silver elevator doors.

"The scan will check you for any contraband, as well as verify your identity using an organ signature."

"Organ signature?" He had never heard the term before.

"Yes. I am not sure what the technical name for it is, but it essentially takes a photo of your heart, lungs, blood vessels – creating a personalized signature. It matches it each time you come in." The guard stepped aside as the elevator opened. "It's all ready for you, sir."

The small space seemed barely large enough for two people. The lights dimmed. Thin blue beams projected from invisible locations and began to trace over his body. The tiny beams danced off the mirrored walls creating a mini laser light show as he waited. A minute passed before the blue lights faded and the normal elevator lighting resumed. Adin noticed there were no buttons and the only indication of his destination was the dark red arrow pointing up, that slowly blinked above the doors. The ride came to a gentle stop and the doors opened to reveal Dr. Cymru waiting for him.

"Surprised?" The aging man grinned, filling the sides of his face with wrinkles.

"Absolutely!" He stepped out of the elevator.

With a large smile Dr. Cymru led him to a spacious corner office. "Good. I hope you like everything. And call me Allan, please."

It was better than he could have imagined. Two sides of the room were wall to wall glass over-looking the city. The other walls had built-in filing cabinets and a small kitchenette. The room held matching leather furniture and state-of-the-art equipment – from the computerized desk to the voice-command espresso machine. It all had a new, fresh smell to it and it filled the room with an energy that he could feel deep inside. This was his place. What he deserved. All his effort and hard work had finally paid off. He had made it.

Dr. Cymru began to talk, but the words weren't registering.

He spun around to face him. "Sorry sir. Could you repeat that, Allan?" The name still felt awkward to use.

"Your personal items. We took the liberty of bringing them up for you." Dr. Cymru pointed at the box resting on the desk.

Atop of the carefully placed items was a family photo with him and Gabriel both hanging onto the arms of their father, happy in that moment. Adin picked up the frame and studied it, setting it down as the first thing on his desk. *I need to fix things between us. He's the only family I have.*

Dr. Cymru pointed to his father in the photo. "Your father was a good man. I miss him. He would have been very proud of you today, I'm sure." He patted Adin on the back and showed him the large monitor on the desk. "Everything should be exactly where it was before. All your files should be there."

"Great." Adin slid around his desk and activated the monitor.

"Adin, I am excited to have you with us. Enough of the office.

How would you like to see the new labs you will be a part of?" Dr. Cymru waved an arm towards the executive elevators.

"Of course!" He could barely contain his excitement as he walked.

After the doors closed Dr. Cymru spoke, "Level SX-2. Absconditus." The blue light quickly encircled their bodies.

"Remember what I just said," Dr. Cymru warned him. "It will be your password into the labs."

He committed the Latin word to memory as the elevator hummed downwards. The red arrow glowed on the wall.

"The researchers and assistants all have other ways into the lab but you will use this elevator only, understood?"

"Yes." The elevator stopped. *Here we go.*

He exited the elevator into a long, ominous-looking hallway with steel doors spaced about ten feet apart along both sides of the walls. A small window was cut in each one. He hesitated, confused. This did not resemble the large, white, sterilized labs he was used to working in. "This is the lab I will be in charge of?"

"Yes. Not our standard lab, but I assure you that what goes on down here is of the greatest importance." Dr. Cymru put a hand on his shoulder to hold him in place. "I want to warn you before we go any further. There are – practices – that will seem chaotic and unnecessary, but they contain impressive amounts of information that we need to further develop our knowledge of the ore. You have accepted a great responsibility by becoming a part of the inner circle we have here at T.E.R.A. Few ever get that opportunity. I have personally recommended you. I have tried to give you everything that you will need but there is still a lot for you to learn. I am telling you this because I need you to be a true scientist while working here. You must be logical. Analytical. Rational. Systematic. Nothing must be taken at face value; everything has a deeper reason and meaning. Like the old saying goes, 'do not judge a book by its cover'. When you are here you must think like a computer. Not a human. Emotions will only cloud your judgement. Remember that."

"I'm not sure I understand. Why are you telling me all of this?" He looked Dr. Cymru in the eyes.

"Before your father's untimely death, we were working on some projects, that to this day, we cannot complete. The research we needed disappeared with your father, we don't know if the systems were tampered with or what exactly happened. The point is, we are running out of time and need to find a breakthrough soon." Dr. Cymru cleared his throat. "Adin, I believe that you can help us succeed. I believe your mind will help us answer the questions that we have failed to answer so far, but above all else I believe a large key to the ore lies within you – in your DNA." Dr. Cymru nodded for Adin to walk with him. "There was more to your father and the ore than most people knew. I believe you and your brother possess some of the those same qualities."

My DNA? *Like Gabriel.* He felt the pit of his stomach turn as the words came out of Dr. Cymru's mouth. At the same time he yearned to be the only scientist who could discover those answers desperately needed by T.E.R.A. If he could only find out its secrets. Continue where others had failed.

Dr. Cymru halted outside the first door in the hallway. "Your father struggled with what we did in these labs. He failed to understand the importance of what we were doing. Sometimes sacrifice is the only way we can solve our mysteries. I want you to put away your emotions, understand the why, before you judge." He urged Adin to look through the small window.

Adin's jaw fell open. Three men, two women and four children lay strapped to gurneys with tubes running from them to a large clear, communal container. Red liquid flowed through the tubes. Inside the container were dull, jagged chunks of what looked like faintly coloured glass. The glass slowly pulsed. A firm hand pressed down on his shoulder, holding him in place.

Dr. Cymru's voice whispered into his ear. "Such a precious thing, blood. It replenishes our bodies with oxygen and nutrients, removes toxins, balances pH, regulates body temperature, protects us from damage and disease. It took us years to make the connection with the ore and human blood. The more blood the ore has access to, the faster it recharges."

"Those people –" He gritted his teeth.

"They feel no pain. There's no need for pity. This is science at its purest form. The truth we need lies in this room." Dr. Cymru's passionate words were convincing but Adin's gut churned. "Our world is starving. Starving for energy to keep the lights on, keep us fed, keep our water clean, and keep us warm. The basic things we need to survive. Despite all of our advancements in solar, wind and bio-energy, and other new efficient methods being found each year, we consume more and more energy. Those who control that limited energy will survive. The ore is renewable but we need more from it. If we can't expand the capability of the ore – get more energy from it, find better ways to recharge it – then we will simply use it up. Like everything else we have found."

He swallowed hard, pushing the lump in his throat down into his stomach. "I don't understand. The ore was supposed to solve the problem. Provide free energy for everyone."

"It does solve the problem but this is how we recharge it. It's barbaric but we don't have a choice. Sacrificing the few for the many is the balancing act we do every day. The ore is our future. And this is why we must find the answers. So we can stop this practice." Dr. Cymru let go of Adin's shoulder and leaned against the wall beside him.

"This isn't right." Adin's eyes were locked on the face of one of the children.

"What do you suggest? We turn everything off? Impossible. They would never allow it."

"They?"

"Those in control. We are not our own masters. I wish it was different but we needed people in power so that we could push T.E.R.A. the way we did." Dr. Cymru frowned.

"But there must be other ways." He pointed at the door.

"Perhaps. But this is the quickest. In the end, when we save humanity, all will be forgiven. We will be heroes. Saviours."

He was torn. Dr. Cymru made sense. Many discoveries in the past were made at the expense of human life. Science celebrated these moments, praising them as leaps forward for mankind. But it felt wrong. Those people in there had had lives – they had families. Did those families know where their loved ones were? Did they know the truth?

"It's time." Dr. Cymru made a motion and Adin realized they were no longer alone.

Two men gripped his arms, pulling them behind his back. "Stop! What's going on!"

"It wasn't an easy decision. But a necessary one." Dr. Cymru stared at the ground.

"What are you talking about?" His heart beat wildly in his chest as he struggled against the guards holding him.

"Your brother is quite unique. I've never seen anyone merge with the ore and not suffer from some residual effects. Most of my experiments augmenting people with ore have failed – the mind simply fractures and they lose control. But Gabriel – he has no side effects. I can only assume you possess that same unique quality. Your brother will be mine shortly – they've already left to collect him. Your father refused to give me what I needed, he refused any experiments, no matter how small. He was the key. He could have changed everything." Dr. Cymru shook his head. "But now, with you and Gabriel, I can fix that. We can recover what your father took away from us."

"You son of a bitch! I trusted you!" He spit at him.

Dr. Cymru stepped back, putting up his hands in defence. "And you should still. I promise you will be fine. Listen to me. They just want a little experiment. It won't kill you. Just – just a test. Think of what we will learn – what you will be capable of!"

"Why?" Adin slumped in the men's grip. Defeated.

"Because this is the next step of evolution. If we all could merge with the ore, we would be able to fix everything. Imagine everyone with the power of ore at their finger tips. No more protection from it, we could harness it freely, bend it to our will. Reshape our world." Dr. Cymru dropped to one knee, looking him in the eye. "I know you don't want to trust me, but you're just going to have to. That office, the promotion – a new future. It's all still yours. Afterward."

He lunged at his mentor. The two guards stumbled forward trying to hold onto him. A sharp pain bit the back of his neck and everything went black.

CHAPTER TWENTY-ONE

Gabriel leaned on the bathroom counter and wiped away the mist covering the mirror. The light glowing in his chest had become an obsession for him and he studied it in his reflection. Drops of water ran down from his wet hair and danced over the shard, clinging to the sharp edges before trickling down his chest. He tightened the towel around his waist and grabbed a smaller hand towel to dry his dark hair.

It felt good to be on his own, hidden away from Adin and any thoughts of T.E.R.A. Adin's betrayal had probably ended their relationship forever. Or had it simply put it back to normal? Pushing that depressing thought from his mind, he focused on getting ready for his date. *I'll set the pace myself and keep things friendly – but still interesting – until the time is right.* A solid plan. He admired himself in the full length mirror. *I'm in control.* He left his room and headed towards the hotel lobby.

He spotted Susan easily. She appeared to be almost floating as she moved towards a lounge chair. This was not the attractive chemist he'd met before. Susan looked sexy in a low cut dress. His stomach began bubbling as his pulse quickened. Control? He stared at her, dumbfounded.

Her eyes met his gaze. She stood up, smiling widely, her red lipstick nearly matching her hair. He did his best to stop gawking as he walked towards her, moving across the tiled floor as gracefully as a clopping horse. He tried to lighten his step and pick up his pace but managed only to trip on the edge of the thick rug spread out under the furniture, barely finding his balance again.

Susan giggled at him. "No one has ever fallen for me like that before."

He felt the temperature of his face rise. "Have you tried any of the restaurants nearby?"

"Several, but I love the little club here best." She smiled.

"The club … yeah it looks okay." He glanced nervously over at the large doorman.

" Wait till you see inside." She stepped towards him, wrapping her arm around his.

He slid his free hand into his pocket, searching for some money to slip the doorman. It was the best plan he could come up with.

"The doorman is a friend of mine." She smiled up at him.

"Yeah, he looks like a friendly guy. If you like friends that could tear your arms off." He swallowed.

Her laugh echoed loudly through the lobby and she caught her lip between her teeth. "You are so cute when you get nervous!"

He sighed. "Well, around you who wouldn't be nervous?" It only took a moment to get lost in her big green eyes.

"Oh really?" She stopped him in his tracks and stepped in front of him with a sly smile.

"Yeah, really. You're smart, beautiful – that's tough on us normal people." He smiled, meeting her gaze.

Susan gave his arm a squeeze and tilted her head. "Are you saying I'm not normal?"

He laughed. "Absolutely."

She joined his laugh and hugged his arm again. The oversized doorman gave them a slight nod as they passed.

The club was dark. The room's only light came from the neon blue glow from hidden lights around the room. The place had an air of secrecy to it. Susan guided them past a circular bar, through the tables and into a private booth against the back wall. It seemed like the kind of place where a couple would cozy up over drinks and share a hidden moment. A sole piano player plunked out soft jazz tunes to the dozen or so occupants around the bar.

When they reached the booth Susan instructed him to sit. "You stay put and relax. I'll go get us drinks."

He stared longingly as she walked away. Her dress showed off her every curve. *Wow.* Susan was setting the pace this evening and he didn't care. He leaned back and took in the scenery, doing his best to settle his nerves. Now that he was actually in the bar, he felt a little more relaxed. He could handle this, he'd had a beer with Nate countless times. He drummed his fingers on the table to the tune of the piano player as he continued to admire Susan's backside. He sure wasn't the only man in there who was looking. He could see the eyes of other men in the bar fixed on her. Her curvy body – silhouetted by the blue lights under the bar's counter – was a delicious sight.

Arriving back at the table, she set down their drinks then slid towards him, only stopping when her body was pressed dangerously close to his side. "A toast to what I am sure is going to be an unforgettable evening." Susan clinked his glass with her own and giggled.

He pushed the straw aside and took a few hard gulps of the blue concoction. It made him feel all warm and fuzzy as it reached his stomach. "So, what exactly are your thoughts for the evening?" he asked, putting down his half-finished drink.

"Wouldn't you like to know …" She gave him a teasing smile.

The sound of her words dragged slowly through his head. He felt himself drifting backwards into the booth, the cushions swallowing him. He grabbed the edge of the table for support but nothing stopped his descent. Susan glanced at her watch and waved in slow motion to someone across the club. He tried to speak but was paralyzed. He slumped hard into the seat as Susan's image began to blur, creating multiple red-headed vixens all pulling away from him.

A man's deep voice echoed through the fog. "Looks like he's had too much to drink, Miss."

"Yeah, poor kid. He's all yours." Susan's familiar voice rang out as he hung on to consciousness, fighting the overpowering urge to sleep.

A man came into his blurred vision, putting a fat brown envelope onto the table. She opened it and thumbed through its contents.

"Nice doing business with you." She left the table and disappeared into the dark.

CHAPTER TWENTY-TWO

GABRIEL JERKED HIS FACE UP. The stale smell of a musty old mattress filled his nose. His head felt clouded and heavy. *Where am I?* Two blurred figures moved in his vision, standing on either side of the only door in the room. His vision slowly focused. The strangers chatted in a language he didn't know. They were obviously guards of some kind, wearing casual clothing with automatic weapons at their sides. Each had the same strange Asian characters tattooed across hands and throat.

As quietly as possible, he pushed himself up and gently swung his feet down onto the dirty cement floor. He kept his eyes on the two chatting guards, trying not to breathe too loudly. His concentration was broken by a sudden loud clang of metal. He turned his head towards the far corner of the room.

Sitting in a chair behind a grey steel desk was a stern looking man. He wore an open collar dress shirt that revealed the same tattoos on his neck and continuing down his chest beneath his clothes. Jaw clenched, he stared at Gabriel. He shouted something at the two guards. They hung their heads in shame and quickly braced, on each side of the door. The stranger turned his gaze back to Gabriel and stood up, not breaking his eye contact. He leaned two heavy fists on the desk and smiled, like a lion baring his teeth.

"So, you're awake?" The strange voice echoed through the concrete room, thick with an Asian accent. "Interesting evening you've had. But who could blame you? Such a beautiful woman. She hides her fangs well. Wouldn't you agree?"

His mocking tone added to Gabriel's confusion. He swallowed hard, still feeling dazed.

The large man stepped out from behind the desk, revealing a strong athletic-looking physique. Gabriel noticed an expensive watch covered in rare stones on his wrist. Money, then. Each fist was lined with glitzy rings, though the hardened, scarred knuckles looked as if they belonged to a cage fighter.

"It is no problem if you do not speak. At this point it is best you listen. I would give you my name but I do not think you would care. All you need to know is that you are now the property of the Tao Sung."

Gabriel's mind flashed to an image he remembered seeing on the news just a few weeks prior. The newscaster had spoken of a criminal group of the same name. They were stealing ore and material on a global scale. They were the ones responsible for the attack on T.E.R.A.'s China transport.

"I am a collector of interesting things and after seeing the footage of you in the labs at T.E.R.A., I can see that you are an interesting thing. I am pleased to have you now, despite your rather high cost. It is not very often we find humans surviving in such close quarters with the ore, but it happens." The man stared smugly down at Gabriel.

"At first I wanted to cut the crystal out of your chest! After all, the white ore is so rare. But my scientist suggests I do not. So for now you are safe." He laughed. "But now I am stuck with a problem. You see, the shard is most likely useless without you attached to it. So, I need you to help me. I don't think you will do so willingly – but then again you are simply a scared little boy!"

That did it. "Go to Hell!" Gabriel straightened.

"Hmmm, brave? Stupid? Which are you, Gabriel Roberts?" The man snapped his fingers and spoke to the guards. They ran over, grabbed Gabriel and forced him face down on the floor. The rough concrete scraped his face. They yanked his arms painfully behind him, handcuffing his wrists to his ankles. The sharp steel around his wrists cut harshly into his skin. "You see," the boss continued, gently rolling up his sleeves on his expensive shirt, "the Tao Sung is not a den of thieves like the world thinks of us. We are a society of enlightened individuals and we live by our rules. All Tao Sung followers wear our decree written all over their body. Set permanently into their skin so that they never forget why we have been called."

He kept talking, but Gabriel ignored him, trying to focus on breaking his bonds with the strength lying in his chest. Nothing happened. His head was still heavy and clouded and the crystal seemed asleep in his chest. He couldn't manage to summon any of its strengths. *Wake up!* His thoughts broke as the man's loud voice increased with passion.

"... and so we became takers of the earth! Nothing in this world is out of our grasp. We will take what we desire and rebuild the world as we see fit. A paradise where the strong will rule and the weak will die!"

"Why am I here." Gabriel twisted his neck to look up at him.

"Because I own you!" The man nodded and the guards hauled him to his knees, his back arched as the handcuffs cut into his wrists. The man leaned down and slapped him across the face, leaving a searing pain in his hand's wake. He walked away from Gabriel, removed several rings from his hands and dropped them onto the desk, one echoing thud after another.

"I want everyone who meets the Tao Sung to understand that we will not be opposed. I don't care if they are men, women or children ..." The man turned, clenching fists and teeth. "Oppose me and you will feel no more! No happiness, no joy or comfort!" The man marched towards Gabriel and struck his face again, toppling him to the ground.

His eye burned like fire and swelled shut. He could feel blood on his face. "Son of a bitch!" The pain was immense.

A kick to his side left him gasping for air and sucking in mouthfuls of dust from the filthy floor. He coughed and spit as he tried to regain control of his lungs. The guards hoisted him up by his collar and the next blow split his lips against his teeth. Blood filled his mouth, choking his breath. They set him back on his knees again. He teetered from side to side trying to keep his balance as he vomited out the blood. The crystal lay heavy and inactive in his chest. Maybe the drugs had destroyed his connection to it? The boss walked away from him, wiping his hands on a silk cloth.

"This is what will happen if you oppose me! I will take everything from you, and lastly – just before you die – I will cut that ore out of your chest myself! Take him and put him with the others!" he barked at the guards.

The two guards rushed over and unlocked the steel handcuffs that had cut their way into his wrists, taking chunks of skin with them. They hauled him up by his arms and dragged him out of the room.

The hallway was dark and musty. Fluorescent bulbs flickered high overhead, casting shadows everywhere. He hung helplessly between the two guards. Pain throbbed in his face and side. They forced him to walk down a set of metal stairs. He lost his balance near the bottom and tumbled down several but they hauled him upright again, hard hands digging into his muscles as they dragged him into a darkened room. A single red bulb glowed to life as they entered. The poor lighting and swollen eye didn't allow him to see much of his surroundings except the steel cage he was tossed into. He lay face down, motionless on the cold wet floor, his head still ringing. He heard a door clang shut, the light went out, and he surrendered to unconsciousness.

He was unsure how much time had passed before he rolled onto his back. If his pain was a good indicator, it couldn't have been long. Even the shallowest breath sent excruciating pain through his ribs. Opening his eyes, he saw only darkness. He reached a hand up and felt the low, cold steel roof of his cage – it was barely tall enough to fit a large dog. He ran his hand along each of the bars on the walls that caged him. The space was no bigger than four feet by three feet, certainly not enough room to stretch out his cramped legs. He also found a small slimy dish of what felt like water and another with some kind of a slop. A foul smelling rag hung on the edge of a bucket in the corner. The odour let him know what the bucket was for. He rolled onto his knees, careful not to knock anything over and strained his eyes to see around the room.

A small slit of light seeped in through a large round wall vent. It hummed and squealed continually as it cycled the stale stinking air. He licked his lips, feeling the sting of a still-open cut, his mouth still tasting of blood. The fuzziness had left him and he replayed the events that had happened to him. He couldn't believe she'd done this. He cursed himself silently in the dark for trusting that viper of a woman. How could he have been so stupid? He wished now that he had gone with Adin to T.E.R.A. He wouldn't be trapped in this hell hole.

"Hello?" A soft, high-pitched voice came from several feet away.

Startled, he turned his head, peering past his own bars and through another set to a blurry movement in the next cage.

"Who's there?" he whispered into the darkness.

The soft voice whispered back. "Lots of people. You aren't alone in this horrible place."

Grunts and other words of affirmations sounded as a multitude of people suddenly came to life in the dark room.

"What is going on? Why are they doing this!"

"Shhh!" she warned him. "Don't speak so loudly. The guards will come back and just be angry."

"Sorry." He lowered his voice to a whisper again. "Why are they keeping us all?"

"They are the Tao Sung. Their leader, Shiro, has an obsession with the ore; he's been collecting it for years, trying to grow his own empire with it." The soft whisper moved closer to his ear.

He leaned his head against the side steel bars trying hard not to miss any of her explanation.

"Everyone in this room is a project to him. He conducts experiments on us – using different types of ore to see what we can do."

"What?" He was shocked. "Why would he do that?"

"Because each of us has some kind of connection with the ore."

I'm not the only one? His heart quickened, his mind going into overdrive. There were others like himself!

"What do you mean by 'a connection'?"

"We each have a special reaction to the ore – some of us even have control over it ... can tell it what to do." Her tone quickly changed. "You must know what I mean. They must want to know what you can do, as well."

They can control it like me? He remained silent.

"I'm sorry if I scared you." She broke his thoughts. "I'm one of the few people who know why I was taken here. I didn't mean to –"

"It's okay. I know what they want from me."

"I'm sorry," she whispered back. "I'm Kyrie."

"Gabriel."

"Nice to meet –" Her words were interrupted as the steel door of the room swung open.

The dirty light from the hallway shone into the room, momentarily blinding him. He squinted hard to focus as two guards walked into the room, casting towering shadows across the floor. For the first time he could make out most of the room; it was larger than he had expected, holding about two dozen cages filled with ragged people clutching the bars with frail fingers. The guards headed in his direction.

His heart quickened as they moved closer. The beam of their flashlight focused on Kyrie's cage beside him. She scooted to the back of the cage like a terrified animal. Her pale face was framed by long, tangled black hair. Her dark brown, oval-shaped eyes were filled with fear and she bit her cracked, lower lip to stop it from trembling. Her tiny frame was badly scarred and her clothes were ripped and ragged. The guards opened her cage and gestured for her to step out. When she refused they reached in each catching hold of a wrist. She fought hard to stay in the cage but one guard slapped her across the face several times and they finally pulled her free.

"Leave her alone!" Rage filled him.

The guards paid no attention to him. He grabbed the bars in anger and the familiar web of light began to glow brightly under his skin. He yelled as he pushed on the cage door. The steel popped and creaked and slowly bent under his strength. The guards dropped Kyrie and stepped back, shouting loudly in their language. Kyrie didn't move. She stared at him. He glared at the guards and began to rattle the door on its hinges

A dark image filled the lit doorway. "Gabriel!"

His concentration broke as he strained to see who called his name. The white beams began to cool under his skin. The door became difficult to move as he continued to try and push it free.

"Gabriel. Gabriel." Shiro strolled into the room.

"Leave her alone!" He spit at the man.

"Hah! Like you have any say in what I do. Kyrie is one of my favourites. But look at you – quite impressive. I will enjoy learning more about what you can do, that is for certain, but right now I need Kyrie … and you need to sleep." He produced two pills from his pocket and handed them to the guard. The guard stepped to the cage with the two blue capsules, holding them out for him to take.

"Take them!" Shiro commanded.

"Go to Hell!"

"Boy! You are stupid, aren't you?" Shiro's voice rose to a full yell. "You don't get it do you? I decide who goes to hell here. I decide who lives or dies! Now do as I say. Or perhaps my dear Kyrie will die today! She is not as valuable as you. " He grabbed her by the hair, pulling her to her feet as she cried out in pain. "Or perhaps I will simply hurt her. You can watch, if you want to stay awake. Listen to her scream."

He took the pills, feeling helpless as he swallowed them dry. He spit at the ground and continued to stare at Shiro, hating him.

"Good," Shiro sneered. "Know this: you try anything, I will not only kill you but every single person in this room."

The threat echoed in his head and his vision began to blur as the medication began to take effect. It must be damping his conscious control of the crystal, too. He tried to fight the reaction but collapsed on the floor of the small cage, unable to hold himself up any longer. His eyelids drooped as Shiro and the guards exited the room with Kyrie, leaving everyone in darkness once again.

He drifted in a sea of memories. He could hear his father's voice, sharing the news about discovering the ore. "... *the ore will change the world; this could save us all ... enhance our ability to farm and provide clean water to the masses!*"

The vision was interrupted by the image of his mother dropping to her knees and crying at the front door of the farm house. Nate stood there with her, apologizing as he knelt down to meet her. The image faded into a blur and moved on to his mother's hand flecked with blood and pinned under the wall of the house. Gabriel tried to scream but nothing left his mouth. If only he could have saved her! If only he had left the crystal to the storm and stayed safe in the shelter with his mother.

Rage filled him and he willed his body to move but nothing happened; he was paralyzed, drifting in a remembrance of sorrows until a thundering crack fractured the images like glass. Gabriel opened his eyes to the steel roof of his cage. Movement beside him caught his attention and he tried to get up, but his body refused. He rolled his head to the side. In her own cage lay Kyrie, her dark eyes half-open. She crawled towards him and stretched out her thin arms through the bars. He could see the gloss of blood down her arm.

"It's okay. I'll be fine," she whispered. "This won't go on forever; my father will find us soon."

CHAPTER TWENTY THREE

The screech of steel on steel startled Gabriel and he jolted up in the short cage, smacking his head on the low ceiling. Something was happening above him. He pressed his face awkwardly against the bars, hoping to catch a glimpse. At the top of the room, light was pouring in from a hole in the ceiling. A hum slowly began and four fan blades spun shadows around the room. Goose bumps rose up over his skin as cool, fresh air floated down into the stale dungeon. The air smelled sweet, almost lush. He inhaled deeply, trying to rid his nose of the musty smell of his cage.

He turned to talk to Kyrie but she was gone. They must have taken her again while he lay unconscious. The steel door to the room opened abruptly and three guards stepped in muttering unfamiliar words to one another as they looked around the room.

One of the guards spotted him, walked over and kicked the door of his cage. "You come with us!" The man unlocked the cage. "Remember what we said! Behave or we will punish everyone in this room!"

Just then an old man across the room screamed as one of the

other guards stomped on the fragile hand he had left dangling out-side his cage.

"Leave him alone!" Gabriel yelled. "I'm coming out!" He met the dark eyes of the guard in front of him.

"Good! You understand."

The other guard laughed and lifted his boot heel from the old man's hand.

Gabriel crawled out of the small cage and stood up. His muscles cramped up instantly. He stumbled towards the guards and they handcuffed his wrists behind his back and blindfolded him.

After walking him through a series of turns and up a flight of short stairs they removed his blindfold and handcuffs. Bright neon lights burned his eyes and he blinked rapidly to adjust. What was this?

"What's going on?"

A shove from behind forced him forwards and a guard told him to sit on the chair before him. Obeying, he sat down on the uncomfortable chair that was bolted to the dirty floor. There was another door beside him, and one of the guards opened it. The smell of bleach burned his nose and throat and he coughed. The side room held a tall steel table with clamps and leather straps hanging from it. A young Asian man stepped out from an adjoining room. He wore thin wire-rimmed glasses and his hair was long and gelled back. A blood-stained apron covered his t-shirt and jeans. He met Gabriel's eyes and grinned.

"So, you are the one with the crystal in his chest?" When he finally spoke, his voice was tiny and thin like the hiss of a snake. "Shiro told me about you ..." He pulled a small electronic pipe out of his pocket and sucked at it deeply. "That's better."

Gabriel stared back at him and said nothing.

"Ms. McCormick gave me very little information on your abil-ities. Perhaps you would be so kind as to explain them to me?" He took another breath from his pipe, exhaling slowly.

Gabriel stared at the floor.

"No response? Come on." The stranger almost giggled. "You know I have seen many people in your spot. Some talk. Some don't. Some even share their own thoughts as to why they can do what they do with the ore. I enjoy the common villager and ill-educated the most. The morons believe they are gods and have powers to control the elements. They realize quickly that they are not a god, nor do they control anything. So, I pick them apart – like a good scientist – and find out how they work. You seem smarter than the usual vagrants Shiro brings me. Make this easier for yourself – and tell me what I want to know." The scientist shrugged.

None of this made any sense to Gabriel. "Why are you doing this? You aren't a psycho like Shiro."

"Yeah, Shiro's crazy. But he brings me the people I need for my research. I don't really care how he finds people like you – I just do my job and I get paid. Really makes no difference to me how I earn the money."

"You greedy son of a bitch. You destroy people's lives by following Shiro. How can you not care?" Gabriel glared at him.

He puffed on the pipe again and laughed. "Oh, I care. I care about what's in this little pipe. It's like a potion of brilliance but it's also very pricy. Once I get Shiro what he wants, solve his mysteries – I'll be set for life. All the drugs, women, and money I want."

"Shiro will probably just put a bullet in your head."

"Ah, you would think so but I have a 'retirement' plan that keeps Shiro on a leash. It's flawless so I win." The young man leaned against the wall grinning. "But back to you! What can you do?"

"Nothing." Gabriel glared at him.

"Too bad." He pressed a small black knob.

Flames of pain seared through Gabriel's body. His muscles locked up and his back arched as the current burned him from the inside out. It stopped just as suddenly as it started. He gasped for air and fell to the floor, his mouth full of blood from his bitten tongue. The doctor skipped over to him, beaming. His shiny leather shoes stopped inches from Gabriel's eyes.

"Again!" The young man snapped his fingers and the guards responded, placing Gabriel back onto the chair, binding him there, this time, with leather straps.

"Observation number one – electricity will slowly cook your organs." He laughed. "Now, what can you do with that crystal in your chest?" He waited again for an answer as he wiped his glasses off and replaced them on his face.

"Water." Gabriel gasped between heavy breaths, the crystal in his chest failing to stop the electricity.

"What about it … What can you do to it?" He scooped up an electronic pad.

"I can boil water." Gabriel was quick to answer this time.

The researcher looked surprised, almost amused. "You can boil water …" He laughed.

"I heat it by touching it." He struggled to slow his breathing down to a steady pace as he fought the urge to pass out.

"The guards told me you nearly ripped the steel door off your cage." The man made another note. "And I know Shiro's methods, but you are undamaged." He peered at Gabriel's face and frowned. "So the crystal accelerates healing despite the sedatives. I have video of a piece of ore becoming energized by your touch, but you … you can boil water …" He looked completely annoyed. "Do you think I am a fool? Do you think that I am clueless?" He turned to walk back to the knob on the wall. "Tell me the truth!"

It was true. Gabriel blinked, his head still fuzzy from the shock. His ribs and face didn't hurt him anymore. "I … I don't know what I can do! Well not everything … the strength is new but I … I can't control it! The red crystal in the lab … I don't know what happened. Honestly, you have to believe me!"

The researcher studied him.

"We were there … at T.E.R.A. trying to figure it out." Gabriel tried to explain.

"We?" The scientist tilted his head.

"My … my brother and I." He felt the shake of fear in his voice.

"Yes … your brother works for T.E.R.A." The scientist's voice slowed as he paced the floor with his arms crossed. "How much does T.E.R.A. know?"

He panicked, searching his mind for answer. "I don't understand!"

"How much does T.E.R.A. know about you and your abilities? What tests did they do on you in the lab?"

"What? No tests! Adin wasn't supposed to tell them! It was just between the two of us."

The doctor went silent again, staring at him. "Why should I believe you?"

Gabriel closed his eyes, praying for no more pain. The researcher said something sharply to the guards. They roughly removed his restraints before hoisting him up by the arms and dragging him into the room with the large steel table.

The doctor walked in ahead of them, tapping several wall mounted screens around the steel table. The screens flickered to life and machines hummed loudly in the small space. A robotic arm lowered a large scanning device into position above the foot of the table. Gabriel's heart began to race, beating loudly in his chest. *What are they going to do to me?* Each breath he took shook his body, his fear growing as he looked around the room. Then he saw her. *Kyrie?*

A glass, coffin-shaped box was set into the wall, radiating an eerie green glow. Inside the clear coffin lay Kyrie. She didn't move. She lay there as if dead, an intravenous line in her arm. The small tank top she wore was stained with so much blood that he couldn't tell what color it was originally. She was covered with wounds that had been carelessly covered with gauze and adhesive. Everything in the room drifted away as Gabriel walked over to the glass coffin. What had they done to her?

"An amazing subject!" The green ore can sustain her life no matter how much harm we put her through: gunshots, beatings, surgeries, whatever Shiro pleases to do to her. What a wonderful specimen to have. We can do virtually anything to her and she will recover, but it does take some time. She often spends days in this chamber after difficult testing sessions. I swear without this little angel I would be years behind in my research."

Gabriel remained frozen at the window, a silent anger building inside him. She was nothing more than an experiment. A lab rat. No longer a human being. He remained in a daze as the guards pulled him away from the glass and strapped him to the steel table. The scientist took scans and pictures of the crystal in his chest, babbling on about its composition and structure. The process took hours and Gabriel remained numb to what was happening. His mind kept replaying the same thought – all of this because his father had found something he should have left in the dirt.

A sharp stab to his arm jolted him out of his misery. "This will keep him sedated for awhile, that crystal will be useless to him." And the scientist sent him away.

Blindfolded again, Gabriel was hauled back to his small cell, the door slammed shut behind him. He lay on the cold floor, staring at the empty cell beside him, his body paralyzed. How long had Kyrie been here, hoping for someone to save her? A chill crawled down his spine. The researcher had noticed that the crystal had healed him. Was his fate to be any different?

Hours past as Gabriel lay on the floor drifting in and out of consciousness, the cocktail of drugs in his body preventing any connection to the ore. Kyrie was eventually tossed back into the cage beside him. He tried to move, to make sure she was alright. She crawled over to him, leaned against the bars, and began to talk quietly.

"I remember my father taking me out for ice cream once a week because he used to work so much that I would be mad at him. He called it 'our time'. A time for him to remind me how much he loved me …" Her voice trembled. "My mother made sure he never forgot and we went out every week no matter how old I got. We kept doing that – even when I left for university – not missing a single week. One day he told me he had quit his job at the government and began to work on the ore with a small group of scientists. They were trying to find a use for it that didn't create the negative effects … so it would be safe. He's looking for me – we just have to be patient. We just have to survive."

CHAPTER TWENTY-FOUR

SEVERAL SHADOWS GATHERED OUTSIDE THE DUNGEON DOOR. Gabriel could see them pace back and forth through the crack beneath it. He couldn't make out the discussion, but it sounded serious.

He reached through the bars and tapped on Kyrie's shoulder. "What's happening?"

She lay on the floor of her cage, unresponsive, her body motionless. He still felt the physical effects of the drugs lingering in his body, but his mind was clear and sharp for the first time in days.

Loud popping sounds rang out somewhere in the facility. *Gunfire.* Orders echoed in the hallway over a speaker. Shadows flickered across the crack at the bottom of the door. An alarm started to bleat. He had no idea how many guards there were but it sounded like hundreds of footsteps running past their door. He needed to escape. He couldn't stay in this hell hole any longer.

"Kyrie, I am going to get help. If I can escape then I can get help and come back." He grabbed her limp hand through the bars and squeezed it. "I'll be back, I promise. Or they will catch me and I'll be back right away ... so basically ... I'll be back."

"Go." Her faint voice was barely audible over the noise outside of the room.

He firmly wrapped his fingers around the bars on his cage door. A deep breath. Then another. He pushed on the steel door. Nothing. *Wake up!* He smacked his chest. Leaning back on his elbows, he hammered at the door with both feet, shaking his cage with each hit. His feet burned with pain and his legs turned to rubber. Firmly grasping at the bars again with his hands, he closed his eyes. *Do something!* His arms shook as he pressed on the bars with all his force. *I need you!*

The crystal sparked to life and waves of heat flowed across his body. He summoned the crystal's strength. Light burst from it, creating a visible glow under his shirt. The light twisted and spun down around his waist and swirled down his legs. It climbed up his chest, around his shoulders and down his arms. It finally reached his hands, bathing them in light.

"Gabriel …" Kyrie sounded frightened.

The crystal's power took away every bit of pain in his body. His fingers gripped the bars, and their cold surface steamed at his touch, then glowed red with heat. He repositioned his body, once again using his feet to push. The hinges made a snapping sound as the steaming door fell onto the wet concrete.

Leaping out of the cage, he felt nothing but the energizing power of the ore pulsing through his entire body. He sprinted to the door on the far side of the room, ignoring the calls for help from the prisoners around him. Of course the door was locked. Being subtle wouldn't help. The webs of light still pulsed in his hands and forearms. He backed away from the door, psyched himself up, and sprinted at it. His shoulder collided with the heavy steel surface and the door ripped out of the wall, its hinges tearing apart. It crashed to the ground.

The ground underneath him shook. A battle raged elsewhere in the building, the alarm was still blaring every few seconds. Sporadic gunfire and shouting echoing down the stone halls. The noise was deafening. He looked back at the room full of prisoners – they couldn't all escape. "Go!" Kyrie yelled at him. "Just go!"

"Come with me!" He charged over to her cage, bending the corner of the steel door back as his skin flared with the power of the ore.

"Stop … I can't even walk … Just go." Kyrie begged him.

There was no time for him to think about her answer, he needed to just listen. Unsure of where to go, he tried his best to remember the steps he had taken on his previous trip to the scientist. The drugs and the blindfold had confused him and he couldn't remember. He decided to head towards the noise, hoping to find an exit. At the end of the hall, he peered around the corner. A staircase. It appeared to be bright with daylight. His heartbeat quickened as he took several steps towards it. The clanging sound of boots coming down the metal rungs of the stairs caused him to halt. His shoes squeaked as he changed direction, ducking back around the corner and bolting through a door he had ignored. He shut the door carefully, trying to make as little noise as possible, then turned to face the room. The only source of illumination, was a flickering ceiling light. He spotted a make-shift counter attached to the concrete wall. A pipe with a tap stuck out of the wall, dripping into a bucket hanging from it. Boxes of rations and unwashed pots rested on the small countertop. This must be where they prepared the slop he had been eating for the last three days. He moved towards the back wall, searching in the shadows for a secret panel or passage that might somewhere else. No luck. The door was the only way in and out.

It burst open. A guard stepped inside, shutting it with a bang as he leaned against it. He clawed at his waist for a fresh clip to put into his weapon, not realizing he wasn't alone in the room. Instinctively Gabriel lunged at him, grabbing at the sub-machine gun strapped around the guard's chest. Caught off balance, the guard slammed against the door but managed to shove Gabriel back several steps. He raised the weapon. Time slowed. Gabriel watched the muzzle of the gun flash brightly with a glowing bullet. His heart stopped as it left the gun, aiming straight towards his stomach. It burnt a hole in his shirt as it pierced the cloth but dropped to the floor with a ting.

The guard's mouth hung open – his eyes fixed on the light bursting from the hole in Gabriel's shirt. Without hesitation, Gabriel grabbed the guard and lifted him off the ground. His hands were webbed with white light, pulsing through the muscles under his skin. He sent the guard sailing across the room to slam against a small table. Scraps of wood and splinters exploded into the air. The guard lay still on top of the debris – not moving. Gabriel leaned against a wall, his head spinning and his body on fire with the energy of the ore.

Another man ducked in and closed the door to the room. Gabriel tackled him. The sheer force and speed of his attack sent the two crashing through the closed door, tearing it from its hinges as they spilled into the open hallway.

"You!" Shiro spit through his teeth as Gabriel fought to stay on top of him.

Anger filled him. His glowing fist smashed into Shiro's cheek. It split open and bright red blood spurted. Shiro punched Gabriel in the side, sending a jolt of pain rattling through his body. The power of the ore was fading. Unleashing his rage, he slammed his fist into Shiro's face, again and again. His arm a blur of speed. A familiar yell rang out behind him. He stopped his assault on Shiro and turned towards the armed soldier. What was he trying to say? *That voice.*

The man, dressed in full camo with an assault rifle, yelled at him, raising his gun. "Gabriel, Get down!"

Gunfire roared in the hallway and the muzzle flash lit up the hallway. There was nowhere to hide. He threw up both of his arms in automatic defence. His hands glowed brightly, and a bubble of light instantly filled the space between them. Bullets dropped out of the air, clanking to the ground. His vision blurred and the dizziness swept over him. His vision tunneled as he slumped over Shiro's limp body.

CHAPTER TWENTY-FIVE

GABRIEL WAS IN THE LOFT OF THE OLD BARN AT HOME. Nate was giving him another lecture about the world as he changed into some clean clothes. Nate's body carried a history of the dangerous path he once walked. Each scar had its own story, carved into his chest, back, and arms. He wore his hair buzzed down as if he was still in the military, and a trimmed beard filled out his face.

Gabriel looked towards the window at the blue sky. Everything felt right. Everything was warm and familiar. Nate's voice continued as Gabriel stood up and walked over to the window, looking down towards the yard. There she was. She had on her flower print apron, her green work gloves and a large straw hat that shielded her from the sun while she worked in her garden. *Mom.* He wanted desperately to run out to her but chose to stay where he was, savouring the memory of her alive, happy, at home. He pressed his hand against the cool glass, his heart aching. This wasn't real. He knew she was with his father now – happier in some unknown place.

Nate called to him from across the room. "Gabriel."

The image blurred and drifted away like smoke into the air. Only the warmth of a hand on his shoulder and a voice calling his name remained. He blinked his heavy eyes. A friendly face met his gaze – Nate.

"You done sleeping?" Nate smiled and helped him sit up in his bed.

"You're alive?" He hugged him, making sure he was real.

"Yeah, as are you. Although – I'm not sure how." Nate patted his back.

Still shocked, he let go of Nate and glanced around the room. "Where are we? That was you in the hallway back there wasn't it?"

"Smart." Nate sat back in the chair beside his bedside. "I was following you after you left Adin's."

"What? You were following me? Why didn't you –"

Nate laughed. "Let me explain. Two known Tao Sung thugs were following you as well. They pulled that stunt at the bar and had you carted away before I could get to you. We got lucky and found you in that Tao Sung –"

He cut Nate off. "What about the storm? What happened at the farm? We thought you were in the barn."

"I went into town late that evening to meet some of my contacts and – It doesn't matter." Nate shook his head. "I couldn't get back in time. The storm hit so fast."

He stared at the sheets on the bed, running a loose thread through his fingers. "I survived … Mom didn't."

Nate looked away and leaned back in his chair. "I know."

Would things have been different if Nate had been there? But he had learned over the last couple of weeks how futile regret was. "Where are we?"

Nate gathered himself and cleared his throat. "Somewhere safe. Don't worry about the details."

Gabriel nodded. Nate had always been cryptic about things.

"You feel up to a walk?" Nate pointed at the door.

The hallway was ugly. White walls with a dingy grey floor.

"This is our medical wing." Nate strolled along beside him as they talked.

"Like a private hospital?"

"Pretty much." Nate shrugged.

Gabriel eyed two men in uniforms walking by, assault rifles over their shoulders. "Hospitals don't have soldiers in them ... Where are we?"

"Look, this a safe place. There's nothing to worry about. The less you know – the safer you'll be." Nate pointed towards a window looking toward a mountain range. The facility obviously was built at the bottom of the valley. "Gorgeous country."

"Nate, cut the cryptic bullshit. Where are we? You back in the military?" Gabriel wasn't in a mood for fatherly protection.

Nate sighed and glared at him. "Your father made me promise to keep you safe. In a day or two you will never see this place again. And I will take you somewhere to start over. So drop it."

"Why! What are you hiding!" Gabriel stopped and faced him. "You can't just pretend nothing has happened. That we could start all over like a happy family. She's dead Nate!"

Nate grabbed him by his shirt and shoved him against the window frame. "You don't think I know that! I have to live with that mistake every day I don't see your mother!" Nate's hands dropped to his sides and he let go of Gabriel.

Gabriel breathed out, his heart racing. "I'm sorry. Everything's screwed up ... I don't even know which way is up." He let his head fall back to rest against the cool window.

Nate stepped away. "Don't worry. We're family ... Let me just find somewhere you'll be safe. I'll finish what I need to do here and then, you and I will start over. A new life. New names. Everything. I promise."

Gabriel didn't want to start over. He wanted his life back. The curse in his chest needed to be cut out and things put back to normal. "What about my life ... my friends? the ranch? What about Adin? Kyrie? The girl! Did you?"

Nate sighed and patted him on the back. "Of course, everyone was taken somewhere safe."

"Where is she?" He needed to see her.

"She's in the medical wing, don't worry about it." Nate smiled at him.

"Stop telling me not to worry!" Gabriel clenched his fists. "How am I suppose to not worry. I was kidnapped and sold to some asshole. Then put in a cage! I'm going to find her." He twisted and left.

He didn't want to look at Nate. He didn't want to hear him say 'don't worry about it' again. He searched on the way back to his room, pausing to look through the small glass window of any door. Where could she be? A final door was left near his room, he crept over to it. A large, clear plastic tent with white zippers filled the majority of the room. Something about the patient lying on the hospital-style bed inside of it seemed familiar. Very familiar. He burst into the room, clumsily pushing his way under the plastic tent.

Kyrie opened her eyes and smiled at the sight of him, reaching for his hand. He scooped up her delicate hand into his. She didn't look any better. She had several IV's running and tubes implanted into her chest. A machine behind her bed beeped and blinked.

"My father found us …" She had an 'I-told-you-so' kind of tone in her voice.

"Just like you said." He couldn't help but smile at her.

Just then the plastic tent zipped open on one side. Nate stepped in with another man in a long white lab coat with a stethoscope around his neck.

Nate introduced the stranger. "Gabriel, this is Doctor Osho. He's Kyrie's father."

Gabriel let go of Kyrie's hand, feeling embarrassed. He offered it out to the doctor. "Um … Good to meet you."

The doctor gripped his hand firmly. "You are a friend to my daughter. I appreciate you being there when I couldn't." He spoke with a British accent that contrasted with his Asian features.

"Dr. Osho is the head of the organization here. He's a friend." Nate nodded.

The thin man smiled half-heartedly at Gabriel, his weary eyes showing a heavy burden.

"I am glad you're up on your feet." Osho politely opened his arm towards the door. "But I must ask you to let my daughter rest now. She needs all she can get."

Gabriel nodded, still flustered. "Of course. I'm sorry. I just wanted to see if she was okay."

Osho shut the door behind them as they exited the room. "Why don't we all talk in my office. I'm sure you have some questions."

CHAPTER TWENTY-SIX

Gabriel sat down, waiting as Dr. Osho went around to the other side of his desk and collapsed into his chair. Collecting himself, he looked at Gabriel, his eyes glistening with tears. "I fear my daughter will not make it. We are doing our best but I am afraid –" His emotions broke through his professionalism. He paused momentarily. "At this point in time, we can simply make her as comfortable as possible and hope she will survive."

He couldn't help but glare at the doctor. What was he saying?

The doctor sighed. "I believed my daughter dead for the last three months. I had accepteqd her fate. I am just happy she didn't have to spend her last days in that dungeon."

"You can't give up! What about the green ore?" He wanted to leap at the man and shake him. "They kept her alive with it before. Do it again."

"Kept her alive, yes." Osho shook his head. "They did not *heal* her wounds; they simply delayed death from taking her."

"But ... you can't –" Gabriel shook his head, horrified.

"I have studied my daughter's condition for years ..." Osho

drew himself up. "She has an amazing reaction to green ore – yes – which can heal her wounds on a small scale. However, she is not wounded on a small scale and I do not have a piece of green ore that is strong enough to regenerate her." A hint of annoyance laced his voice. "The internal bleeding alone is nearly impossible to deal with. Her organs are beyond any surgeries we can perform. They damaged her too much."

Gabriel went silent. His mind searched desperately for a solution. There had to be a way to save Kyrie.

Nate reached out and put his hand on Gabriel's shoulder. "Gabriel, we all would like to save her. This is hard enough for Dr. Osho. Please let it be. Everything that can be done is being done."

"No!" He hit Nate's hand away. "We didn't get out of there just so she could die!"

"I'm sorry, but –" Nate stood up and moved between him and Dr. Osho.

"You can't let her die!" Gabriel stood and slammed his hand down on the arm of the chair.

Nate pointed at him, a stern look on his face. "Gabriel! This is not your place!"

There had to be a way. He paced the room, refusing to accept the facts as final. "If you had some ore strong enough, would it help?" He pointed at Osho.

"Well, yes, in theory. But we don't have anything that can amplify the effects." Osho leaned forward in his chair, elbows resting on the desk.

"I can!"

"What are you talking about?" Nate frowned.

"It happened at T.E.R.A. – I touched a red shard and it ... it glowed so bright." Gabriel looked down at his hand, mimicking the shard in it.

"You're saying your touch increased its energy output?" Osho sat up in his chair.

"It did something. Let me try." He wasn't asking. "Give me the largest one you have."

Osho glanced to Nate.

"It's too dangerous. No – we will think of something else." Nate's expression was troubled.

"Like what?" Gabriel looked Osho in the eyes. "How much more time does she have?"

Osho stared silently at him. "She doesn't … I want him to try."

"What!" Nate shook his head. "We have no idea what will happen! The crystal could explode for all we know."

"If he is willing to take the risk, then so am I." Osho nodded at Gabriel.

"Please, both of you listen to me …" Nate was quickly cut off by Osho.

"She's dying Nathaniel … she's my only daughter. Even if it is just a chance – I have to try." Osho's eyes welled with tears.

"Let's do it." Gabriel stood up and turned to leave the office.

The three exited the office and headed directly to Kyrie's room. She was asleep struggling to breathe. Gabriel needed to make this work. Dr. Osho unlocked the bedside cabinet, opened the drawer, and pulled out a small metal box, much like the ore storage boxes Gabriel had seen in the labs at T.E.R.A.

Setting it on the small table, Osho looked at him, his face full of pain. "We have tried several sessions with it already but nothing has helped. She keeps fading."

"I just need the ore." Gabriel rubbed his chest. I need you.

"Be careful. I have a team waiting outside just in case." Osho ushered Nate out of the tent area. "There is no lock on the box and this tent will keep the radiation in." The doctor zipped up the wall behind them. Their exit woke Kyrie. Gabriel took his place next to her.

"What's going on?" Her voice was weak.

"Trust me." He smiled and opened the small steel box beside her, revealing the eerie green crystal.

He reached into the metal case. His fingers brushed along the foam padding that supported the ore. The green shard was the size and shape of a softball. It gave off a small pulse of light, awaiting his touch. He picked the green orb up. The gentle glow intensified, washing the whole room in a sea of green light. He moved it towards her. She breathed sharply as the ore touched her just below her neck. She looked at him, her eyes filled with fear.

"Shhhh." He touched her forehead with his other hand. "Just close your eyes."

She shut her eyes and tears slid down the sides of her face. She took a few deep breaths, then her breathing slowed to a steady pace. He followed suit, shutting his eyes and focusing on the green ore in his hand. Mentally, he pushed everything he had into the crystal in his chest: his thoughts, his will, everything he could muster. *You have to help. Make her better.*

The crystal flared in his chest. His eyes snapped open. A rush of white light rushed down his arm, cascading like a waterfall towards the green crystal until it reached its surface, encircling it. The green ore pulsated more and more brightly until it overtook the white light completely, changing his hands into a silky green. The light continued to brighten until the room was bathed in a brilliant green aura that banished every shadow in the room. He watched as the bruises on Kyrie's body faded and the cuts shrank and healed in moments. Her swollen abdomen began to look normal and color flushed her pale face.

He glanced over at Osho outside of the tent. Tears were rolling down the doctor's cheeks. He grabbed Nate by the front of the shirt and shook him. "He's – He's healing her! Her organs … I don't – I can't believe this."

Gabriel smiled at Osho. His arm began to shake as the brightness of the green ore faded. Alarms on all the machine behind her beeped wildly. Kyrie began to shiver as she fell into shock. The white glow surrounding his hand faded, retreating up his arms and into his chest.

"Gabriel! Don't stop! Her body can't handle the shock," Osho cried out to him.

His mind fought the ore, forcing the white light to stop its retreat. It snaked back down his forearms again, rushing to meet the green shard he clung to, filling the room with the green brilliance. Kyrie fell still and the beeping stopped. He pushed himself to the limit of his strength, holding on for several more minutes. A thundering crack split the air. He crumpled to the floor, falling hard into the bedside table. The room filled with darkness as the green ore slipped from his limp grasp.

"Nate! Wait! The ore is still exposed." Gabriel heard Osho's voice as if from a great distance. He stayed on the floor, waiting for the room to stop spinning.

Dr. Osho slipped into the tent, wearing a white protective suit. He helped Gabriel off the floor then nodded at Nate. "He's okay."

Osho carefully collected the ore, returned it to the steel box, and shut the lid. He signalled to Nate to turn on the fans above them. Gabriel smiled at Kyrie, and stepped out of the tent still unsteadily – collapsing into Nate's arms. Osho removed his helmet and sat on the edge of the bed as he pulled off his glove and touched Kyrie's face.

Her smile sent him into tears. She kissed his hand and reached towards his face. "I'm okay, Dad."

Nate pulled Gabriel's arm over his shoulder. "You alright?"

"I'm fine." He leaned heavily into Nate. "Just need some time." "I don't … How did you … I mean …" Nate was completely flabbergasted.

He smiled at Nate. "I'm going to have to tell you all about this." He touched the crystal.

"Thank you!" Osho rushed over and hugged him.

Gabriel steadied himself and patted the short man on the back. "I'm glad it worked."

Osho wiped his eyes and stepped back from him. "Your father would be very proud."

My father.

CHAPTER TWENTY-SEVEN

"What about my father?"

"Damn it, Osho." Nate glared at the doctor.

"Nathaniel, I understand your desire to keep him safe but he deserves to know." Dr. Osho put his hand on Gabriel's shoulder. "I'm sure Calvin regretted never being able to tell him himself. Let's speak in my office."

Gabriel stuck close to Osho, following him out of the room and across the facility to his office. Nate stayed behind them, clearly annoyed at Osho. As they all entered the office Gabriel couldn't wait any longer. "How do you know my father?"

"Calvin and I started this whole place after he discovered the ore in what used to be Iran. This research facility is owned by the Ingenius Pluris." Osho smiled at him and shut the door. "The IP has been continuing your father's research since his death. I haven't seen you since you were a little boy, sitting in your father's lap."

"I don't understand." He quickly took a seat in front of the desk. Nate sat beside him. "Why wasn't I told?"

Nate sighed. "The only way your mother saw to keep you two

safe was to never be a part of this again. She didn't want anything to happen to you boys and you would be at risk if you were attached in any way to what your father did. I moved in to watch over the family. Your dad wanted to make sure everyone was safe."

"Safe from who?"

Nate's response was blunt. "Dr. Cymru. From T.E.R.A."

Gabriel sighed. "Nate, I've met the man, he's not the monster you think he is."

"Gabriel, the man is a snake. He's only interested in you because of your ability with the ore."

Gabriel rolled his eyes. "He didn't even know, Adin never told him!"

"He knew about your father, which means he knew there was a possibility that you and Adin might have inherited his unique connection to the ore." Dr. Osho cleared his throat and settled in behind his desk.

"What abilities? What are you talking about? I'm the one with the crystal in my chest, not Adin. And Dad died from ore radiation!"

Nate stared at him. "Your father was like you. He was immune to the ore's effects. It didn't kill him."

He stared at Nate. "You're saying Cymru killed him?"

"No ... the man's a coward. But he most definitely had a hand in it." Nate's nostrils flared.

Osho sighed. "Once the ore was found, it didn't take long for Cymru's good intentions of helping humanity to give way to a hunger for power and control. Calvin disagreed with that choice of direction. The experiments Cymru conducted on people were horrid. His desire to become like Calvin drove him to do unspeakable things. The kidnappings and illegal experiments became too much for Calvin. He broke with Cymru and started working on his own research. He started to pass vital information to me. He then began to send me shipments of ore; just a single crystal or two for study. We needed to increase our knowledge and test our theories. It got riskier as he redirected more and more shipments, off-loading some of the ore before the shipments got to their destination. Soon afterwards, his 'accident' happened." Osho sighed. "Gabriel, your father believed what he was doing was right. He believed it needed to be done – even if it cost him his life."

Gabriel stared at the floor in silence, his mind whirling as it tried to process this new information. Too many 'what ifs' filled him. He didn't understand. Why didn't his father just leave, why risk everything? He felt numb.

"Look," Nate put a hand on his shoulder. "I loved your dad. He was my best friend. I hated his decision as much as anyone but I can see now he needed to do this for all of us. He didn't want his discovery to be what enslaved all of mankind to a corrupt few. He needed to put things right." Nate turned and opened his arms to their surroundings. "Look around you! It made a difference. This whole organization fights for the same thing he did. We are searching every day for ways to utilize the ore safely. I know you don't understand this now but in time you'll see how his decision shaped our future. Sooner or later you're going to have to accept that what he did was right. Be proud of that!"

"Does Adin know the truth?" He continued to stare at the floor.

"Your brother chose his own path. Did he know everything? No. But your mother believed he knew enough to decide for himself. And I think that she thought he would be safer working with T.E.R.A. then against them. Especially with Dr. Cymru so interested in him." Nate rubbed the short beard on his face.

Osho shifted at his desk, stood up and came around to lean against the front of it. "I examined you when you first arrived. The crystal seemed to be inactive but you were stable. I figured you would have a connection to it but, I never would have guessed how much. Your father had a special reaction to the ore as well. When he first went to the discovery site, he said it was as if he could feel it beneath the ground, as if it called to him."

Gabriel looked up at the doctor. "Could he control it?"

Osho shrugged. "I don't know. The ore's energy acted like a homing signal to him. When it 'called', he would feel it. He was meant to find it – no one else. Soon after the first chunks of ore were unearthed, we found out about its negative effects. Many of the initial team were quite weakened by the ore and had to leave the site. But your father could handle it without any protection. That's why the 'accident' at T.E.R.A. didn't make any sense. Your father could not have died from ore exposure. Soon afterwards, messages started to arrive from Calvin – he had planned for his own death."

"Dr. Cymru seemed so sad when he talked about Dad's death. Are you sure?" Gabriel frowned. How did I not see through it?

Dr. Osho shrugged. "I don't doubt that Cymru had some regrets. They were very close. They were research partners for years when T.E.R.A. was first created by the government. But despite that bond, Cymru was consumed by Calvin's relationship to the ore. No matter how much time Cymru spent studying the ore, Calvin would always know it better. He demanded to study your father – to find the secret but your father refused and Cymru was enraged. After that, their research began to go down separate paths. Cymru demanded that Calvin turn over his findings. Of course your father refused. Soon, afterwards Calvin was discovered dead."

"What was Dad researching that was so important to Dr. Cymru?"

"The white and black ore. The white ore was one of the rarer finds Calvin unearthed. If I remember correctly, there were only a couple of crystals found in total and all in the same small area. We assumed they were part of a larger piece." Osho moved back to his chair. "Calvin removed them from T.E.R.A. without much of a problem as they didn't seem to have any power. I see now it had a different purpose. It needed something. A master. A symbiote." Osho smiled at him. "You."

Gabriel sat silent, pondering Dr. Osho's words.

Why me?

"The black ore is a mystery as well. Calvin had made a

breakthrough but his discovery died with him, unfortunately." Nate shrugged.

Gabriel finally spoke. "Adin and I were working on what I could do with the ore, before I left."

"Adin?" Nate looked shocked. "He knew?" Nate looked over at Dr. Osho.

Osho looked to Gabriel. "Does Dr. Cymru know about you?"

"I would guess he does now ... I don't know for sure but that's what we fought about when I left. Adin had always wanted to tell him about me and I wanted to keep it hidden." He shrugged. The sting of Adin's betrayal was still fresh. "Why?"

Nate looked over the desk at Osho again. "Cymru must be looking for him. That might explain —"

Osho lifted his hand to Nate, putting the conversation on hold until another time.

"Explain what?" Gabriel looked from one man to the other. .

"How much do you know about T.E.R.A.'s activities?" Osho tilted his head at Gabriel. "Well, I saw the labs Adin showed me and nothing there looked dangerous. Dr. Cymru just talked about free energy and solving the energy crisis." He was confused by his question. "Why?"

Osho shifted in his chair. "Whether this comes as a shock or not, there are certain things you need to know about T.E.R.A.'s operations. First: everything they claim about the ore is a lie to hide their secrets. The ore is not sustainable forever. It does not possess an unlimited source of power. The ore's energy can be used up and once that happens there is only one way to recharge it." Osho cleared his throat as he continued. "The only known way to recharge the ore is to trade it for human life – something they have been practising for years to keep the ore replenished. When a human is exposed to the ore, it slowly recharges itself, ultimately killing the person. It doesn't produce dangerous radiation, the way Uranium does. It steals life energy. But T.E.R.A. has made people believe that ore radiation is dangerous to account for the deaths that they bring about purposefully." Osho drew a deep angry breath. "Experiments were done on other life forms – lab rats, plants, bacteria – with no success. It is believed the ore draws on what is commonly known as our souls. The site in Iran where we found the ore was believed to have been the site of Eden. Many believe the ore effects were the curse that God placed on the Garden of Eden after man was banished from it."

"Secondly: Dr. Cymru has been conducting experiments on humans and the ore ever since they discovered it. He's been surgically implanting ore into individuals, trying to force some kind of evolution. Individuals such as yourself, and my daughter, are anomalies. Your genetic code is no different than Nate's or mine but you have an inherit relationship to the ore. Cymru is searching for the reason why. This makes you a target for not only them but others as well."

Gabriel could feel the hairs on the back of his neck stand up and a chill went down his spine. "Others?"

"The Church of Humanity for one." Nate looked at him. "They at least hope to use the ore for the good of mankind but individuals like yourself are considered abominations. 'Ore users' as they're called. For years, they have either exiled or executed the users they find. Depending on their strength."

"This is ultimately why we exist – to balance the equation." Osho nodded at Nate. "Your father believed in a world where the ore would save us, not enslave us. We seek to find other means of re-energizing the ore without trading it for human life. To find harmony with mankind and the ore. The more the world uses the ore, the more people will need to die in order to keep it recharged. I tell you all of this because I hope you will help us."

"Gabriel." Nate spoke up suddenly. "Back at the ranch – up in the loft – there was a strongbox. I went back to look for it but it's missing, do you know where it is?"

"Yeah, the chest is at Adin's. I took it there after the storm. I didn't think you were alive and it somehow seemed important."

Breathing a sigh of relief, Nate sat back in his chair. "Smart. We need to get it before Cymru clues in." He looked meaningfully at Osho.

"Thank you for that information. We need to discuss some things in private. Gabriel, could you excuse us?" Osho pointed to the door politely.

"Get some rest. We can talk some more later." Nate patted him on the shoulder.

Gabriel's heart was heavy. The news of what happened to his father just seemed surreal. He wished Nate would explain it further but he and Osho were still holed away in Osho's office. He wandered back to his room after a dinner alone. Evening had already passed and the facility was bathed in the light of a new moon. It cast an eerie glow along the white walls. Everything was quiet as he approached his room. He paused a moment at the door to Kyrie's room then, looking behind him, he slid into the room. The plastic tent was gone from over her bed and only a single machine remained.

"Kyrie?" He spoke softly. "You awake?"

"Yes." She smiled widely at the sound of his voice. "Sneaking around are we?"

"Ah ... it's late. I just wanted to know how you are doing." He came over to the bed.

"Much better, thanks to you." She breathed deeply.

He smiled, glad the room was dark.

"So ... you're Gabriel Roberts, Uncle Calvin's son ..."

"Uncle?" He blinked. .

"Sort of ..." She giggled. "Your dad was around a lot."

What? He felt a brief shock. He'd spent time enough with her to be 'uncle'? He was never home ...

"He came to see my father a lot when I was growing up. I would sit on the floor playing as they talked about the ore, T.E.R.A. and the IP." She smiled. "He was the one who found out I had a reaction to the green ore."

"Really?" He forgot about his jealous thoughts and listened to her story.

"Yes, he had a small shard in his bag one day when he came over and I found it. He came out and I was playing with it. I remember that he just watched as a scrape on my knee healed over in minutes. Your father felt responsible, you know, for finding the ore and giving it over to T.E.R.A. All the horrible things Dr. Cymru did were because of what he discovered. That defined everything he did. He wanted to change the ore's fate."

Gabriel sighed loudly. "And he died for it. Not sure how that changed anything for the good."

"But it did." She rolled to her side to face him, carefully moving her IV out of the way. "His death had a purpose … just like your life has a purpose."

"Purpose? Hah!" He looked away. "Things are a mess; I don't even know which way is up lately. You know a couple of weeks ago all I had to do was to pick a college … that was the biggest choice in my life. Now … I don't have any purpose …"

"You do have a purpose … and a purpose gives you direction. Maybe you need to look closer and you will know which way to go." She leaned back comfortably on her pillow and closed her eyes with a slight grin on her face.

He stood there in silence, thinking about everything that had happened in the last month. Was there truly a purpose in all of it? His heart was heavy and thoughts of Adin crept in. Had he abandoned his brother to T.E.R.A.? Gabriel felt like a twig caught in a strong river – swept along from one danger to another with no hopes of finding a path.

"Kyrie?" He looked over at her.

"Hmmm." She was drifting to sleep.

"Goodnight." He left the room quietly.

Lying back in his own room, he rested his hand on the cool edge of the ore in his chest. Feeling too exhausted to find any more answers today he drifted off to sleep.

CHAPTER TWENTY-EIGHT

GABRIEL AROSE EARLY THE NEXT MORNING AND DRESSED IN A CLEAN SET OF CARGO PANTS AND A PLAIN BLACK T-SHIRT THAT HE HAD FOUND WAITING FOR HIM ON TOP OF HIS DRESSER. He piled his dark button-down shirt and jeans on a chair in the corner of the small room. Staring at them he realized that this was all he owned. Everything was either covered in dirt and blood or lost to circumstance. Was this his future – wandering from place to place, leaving no traces behind?

"Morning," Nate interrupted his thoughts, stepping into the room, carrying a box. "You sleep okay? You seem to have a lot on your mind."

"I guess … yesterday was a heavy day." He plopped down on his bed.

"I bet." Nate sat down on a chair and set the box on the ground.

"All I have is a bunch of dirty clothes … What does that mean?" He sat down on the bed and pointed at the pile of laundry.

Smirking, Nate motioned to the box he left on the floor.

"When you didn't come out of the bar, I headed to your room and took everything I could. It should all be there."

Gabriel rushed to the box and dumped it on the bed. His clothes, toiletries, and some small electronics tumbled out. *It's all here.* The sight of the items almost brought him to tears. He wasn't completely lost – he still had something. He shook his head. "Thanks, Nate ... I was an idiot ... She played me."

Nate laughed and kicked him lightly. "Relax, she would have had the same effect on any man. The way she looked that night, wow!"

"I wonder how much I was worth?"

Nate hesitated a moment. "Whatever it was, she didn't have time to spent it. She was found the next day by some of our people in her apartment. Authorities ruled it as a suicide which makes no sense if you saw the place."

"What?"

"She looked ... it was like someone had drained all the life out of her. There was definitely a struggle in there and she was in bad shape." Nate shook his head.

"Shiro?"

"Can't say. Somebody took their time with her. Punished her. She had a strange diamond shaped burn on her neck." Nate ran his finger along his throat. "There wasn't much time to look for any clues before the police arrived."

Susan. Gabriel's stomach twisted as he thought about what they might have done to her that night and how she must have suffered. Despite what she had done, he couldn't help but feel pity. The world had become a horrible place over the last several weeks. None of it felt real.

Sitting on the bed he looked up at Nate. "What's going to happen to me?"

"That's up to you. Everyone needs to find their own path." Nate shrugged. "I would like you to stay with the IP and me until we get a better understanding of what's happening."

Gabriel nodded in agreement. "You mentioned the chest yesterday."

"We need to get it. You still have access to Adin's apartment?"

"I think so."

"Good." Nate stood up. "I'm hoping things will be easy. I figure we can enter the apartment through a service entrance. I have already arranged covers for us to get in there … then we can just head straight to his apartment. In and out fast … no problems."

"Wait. I'm going with you?" His heart skipped a beat.

"I don't like it either but yes." Nate shook his head. "T.E.R.A. is looking for you. I expect they will try and trap us in the apartment and call for help once your thumb touches the lock."

"Then why are we going?"

"The chest. It's a key to something we need. If Cymru knew it was there …" Nate chuckled. "Anyhow, the best way to get out of trap is to set one of your own." Nate grinned at him slyly.

"I hope you have a plan?" He trusted Nate.

"I've called in a favour. We'll be fine." Nate winked and pushed him towards the door.

They travelled out of the facility in a plain white van, driving under a canopy of trees. The gravel road led to a gate with a small guard shack. Nate was quickly recognized by the guard and waved through. They passed two more checkpoints, increasing in size and defensive strength.

"Where are we?" Gabriel stared at the landscape of pine trees and thick brush.

"In the mountains, west of Denver."

"So, this is what you do?" he asked after seeing the guards' response to Nate at the security points.

"This is what I do." Nate slowly nodded his head.

"I always thought you were a good rancher." Gabriel opened his window, letting the smell of the woods fill the cab.

"I was. I am. It was my home." Nate's mouth tightened as they continued along the gravel road.

"Well, at least we are together again." He smiled and jabbed Nate's arm.

Nate reached over and squeezed his shoulder. "Absolutely, let's not change that anytime soon."

"You never talked much about the army." The bumpy gravel road ended and they pulled onto a paved road heading towards the freeway.

"Not much to say. You learn to leave your memories behind. Leave them with the dead. Otherwise, you go crazy." Nate half-smiled at him.

"I guess I never thought about it that way." As a kid, he'd loved to hear Nate's stories – the glorious victories – but those were just stories. He left it alone. "What about starting at T.E.R.A.?"

"I was a Ranger in the Army. Only option after you leave is security. Started with some small jobs ... escorts, protection ... little things. It's all I ever knew and never thought to get a real job like your dad. Anyhow, I ended up at T.E.R.A. as a regular and that's when I met your Dad."

"That must have been interesting." He smiled at the thought of their first exchange and how they seemed like such opposites.

Nate laughed. "He was always on the move, couldn't sit still. Half the time he never had permission to be digging around in someone else's backyard, but it didn't stop him. The pay was good so I started to book more and more missions with him. I started to get to know him. What he was all about."

"Sounds like he was a real pain!" He smiled widely at the thought of his Dad ordering Nate around.

"He was. Kept taking us into rough areas, one after another. No island paradises for him. But then we found the ore and things started changing – real fast. One day he said to me 'This is a mistake ... I never should have dug this stuff up.' He was so mad at himself. Everything shifted in his mind. He started misdirecting shipments – setting up hidden caches of ore all over the place. He started lying on reports ... I had half a mind to turn him in ... but

I trusted him. Things caught up to us quickly though. I was put on another team by Cymru and a couple of weeks later, his accident happened. I should have stayed with him." Nate went silent.

"You miss him?" Gabriel stared straight ahead to the road.

"Of course. A couple of days after his death I got a letter from him telling me what he needed me to do. He knew it might happen. I left T.E.R.A. and came to the ranch. He was certain Cymru would direct some kind of punishment at the family. I'd be damned if I was going to let anything happen to your mom or either of you boys. Years went by and nothing happened. Cymru didn't make a move on anything at the ranch but he watched it like a hawk for years. Once I felt you all were safe, I started looking into things. I remembered your dad mentioned his relationship with Dr. Osho ... so I tracked him down and signed up for the IP."

"Why did you do it? Why didn't you just stay with us ... I mean, I know you stayed, but you could have left it alone."

"I could of but I wanted to continue what your dad had started with the IP." Nate kept his eyes focused on the road. "You live a life like I do long enough, you lose that feeling. That fight. Standing up for something bigger than you. I guess I didn't want to lose that."

Gabriel always thought of Nate as family and was pleased that Nate sort of felt the same. They travelled the rest of the way in silence. The lights of Denver clicked on in the distance as the sun set. Gabriel thought of Adin as they moved through the busy city. The streets were full of hurried people finishing their day-to-day lives with no thought of the ore and the horrors it caused. He envied them. Would he ever get the chance to lead a simple life again?

They pulled into T.E.R.A. Towers, entering through the service entrance. A guard approached the driver side window.

"Ignore the guard." Nate grabbed an ID badge from the dash board and handed it to the guard. "How you doing?"

Gabriel looked out the window, trying not to make eye contact with the guard.

"Your ID matches the appointment in the books. How long you planning on being?" The guard handed him back the badge.

"Um … an hour. You never really know working with these optic lines." Nate shrugged at him.

"I'll mark down an hour. If you go over you need to come back and see me for more time. Who's that with you? The book didn't mention another person."

"Doesn't surprise me. He's one of the apprentices." Nate's voice sank to a whisper. "Boss's kid, pretty useless. Didn't have much of a choice."

The guard nodded. "Alright, just be quick. Under an hour. Otherwise, security will come looking for you. You can go ahead once we scan the truck. Second floor service elevator will be unlocked."

"Second floor. No problem." Nate pulled ahead on a platform as the guard walked away.

Nate removed a pistol from the bag beside him. He dismantled it in seconds, handing everything to Gabriel but the clip. "Put them in the glove box."

He followed the instructions, dumping the metal pieces into the small space. "Done."

"Stay put." Nate jumped out the door and hollered at the guard. Gabriel twisted around in his seat to see Nate waving at the guard.

"Hey!" The guard rushed out of the shack, yelling at him. "You need to stay in the truck during the scan!"

"Sorry!" Nate shrugged. "I just wanted to take an hour and half to be safe. Save me from coming back down here."

"Fine, whatever. Get back in the truck." The guard pointed to the vehicle, stomping back to the shack.

"What was that all about?" Gabriel asked as Nate got back in the cab.

"The scan would pick up the bullets in the clip. And the gun for that matter, but now it will just look like parts of something else." Nate kept his eyes on the side mirror.

"What did you do with the clip?" Gabriel fidgeted, twisting to see the guard shack again.

"Stop moving and face forward." Nate poked at him. "The clip's on the ground outside."

Gabriel stared straight ahead. "What?"

"Relax, I'm going to pick it right back up, once the scan is done." Nate popped the door open and stepped out.

Gabriel couldn't help but turn around and watch. *What the hell is he doing?*

"Hey man, you know what? An hour is fine." Nate hollered at the guard.

"Sir! Get back in the veh –" The guard looked down at screen in front of him. "Fine. Just go."

Nate jogged back towards the van, popping down for a split second and jumping back into the cab. "Piece of cake."

They drove up the concrete ramp and looped around the structure, pulling into a large parking area. The space was painted in yellow, with number two's all over the walls. Nate pulled the van into a stall close to the elevators and quickly reassembled his pistol. They exited the vehicle and walked briskly to the service elevators. Gabriel tried to stay calm but his nerves were tense. Nate punched a key code into the panel on the wall, opening the two steel elevator doors. Inside, another panel rolled out near the elevator's holographic buttons. Its small blue screen outlined the imprint of a hand.

"Do I need to –" Gabriel hovered his hand over it.

"No. I don't want them on to us yet." Nate slipped on a black glove covered with small wires and metallic pads.

The palm of the glove touched the screen and emitted a series of clicking sounds. The screen turned green. Nate removed his hand, leaving an imprint of a palm and finger prints on the screen.

The panel flashed the image and replied with an automated voice. "Welcome, Josh Harper." The screen listed the name of a cable optic company and an employee number.

"Neat!" He whispered and pushed the button for the eighth floor.

Nate stepped out into the hallway first. He followed. The hall was completely empty. Gabriel looked up and down the halls, getting his bearings. "This way."

He led Nate through a series of hallways until he found the door to number 871. He pressed his thumb into the lock, and it clicked open. Nate slid past him and drew his pistol from his bag as he moved through the apartment. Gabriel shut the door behind them and stared around the room, the tight knot in his stomach twisting. *Adin.* This was where he'd seen Adin last, right where he stood now. The fight was fresh in his mind.

"Where's the box?" Nate tucked the pistol back into his bag.

"Ah ... back bedroom on the right."

Nate disappeared down the hall.

Gabriel slowly moved through the kitchen. The counters. The sink full of dishes. *This can't be right.* Everything was the same as it had been when he left, right down to the broken chair. Nothing had moved. A bowl sat on the counter with hardened food in it. It was the last thing he had eaten, right before their fight. Spinning around, he looked for something new in the room – some kind of change to prove someone had been here in the last couple of weeks. His heart sank into his chest. Nothing had changed.

"Let's go." Nate headed straight for the door, bag in one hand and the strongbox in the other.

"Wait!" He shook his head. "Nothing has changed ... This is the same bowl of food I left here." He pointed at the dish.

"Forget about it ..." Nate said harshly. "We need to get ready!"

"Let me just check his room, or the bathroom ... just so I know he's been here." He moved towards the hallway.

"Gabriel!" Nate's voice rose. "We know he hasn't come back here. We need to get ready!" Nate pulled on the door. "They've locked down the apartment. They know we are inside." Nate dropped the chest and dug through his black duffle bag. "Time for the trap."

"What ... I ..." Gabriel rushed to the door and pressed his thumb into the lock. "What do we do?"

Nate smiled as he found what he was looking for. "My job. I need you to focus. Try to act normal ... A guard is going to come through this door in 3 minutes."

"What? How do you know that?"

"Like I said, a trap within a trap." Nate pulled out two small black bars about a foot long. He placed one over the door frame, the other he set on the floor just far enough away for the door to swing open easily. "Time to charge them."

A high-pitched sound resonated in Gabriel's ears but quickly disappeared. "What are those?"

"Sonic disruptors." Nate carefully flipped the switch on the unit stuck over the doorframe. "Once they charge – in about a minute – whoever walks through this door is gonna get blasted by a powerful sonic wave. Basically, blowing the ear drums and knocking them out."

"What about us?" He stared at Nate unsure whether or not to cover his ears.

"As long as we are on this side of the device, we're fine. Just be ready." Nate moved behind the kitchen counter and knelt down. Gabriel dropped down beside Nate but Nate shook his head. "I'm hiding. You need to look normal so they come inside."

Gabriel's head felt like it was full of soup. "Right." He tried to stay focused but wanted to know more about Adin.

"How long have you known?" He stared at the door, waiting for it to swing open.

"Ten days." Nate's voice was quiet behind the counter.

"Why didn't you tell me?" He could feel the sting of tears on his eyes.

"Because I don't know whose side he's on. I couldn't risk you trying to contact him. I'm sorry. It just had to be that way."

He breathed deep, his chest quivering as he fought to keep control of his emotions. "Will you find him?"

"We haven't stopped looking." Nate shifted as the door lock clicked from the outside. "Get ready," he whispered.

The door swung open. Two guards rushed in almost beside each other, barely fitting through the doorway. A pop echoed in the room and Gabriel's ears started to ring. The two men dropped to the ground instantly. Nate popped out from behind the counter, rushed over and disarmed them both. Gabriel joined him, unsure of what to do now.

Nate slipped a silver disk from the back of a guard's head, sliding it behind his own ear. "Apartment breached, searching the premises."He gestured for Gabriel to help him collect all the electronics on the guards. Silently, he frisked the men, looking for anything he recognized, handing things to Nate who dropped them into a reflective black bag he pulled from his vest.

"Moving to back bedrooms." Nate continued to impersonate the guard.

"What now?" Gabriel mouthed the words.

Nate pointed him to the door. "Target is barricaded in. Give us a couple of minutes to collect him. He's alone."

He poked his head into the hallway – it was empty – calling back over his shoulder, still trying to be quiet. "No one."

Nate slipped off the silver disk and dropped it into the strange black reflective bag. "Alright. We got payment. Grab the chest and let's move."

Gabriel didn't understand what Nate was talking about but knew the hall was full of cameras. "They're going to see us." He hoisted the strongbox in his arms.

Nate looked down at his watch. "Not in 26 seconds. The whole floor is about to be hit by a jammer. It should disrupt the feeds so we can slip pass. Won't last long though, maybe 2 minutes. We need to get to another floor through the stairs. Elevators will be locked down on this floor."

Gabriel waited as Nate counted down the last five seconds and signalled for them to leave. They sprinted down the hall, keeping close to together. Another two hallways, a right then a left and they were there.

"Shit!" Nate shook the door handle. "The jammer may have locked us in." He dug around in his black duffle bag.

"What now?" Gabriel put the chest down on its side.

"Give me a second." Nate pulled out a strange looking roll of tape. He stripped three pieces of tape carefully off of it. He covered each of the large hinges on the door, and placed a final piece beside the handle. He tossed the roll back into his bag and pulled out a strange flashlight. It glowed blue across the surface of each piece of tape – and each one began to bubble.

"Grab the chest!" Nate pointed at it and stood back from the door.

"What's that smell?" Gabriel's noise twitched. The air had become thick with a horrid odour.

"Our way out." Nate pointed at the hinges.

The tape – clearly it had released some sort of acid – was eating its way through the wooden finish of the door and in no time had started to work on the steel hinges and lock. After waiting another couple of seconds, Nate began forcefully kicking the door – hammering it again and again until it buckled. A final blow and it came crashing down into the stairwell.

Nate walked over the broken door. "Stay close to me!"

He vaulted down the stairs, taking several at time. Gabriel struggled to keep up, the chest swinging awkwardly back and forth in his arms as he aimed for each step – trying not to trip. He made it down two floors and caught up to Nate who was peeking into the hallway behind the steel door.

"Looks like one guard on this floor." Nate glanced at his watch. "He'll pass back this way in about 30 seconds."

"Then what?" Gabriel sat on the steps, to catch his breath, the chest resting on his knees.

Nate didn't say anything and disappeared behind the steel grey door.

"Shit." Gabriel hopped up and caught the door with his foot, pushing against the door and chased after him.

Nate sprinted down the short hall and met the unaware guard in the middle of the hallway. Without missing a step, Nate slipped around behind the guard – covering his mouth. He accurately drove his right heel down on the man's knee, resulting in a sickening crunch. The guard dropped to the floor in pain, toppling over on the broken knee. Nate caught the man's neck in a choker hold and held him until he passed out, then dropped the man to the floor and continued towards the elevator. "Keep up!"

Gabriel reached the elevator and set the chest down. Despite its light weight, he needed the break. Nate grabbed his hand, pressing it awkwardly against the light blue screen on the elevator panel. The screen flashed red. Locked.

"Damn, they acted quicker than I thought." Nate slammed the wall of the elevator. "We're locked in."

"What do we do now?"

"Let me think." Nate tapped the close door button on the elevator.

Gabriel's patience was disappearing. Voices filled the hallway. Nate put his finger over his mouth, signalling him to keep quiet. Both of Gabriel's hands were clenched, his nails digging into his own skin as they waited, trying to be invisible to whoever was outside the elevator doors.

The elevator suddenly began to descend.

"Thank God." Gabriel looked up at the numbers counting down. He grinned at Nate who pulled a pistol out of his bag and pulled back the slide.

"Someone else is moving the elevator." Nate readied himself, pointing his gun at the doors.

"Oh shit." Gabriel wasn't sure where to hide.

The doors opened with a ding to a concrete underground, Nate held his gun to the face of the guard standing in the doorway.

CHAPTER TWENTY-NINE

GABRIEL FROZE, HIS EYES BOUNCING BETWEEN NATE AND THE GUARD.

"Glad to see you recognize me." The guard stared at Nate. "You don't have much time. Your vehicle is marked, abandon it and get outside the perimeter."

Nate lowered his gun. "You're lucky I remembered that day at the restaurant."

"Well, I'm not bleeding, so I guess it made it a little tougher for you." The guard stepped into the elevator. "Get out."

"What is Riley after?" Nate pushed Gabriel out of the elevator.

"Ask him yourself. There's a spray in a bag by the back tire of the blue sedan outside. Use it. This is the only floor with street access. Everywhere else is locked down. Good luck."

The doors shut and Gabriel sighed. "Who was that?"

"One of Riley's men." Nate ran over to the sedan, searching the tires.

"Riley?" Gabriel chased after him, totally confused.

"Bishop Riley. For once I am happy that the Church is

watching." Nate scooped up the bag and pulled out the spray can. "Close your eyes."

Gabriel held his breath as the spray covered him. He tried not to breathe but was running out of air. As Nate finished, Gabriel took two steps away from him, coughing at the horrid smell as he sucked in some air.

"Yeah. awful stuff." Nate started to spray down his legs and arms.

"What is it?"

Nate handed Gabriel the spray to finish him off. "It's a thermal blocker. They use infra-red to keep track of people down here." Nate closed his eyes as Gabriel sprayed his face.

"Can we wait them out?" Gabriel finished covering Nate's back with the spray.

"Too risky. The street is our best chance to lose them." Nate pointed at a ramp, leading upwards to the next level. "If we can get to street level without being see we stand a chance."

Hunched down low, Gabriel followed as Nate darted between the vehicles along the concrete walls. They stuck to the darkness, avoiding any open, lighted areas, weaving between the cars – even slipping past two guards who were circling through the parkade and checking everyone for ID badges.

Nate pointed. "There it is."

Gabriel glanced over the hood of the car they were hiding behind. The gate was cluttered with guards.

"Too many." He shook his head as the guards checked every vehicle that passed through the gate – scanning each of them before letting them in or out.

"Doesn't look like we can hitch a ride out. They're pretty backed up with that line of traffic. Still, we could use a distraction."

Gabriel stared at the entrance, hope fading. There was no way they could sneak past the dozen guards.

"Stay put." Nate shifted around behind the vehicle and disappeared from Gabriel's view.

He kept watching the gate, waiting for Nate to come back with a plan, "Turn around slowly!" Someone shouted from behind him. "East residential exit. On your knees – hands in front." He twisted around to see a gun pointing at him.

His heart thumped in his chest as he dropped to his knees. The guard reached forward and draped a loose chain across his wrists. It came to life on its own and tightened around them. The guard suddenly jerked backwards, struggling. His weapon fell to the ground with a clang as Nate chopped his arm. Gabriel stood frozen. The guard glared at him, his eyes popping as an arm tightened around his neck, then rolling upward as he sagged in Nate's arm.

"Let's get you out of –" Nate was tackled from behind – a massive body pinned him to the rough concrete. It was Anthony, the hulking guard who had coded Gabriel into the building.

Gabriel struggled against the chain binding his wrists. Nate got in a quick elbow to the side of Anthony's head. "Go! take the box and go!"

He didn't want to listen to Nate but more guards would arrive soon. Nate could take care of himself – he needed to get the strongbox to Osho. A blast of heat pulsed from his chest, as he snapped off his bindings. He grabbed the steel box and ran towards the concrete outer wall – between the ceiling and the wall there was a small space. Not enough for him but it could fit the chest. He managed to get it far enough into the hole that it dropped outside the wall. He twisted to see Nate still fighting the giant.

Nate's right fist drove into Anthony's jaw, knocking the massive man to the ground. Anthony roared as he got back up and charged him. The beast picked Nate up off the ground – continuing his charge into the hood of a parked car. The fibro-steel cracked as Nate's back slammed against it. Anthony held him there with one arm and hammered him with a closed fist – the barrage of strikes missing Nate as he scrambled to stay out of the way. A single blow finally connected, then another. Nate slumped against the hood, losing the fight. Anthony wrapped his huge hands tight around Nate's throat. Gabriel sprinted towards the giant.

A blast of blood erupted out of Anthony's massive back, ending the brawl. Nate crawled out from under the lifeless body and staggered to his feet, his face bloody. Leaning against the car, he coughed and spit blood. Gabriel barely caught Nate as he dropped to the ground. A spray of bullets pierced the car, exploding glass all over them. Two gunman rushed them, outfitted with automatic weapons and tactical armour. Nate returned fire. His shots slammed straight through the chest of one of the gunmen, exploding blood into the air. The other dove for cover behind a concrete column. Gabriel dragged Nate behind him as he barrelled towards a steel door set in the concrete wall.

The ground blurred beneath him as he sprinted. He dashed at the greyish steel rectangle – the only way he could see out. Before he knew it, he was only a dozen feet away. Letting go of Nate, he braced for the impact, twisting his shoulder to hit the steel first. An explosion set his ears ringing as the steel frame ripped free from the thick rock wall. It crashed to ground outside, its warped shape bucking him free as it rocked back and forth, the steel door bent from the impact. Pain drummed through him as he twisted on the ground, trying to get his feet back underneath him.

"What the hell was that!" Nate's eyes were wide, as he lifted Gabriel off the pavement.

"We needed out!" Gabriel stood on his own, despite the pain. "That wasn't much a door."

"Where's the strongbox!"

"Just up the path!" Gabriel pointed at the steel box resting on its side against the wall fifty feet away from them. Nate ran towards it but dropped as a bullet hit him. .

"Nate!" Gabriel screamed.

It was too late. They were quickly surrounded by armed guards.

CHAPTER THIRTY

SIX GUARDS SURROUNDED GABRIEL AS HE SAT OUTSIDE THE BROKEN CONCRETE WALL OF THE PARKING AREA. His heart pounded in his chest, each beat drumming pain through his ribs. They dragged Nate over by his vest, and dropped him on the ground. Nate clutched his shoulder and winced as he hit the rough payment.

"You alright?" Gabriel helped him sit.

"It passed through. I think it missed the bone." Nate gritted his teeth.

"Shut up!" One of the guards stepped forward and jerked his chin at the other guards. "Secure them!"

One of the guards walked towards them, pulling two of the magnetic chains from his belt. His helmet jerked and the material burst out the opposite side. His eyes froze as blood dripped down his face. A second later he collapsed – dead. The other guards stared at the body, stunned. Seconds later, more shots pierced the heads of the unprepared guards – killing them instantly. The two remaining guards fled to the cover of concrete parking area. Only one of them made it, screaming "Sniper! Sniper!" to his wrist.

A black van barrelled down the alleyway, barely stopping long enough for someone to scoop up the steel strongbox. It continued towards them, skidding to stop as the door popped open and a man jumped out with a mask over his face. "Get in!"

Gabriel helped him lift Nate into the open van door and dove in after him. The tires screeched as they pulled away, bouncing over the broken pieces of concrete and door scattered across the road.

The masked man pulled his hood off and pointed at Nate. "Get him fixed up!" He left Gabriel to try and figure out what to do as he climbed up into the front seat with the driver. "Get to a safe house fast!"

Gabriel stared at Nate. "What do you need?"

"Pills and … side pouch … black vial and the small plastic box …" Nate pointed at his bag, his hand shaking.

Gabriel fumbled around with the bag's side pouch, finally dumping all of its contents onto the floor of the van. He grabbed the bottle of pills as the van cornered hard and the rest of the items slid. Nate popped the top of the bottle with one hand and drank from the pill bottle. He coughed and in a few moments, the shaking stopped and his words became more coherent.

"Riley, I need some light!" Nate hollered and the cargo lamp flipped on. "Good … the black vial now … hand it to me."

Gabriel handed it over, trying to keep all the items in a pile and stop them from sliding away. Nate removed one end, exposing a long thick needle. He jammed it into his wounded shoulder and cried out in pain, his foot thumping against the ground, his eyes closed tight, as he fought it. Gabriel felt helpless.

"Help me out of my jacket."

Gabriel carefully peeled the sticky fabric off of Nate's shoulders.

"In the plastic box … there's a tube of paste. It needs to go on the wound. Whatever you do, don't touch it." Nate instructed him.

"What is this stuff?" Gabriel opened the tube. His nose twitched as the strong smell filled the air. Squeezing it out onto the dark hole in Nate's shoulder, he pulled his head back as it began to smoke. The air smelling like burnt meat.

"Ugh! What's happening" He watched as it bubbled and oozed in the wound.

"It's a chemical that reacts with our blood by pulling the plasma to the surface to seal the wound. It stinks to high heaven but it will seal the wound temporarily and stop the bleeding." Nate waved the stench away with his hand.

"And the pills?" He pulled Nate forward to reach the back of the shoulder with more of the smelly paste.

"Adrenaline spikers. Stops me from passing out on you."

"You're going to be ok, then?" He focused on emptying out the tube onto the wound.

"It will hold me together until I can get some proper treatment." Nate leaned his head back against the wall, closing his eyes. "My own little first aid kit ... never leave home without it." The man from the front seat climbed back to join them. "Looks like you do good work, Gabriel. The name's Riley." He patted Gabriel on the back then turned to Nate. "You look like shit."

"Aren't you a bishop?" Nate grinned at him.

"Ah, just a title. You know that – still they saved me from myself so I owe God something. So, I'm in the service but still a sinner to the core. Now, saving isn't cheap – what do you have for me?" He tilted his head and grinned at Nate.

"You haven't changed." Nate laughed and pointed at his duffel bag.

"Let's see." Riley crawled around Gabriel to the duffel bag, pulling out the reflective black bag. "They still good?"

"Put them in right after we disabled the two guards. Should be perfect." Nate hoisted himself up with his good arm.

"What are you talking about?" Gabriel was completely confused by the two men.

"The guards' little toys here – radios, ear pieces, trackers – if you want to steal them, you gotta be ready. Some smart asshole designed a system to disable them remotely. Stops people like me from impersonating your guards."

"The bag blocks it." Gabriel tapped the shiny surface.

"Exactly." Riley smiled. "You see – information beats a bunch of soldiers any day."

"And you don't get shot." Nate added, his eyes shut as he leaned against the van wall.

"These will help us keep an eye on T.E.R.A." Riley grinned. "Sit tight." He returned to the seat up front.

"You two friends?" Gabriel put all of the items back into Nate's bag.

"Friends? No idea but he's there when I need him. My team rescued him after he was captured. We found him half insane and nearly beaten to death. That was around 15 years ago. The Church managed to put him back together so he's been with them ever since." Nate tried to move his shoulder, grunting at the pain.

"How did he know about today?" Gabriel set the bag down on the chest, keeping his balance as the van shifted left. "We wouldn't have made it if they hadn't shown up."

"Agreed. I wonder what they were up to in there?" Nate whispered. "The guard at the elevator is a collector for Riley – I've bumped into him before. We'll see what Riley knows." The van stopped abruptly. "This must be our stop."

Riley offered to stay with them until one of the Church's doctors could patch Nate up and then they were on our own. The safe house was more of a room than any kind of house. Gabriel stared at the empty space and sighed. There was no furniture – it was simply a twelve by twelve room with no windows. A single bulb illuminated the room and a small fridge hummed in the corner. Despite the lack of basics, he was simply happy to have somewhere safe for the moment.

"There's a jug or two of clean water. That's about it. I need to check in with my teams. You'll be safe here, just try to relax. I'll be back." Riley shut the door behind him. Nate put his shoulders against the wall and slid down to the floor.

Gabriel hoped it was true. He turned his attention over to the chest, dragging it across the floor towards Nate. Rubbing his hand across the top, he asked, "So what is so important about this thing?"

"Reports by your father, locations of ore caches, things we will need soon." Nate explained. "And something you might find familiar."

Familiar? What could that be?

Nate reached into his shirt, pulling out his dog tags and a small key that dangled with them. He snapped the key free from the steel string and held it out to him. "Take a look. We are going to be here awhile, until things calm down."

Gabriel slid the small key into the lock on the front of the chest. A mechanical buzz filled the room and a slight hiss came from the box, as an internal pressure seal was released. He opened the lid to reveal a set of files, some journals, and some strange looking discs. Puzzled, he looked to Nate. Nothing was familiar.

"Look deeper ... it isn't going to jump out at you."

Removing the files and journals, he stacked them on the dirty floor of the room. *It can't be.* A small white crystal glowed weakly inside a plastic case. Without hesitation he picked it up and pulled it free. The small crystal came to life at his touch.

"Why did he have this?" He rotated the crystal in his hand.

"Not sure." Nate gave a one-sided shrug. "There were only a few of them ... maybe he knew how special they were. Anyhow, I figure the crystal's yours now, seeing as you're probably the only one who can use it." He leaned his head against the wall and closed his eyes.

Gabriel traced his fingers along the smooth grooves and sharp angles of the crystal. Something about those angles and grooves seemed familiar. As he rolled it around in his hands, a pulling sensation came over him.

"Strange ..." The small crystal vibrated with each beat of his heart.

"What's that?"

"It isn't reacting much." He was disappointed. "But there's something about it ..."

"And ?"

"It has a pull to it." He was confused by the sensation coming from the ore. He held it closer to his body and the crystal shifted in his hand. "Look!" He was stunned by the movement.

Nate shook his head and closed his eyes again.

It's like magnetic. I can feel it wanting to move. Determined to understand what just happened, he held the crystal nearer to his chest. It teetered on its edge, as if something invisible was pulling it towards him. He continued drifting the new crystal towards himself. Inches away from him, it vibrated in the palm of his hand.

"Do you see this?" He held it out to Nate.

"Gabriel, my eyes are closed. I don't care to see anything right now."

He set the crystal down on his lap and lifted his shirt, tucking it under his chin. Rubbing his fingers across the smooth surface of his crystal he noticed a small cove along the outside edge. He glanced at the crystal in his lap. *Is this a part of the one in my chest?*

"I think they fit together." He picked up the loose crystal, checking the shape once again.

"Gabriel, you're imagining it." He didn't open his eye. "If we went outside we could find two rocks from totally different places that would seem to fit together ... it doesn't mean anything."

Annoyed by Nate's comment, he kept tracing the piece in his hand.

"But they were all found together right?"

"I think so. It was a long time ago."

Gabriel watched as the two pieces began pulsing in unison – without touching. *The two must match.* As he narrowed the distance between the two, he could feel the pull from the small crystal. Their pulsing lights grew brighter and they surged in unison.

He pushed the new crystal into the small cove on the shard in his chest, adjusting it slightly until it felt just perfect. Immediately, the two shards glowed even brighter. The light filled the small room. He let go of the crystal and covered his eyes. The new crystal seemed stuck to its larger counterpart. A pool of light burst from his chest, swirling tightly around the two pieces. He felt electrified. His skin sizzled. The crystal sent waves and waves of energy crashing over his muscles, vibrating through his bones. He tried to cry out to Nate, but nothing left his mouth. The energy continued to swirl around his chest, burning his skin. A volcano erupted in his chest as the light grew brighter – like a mini sun burning a hole in his chest as it seared his skin away.

"Gabriel!" Nate's cry reached him through the intense light.

Gabriel clenched his teeth at the pain, so hard, that they felt as if they could shatter at any moment. His rib cage split apart and his skin tore open. Paralyzed, he lay on the hard floor unable to respond.

"Gabriel!" Nate sounded frantic. Gabriel felt his grab, trying to pull him free of the light.

CHAPTER THIRTY-ONE

NATE WAS ALMOST BLINDED BY THE GLOWING WHITE LIGHT CONSUMING GABRIEL. He wasn't sure what had happened but he wasn't going to just sit there. He groped along the smooth floor as he crawled towards the source of the light. He forced his eyes open, and could just make out the outline of Gabriel's limp arm on the floor.

"Gabriel!" He grabbed it, and yelled. Gabriel's arm felt like hot steel.

There was nothing he could do. He could only close his eyes and wait for it to stop. Something grabbed his leg and dragged him away from the burning light. He could see the door outside was wide open.

"Come on! Get outside!" Riley pulled Nate up on his feet.

He stumbled down the steel steps away from the room. Riley slammed the door shut behind them and dragged Nate away from the entrance.

"Stop!" He pushed back against Riley, halting their retreat.

Riley's eyes were wide and his face was nearly white. "No, we need to leave. He's an ore user! He could blow this whole place up!"

"I can't leave him! He's my responsibility! I need to get back in there." He stumbled towards the door but Riley grabbed him by the shirt and twisted him around.

"He needs to burn out first – he could kill you if you stay there with him!"

"What are you talking about?"

"I've seen them lose control before. You can't help him." Riley let him go, ran his hand through his hair and sighed. "Shit. This is a problem, Nate!"

"What are you talking about? How do you know so much about this?" Nate pushed past Riley and sat on the metal steps. "You said he would burn out. So, this will pass?"

"Of course, I've seen it before." Riley rubbed his hands together. "I hunt them."

Nate glared at him. "You touch him and I kill you. I swear to God."

Riley shook his head. "I'm not calling in a team, he'll be safe. That's not the problem." Riley walked over and knelt down in front of him. "The Church is looking for him."

"What?"

"We were in T.E.R.A. towers to intercept an ore user they had laid a trap for. I didn't know it was him we were looking for. T.E.R.A. is putting a lot of resources into finding him – we weren't going to allow that to happen." Riley cleared his throat. "We were sent in to get to him first."

"Why would the Church want Gabriel." Nate couldn't believe what he was hearing.

"To kill him, to exile him. I don't know. Maybe just to stop T.E.R.A. from getting their hands on him." Riley took a deep breath. "He's an ore user. They're dangerous, Nate."

Nate shook his head. "Gabriel is not a danger to anyone."

"Maybe not yet but they get stronger the more they learn to control the ore. Listen to me – no one should have that kind of power. I've seen a fire user ignite the air in your lungs. A water user sucked all the moisture out of a soldier's eyes! It's not human – they can't be allowed to have that kind of power."

"Still conducting witch hunts for those that are different from what you define as normal." Nate shook his head. "Same old Church."

"I don't make the rules, I just try to follow them."

"So where's that leave us?" Nate stood up and pointed over his shoulder. "He's like my own son, I'm not going to let you take him." Riley stayed silent, his foot tapping against the concrete. "Well?"

"You brought me back from hell once – that kind of debt you can't ever repay. I'll take you to Sarge. He can patch you up." Riley stood up. "I'll find out what they want with him. It's the best I can do, but you need to keep him hidden."

"I appreciate it. I'll get him back to the IP." Nate held out his hand to Riley.

Riley shook his hand. "Be careful, Nate. As long as you stay with him, you'll be hunted and not just by us."

CHAPTER THIRTY-TWO

GABRIEL SAT UP IN A BED AND LOOKED AROUND. The room wasn't familiar to him. *How did I get here?* The last thing he remembered was an immense pain – as if his chest was splitting open. He slid his hand under his shirt. Pulses of heat radiated across his palm as he touched the ore. It had worked! The two pieces of ore had forged into a single larger piece. Jumping up from the bed, he felt especially alert. His eyes picked up the details of everything in the room. His ears twitched at the muffled voices coming from behind the door. All of his senses were keener than normal.

He surveyed the room, starting with the small army cot he was lying on. It was old and smelled – there was some mould growing in the fibres. It had patches of army emblems sown over the torn cloth. They listed different platoons and companies from across the last fifty years. Nate wasn't that old.

On the wall next to him was a tall dresser that looked like it had been discarded on the street in some rundown neighbourhood. Half the varnish had been eaten away by time and the whole thing stood at a slight slant. The top of it was covered in dust and he guessed the drawers would be much the same – empty and forgotten. The room was more of a closet, no bigger than ten by ten. It was dimly lit by a glass light bulb. He was surprised it even worked. Turning to the only door in the room, he grabbed the handle and pushed it open.

Nate was bare-chested and hunched over the back of a small wooden chair. A large bald man wearing blue surgical gloves pulled thin black thread as he sutured the back of Nate's shoulder. His hands were steady as they worked the hooked needle and thread through the skin.

"Hurry up, Marlin. Just another scar to add to the collection." Nate laughed, failing to notice Gabriel's entrance to the room.

"Quit your belly aching … I'm almost done here." The bald man took notice of Gabriel through his narrowed eyes. "You feeling alright, soldier?"

"Yeah, I'm good." Gabriel nodded quickly, hoping to avoid an examination.

"Told you that bed would be fine!" Marlin slapped Nate's wound, causing Nate to grunt as he gritted his teeth.

"Glad to see you're up." Nate twisted to face Gabriel.

"I told you he was fine, nothing wrong with him." The old man finished his last stitch and slapped a large piece of strange coloured tape over the wound, making Nate grunt in pain once again.

"And I promise this is the last time."

"Sure, sure … keep those patches on for a few days and you should be all healed up." Marlin took off his gloves and tossed them on the table with the rest of the medical supplies.

"Sarge, this is Gabri –" Nate words were cut off by the grumpy surgeon's roar.

"I don't want to know his name! Or what you two are up to! I am old and retired. I lead a quiet life now and don't need none of your crazy crusades messing that up. Now get out of my house!" The man glared at Nate through squinted eyes.

Nate rolled his eyes, shaking his head. "You grumpy old bastard! Never going to change are you?"

Gabriel couldn't help but grin at the remark as Nate began gathering their things.

"Well, if you're done being a pain in my ass, Reinhart. I'll get back to my day." The old sergeant huffed and left towards the front of the small house.

Nate looked Gabriel up and down as he finished stuffing some things into his black bag, "What happened with you, anyways? You glowed like a match head and burned me when I tried to touch you."

"They merged." He tapped his chest.

Nate stared at him with an odd expression. "What are you talking about?"

"The crystals combined!" Gabriel smiled. "I knew it."

"Combined!" Nate was shocked. "What does that mean?"

"No idea!" He laughed.

Nate stared at him for a moment. "Ah, forget it. I'll wait for Osho to explain it. Grab the strongbox and let's go before that old dinosaur comes back in here and yells at me again." Nate leaned out, looking down the hallway where the Sergeant had disappeared..

Gabriel picked up the steel box. "Please tell me we can get rid of this thing soon. I am really tired of carrying it."

"One more stop. Got a new vehicle out back. Courtesy of Bishop Riley. He thought we would be safe here." Nate nodded at him. "You seem to be a hot commodity. Even the Church is looking for you."

"What? Why?" It didn't make any sense to him. He had nothing to do with the Church.

"Riley's trying to find out. We can trust him. In the mean time we'll have to be a lot more careful from now on." Nate pulled a new T-shirt over his head. "Sarge!"

"What!" A nasty holler came from the front of the house.

"Love you!" Nate shouted as loud as he could.

"Shut up! And get off my property!" the old man roared back.

Gabriel followed Nate through the side door of the old house, laughing with him. A blue SUV waited for them in the alley. It was obvious that Nate had taken care of all the details and there wasn't much for Gabriel to do but carry that chest until he was finally told to stop. As the two walked down a flight of rickety stairs at the back of the old house he asked, "What's the deal with him?"

"Mr. Charming? He was the first sergeant major I served under in the Special Forces. Always there to help out when I'm in a tight spot. Not much for talking though but a damn good field surgeon. And, despite his grumpiness, he's a good guy. Outside of you – he's the closest family I've got." Nate stopped walking and turned. "Speaking of 'what's the deal' … What were you thinking? Here I am shot and you go do something crazy with the ore! You're more like your dad then you know. Next time give me some warning." Nate opened the hatch of the SUV, and threw his bag on the back seat.

"Yeah, sorry about that." Gabriel slid the strongbox into the back then climbed into the front of the vehicle. "What about the Church? Does Riley know?"

"He pulled me out of the room, afraid you were going to go off like a bomb." Nate opened the driver door. "I don't know all the details but it sounds like they've run into some users just as strong as you."

Gabriel stayed quiet. Just as strong as him? Or stronger? Was the ore imbedded in them as well?

"Anyhow, Riley will keep the Church at bay for now, but it's best if we don't draw any new attention to ourselves." Nate checked the mirrors around the vehicle.

"So, back to the IP?" He was eager to talk to Dr. Osho about the ore combining.

"Actually, that's something I need to talk to you about." Nate paused before starting the engine. "I need to go back to the ranch – our ranch."

"What! Why?"

"There're some things I need from there … look I know it isn't the most comfortable idea going back there for you but," Nate turned the key, "I think you should see what's there."

Gabriel's gut twisted as he thought about the wreckage of the house and the body of his mother trapped under the fallen wall. Her lifeless hand covered in blood. Nate grabbed his shoulder. "Whether you want to go or not, one day you will need to deal with it. We will all need to deal with it. It's our home."

The words "home" bounced around inside his head as they drove. Neither he nor Adin had discussed what was going to happen to it. The large steel container held the remnants of his former life. It would remain there until he chose to move it. No one else could.

Swallowing hard he nodded his head and looked at Nate. "You're not really giving me a choice … are you?"

Nate put the car into gear. "It's something you should probably just see."

They left Denver's smoggy skyline in the distance as they headed up an on ramp to the main highway to the west. Neither of them spoke much during the drive. The trip was a somber reminder of where he had come from and where his life was now. He had been thrust into a whirlwind of life and death, trying to discover his father's secrets and a world hidden behind a veil of lies.

Driving the highway for the first time with Adin had felt like entering a different world, leaving behind the one he loved and knew so well. Death and fear had ruled so many of his days over last several weeks and months. It was a harsh reality that he wanted to run away from, but he knew he couldn't. Too many secrets. Too many lies. He needed to know the truth. It held him on this path. A path his father had chosen to walk and now a path he would follow. As they neared the ranch, the familiar sights of broken homes and destroyed lives rolled past his window. His mounting anticipation became physically uncomfortable as he shifted in his seat. The long driveway of the ranch was just ahead of them. He breathed out loudly, pushing his emotions aside and trying to focus on the present. Nate surprised him by continuing past it, failing to slow down at all.

"You missed the turn." The small dirt road zipped by the driver's side window.

Nate smiled. "No, I didn't. We will come in on the backside. Just in case there are any surprises waiting for us." He remembered the old back road. The plan made sense. He still wasn't used to the idea that people could be following him.

They turned onto the beaten up country lane, full of pot holes and washed out tire tracks. Rounding the hillside on the back of the farm, Nate brought the SUV to a stop, just out of view of where the house once stood. He jumped out. "Wait here. I'm just going to take a quick peek." He ran up the side of the hill, carrying a pair of electronic optics.

During the moments alone, Gabriel's mind ran through different scenarios of what would happen to them if T.E.R.A. was there. He imagined patches of grass coming to life with guns, helicopters roaring up over the hills towards them and him going back into a cage. He focused on calming himself. *Breathe. Who would realistically be there anyhow?* He tried to think positively. Perhaps Adin had come back or left a note for him.

Nate came jogging down the hill, jumped into the car and started it up again. "Place looks empty. Let's go."

They continued down the road at a slow pace. Gabriel kept his eyes open to their surroundings, mindful of any movement. It hurt to see what used to be his home and was now just rubble left by a storm. The fields were still torn up but small green shoots of wild grass had begun to fill in across the black soil. Most of the fencing lay half knocked over, the posts broken off at the ground. The old farm equipment was flipped over, littering the area with rusted steel. Parts of the house and barn were scattered all over the yard, broken and looking as if no one had been there in years.

They coasted towards the barn and came to a stop at the edge of the wreckage, leaving just enough room for the doors of the vehicle to open. Nate stepped out first, surveying the scene before waving to

Gabriel to join him. This was Nate's home as much as it was his and the pain was visible on Nate's face.

Gabriel stepped out the other side of the SUV, tears stinging his eyes. Each piece of the wreckage was a memory and something special. Gabriel did a complete three sixty. Everything was gone. The storm had spared nothing.

"Gabriel! Over here!" Nate called out to him.

The barn was a mess. He climbed over the broken walls, half destroyed by the storm then eaten by the harsh chemicals of the rescue team. Nate had moved some of the wreckage off one of the old wooden support beams.

"We need to lift this off." Nate kicked at it.

Gabriel shrugged and strolled over to the beam, placing his hands under the rough cut surface.

Nate laughed. "It will be a nice try, but we're going to need a lot more to move that thing than your tiny arms."

The sleeping giant under Gabriel's shirt came to life at his command, sending strings of white strength down his arms and legs with a rush of heat. His muscles twitched at the energy, eager to be used. He strained against the huge beam as it lurched upwards, creaking loudly as it broke free at one end. Pieces of debris slid off of it as he raised it. He focused. The crystal flooded a new strength through his body.

He thrust the beam away from him with a roar, sending it crashing to the ground like a great tree falling from a logger's axe. As the dust cleared and the ground settled, Nate stared at him, dumfounded.

"Tiny arms, huh?" He laughed aloud.

"How?" Nate shook his head, joining his laugh.

He tapped on his chest as the rush of energy raced back into the crystal, leaving him feeling refreshed and slightly buzzed.

Nate moved over, prepared to catch him if he fell. "You okay?"

"Yeah ... I don't feel dizzy at all!" He grinned.

"Good. I don't want to have to carry you again." Nate chuckled.

He finished moving some of the remaining rubble off the old wood floor.

"I don't feel sick at all." He hadn't felt the slightest drain from using the crystal. "Nothing. Absolutely nothing!"

Nate looked up from his work. "Good, help clear the rest of this off."

"Clear the floor?" He didn't understand. "Why?"

"Because I need to get into your Dad's lab." Nate finished the job himself.

"Dad's what?"

Nate stopped, hanging his head. "Gabriel, there are lots of things you didn't know about. That is why I wanted you to see it. Lots of things were hidden from you and your brother. It was for your own safety."

"Did Mom know?" He crossed his arms, annoyed.

"Probably. She was sleeping with the man," Nate said bluntly and slid a small steel rod into the floor. A panel slid open and he punched in a code. "I hope this still works."

CHAPTER THIRTY-THREE

WHY DID DAD HIDE SO MUCH? The floor below Gabriel's feet rumbled as something came to life under the old wooden boards. A section dropped down several inches then slid to the side to reveal a steel hatch. It released, opening upward to reveal a dimly lit stairwell leading below the barn floor.

"Good." Nate barrelled down the stairs. The room illuminated with a soft glow as he hit the final step.

Gabriel crept down after him, looking curiously at the floor and even the stairs, shocked that they even existed. The room was spacious, despite feeling like a dungeon, with tables along each of the walls and a single large desk in the centre with a small computer terminal on it. Each of the tables was covered in scraps of paper with Calvin's scribbles and thoughts all over them. Nothing was organized. Gabriel felt as if he had stepped into a stranger's mind, rather than his father's lab. His father was always organized, loved systems and structure. This was chaos. *This can't be Dad's.* He looked around. Random thoughts were everywhere in notes taped to the walls and the ceiling with no connection to each other. There was no technology in the room, outside of the old computer. Confusion filled his mind as he wandered around trying to understand what had taken place in this room. This wasn't a laboratory – this was just a collection of thoughts.

Nate rummaged through pieces of paper and old journals, collecting a small pile of things he needed. It was obvious by the speed of Nate's movements that he had been in this room before. Gabriel passed the centre desk and mindlessly ran his finger along the computer screen as he looked around the room. A small beep came from the machine, as the screen activated. Underneath some of the papers surrounding the terminal, was a glowing blue screen much like the ones in the elevators at T.E.R.A. Towers. Sliding the papers aside, he placed his hand onto the rough blue screen. The rough surface became sharp as thousands of small hair-like needles stuck in his hand. The sensation caught him by surprise and he jerked his hand back.

"Ow. What the hell?" The terminal activated.

Nate stared back at him confused by the new noise in the room. "What did you do?"

"I put my hand on the scanner and it … poked me or something." He scratched the palm of his hand, trying stop the lingering sensation.

"Poked you?" Nate mocked him.

"Yes, it poked me."

"My guess is it's encrypted. Only your dad would be a match …" Nate headed over to him.

"So?" He shrugged.

"Put your hand on the scanner again."

He pressed his hand against the scanner. The strange sensation returned as the rough surface changed, filling every groove in his skin with something. The scanner changed to green and the terminal booted up.

"Well, I'll be damned … your Dad coded you into the system. If you can open this, I'll bet Adin can too."

"Why would he do that?"

"No idea." Nate shook his head and shrugged.

The screen opened up to a series of files, all dated years before his Dad's death. Nate tapped on the first file, opening it to the worried face of Calvin Roberts. A video log.

"I transferred another shipment of ore into the hands of Dr. Osho. I only hope it gets there undiscovered. We have been conducting research to find new ideas of how to charge the ore back up to strength without the loss of human life. The experiments have been unsuccessful at locating a proper specimen that can even get the slightest reaction to the ore. Osho still believes it has something to do with the soul but I think it lies within the DNA structures of ..." The digital voice of Calvin was cut off by Nate pressing another button.

"Hey!"

"Sorry," Nate explained. "I just need to check something else."

He waited as Nate navigated the system to several other documents.

"I think this it ... it looks like his code." Nate hit the print button and a printer across the room started to spit out sheets of information.

"Code?"

"Your father developed his own code. There were only three of us who could read it and only your dad could write it. This place was where your dad put all of his secrets – outside of this computer, no electronics. This was his safe house." Nate headed for the printer on the desk.

As Nate left to collect everything, Gabriel glanced at what he had just printed. There were no words, just a series of symbols; similar but all subtly different. He closed the document and tried to find his way back to the video diaries of his father.

"These are coordinates to some of the secret ore caches your father hid before he formed the IP. There are about seven of them all over the globe but two are close – I recognize the coordinates." Nate explained. "Also, some of these journals are written in code – some of his discoveries were never made known. He kept them hidden from Dr. Cymru. Osho needs some of his work to keep our research going."

Pocketing the paper, Nate headed back over to the boxes of files and rummaged through things, discarding what he didn't want into a large pile of papers in the corner. Gabriel continued to navigate the computer system until he found a file saved two days before his father's death. Activating the file, he sat there glued to the screen waiting for his father's face to appear.

"I fear my finding of the ore was a mistake." A digital image of his father rubbed at his forehead. "I have been unsuccessful at finding any alternative means to recharging the ore. Dr. Cymru and the others are ignoring my pleas to continue searching for a solution. I am afraid the laws won't stop their next action."

The digital Calvin rubbed his eyes and face with both hands, breathing out loudly at the screen.

"Allan has changed drastically. His desire to use the ore to help mankind no longer exists. Our partnership is over. My own actions are now being monitored heavily; Nate has been assigned elsewhere along with most of my trusted research team. I am uncertain about what may lie ahead. The truth of the ore has remained a secret to the general public and I believe Allan has plans to keep it this way for as long as possible. The IP is still immature in its development and could not confront T.E.R.A. without dire consequences."

"I feel trapped and I fear for my family daily. I find myself in a position of wishing I was the destroyer of the ore rather than its discoverer. I have been conducting personal research into any means of destroying the ore safely rather than leaving it in the hands of those who would do evil with it, but nothing has worked. My only hope lies in the pure white ore that we discovered. While its properties currently evade me, I believe, and hope, my answer will lie with it. However, my research will have to remain on hold for now, as I am being watched so closely by T.E.R.A. I pray that my actions carry no fallout for my family and, God willing, my boys will not have to grow up in a world enslaved by this ore."

The recording stopped, leaving Gabriel to ponder his father's words. Even Nate had stopped his search and listened to his best friend's voice from the corner of the small lab.

"Is there anything that can be done to stop Cymru?" Gabriel wondered aloud.

Nate sighed. "It's why we are still fighting and will keep doing so … T.E.R.A. hasn't even begun to show what it's capable of, I'm afraid. Things will only get worse as they gain more control. Right now it's just about energy and profits." Nate walked over, patting him on the shoulder. "I miss him too." He knocked the computer terminal to the ground with a crash.

Gabriel jumped up, shocked. "What are you doing!"

"Unfortunately, we can't leave anything here." Nate ripped apart the terminal with the blade of his boot knife, finally prying a small round steel disc out from it. "Here … that's yours." Nate tossed the disc to him. "I'm sure you will find some answers there but right now we need to leave."

Nate finished putting some journals into his bag and tossed the rest of the filing boxes onto the large pile he had made in the corner.

"Why are you doing this? This is all of Dad's stuff and –"

Nate cut him off. "Because I can't leave anything for Cymru to find … he can read the code as well as I can … everything in this office has to be destroyed. It's too dangerous to leave it hidden here. They would eventually find it. We got what we need and Dr. Osho has the rest of the research. It's just what needs to happen."

He nodded, understanding Nate's point. If Cymru ever found this place and resurrected any of the data stored there the IP would be completely exposed as an enemy – but he still felt torn. This was a piece of his father; these were his thoughts, his deepest secrets. He longed to know more. He needed to find answers about why his father made these decisions.

Nate slammed a flare on the table, lighting up the room with a red glow. He threw the flare into the pile of papers.

"It's time to leave." Nate pushed him towards the stairs. "The room will soon release a gas and ignite everything."

As he left the office, he allowed himself one more glance at his father's private world. The answers he searched for were now lost in black smoke. The questions remained. When they reached the SUV, just outside the barn, he looked around. "There's nothing left here for me."

"Another day, there will be." Nate opened the door to the SUV. "This is still our – Gabriel, don't move!"

A loud shot rang out and a blaze of light hit the ground beside them. Nate raced over to him, drawing a pistol – scanning the direction from where the shot came.

"They missed!" Gabriel said reached for the optics on the front dash of the SUV to see who was out there.

"No, they didn't. They're letting us know that they can kill us if they want to. It looks like they just arrived – the SUV should still be good." Nate kept both his hands on his gun.

"Welcome home!" a loud, distorted voice called out from beyond the rubble of the house. A man in a black suit and a trilby hat, pulled down low across his brow, strolled towards them. He kicked through the rubble with no respect and stepped on anything that would break.

"Quite the mess!" His voice rasped, as if it had been stripped of its harmony.

The stranger leaned down and picked up a broken dish examining it for a moment then threw it to the side, shattering what remained of it.

As the man in the suit neared them, Gabriel held up the optics and could see his disfigured appearance. Despite the trilby hat, the face of the stranger was still visible. Blackened, calloused skin covered the whole left side of his face, including his eye. The sharp features of his face were enhanced even further by the grotesque skin that clung tightly to the bones. It was as if it had been burnt over and over, and never had a chance to heal. Streaks of blackened veins under the pale skin that remained on the right side of his body gave him a tiger-like appearance. Even his hands were different from each other – one was as black as his suit, the other looked normal, with an expensive watch hanging loosely around his wrist.

Setting down the optics, Gabriel watched in terror as rough looking gunmen stepped out from the rubble around them. They looked like street thugs, sauntering left and right over the area until they took their final positions surrounding him and Nate. Their rifles were at the ready. Two men leaned against some rubble on the left wall of the house, three more moved around the back of the vehicle near an over-turned tractor, and the last stood lazily beside the man in the black suit.

"Gabriel ... did you think I would forget about you?" The strange man cackled, his voice was as damaged as the rest of his body.

"Stay calm," Nate whispered to him.

"Caught like rats in a trap aren't we? And in such a pitiful place." The disfigured man waved a disparaging hand at the ruins. "Needs a bit of cleaning."

"What do you want?" Gabriel yelled, locking eyes with the stranger.

"What everyone wants – the lab." The man revealed a set of shiny black teeth behind his wicked smile.

"Keep him talking ..." Nate whispered. He inched closer to the door of the vehicle.

"You seem to know an awful lot about something that was a secret." He called out to the disfigured man, stepping in front of Nate. The crystal in his chest surged with energy, waiting to be released.

"No more secrets! No more lies!" The man pulled his hat down tight over his head, like there was a fight inside his own head. "He hid it! I should have been told! It's mine!"

"Who are you?" Gabriel couldn't help but think of the horrors that might have happened to him.

"You should know." The disfigured man laughed with a high-pitched cackle. "I am your death!" He gave the signal for the troops to move in. "Take them alive!"

Two shots blazed out over Gabriel's shoulder. They struck the power cell still left on the broken wall of the house. The high velocity round punctured the cell, spraying its blue acidic contents high into the air and over the two thugs positioned there. The acid instantly ate into their armour and weapons. Within seconds the men were screaming in pain, dropping their weapons and attempting to flee from the acid, their clothes billowing in white smoke.

"Open fire!" The disfigured man screamed. The thug nearest to him fired on Gabriel.

Gabriel raised his hands and a luminous bubble filled the space in front of the SUV, absorbing the impact of the shells. It held strong, his hands raised and spread apart, glowing in sleeves of pure energy that produced the fluid-like wall of light. He glanced over his shoulder to see Nate engaging the thugs behind them. His accurate shots punched through the chest of one of them, a cloud of red blood bursting out the back of him. The other two scrambled for cover, retreating. Gabriel kept his focus – his shield was impenetrable. He watched as more men came in from the road.

The man in black ripped a half-broken wall free from the rubble, hurling it at Gabriel. The large piece shattered against the shield. Gabriel stumbled back, surprised by the show of strength. He kept up the shield and moved towards the SUV as Nate spun it around to make an escape. The passenger door hung open to him and Nate yelled for him to get in.

A deafening crack rang out in his ears. The fluid-like surface of Gabriel's shield hardened, cracks running through its surface. He froze. The ore in his chest struggled, as the disfigured man's smoking black fist crashed through the shield. The sound of broken glass filled the air. The shattered shield broke into fragments of light.

Bolts of light filled the air as the thugs attacked the SUV, filling the back with holes from each shot. The disfigured man attacked Gabriel. He tried to block the incoming strikes but each hit felt like a baseball bat striking against his forearms. His skin seared in pain, as he came in contact with the disfigured man's smoking black fists.

Without thinking the ore surged through his body, sending streams of light rushing down around his hands and arms. The next strike was painless, bouncing off his forearm as he went on the offensive. The man in black was skilled, dodging each attack as he moved backwards. He was too fast for Gabriel to hit.

His blackened teeth glinted as he grinned at Gabriel, circling him like an animal patiently waiting to kill its prey. Black smoke rose from every part of him, blurring his image as he moved back and forth. He closed the gap between them in a rush of black smoke. Gabriel's jaw wrenched sideways as he was struck across the face. Another hit rattled through his ribs, as the disfigured man's arm blurred with speed. He fell backwards to the ground, staring up at his attacker. The white ore in his chest raged like a fire, burning a hole through his shirt, flooding his limbs and chest with white light. The disfigured man halted his attack and, as if mesmerized by the crystal, he stepped back from Gabriel.

"You ..." His eyes focused on the shard as he struggled against something. He put both of his hands against his face, pressing tightly against his skull as if in immense pain. A ragged scream burst from him.

Just then a helicopter came in overhead, hovering low to the ground, sending dust and debris everywhere. Soldiers descended on ropes just beyond the debris of the house, as shots targeted the thugs from heavy caliber weapons aboard the choppers.. The man in black glared at Gabriel, then disappeared in a blur of smoke towards the helicopter. Screams rang out in the air and sprays of bullets erupted from both sides. Nate yelled at him to get in the car. Gabriel watched in terror as the man in black attacked the soldiers like a rabid animal – tearing one of them apart. Gabriel retreated and lunged for the passenger door. Nate floored it, the SUV swerved all over the yard, trying to get back to the old road. Gabriel twisted to look behind them – the scene played out like a war, men on each side dropping as bullets slammed into their bodies.

CHAPTER THIRTY-FOUR

THE BULLET-RIDDLED SUV SCREECHED OUT ONTO THE OPEN ROAD OF THE HIGHWAY. Nate pushed the engine to its limit as they tried to increase their distance from the ranch and their attackers. Gabriel stared out the back of the SUV. No one following them.

"Who was that?" he yelled over the noise of the wind.

"The helicopter? T.E.R.A. special ops team, for sure." Nate snapped his seat belt.

"Not them, the other ones!" Gabriel kept watch. If T.E.R.A. had come looking for him they wouldn't be too happy to let him disappear into the night.

"No idea. They were sloppy! Hired thugs I'd guess." Nate changed lanes abruptly, sliding deftly between two cars.

"What about the guy in black – he was an ore user, wasn't he? He broke through my shield."

Nate's eye met his from the rear-view mirror. "You sure? Didn't think that was possible."

"His fist went right through it!" Gabriel turned around and strapped himself in.

Nate continued to speed down the highway. "Maybe it just got weakened with all those shots."

Gabriel didn't believe it. The way the man ripped up that broken wall and threw it, how he attacked those soldiers. He's like me. "He could have killed me."

"I doubt that! Looks like your crystal was going into overdrive. There's a fresh shirt in the backpack." Nate pointed to the pulsing glow of the crystal visible through the hole in his shirt.

Gabriel leaned over the seat and rummaged through the backpack, pulling a black t-shirt out. "I dunno, he just stopped. He stared at the ore and screamed. Like he recognized me all of the sudden."

"He certainly didn't seem like he was all there ... I sure hope we destroyed the lab. I guess T.E.R.A. finally decided to come look for it."

"Shouldn't we be getting back to the IP?" Gabriel thought about Dr. Osho and Kyrie.

"We need to get clear of here first. Don't want anyone following us home." Nate dug into his pocket and pulled out a silver disc.

"Who you calling?" He watched as Nate slid the disc up behind his ear.

"Alex. My contact in Burlington." Nate stopped talking for a moment as Gabriel changed into his new shirt, tossing the old one back into the backpack. "Shit!"

"What?"

"Something's wrong. He left a coded message at the store." Nate slid the disc off.

"If we can't go back to the IP, where do we go?" The IP was the only place Gabriel had felt safe. He hoped everything was alright.

"I know where they'll be." Nate took an exit off a side ramp and changed their direction.

The night was taking over the sky as they neared their destination among a strip of old warehouses, outside the north end of Denver. Gabriel noted the high fences and hazardous waste signs all around the property as Nate slowly pulled in. A small guard shack stood at the entrance of the parking lot, surround by six abandoned buildings. A casually dressed man stepped out of the shack and walked over to the beat up SUV. He could see an automatic weapon tucked beneath the stranger's jacket.

"Good to see you safe, Mr. Reinhart." The friendly guard nodded at Gabriel as he spoke to Nate.

"What happened?" Nate put the SUV in park.

"Not to worry sir, most of our people got out and everything was already moved prior to the raid from T.E.R.A.." The guard looked grim. "But sir ... they had full government support to deal with us as they saw fit – no interference or regard to the law."

"Government support? I don't understand ... How did we find out about the raid?" Shock registered on Nate's face.

"An associate of the church tipped us off to the raid. We followed protocol as fast as we could, evacuating the essentials first and moving the majority of the ore we had to a safe location. The remaining non-essentials had to stay behind to make T.E.R.A. believe the raid was a success."

The story confused Gabriel. Essentials? Non-essentials?

"The others are already inside, and the essentials have been accounted for."

"Good work, Tony. Double the watch and get people moved out of the area. I don't want anything else left for T.E.R.A. to try and snatch up." Nate patted the guard on the shoulder.

"Consider it done, sir." Tony stepped aside and opened the reinforced gate.

"Essentials? What is going on?" Gabriel stared at Nate.

"Our supply of ore," Nate snapped.

They parked and Nate led him to a metal door at the side of the warehouse. He banged on the door and it popped open promptly. Gabriel followed Nate warily into orderly chaos hidden behind the old steel walls. Nate leaped into action, leaving Gabriel trailing behind him, carrying the chest once again.

"Mr. Reinhart!" A man in army fatigues raised his hand and strode towards him.

He nodded to Gabriel briefly, and faced Nate. "Sir, the trucks are being loaded with the remaining essentials. They will be shipped out tonight to secure locations across Europe as well as our remote northern locations near the old Canadian border." The man handed Nate an electronic clipboard. Nate nodded as the man continued to explain the shipments and routes listed on the clipboard. Gabriel's eyes wandered around the warehouse as he jogged after Nate, dodging people and machinery as they off-loaded crates from a revolving series of trucks.

"We will have operations back up to eighty percent in five days max, full capacity by the end of the week." The man stuck close to Nate as the two moved through the busy floor.

"How much did we lose?" Nate barked at him.

"We lost one percent of the essentials, twenty-one percent of the non-essentials and thirty-four percent of our combatants, sir."

"Where's Osho?" Nate handed the man back his clipboard. "Pen."

"Third office, sir." He traded Nate a pen for the clipboard then pointed to a set of steel stairs leading up to a few rooms overlooking the warehouse.

"Turn around." The soldier obeyed and Nate used his shoulder as a writing surface. "I want these trucks gone in four hours and I need extraction teams to retrieve the ore at these coordinates ASAP." Nate handed the man the piece of paper from the lab under the barn. "Empty these two caches in the next 24 hours or less, otherwise T.E.R.A. will most likely find them. By the way, that piece of paper you're holding is the only copy so don't lose it!"

The man yelled orders at some of the loaders as he tucked the piece of paper into his chest pocket, making sure it was zipped shut.

Their feet clanged on the steel stairs as they climbed to the second floor. Gabriel paused at the top, looking over the railing at the workers moving around the warehouse. He spotted Kyrie among the crowd and attempted a wave but she didn't see him. She had joined a line of people passing boxes to a truck. It was good to see her up and moving.

"Gabriel!" Nate hollered from the third office door. As they entered, Gabriel spotted Osho seated at a crowded table, in the midst of a heated discussion. The room fell silent as everybody looked up. Some of the faces were angry.

Nate walked straight over to the table and slammed down his things. "What happened?"

"Nothing we foresaw eventually happening. T.E.R.A. was just quicker than we assumed." Osho's usual calm, cool manner didn't falter.

Nate clenched his hands into fists as he stared at Osho.

"We will bring you up to date shortly, I promise." Osho nodded at Nate. "Let me first introduce Father Clarence and Cardinal Vincent from the Church of Humanity. These men saved us from what would have been a devastating assault on our operations."

Nate nodded at the guests.

"This is Nathaniel Reinhart, our Chief Security Officer, and Gabriel Roberts." Dr. Osho finished the introductions.

"Roberts?" The cardinal pursed his lips. "Calvin Roberts' son?"

"That's correct," Osho confirmed.

His eyes met the cardinals' and they exchanged a nod of acknowledgement. The cardinal stared at Gabriel, not saying a word. Gabriel set down the strongbox and used it as a seat, tired from carrying it for most of the day The meeting resumed and he tried to pay attention without drawing too much attention to himself.

"The last forty-eight hours have been busy for T.E.R.A. on a global scale. Let me bring everyone up to date." Osho recapped the last two days like a news anchor.

"T.E.R.A. openly attacked the so-called 'Horsemen' in China, completely destroying their suspected headquarters and seizing what remained of their ore. While no direct support came from the Chinese government, no issues were made about the attack and

T.E.R.A. was allowed free passage. The reason for the attack is still unknown as T.E.R.A. has always tried to stay clear of the Horsemen. Something got their attention or they wouldn't have been so bold. After close examination of the camp my daughter was rescued from in Denver, we can confirm that the Tao Sung were working for the Horsemen, but we have no idea of their goals."

"Across the globe, T.E.R.A. has been setting up offices and facilities. Most countries are welcoming them, hoping for access to the ore. Several new T.E.R.A. locations have been confirmed across Europe as well as on the eastern continents. Our friends at the Church have been watching this with a close eye."

"A new global message has been issued by Dr. Cymru listing demands that all nations must comply with if they want access to the ore. The list requires the nations to replace all old technology with ore powered equipment – this includes manufacturing, agriculture, logistics, and some retail components. That means ore will be used on a global scale – and the people needed to recharge will increase dramatically. By the time the public realizes what is going, on they simply won't have a choice anymore. They are also proposing new laws to allow trial experiments on humans that have a relationship with the ore, claiming it is needed for research. This would mean regulated testing for everyone, and most likely every person with a relationship to the ore would be put into camps. T.E.R.A. also wants all companies involved with the ore and its research to come under their control – peacefully or not. Our government is in full support of their recommendations. It won't be safe for us here anymore." Osho sat down at the table.

"No one is against this?" Nate sounded overwhelmed.

"Our government is leaving them to do what they feel is necessary. I am sure the paperwork to commandeer our facility was filed at a very high level, which means we don't have a lot of options." Osho shrugged.

"How can people believe them? It sounds insane!" Gabriel finally spoke up. .

"And no wonder, for even Satan disguises himself as an angel of light, Second Corinthians eleven verse fourteen. The power of deception can be quite strong over the masses." The cardinal stood up from the table.

"It's true." Osho nodded at the cardinal and turned to Gabriel. "T.E.R.A. is promising a way to turn back the clock for the planet, assuring everyone that the earth can rejuvenate itself if the ore is used properly. In theory, it *is* possible."

Nate sighed. "We don't have as much research into the ore as T.E.R.A. does. No one does. But knowing their intentions, these moves are intended for control. If everyone is forced to depend on them for energy, then we will see more people sacrificed to keep up with demand. Things will only get worse after that."

"I have to agree with Mr. Reinhart." The cardinal nodded. "I think we haven't even begun to see true terror from them yet and that is why you must join us. You have to trust us." He turned to Osho, his hands together as if in prayer.

"Trust you? What are you talking about – trust you with what?" Nate's voice rose.

"We are compromised here." Osho wouldn't meet Nate's eyes. "Which is why we have been discussing placing ourselves under the control of the church."

Nate bolted to his feet. "The Church? We know nothing about them! Just because they warned us about today's attack doesn't mean they aren't on the same side of the power struggle as T.E.R.A. is!"

Osho remained silent but Cardinal Vincent cleared his throat. "Mr. Reinhart, how many did you lose … how many souls were sent home today because of what happened?"

Nate glared at the cardinal. "I lost one third of my men!"

"And you were given a warning. Next time you may not have us to help you. How many more are you willing to lose before you see that you cannot stand against this devil alone?"

"I have looked at this option many times over the years." Osho's tone was calm, but a note of pleading lurked beneath his words. "Nate, you know this to be true. We can trust them. We cannot stand up to another raid. With the government behind them, we don't have much of a choice."

"The IP will simply fall under our protection ... you will still be able to continue your ore research. If you are working with our current researchers, we might be able to find something to change the course of this world." Father Clarence finally spoke, his eyes on Nate.

"What about our people? Some of them might disagree with your practices." Nate's nostrils flared, his chest moving rapidly.

"I offer a sanctuary, nothing more. Their futures will be decided by their actions not ours." The cardinal met Nate's stare unafraid.

"Gentlemen, please." Osho did his best to settle the room.

"Dr. Osho is right. Our beliefs might be different but our enemy is the same." Father Clarence put his hand on the cardinal's shoulder.

Nate looked at Dr. Osho, and Gabriel watched a silent conversation pass between them. He turned to Gabriel finally. "What do you think?"

"Me?" Gabriel was dumbfounded. "What would Dad have done?"

A small grin creased Nate's face. "He would fight ... but he wouldn't do it alone." A minute of silence past in the office. "Transfer all the essentials over to them. Make sure our people are safe!" He looked back to the cardinal. "All of them."

CHAPTER THIRTY-FIVE

Everyone in the room sprang into action. They organized the trucks to carry materials to new locations and IP personnel were moved into Church safe houses across North America. Gabriel moved into a side office, trying his best to stay out of the way. He sank gratefully into the only chair in the office. Not sitting on that hardened steel chest felt so much better. Osho and Nate followed after him. Nate leaned against the desk and sighed.

Osho put his hand on Nate's shoulder. "It's for the best ... we couldn't have survived much longer. The Church has always been good to us, you knew this day would come."

Nate gave a half-hearted smile. "Yeah, I just didn't know it would happen so soon."

Osho turned to Gabriel. "I believe your father would have agreed with this choice."

"You knew him better than I did." He shrugged.

"While it may seem that way, his thoughts were always of his family first. We came second. Don't ever believe differently."

Dr. Osho's comment felt like a hollow truth, something you

tell a child so they aren't hurt by reality. His father had led a double life, a life full of secrets. One that had led him to his death, leaving his family lost.

"Did you recover anything out of Calvin's office?" Osho peeked through the blinds at the warehouse below.

"Yeah, we have new coordinates to some of the ore caches. I found the coded journals you were asking for and the hard disk out of the computer. Teams will retrieve them in the next 24 hours, but we were ambushed on the ranch." Nate ran his hand through his hair.

Osho frowned. "By who?"

"Another ore user." Nate glanced over at Gabriel.

"He was strong. A lot stronger than me." He nodded at the two men.

"How did you get out then?" Osho looked shocked.

"T.E.R.A. raided the ranch. I guess with the new law in place, Cymru saw it as a good opportunity to go for the lab. Anyhow, the two groups turned on each other – we managed to slip out in the confusion." Nate sighed.

"That man." Gabriel shook his head. "He had me beat but he turned and attackd them, like he hated them."

"What about the lab?" Osho looked at Nate. "What was left?"

"Nothing. We burned everything." Nate shrugged. "They shouldn't be able to salvage much."

"That's a loss but for the best I suppose." Osho rubbed his unshaven chin. "The mysterious man – he wanted the lab as well?"

"How would he have even known about it … I think he came for Gabriel."

Gabriel shivered.

"Not surprising, considering what you can do." Osho thought for a moment. "We will need to get everything moved. I fear anything left in the hands of the IP will belong to T.E.R.A. by an order from the government. I want you both to come with me to meet the council of the Church."

"No! I need to stay here. Make sure our operations are safe."
Nate shook his head.

"I understand how you're feeling after the raid, but others
can do that. I need you to help me make sure we are 'safe' within
the Church. Gabriel will be a threat to them," Osho said flatly. Nate
sighed. "Of course."

"Why would I threaten the Church?" Gabriel blinked.

"Not you, kid. What's in your chest. Riley mentioned that
they've been hunting more – tracking more users down." Nate
scratched at his beard. "Can we keep it hidden?"

"Gabriel has done a good job of that so far." Osho patted him
on the back. "We will just have to keep up the charade."

Gabriel nodded. He had grown accustomed to keeping the
crystal hidden. "Where are we headed?"

"Saint Petersburg in the Northern European Commons."
Osho smiled at him. "We leave by jet in twenty minutes with Father
Clarence and Cardinal Vincent. Don't worry about clothing or personal effects of that nature. We will find everything we need once
we arrive."

"You're sure we're doing the right thing?" Nate stood up.

"I don't think we have much of a choice, Nathaniel. Now if
you will excuse me. I must see to my daughter and family." Osho left
the room.

"How do we know the Church isn't going to freak out once
they find out about me?" Gabriel hunched his shoulders.

"Well, firstly, we aren't going to tell them. And secondly, if
they do, well, that's why I'm coming." Nate's grim tone didn't give
Gabriel much reassurance. "Let's get our stuff."

They drove to a nearby airstrip, taking only what they could
carry: Nate's bags of tricks, the chest, and Dr. Osho's steel briefcase.
Boarding the small Lear jet, they found Cardinal Vincent already
seated while Father Clarence was performing a pre-flight checklist.
Once everyone was buckled in, Father Clarence piloted the small jet
down the short runway. Gabriel leaned towards the window as the

ground drifted away from him. They lifted high into the sky, passing through the thick layer of clouds and up into the night.

Cardinal Vincent spoke first as they settled in at their cruising altitude. "The IP will fall under Church rule without question, no demands will be made of you. However, we request a penance for the young man here." The cardinal stared at Gabriel.

"God damn, Riley." Nate rubbed his beard and shook his head.

"Mr. Reinhart, I would ask you to refrain from using those terms around me. And your friend, Bishop Riley, is the only reason I even allowed the young man on the plane." The cardinal's face was stern.

"What is it you desire?" Osho put out a hand to calm Nate.

"It is not a desire but our mission." The cardinal smiled at Osho. "Calvin Roberts was an expert in the study of the ore. No one on earth knew more about it than he. In his final days, we understand he was researching ways to dispose of it – to destroy it. The black ore is evil – it is the embodiment of sin. Our research into the black ore has failed to reveal any way of abolishing it."

"You want my father's research." Gabriel interrupted him.

"Yes." The cardinal faced him. "We will give you exile within the Church. A safe place for you to live out your days. And in return, you will give us everything Calvin knew about the black ore."

"That's not really much choice, seeing as we are already on route to St. Petersburg." Osho leaned back in his chair. "If we refuse?"

Cardinal Vincent half laughed. "Then he is an enemy of the Church and will be treated as such."

Dr. Osho cleared his throat. "That's fine. There was no need to threaten Gabriel, we would have shared it regardless."

"Then I must ask for your forgiveness." The cardinal bowed. "The patriarchs would not have it any other way."

"Why are you so afraid of ore users?" Gabriel had to ask.

Cardinal Vincent sighed. "It is not the individual we fear. It is what they are capable of. The ore is God's gift back to us, a chance to redeem this world. That power must be governed by the righteous, the most pure of heart. They must protect it and use it for the good of everyone around them. Ore users disrupt that control – they govern the power the way they see fit. Sometimes they use it against what it was intended for – a perversion of the gift. Their lust for power can overwhelm them and they become lost, losing control of themselves. They mutilate themselves with the ore, seeking more power from it. We have no choice but to destroy the abominations they've become."

The words gave no comfort to Gabriel. He didn't have a choice with the ore – fate had fused it to his chest.

"I'm sorry if my words upset you. It is a harsh reality but it is part of our task as stewards of the ore." The cardinal half smiled at him. Gabriel stayed silent. "Are we free to speak openly? There are other matters to be discussed." He looked at Osho then at Gabriel.

"This young man is as much a part of this as his father was." Osho patted Gabriel on the knee.

"He's saved my life once or twice." Nate smiled at him then stared at the cardinal. "I trust him more than I do you."

"So be it." The cardinal looked annoyed. "We have just received some new information from one of our operatives stationed at a border around old Kazakhstan. An old factory north of the border has been receiving a mass influx of supplies and personnel in the last few weeks. Satellite images confirm a huge spike in activity within the last few days. Our border operative says shipments of ore have been heading there. She cannot tell from where they come or whom the personnel at the old factory are working for."

"I thought most of the ore was under your control." Nate raised an eyebrow at the cardinal.

"Our stocks have all been accounted for. It's coming from outside of Europe. The council believes the Horsemen are behind the operation." The cardinal handed a folder to Nate. "Here's everything we know."

"Paper?" Nate was surprised.

"It's much easier to delete. Fire works best." The cardinal smiled.

"Sounds familiar." Nate flipped through the pages.

"Why would the Horsemen be in Kazakhstan? After T.E.R.A.'s move against them how would they have the resources to put this together?" Osho leaned towards Nate, eyeing the folder.

"We're unsure. We have many operatives within the European government looking for the source, but they aren't finding much information." The cardinal pulled out his rosary and thumbed through the beads.

"So, what's the big concern? You want the ore." Nate leaned back in his seat, surrendering the folder to Osho. His eyes focused on the cardinal.

"Not exactly, Mr. Reinhart. From what we know of the history of the building, it was once a weapon factory. Now, judging by the equipment being reportedly moved into the area we guess that the facility is being retro-fitted to produce some kind of weaponry." The cardinal shrugged. "Rumours are circulating that the weaponry utilizes ore."

"Weapons with ore … how?" Nate leaned forward.

The thought sounded terrifying to Gabriel.

The cardinal silently thumbed his rosary for a moment. "We don't know. As I said, everything is just a guess but I was hoping Dr. Osho might have some thoughts."

Dr. Osho stayed quiet.

"It could be a threat to us. Its position in Europe makes us the most realistic target." The cardinal clasped his hands together and leaned forward. "I understand that trust is difficult. But it is something we cannot move forward without. Now, I trust you. And my superiors have trusted my judgement in making you a part of our flock."

Dr. Osho bowed his head in apology. "Of course. Now, the Horsemen are a crime syndicate. They don't openly wage war. They kill from the shadows. T.E.R.A.'s attack might not have disrupted anything. The possibility that they are behind the weapon facility still remains, but weaponizing the ore – that kind of technology would be very advanced."

"I have to agree. Taking out the headquarters doesn't mean much. Another would simply rise to power and continue their operations." Nate's tone was grimly matter of fact.

"We have a stronger position than they do in Europe but we don't know their numbers. Some of our own people might even be assisting them – their corruption knows no bounds. With the majority of their operations in the shadows, we have no idea about their real numbers." The cardinal thumbed the rosary again. "If they become equipped with the right technology, they could amass a powerful army. If a war breaks out between the Church and the Horsemen our government relations might not give us any support. Then there's T.E.R.A. Certainly, if the Church is in a weakened state, they might try to capitalize on that."

Osho handed the folder back to the cardinal. "They still control more than two thirds of the world's estimated ore supply and if everyone is forced into using it as a power source, they will want to expand. This might be motivating the Horsemen into action."

"We will be meeting with the council when we arrive to discuss what will be done about this situation. All your assets will be transferred to our facilities but you will still maintain control of them, I promise you that, Mr. Reinhart. However, while you are under our protection, I would like you to work with our combative lead – Father Clarence." The cardinal pointed to the cockpit.

"A priest?" Nate couldn't help but laugh.

Smiling, the cardinal pointed at him. "You have a lot more in common than you think. Clarence was a highly trained soldier before the Lord called him into service. His fatherhood is more of a title than a lifestyle."

"To keep an eye on me?" Nate crossed his arms and raised an eyebrow.

"To help you. Dr. Osho, please continue your research into recharging the ore as well as assuming control of our resources for your efforts. I am sure your studies are far ahead of our own." The cardinal handed him a thick red folder with *Classified* written on the side of it. "You will find everything you need in there but I do ask that some efforts be put into developing some kind of defence against this rumoured weaponry."

Osho nodded and flipped through the pages, leaning back into his seat. "And me?" Gabriel couldn't help but ask.

The cardinal frowned for a moment, then his expression lightened. "If you're anything like your father you will find your place, I'm sure."

Nate nudged him on the arm. "You stick with me. You're pretty handy in a fight."

CHAPTER THIRTY-SIX

GABRIEL SAT ON A WOODEN BENCH. Its old iron legs and worn wood matched the age of the tall rock wall it sat under. He stared out across the gardens and sprawling lawns surrounding the Church's research facility in St. Petersburg. From the outside, the facility looked like a 300 year old church. Aged stone exterior walls and tall narrow turrets hid the technology within. Only a third of the facility stood above ground, the rest lay deep beneath the earth. On the lowest floor was one of the largest ore vaults in Europe. The other floors housed laboratories and living quarters for its security force – a small army. Still, the grounds had a peace to them. That was a feeling he had forgotten over the last several weeks. He stretched out his legs and stretched his arms along the back of the bench, relaxed and waiting.

Since his arrival, Cardinal Vincent had taken it upon himself to educate Gabriel. They believed the ore was placed in the Garden of Eden when God created the world. It was the ore's powers that had shaped the garden – blue ore produced pure water for man to drink, green allowed the garden to flourish with food and calm the animals, red kept man warm despite the seasons. The Church also believed that the white ore was reserved for Adam to use to govern the garden. When man fell, it shattered, rendering it useless. In the end, man was cast out for his disobedience. A ring of black ore was placed around the garden, killing anyone who tried to come near it.

The Church had spent years collecting any piece of ore they could find. The bulk of the collection was held within the Vatican City in Rome. Their desire was not that much different than the mission of the IP. They believed that the ore was to be governed by them alone and not by the governments or any independent groups. They claimed to be the ore's overseers, ordained by God to use and govern.

He sat patiently on the bench wondering about the story. If the original crystal Adam had used had shattered, why was he able to put two pieces back together? There was nothing holy about him, he wasn't even sure he believed in God. Was this an evolution of man or a return to how humans were meant to be? He hadn't forgotten what Shiro had told him – others were being hunted for their connection to the ore. He wasn't the only one. The ones the Church didn't execute were called exiles – they were protected and cared for but weren't allowed any contact with the ore. They could live out their lives in special communities – a future Gabriel found depressing. The cardinal told him about one exile in particular, Claire Bennett. She had been given special permission to be a research assistant at the facility. It was her, he sat waiting for.

She appeared suddenly, hustling across the green space, heading towards one of the several entrances to the underground facility. He almost missed her and sprinted after her. As he quickened his pace, he dodged around a gentlemen in a white lab coat, strolling towards the same entrance.

"It's rude to chase after strangers!" Dr. Osho's familiar voice sounded behind him. "There are easier ways."

He gave up his pursuit and turned to see Osho grinning at him. "I wasn't chasing. I was trying to catch up."

"Gabriel, I watched you racing after the poor girl." Osho laughed.

Smiling at the humor in Osho's voice he asked, "You mentioned an easier way?"

"I have a task just for you, and perhaps Ms. Bennett can assist us. How's that sound?"

"I guess better than this."

"Yes. Shall we then?" Osho held out a box of cubes for Gabriel to carry, as he led the way.

He scooped up the electronic files in his arms, smiling at the doctor and headed toward the entrance doors. They entered the building and stood in line, waiting for the busy elevator to take them down below the ground. He teetered on his toes, scanning the room hoping to catch a glimpse of Claire. The ding of the elevator opening shifted the people around him. He shrank back down to keep his footing as they stepped up for their turn.

"You are certainly interested in this girl. Just relax and wait. She will be more than happy to join us soon." Osho continued to grin at him.

"Yeah … I just want to know what she can do." He kept his voice down. "I mean with the ore. The cardinal said she could handle all of them but the black."

Osho glanced around, speaking at a whisper. "I am sure you are quite different from her. She is unique though. Lots of individuals have a relationship to the ore, whether they know it or not, but it is usually to a single kind. Having the ability to interact with all of them is certainly interesting and rare."

"Do you believe the story of the garden? I mean, do you really think the ore came from God?"

"The ore defies many scientific theories. It could be possible. Its existence and properties are reflected in the natural world but not in such great strength." Osho pointed to the opening elevator door, guiding Gabriel through it.

"Cardinal Vincent said Adam controlled the garden with the white ore before it was shattered. What does that mean about me?" he lowered his voice to a whisper as they piled into the cramped space.

"I do not know." Osho shook his head and smiled. "But I do know your father found it for a reason; it was his purpose. Your connection to the ore ... it has a reason, a purpose. Instead of asking why, ask how. How are you going to change things?"

Gabriel thought about Osho's words as the elevator hummed down below the ground.

How could he change anything?

He stepped out of the elevator and passed through the security check point that scanned the ID badge given to him when they had first arrived. The walk to Dr. Osho's office was short.

"Come in, my boy." Osho opened the door wide to let him through.

Gabriel stepped past him. Osho had obviously been working in his office nonstop for the last couple of days. His desk was a mess of cubes. The small couch in the corner of the room had been turned into a make-shift bed and stacks of plates stood on the small table. Osho cleared off one of the chairs and invited him to take a seat.

"I apologize for the mess. I actually slept in a bed last night for the first time in days." Osho gathered up some more of his things.

"It's alright. So, what's this task?"

"First, I wanted to ask you some questions about your trip into the T.E.R.A. labs. Where did I put that cube?" Osho found an empty cube to take notes on and sat down behind his desk.

"Sure. Um ... is there any new information on Adin?"

Osho stopped what he was doing. "Of course ... Nathaniel has been quite busy with his new tasks. I'm afraid we still don't know anything for sure but in the confusion over the last week I must admit it has dropped down the priority list. I will speak with him about it."

"It's been too long hasn't it?" He found it difficult to stay positive about Adin.

"There is no length of time that is too long. Kyrie was gone for four months ... we didn't stop looking. We will find Adin, one way or another. I promise." Osho nodded then adjusted his glasses and changed the subject. "When you were at the labs did you see, or get an idea from Adin, as to how much ore was there?"

"No idea." He shrugged. "The lab seemed to be more of a show-and-tell for the new equipment that used the ore. They had some small pieces stored in drawers but not a lot."

"That's unfortunate." Osho sighed. "What about the black ore? Was it used in any of the equipment?"

"Not that I can remember. Adin never actually talked about the black ore. None of his research involved it. Why all the questions?"

Osho removed his glasses and rubbed his eyes as he leaned forward on his desk. "I have been going through all of our research information searching for some kind of defence against the black ore and have come up with nothing. We know the black ore can affect other types of ore – polluting it – slowly changing it black over time. We know the black ore is lethal to anyone who comes in contact with it, even those who have connections to the other types of ore. In most cases, exposure happens so fast, it's difficult to even move without proper protection from its radiation. Even the smallest crystal can contain a massive amount of kinetic energy. Everything else about it is a mystery. We have no way to neutralize it. I have no idea how we can prepare any defence against it."

"Is any of the black ore here?"

"Yes, we have a small supply on site but –"

"Let's go see what I can do to it." He cut Osho off. "Dad was studying the relationship between the white and black ore. It's in his notes." He drummed on the crystal in his chest.

"What?" Osho stared at him shocked.

"I can interact with all the of the ore … I'm guessing that includes the black."

"Well, what do you … I mean what are you planning on doing with it? You do realize how volatile it is? It could explode in your hands." Osho looked quite alarmed.

"I don't know the science but I can push energy into any ore … red, blue, green … it doesn't matter what kind it is. So, something must also happen when I come in contact with the black ore." He stood up and pointed at the door. "Let's go find out."

"But – I –" Dr. Osho threw up his arms in defeat. "Alright. There really is no other way to find out except to let you get close to it. Let's head down to the lower levels."

Osho collected a small silver box from a locked drawer and they exited the office. At the elevators, they dropped deeper into the underground facility.

"So where are we headed? Security didn't let me explore the lower levels."

"The containment rooms in this section of the facility were designed for experimentation – able to withstand explosions, radiation, poisonous gases – anything that could go wrong." Osho stood aside as the elevator doors opened to a security checkpoint.

A guard took their ID's and scanned them and waved them through. Gabriel noticed one of the specialized rooms was already occupied. He glanced through the reinforced glass viewing panel. There, dressed in a long white lab coat and oversized safety goggles, Claire Bennett handled several pieces of ore.

He stared at her, studying all of her features. Her brown hair was tied back in a pony tail. Her eyes squinted behind the safety goggles as she focused on the ore in her hands. The ore pulsed at her touch. *It's the same as me, just weaker.*

Osho stepped beside him and rapped on the glass, shocking both Gabriel and Claire with the noise. Gabriel scrambled to look busy but found nothing to do but tie his shoelaces. He ducked down below the window and fumbled with them. He sheepishly glanced back at the window to see Claire staring down at him. She looked annoyed as he gave an awkward wave of his hand.

Dr. Osho pressed a button for the speaker in the room. "Sorry to disturb you, Claire, but I could use your help."

She smiled at the short doctor. "Of course, I would be happy to help you." Her cute accent only added to Gabriel's attraction to her.

"Great." Osho smiled and walked towards the next room.

"Gabriel, your shoe is tied well enough by now," he called back over his shoulder.

Gabriel felt the blood surge to his face as Claire walked by, completely ignoring him. The door shut behind her, sending a rush of cool air across his face. He stood and followed her into the small containment room. The silver box rested on a steel table that was firmly bolted to the wall. Osho was directing Claire into a side room. The door closed behind them, a mechanised lock activating in the door. Gabriel was sealed alone in the room, being watched by the other two through the reinforced viewing window. *Now what?* Not sure what he should be doing, he shrugged and stared at Osho for some insight. Osho flipped a switch on the outside wall.

"Go ahead, Gabriel. It's on the table." His voice rang out through a speaker mounted high in the corner of the room.

Right, the box. He nodded and flipped the small box open, revealing a dark sleek crystal, the size of his palm. A weak draining sensation came over him immediately. He reached his bare hand into the box, without much thought and picked the shard up. He dropped it on the table immediately. The ore banged against the flat steel, blasting sparks across the steel surface.

"It burns to touch!" He turned to Osho, rubbing his hand as it throbbed in pain.

Claire grabbed Dr. Osho's arm. "Of course, it will hurt if he touches it! That ore will kill him if he stays in that room any longer!"

Gabriel grinned, listening to their conversation on the speaker. I *doubt that.*

"Don't worry." Osho looked at her and shook his head. "Gabriel isn't exactly normal. He's an ore user."

"What! This is too dangerous." She looked at Gabriel then back to Osho.

"He will be fine, I hope." Osho looked at Gabriel, calling out over the speaker. "See what you can do."

Nodding, Gabriel turned and contemplated the black crystal on the table, unsure of how to touch it without hurting himself. He rubbed his hands together and breathed out as a strand of white light exited his shirt sleeve and pooled in his hand, forming a glove that covered his hand. The room grew brighter as he picked up the small crystal. Holding the shard without any pain, he turned back to the window to present it to Osho. Claire's eyes widened.

"It's draining. Like the white crystal is struggling against it." He tried to explain his feelings to Osho.

"I want you to focus your energy into the ore but do it carefully ... no sudden pulses," Dr. Osho directed.

He nodded and set the shard down on the table. He stretched his neck out from side to side, readying himself for the unknown. *Alright.* He summoned protection around both his hands. With his hands clasped around the black crystal, he focused. His body felt weak and achy, like he suddenly had the flu. He was short of breath. His white ore pulsed as he sent more energy towards the small shard. Wave after wave, more and more energy poured into his hands. The small black shard felt as if it had come to life, fighting to stop the process.

An explosion erupted in the room. The blast sent him flying backwards against the glass panel, webbing it with thousands of cracks but not shattering it. The walls split, sending chunks of concrete crashing to the floor. A cloud of thick grey dust enveloped him, blinding him.

"Gabriel!" Osho's yell echoed into the small room as it filled with darkness and dust.

"Son of a bitch! That hurt!" His hands stayed clenched as he waited for the burning sensation to stop. The room's emergency lighting flashed on and a loud fan pulled the dirty air upwards, clearing his vision of the room.

"I'm alright." He called out as he stood up and twisted. He could see Dr. Osho and Claire pressed against the fractured window.

"Thank God." Osho rushed over to the door, punching in a code that released it from the override locks. Gabriel watched as an emergency crew moved Claire away from the broken window. She stood at the doorway, her mouth wide open. The team followed Osho into the room.

Carefully stepping over the debris, Gabriel met Osho with a huge smile. He opened Osho's hands and raised his own closed fist above them. As he opened his fist, a dull green dust sifted between his fingers. "Not much left."

Osho stared down at his hands. "I need to put this in something." He looked to a member of the decontamination team who was quick to hold out a plastic container. He emptied the dust into it.

"Sometimes the stupidest method works the best!" Gabriel patted Osho on the back and laughed.

"Outstanding." Osho joined in his laugh.

"Sir, we're going to need you to come with us." One of the decontamination team put a hand on Gabriel's arm, pulling him away from Osho.

"I'm his physician!" Osho pointed out to the team. "I'll be coming with him."

The team escorted Gabriel towards Claire, and she abruptly stepped out in front of them. "I'm Claire. Claire Bennett."

"Gabriel." He smiled at her as the team stepped around her, prodding him along, Osho right beside him.

When they reached one of the medical bays, Dr. Osho ushered everyone out, demanding privacy during the examination. Gabriel was thankful and removed his shirt as he lay back on the bed.

"Let's do a quick inspection, then they will want you to shower down." Osho gathered some equipment on a tray.

"What for?" Gabriel knew nothing inside that room could hurt him.

"Just residual contamination. Best just to go along with it. We've already drawn enough attention to ourselves." Osho pulled the tray over to the table and began to examine the shard. "Either I am getting too old or this shard is larger than I remember."

Gabriel laughed. "I had totally forgotten. I merged it with another shard from Nate's box."

"You what?" Osho's mouth hung open.

"Ah – merged. They became one. Two shards –" Gabriel was unsure how to explain it any better.

Dr. Osho rolled his eyes at him. "I understand what merged means ... but how?"

"I just touched them together." He shrugged.

"Really ... That's it?" Osho crossed his arms.

"Well, my chest felt like it split open and my skin was on fire." Gabriel nodded. "That was about it."

Osho sighed. "Please, next time you are so bold, just let me be involved. Seeing that you might be the only person in the world who can do that. Let's not be so rash next time."

He smiled and chuckled. "It's not like I knew it was going to happen."

"Precisely, why I should have been there." Osho pulled a scanner over the top of the table. "Stay put while this runs." He flipped the switch.

Gabriel stretched out on the table to get comfortable. A minute or two into the scan, shouts erupted from outside the room.

"Stay put. I'll see what's happening." Osho walked towards the door. Before he could open it Cardinal Vincent burst into the room, slamming the door behind him.

"I thought we had an understanding!" Vincent yelled at Osho.

"I believe we did. Gabriel please don't move until the scan is done." Osho seemed completely calm but Gabriel's heart was racing.

"Then what were you doing in the containment rooms giving ore to him!" The cardinal pointed at Gabriel. "He should never be allow –" Vincent's jaw dropped as he stared at Gabriel's chest.

"As you can see I don't have to give him anything. He has his own." Dr. Osho offered the cardinal a chair. "Sit. Please."

Cardinal Vincent was silent. He stared for a full minute, caught in a daze of disbelief, then collapsed into the chair.

"What you see here is not an experiment, he isn't artificially augmented like so many other ore users. Gabriel was impaled with the white crystal during an unfortunate storm that killed his mother. The ore has since taken on a symbiotic relationship with him. I believe they sustain one another. His mastery of it is quite impressive." The scan finished and Osho continued to work while he talked. "In fact, he is the answer to the question you have been searching for."

The cardinal stumbled over his words. "What – What question? What do you mean."

"I watched Gabriel destroy a fragment of black ore in the containment room downstairs. If you've seen the room, you understand the magnitude of what he is capable of." Osho put everything back on the tray beside him. "You're all done – perfect as usual – put your shirt back and go shower in your room privately. I will take care of things here."

Gabriel nodded at him, agreeing that it was best for Dr. Osho to deal with the bewildered cardinal. As he headed to leave, Vincent grabbed his arm.

"You destroyed it?"

"No, I just returned it to what it once was. A fragment of green ore." He smiled at him. "Perhaps your mission of exiling and killing ore users is the whole reason you've failed to destroy the black ore." He gently removed the cardinal's hand and walked back to his own quarters.

CHAPTER THIRTY-SEVEN

"GET UP!" Nate was shaking the mattress.

"What is wrong with you?" He pulled the covers over his head in protest. "The council meeting isn't until this evening ... no need to get up!" He poked back out and checked the clock beside him. "Five thirty! Man, don't you remember what sleeping 'in' means. We don't even get up this early at the ranch. "

"You did sleep in! I could have come here at five when I was awake." Nate grabbed him by the head and shoved it into his pillow.

"Alright!" He flailed at Nate and missed. "Man, I was having a good dream, too!" He kept the sheets around his waist.

"About a brunette Brit, I don't doubt." Nate laughed, tossing Gabriel his jeans. "Get dressed!" Nate stepped into the hall, closing the door behind him.

He staggered out of the room, still half asleep. Nate held a tall glass of hot tea up to his nose for him to sniff. "Tastes awful but it'll help wake you up."

Having no energy to argue, Gabriel choked down the hot liquid. It sent shivers through his body and his face scrunched up involuntarily as the aftertaste hit him.

"You will be wide awake once that kicks in!" Nate gave him a pat.

He burped up something awful. "If it stays down."

They headed out of the sleeping quarters, towards the exit. Gabriel must have swiped his badge two dozen times, trying to get outside. Normally, moving around the facility wasn't difficult but security had turned from cautions to a hassle in preparation for the council meeting.

"I'll be happy when this is over." Nate pointed at a little red car. "Let's get out of here." Nate smiled, pushing Gabriel around to the left side of vehicle as they approached. "Other side, sleeping beauty."

They left the compound, passing through the last security check point and turned onto a wide stretch of road. Gabriel nestled into the small front seat to catch some more sleep.

Nate laughed. "That won't last."

Gabriel ignored the comment but soon the effects of the drink raced through his body. A minute later he sat up, giving up on a nap. "So, where have you been?" This was the first time he had any one-on-one time with Nate in the last week.

"Busy sorting out the mess we left back in the Denver."

"How's that going?"

"T.E.R.A.'s expanding … eating up everything to do with the ore. Heard you blew up the lab or something."

He put his hands up in defence. "That wasn't my fault. Blame Osho."

"He was pretty excited about the whole thing. Heard you're no longer considered an exile."

"The cardinal changed his mind did he?" He laughed. "Apparently, now we're useful."

"Well, at least we don't have to worry so much about you. I'm just happy you can deal with the black stuff." Nate smiled at him.

"It was a small shard – knocked me across the room. Anything bigger could be a problem." He wasn't excited about the results. "You believe the rumours?"

Nate shrugged. "Developing some kind of ore weapons? Probably nothing to worry about; if Osho can't crack that technology then I doubt anyone else can. The black stuff is highly explosive and unstable as hell. Even if you could weaponize it, you might blow yourself up just handling it." Nate imitated the explosion with his hands. "Like when we first started to dig it out. We lost so much machinery." He laughed.

"Should have left it in the ground. I would be back in Burlington with my family. Who knows where you would be." Gabriel shook his head.

They turned into a large abandoned stone quarry. The air became thick with dust as the little car came to a stop at the back of a hollowed out pit. A small table was already set up overlooking several targets; black silhouettes of bodies in different positions at various distances from the table. Gabriel stepped out of the car and followed Nate to the trunk.

"I know it's been awhile but I figure it's time you remembered how to use one of these." Nate took out a pistol and placed it in Gabriel's hand.

His heart quickened as the cold steel touched his skin. He hadn't handled a gun in months. The two of them had a history of training days – practising shooting and fighting on the ranch. Even Adin took part back in his younger days.

"Come on." Nate led him over to the table. "You remember the rules: Don't point it at me or yourself, always at the ground. Only put your finger on the trigger when you're ready to shoot, otherwise keep the safety on. We only go out to the targets together and the guns stay at the table, unloaded."

"I remember."Gabriel nodded at the familiar instructions and turned towards the targets, trying to focus, but he couldn't hide his smile as Nate explained the weapon.

"Got some new toys today. Little different from the rifles at home. That is a HVP Mark 6. Your standard military sidearm. The design on hand guns hasn't changed much since the cowboy days."

He pointed at the pistol. "Basic grip, firing hammer, and barrel. Now what has changed is what is inside."

Nate took the handgun from him and dismantled it into pieces on the table in seconds.

"The grip holds a hydrogen cell that feeds the magnetic rings in the barrel of the gun, the cells last about a year before you have to change them out." Nate picked up the barrel and handed it to him with a small flashlight.

"You see the rings inside? High powered magnets. These are what accelerate the bullet, making any drop in distance negligible."

"So … point and shoot?" Gabriel was eager to move past the theory lesson.

"No. You need to get used to the rhythm of the recoil as you fire but just focus on aiming … one shell at a time." Nate slid the barrel and the grip together, showing Gabriel how to release the slide on the barrel. He then picked up the magazine and popped out one of the shells for him to look at. "Alright, your magazine works on a simple rotator. You can hold 25 rounds. To load it just keep pushing the shells down and to the right until you can't anymore."

"Easy enough to remember."

"Now the bullet. Technology has made them smaller – thinner – but they still have the same hitting power as the old school copper heads. Gunpowder in the casing with accelerants painted into all the grooves along the bullet." He pointed closely to the thin black lines swirling down the head of the bullet. "These are like little rockets, causing the bullet to spin even faster. This, combined with the magnets, is how the bullets get to such a high velocity. Those are the basics. Let's do some shooting." Nate winked at him.

Gabriel stared down the thin sights of the pistol. He tried to remember to stay loose.

"Squeeze the trigger – don't pull it." Nate hovered beside him.

The pistol rocked back as the first round was fired. His arms weren't ready, spoiling his aim as he shot.

"Move with its rhythm. Let your arms absorb the shot and put the pistol right back to where it came from."

He focused on Nate's instruction.

He kept his eyes on the target – letting his body move with the gun as it kicked backward towards him. The pistol came right back to where he had started.

"Beautiful." Nate clapped. "Center of mass. Good shot."

"Thanks." He focused, sending another round of light at the black target.

"Good. Again. Faster."

Two more shots. His arms held steady, absorbing the kicks and returning the pistol to his sights each time.

"Alright. Now, 25 yard target. Three quick shots. Take a second between each shot, make them count."

One. The shot glowed as it left the barrel. Two. Gabriel breathed out. Three. Eyes on the target. The black target bucked backwards, as the final shot landed just inches from the other two.

"You're picking this up fast. Let's change it up." Nate pulled the pistol from his hand, replacing it with an assault rifle.

Gabriel shifted at the table to adjust for the size difference, grasping it with both hands.

"That's too easy. Let's move away from the table and get into a kneeling stance." Nate tapped his shoulder.

He let Nate guide his position on the ground, brushing away rocks under his knee. "Like this?"

"Yeah, that's good. Kneeling shots give you three points to be stable on." Nate gave him a shake. "Good. Feel yourself get pulled down into the position. You and the ground are the same thing."

Nate pressed the butt of the gun into his shoulder.

"Tuck it in, don't let the recoil move you as much on this one. It's not a pistol and it'll kick a lot more. Keep rigid – strong. Send out the rounds in bursts. Stop to aim and evaluate each time." Nate slid the clip into the bottom of the weapon. He flipped off the safety. "25 yards! Fire!"

The rifle rattled in Gabriel's arms, as he let out a burst of light at the target with a single squeeze of the trigger. He tightened his grip on the rough grooves of plastic. Breathing out for each burst, he focused, hitting the black cut-out with a spray of bullets.

"50 Yards!" Nate barked.

Gabriel twisted. He kept his toes and knee dug into the dirt, not lifting anything. The gun's small lunges tested his grip as each burst left the barrel.

"Again."

He stayed focused. Breathing. Stance. Squeeze the trigger. The bolts of light found their target.

"Think of your home!" Nate knelt beside him. "Fire!"

Gabriel shook his head, refocusing on the black target. The rounds left the gun abruptly, shaking his grip, hitting the target low.

"Think of your brother!" Nate bumped him. "Fire!"

Two more shots hit the black target but Gabriel could feel his aim was off. He tried to ignore Nate's shouting – focus on the target in the steel sights.

"They took Adin! Shoot them!" Nate's shout echoed in the empty quarry.

Thoughts flooded into his mind. He took aim, trying to remember his list. Breathe. Squeeze. The round of shots set him off balance. He shifted his feet to reposition.

"Faster! Your brother is in trouble! Faster!"

He couldn't ignore the thoughts of Adin filling his mind. Round after round kicked up the dirt around the target.

"Again, kill that target! Hold down that trigger!" Nate commanded.

Gabriel's arms filled with tension, as he held down the trigger, the continuous fire throwing his aim off. He failed to adjust. The gun jumped around as he tried to stare down the sights. Then it stopped. The final casing clinked to the ground beside him as it exited the chamber. He breathed out, his chest rising and falling. Nate carefully took the rifle from him. His hand was sore from the grip. He glared at Nate.

247

Nate cleared his throat. "Every bullet you send down the barrel carries a thought with it. If you can't control that, you can't control the shot. It's a tough lesson." He took the magazine out of the rifle and set both down on the table.

"Where is he?" Gabriel faced him.

Nate breathed out and shrugged. "We don't know."

"Have you even been looking?"

"Of course we've been looking!" Nate glared back at him.

"Well, give me something! Give me a reason to not think he's dead!"

"No one has filed a missing person's report. His apartment is still in his name. T.E.R.A. moved his vehicle into long term storage. They paid him last week! All his bills were paid on time this month!" Nate threw up his hands in frustration. "The systems all say he's alive and active. But we can't find him. No pictures, nothing. Not a glimpse of him anywhere."

Gabriel shook his head. "So, I just have to wait. Wonder if he's out there somewhere? What am I supposed to do in the mean time?"

Nate pointed his finger at him. "You do everything you have to, so we can go home."

Gabriel stayed silent, grinding his teeth

"We push ourselves. We fight. We take down whatever stands in our way. We do what the Church needs us to do, then we go home. They'll make sure we are safe. And once we get there, we will find him. No matter what! So, don't you give up!" Nate reached out and hugged him. "Don't ever give up."

Gabriel grabbed onto him, his lungs quivering as he drew in a deep breath. Nate was right. Everything here was temporary. This wasn't his home. He needed to fight. To never stop until he found Adin. Until they were both home.

The two stayed at the quarry until well into the afternoon – shooting, loading clip after clip, wreaking havoc on the black targets. Despite the hard lesson from Nate, Gabriel enjoyed the time; it reminded him of better days – good memories of the ranch.

Evening arrived as they returned to the facility. There was a buzz of activity as everyone prepared for the council's arrival. Gabriel spent most of his time by Nate and Osho, helping them gather notes and documents to present to the council on their findings about T.E.R.A. The three were summoned from Osho's office and preceded to the church's main sanctuary. They descended a small set of iron rod stairs, deep below the huge cathedral.

Security was tight. They passed through several armed guards, holding positions along the doorways and corridors below the sanctuary. By the time they had reached the meeting room Gabriel felt dizzy, lost in the maze they had taken to get to the final room. They were instructed to sit, taking spots around a large stone table that must have been built in the room three hundreds years ago. There was no way it could have fit through any of the doorways. The whole room was supported by stone blocks perfectly shaped, standing one on top of another, stretching into massive columns that came to a peak at the high vaulted ceiling. A huge fire roared in the enormous fireplace on the side of the room, giving the cold stone a more comfortable temperature. Another doorway on the far side of the room was closed, a sentry posted on each side, eyeing everyone who entered the room.

People filled the space in the room, taking seats around the great slab of stone, including Father Clarence and Cardinal Vincent who both nodded as they sat at the great table. More arrived. They lined the walls on small wooden benches. Claire entered and took her place, smiling at him. He turned back to the table to find Nate looking at him. "Pay attention."

The room quieted as the door everyone had entered through was shut and locked from the outside. At the same moment, the guarded door on the other side of the room was unlocked and opened. The guards in the room stood at full attention. Five men strolled through the doorway. Each was older than most of the people in the room, with silver hair peeking from under a crimson cap. The Patriarchs all wore long crimson robes with gold rosaries hanging down from a small pocket on the waist. They took their spots around the table efficiently, each allowing the one before him to sit before seating himself. Following behind them was a group of black-robed monks, shaven bald and carrying leather cases by their sides with ropes attached to them. They each stood behind a Patriarch and set the leather case on the stone table, opening it up for the Patriarch.

He remembered the quick lesson Dr. Osho had given him on the council. "There are always only five of the nine Patriarchs at the council meetings. The other four remain hidden, in case disaster strikes the meeting and the five are killed. The remaining four would elect a fifth member and the council would continue to function while they searched for new Patriarchs."

The monks called out their superior's name in sequence from left to right.

"Patriarch Romaniski."

"Patriarch Laurent."

"Patriarch Schmidt."

"Patriarch Goodwin."

"Patriarch Milani."

CHAPTER THIRTY-EIGHT

Patriarch Goodwin stayed standing, as the other Patriarchs took to their seats on the stone floor. The round room remained silent as he addressed everyone. Gabriel took one last look at Claire, then prepared himself to listen.

"We all know why we are here." The deep English accent of Patriarch Goodwin filled the room. "T.E.R.A. is positioning itself in Europe and this is of concern to the council. They are in opposition to our views and threaten our sanctity. Also, a possible threat has emerged in old Kazakhstan." He paused as the other four crimson-robed men responded with a series of "yes'" until each of them had agreed with the statement.

Gabriel's eyes wandered between each of the Patriarchs, studying their expressions as Patriarch Goodwin continued his speech. It was challenging not to despise them. Their beliefs would have put him to death just a week ago and now here he was, trying to help them. He needed to be calm and leave his emotions out of this discussion. In the end, all men make mistakes, he reminded himself, but not all men learn from them.

"Lastly, we find ourselves becoming united under a common goal with new friends, the Ingenius Pluris. They have chosen to stand with us, against the evil that is growing in this world. An evil that threatens the gift our Lord left behind to one day save us from our own actions, as he did before. And until his return, we will uphold the righteous and do battle against evil. The decisions before us tonight must be taken into careful consideration. While it is not our way to be aggressive, we will defend ourselves and all the Lord has given us." Goodwin was quite tall and thin and his robes hung from him like a tent. He sat down at the table.

"It's what must be done." Patriarch Laurent leaned forward to look at the other Patriarchs. His thin pointed moustache was trimmed perfectly and his thick hair was slicked back under his crimson cap.

Father Clarence stood up and clicked a small remote in his hands. A 3-D image cascaded down over the table from above. He was firm as he spoke, his voice not faltering. "Here is what we know. Most of our churches in North America are currently safe. The area is now considered to be under the complete control of T.E.R.A. We know they manipulate the government and will set the stage as they see fit so that they can rule."

Gabriel was shocked as the slide revealed hundreds of locations across North America. There were more offices than he had ever thought T.E.R.A. could have. Staring at all the dots he thought of Adin. *Could one of those be him?* The image faded and was replaced with a large map of Europe. Red dots spread out across it, one after another, revealing dozens of new offices and facilities.

"T.E.R.A. has set up new facilities across Europe within the last 72 hours. While most of these pose no threat to us, their intentions here do. This is considered our number one priority and it cannot be ignored. They will begin to put more pressure on the European Commonwealth to agree to increases in ore usage by all sectors." The slides started to scroll through 3-D images of some of the new manufacturing equipment being released by T.E.R.A. "If they succeed in their plans, they will have control of all manufacturing in Europe." Father Clarence sat down and waited for a response.

The room remained silent. Gabriel focused on Father Clarence's final statement, Adin forgotten. Patriarch Goodwin stood up and addressed the room again. "Things are beginning to break down in the European government. While we still have influence, we will not be listened to for much longer if T.E.R.A. is allowed to expand. They will poison this land and we will not be able to stop it. We are all here to be stewards of the ore and protect what is ours."

Patriarch Schmidt spoke up, his voice rising. "They must not be allowed any foothold in Europe." The passion in his voice was unmistakable. He was clean shaven and wore small rounded glasses – he looked more like a man of science than a man of god.

Patriarch Milani's brows rose. "Risk open warfare with them? Is that what you are willing to gamble?" He was oriental with a very round face and he looked like a toad when he frowned.

Father Clarence stood back up. "We have the resources. Strike them now before they continue to grow!" He slammed his hand against the table, despite Cardinal Vincent's attempt to hold his hand back.

Patriarch Milani's lip curled. "Your priesthood doesn't hide your years of war-mongering very well. If we strike, we put ourselves at the edge of the abyss. It could push us into war."

Patriarch Laurent now stood. "And what kind of power does T.E.R.A. hold? We have operatives who can confirm they research things in secret and have done so for years. How would we fight that?"

"If action is taken against T.E.R.A. and I do mean 'if' ..." Patriarch Goodwin looked around the room, "it must happen in secret. We cannot openly stand against them unless we have the European Commonwealth behind us."

Patriarch Romaniski finally spoke in a thick Russian accent. His full brown beard hid most of his face. "A well placed strike – fast and direct – could slow them for now but it will take war to kill the beast."

"Our way is not war." Patriarch Milani objected.

"We also do not allow evil to flourish!" Patriarch Romaniski glared at him.

Patriarch Goodwin stood. "SILENCE!" He slammed the leather case against the great stone table, causing a deafening slap in the stone room. "We will not get anywhere unless we are united in our decision!"

"May I speak?" Dr. Osho raised his hand.

"Of course, doctor." The Patriarch bowed, giving him the floor, and sat back in his chair.

"The IP has always tried to find the good in the ore, looking past the evil. We believe there are ways to live in balance with the ore, use it to feed our civilization, without damaging what is left of this fragile planet. However, I have personally seen what T.E.R.A. is capable of back in North America. I am sorry but if you do not take a stand against them, you will certainly lose. No one will be allowed to live in harmony with T.E.R.A. Their greed for power will not allow it."

"We all agree with your heart-felt statement doctor, but how does one take down an organization as large as T.E.R.A.?" Patriarch Goodwin shook his head.

"To take down a giant, you need but one well-placed stone. I believe you all know the story?" Osho smiled gently.

Nate stood up beside Osho. "We've found a crack in their wall, if you will, in T.E.R.A's operations." He nodded to Father Clarence to activate a new image over the huge table. A large blue globe with red arrows indicated movements around the world.

"T.E.R.A. is stretched thin. Too thin. They are over-extending themselves as they push for rapid expansion around the world." Nate pointed to the many red dots moving across North America, as well as Europe. "They are transporting ore and equipment all over the country. The new manufacturing laws in North America require the use of ore technology. Several new facilities are opening in Europe. They are also integrating several smaller companies into their corporate tree as they assume control of the energy market in North America. This is leaving holes in their security systems."

Nate motioned the projector off. "A large enough distraction could disrupt their chain of command enough that we could scramble a series of smaller operations throughout North America, as well as Europe, targeting key materials, particularly the ore shipments. If we succeed in collecting enough ore, it would paralyze them for a short period of time forcing them to retreat back to North America and allowing us time to fortify our position here."

"You are asking us to organize a lot in very little time." Patriarch Goodwin crossed his arms.

"Not necessarily. My teams are already set-up in North America using what is left of the IP's network. If these positions could be strengthened with additional soldiers, we could attack dozens of areas in a single moment." Nate faced him.

"And those targets – how would they be chosen?" Patriarch Laurent frowned at Nate.

"The new companies T.E.R.A is forcing under their control still have to integrate their computer systems into T.E.R.A.'s global network. This presents some vulnerability in their networks. With so many new users being put into the system, it could be overloaded. We already have people in place to hack the network and discover their movements. We then simply need to disrupt the signals to all the shipments, sending them off course." Nate smiled. "Then we wait for them to walk into our traps."

"Impressive, Mr. Reinhart," Patriarch Romaniski spoke up. "But what target would be the fulcrum of this attack? What do you plan to do to focus their attention? What would blind them enough to give you the time you needed to succeed? I'm sure reinforcements would arrive quickly."

"The IP itself." Dr. Osho volunteered the answer. "If we let them believe they have found what they missed in their raid on us, I guarantee they will put substantial resources into getting it. We have a series of caches hidden by one of our founders. If we combined several of the locations into one single 'Jackpot' T.E.R.A. wouldn't pass up the opportunity to get their hands on that quantity of ore."

Patriarch Milani stared at Osho. "If you fail, all you have done is given them more ore."

"We won't fail." Nate stood beside Osho.

Osho removed his glasses. "You will not see another opportunity like this again ... and even if we succeed on 60 percent of the targets, we will come out ahead. We will have more ore than they find in the cache."

Patriarch Goodwin grinned from ear to ear. "What must be done?"

Osho put his glasses back on and smiled at Nate. "Most of the plan has already been put in place but we need some additional resources. Mainly we need soldiers."

Nate crossed his arms, nodding. "Our requests are not negotiable. We need them to succeed."

"Careful of your pride, Mr. Reinhart. We, who are present, may agree but our missing brothers may not." Patriarch Goodwin rose, collecting a sealed envelope from one of the monks. He drew a small dagger and slit the seal – read it and handed it to the other Patriarchs.

"You may have your resources but this operation will be done from the shadows. Only those involved may know about the attack." Patriarch Goodwin frowned. "Secrecy is key. We will discuss this more later. Now, what shall be done about the threat in Kazakhstan?" He opened the question to the room.

"Thank you." Osho bowed at him and sat down with Nate.

"The site is an old weapons factory outside Kazakhstan." Father Clarence stood, activating the projector. A satellite shot of the compound glowed across the stone table. "Activity there has spiked. Ore shipments are coming in daily, and the facility is being retrofitted for some kind of weaponry assignment. Our latest reports say the time table has been accelerated and the project should be completed within days, not weeks, as we originally expected. Also, a large number of refugees have been moved into the facility. We are still working to find out why they are there. We are gathering more information daily, but if we allow this facility to become fully operational, we will eventually have to face what they are building there."

"What of the rumors?" Patriarch Milani stood. "Are the weapons designed to use the ore?"

Father Clarence sighed and shook his head. "We don't know. It has been difficult to find out about all the ore shipments but, yes, we do know they have all types of ore on site. Including black."

"The Kazakhstan weapon facility could also be assaulted if the European Commonwealth acknowledged it as a national threat. They would allow the church to handle the situation. If we are seen as preoccupied with it, the attack on T.E.R.A. would draw less suspicion, hiding our tracks," Nate pointed out.

Patriarch Romaniski laughed deep in his belly. "You are a soldier aren't you? Let's say you succeed at getting through the security at Kazakhstan. What then? You can't detonate the store of ore. You don't even know whose base you're attacking!"

"With government support, we would be sanctioned to assume control of the compound." Patriarch Goodwin eyed his counterpart carefully.

"What of reinforcements? Could be a commonwealth facility for all we know." Patriarch Milani joined Patriarch Romaniski's side.

"No." Goodwin shook his head. "We know for a fact it is not with the European Commonwealth. They see it as a threat as well and they leave the stewardship of the ore to us."

"The owners of the facility are the threat, not the technology and ore within," Patriarch Laurent said slyly.

"You know the laws, Laurent. Anything involving the black ore is sealed away and never disrupted again. That is the reality of our stewardship. We will not be using any weapons we find." Patriarch Goodwin spoke firmly, forcing the other Patriarch to bow his head, acknowledging his mistake.

"The black ore could be destroyed at the —"

Nate was quickly cut off by the mockery of Patriarch Romaniski. "Destroy the ore! You must be joking. There is nothing that can destroy it! Even if you broke it into hundreds of pieces the poison still remains."

"With all due respect, you are wrong." Dr. Osho stood up. He poured the contents of an envelope onto the grand table – a simple sand with a light green sheen.

The Patriarchs eyed the substance and stared back at Osho, curious.

"See this? This is a simple crystallized ore void of any energy … any radiation at all." He picked up the fine dust with his bare hands dropping it onto the table. "This is all that remains when the black ore is properly destroyed."

Pandemonium broke out in the room. Mockery, shouts, and questions filled the air as everyone demanded Dr. Osho explain himself. Patriarch Goodwin raised his hand, quieting the room as he spoke, "Why were we not informed of this before?"

"Because we only discovered that it could be done yesterday." Osho bowed his head briefly. "The power to destroy the ore lies within this young man." He rested his hand on Gabriel's shoulder.

"They are lying!" Patriarch Romaniski barked. "He's an ore user. Why would he destroy his own power?"

Gabriel glared at the man. "The ore has destroyed my life. I would gladly be rid of it."

"The ore is our future, we only want to destroy what has been polluted." Patriarch Milani shook his head.

"This young man wants a reckoning. Why should we trust him with anything?" Patriarch Schmidt's eyes drilled into him.

"Because by the time we find another option, there won't be any time left." Dr. Osho pointed at the table. "The proof is right there. Question it all you like."

"They are trying to deceive us!" Patriarch Romaniski remained hostile.

One voice rose above the room. Claire ran over to Gabriel and

Osho. "It is true!" She faced Patriarch Goodwin. "I saw it with my own eyes. They are telling the truth."

Gabriel felt indebted to her. She was standing up for him to the Patriarchs, asking them to trust his strength.

Laurent looked down his nose at her. "Why would we believe an exile?"

"Watch your tongue, Laurent. Ms. Bennett will be counted as a witness." Goodwin glared at the other Patriarch.

"Then you may also count me." Cardinal Vincent stood up. "While I was not present – I have seen enough to believe their claim."

The room remained silent for several moments as the Patriarchs whispered amongst themselves. The door the Patriarchs had entered through burst open, and a monk entered carrying another sealed envelope. The monk handed it to Patriarch Goodwin who broke the seal and read the message then passed it to the other Patriarchs for confirmation.

"Our missing brothers of the council are eager for a demonstration. As am I." Patriarch Goodwin stared at Gabriel.

Dr. Osho nodded his head. "Of course, I can prepare a containment room and we can –" He was cut off by Patriarch Goodwin.

"No preparation, we need to see it now. We must know he can do this by command, that it is not a lengthy process." Nods of agreement came from around the room.

Dr. Osho looked to Gabriel. "You will have to control the blast – surround it completely."

"I'll try." Gabriel nodded.

"No." Nate looked him in the eyes. "You have to make this work. We do whatever we have to, remember.?"

"Right." He remembered his commitment. Anything to find a way home.

Nate moved several others, including Claire, away from Gabriel as Osho pulled out a silver steel container and placed it on the table.

"I thought they might want to see it so I came prepared." He smiled as he placed Gabriel's hand on the case and stepped away from him.

The container was the same as before. It contained a smaller shard, about the size of his thumb. Relieved, Gabriel removed the clear protective casing from around the sleek black shard. The effect was immediate. He could see everyone in the room looking suddenly drained, as the shard was exposed. Bright white gloves formed around both his hands. The room filled with muttering as he tried to stay focused. He picked up the shard, covering the whole thing in both his cupped hands. The Patriarchs whispered amongst one another.

Gabriel started to push energy from his chest into the small black stone, causing his hands to grow brighter and brighter, blinding those who were too close. The reaction was close to complete, the black shard vibrating in his hands. Another globe of white light pulsed into the air, circling around his hands as he added extra protection. He closed his eyes. A muffled bang erupted in the room and Gabriel's arms absorbed an invisible shock. The thin shield disappeared first then the two gloves retreated from around his hands. He opened them.

A dull blue dust rested in his palms. He poured the grains of bluish sand on the table, covering the green dust left there. He swallowed hard, breathing in deeply as he tried to control his nerves.

Dr. Osho smiled and leaned over the table cupping some of the sand into his palm and dropping it back on to the table. "Satisfied?"

Each of the Patriarchs leaned over in amazement, staring closely at the blue and green sand resting before them. Some lifted the sand into their palms, dropping it back on the table. The room filled with chatter until again Patriarch Goodwin raised his hand to silence them all. He looked at the other Patriarchs who nodded in agreement.

"Contact the Commonwealth. We need to speak to them."

CHAPTER THIRTY-NINE

THE NEXT DAY WAS A WHIRLWIND OF ACTIVITY. Secret communications were sent to the remaining IP members in North America, strengthening their numbers with operatives of the Church. Access into the T.E.R.A. mainframe was acquired, as they broke through security weak points. Operatives waited to disable T.E.R.A.'s central communication hub. The trap was set. Targets were selected all over Europe and North America. Gabriel stuck close to Nate and Father Clarence. They studied local maps and roadways for each target, choosing the optimal position to attack. Exposed stretches of isolated road, manufacturing facilities and warehouses were all picked apart, as they determined the best areas to strike. Dr. Osho coordinated locations where the teams could retreat to after their assaults and to hide the precious cargo. Safe houses were set up within churches all across North America with hidden vaults inside for the ore.

A final secure meeting with the council was called to review the operation. The lights in the room dimmed, as Gabriel found a piece of wall to lean against, while Osho took a seat near the front of the room. The wall at the front of the room glowed with red letters. A list broke apart and reformed under three columns.

Father Clarence started the meeting. "These are the targets for this operation; 31 in total. Our operatives have hacked into T.E.R.A.'s mainframe through the exposed networks of the acquired companies in North America. From there they can attack the network and disrupt any communications. This will give us the time we need to strike. Twelve of the targets are ore transport trucks, heading to manufacturing plants around North America. Teams are positioned to hit them on open stretches of highway, well outside of any of the cities and far from any additional support. Fifteen of the targets are new laboratories. Teams included in this leg of the operation will be straight assault, demolition, and ore retrieval. The IP will handle the majority of these with their people. The last four listed are testing sites for experimentation. These are human testing facilities – which is now completely legal in North America. I know this might be a challenge for some of you, but the goal is to destroy these facilities. Minimal efforts will be made to save any prisoners. From what information we have, most of them are already lost. May the Lord forgive us."

Mumbles and whispers filled the room, but no one objected. Gabriel could see everyone knew what had to be done and no one questioned it.

As Father Clarence took his seat, Dr. Osho cleared his throat and stood up. "Soon, we will expose the bait. Everything depends on this. The leak about a major cache of ore the IP had kept hidden will trigger the attack. Judging by the amount of resources put into the first attack on the IP, and knowing T.E.R.A., they will react immediately. We expect them to divert a large piece of their team to assault the cache we have set up. We've developed an elaborate series of defences that should slow them down."

Dr. Osho returned to his seat and Patriarch Goodwin took the floor. Gabriel was surprised to see him dressed, not in his red robes, but in black. Large brass buttons ran down the front and a red sash was tied around his waist.

The Patriarch took the time to look around the room at each

person before speaking. "There are going to be causalties – for T.E.R.A. and ourselves. Our Lord will forgive us, but this is an act of war. All teams are instructed to shoot to kill, making sure no witnesses are left. If a brother in arms falls beside you, you will bring him home. The operation needs to be as covert as possible, leaving no trace of our involvement. We cannot risk this becoming open war." He ended by bowing his head and saying a prayer in Latin. Gabriel couldn't help but think about Goodwin's words. What sacrifices would be required to get the ore into the hands of good, honest leaders? He just wanted to end the tyranny attached to the ore. To be able to walk away from this, and leave it all behind.

As the prayer finished, Gabriel stayed against the wall. The room emptied leaving only a few remaining. An image of the weapon facility appeared on the wall. He walked down to sit in the front with the remaining twelve soldiers. Father Clarence handed each of them a small booklet. It mapped every wall in the weapons facility.

Nate cleared his throat. "Memorize that. The initial assault will begin from the European Commonwealth. Our team will secretly enter the base. Once inside we split up – Gabriel will enter the vaults alone to deal with any black ore. The rest of us support him and find out who is behind the facility. Those beside you are all that we will have. The Commonwealth will not recognize our actions or protect us in anyway if we fail."

Nate's words scared Gabriel. His heart raced as he imagined what he might encounter on his way to destroy the main black ore supply. The amount of the black ore in the facility was still unknown. He was certain he could dispose of several large shards but didn't know how it would affect him. Osho predicted there would be dozens of samples. The largest would only be as big as a bowling ball, which seemed like a challenge – but not impossible. He hoped.

The meeting continued for another two hours, becoming a blur in his mind as he sat in the room going over the 3-D images of the facility, listening to Nate lecture them on how important each of their tasks were.

Finally allowed to leave, he retreated down to the vaults. They were the only vacant hallways in the whole structure where he could find some peace. Unfortunately, the guard didn't quite understand.

"I'm not here to take any of the ore. How many times do I have to say that?" Gabriel repeated himself again for the guard. "I was looking for a quiet place to relax, have you been upstairs lately?"

The guard didn't blink. "If you have no business here, please head back upstairs."

Claire stepped up beside Gabriel and smiled at the guard.

"Ms. Bennett, do you need access into the vaults?" The guard returned her smile, ignoring Gabriel.

"Yes, I just need to get some samples for some testing." She held out her badge. "I can take Mr. Roberts in with me."

The guard frowned and stared at Gabriel.

"I can get Patriarch Goodwin's approval if there is a problem?" she suggested politely.

"No." The guard shrugged. "You've been given open access to the vaults, I wouldn't want to bother the Patriarch at this time."

"Good." She smiled again and took Gabriel by the arm. He stayed quiet, enjoying the moment with her. She led them to a large steel door with a keypad on the side of it. A small lens stared at them pulsing with blue light. Claire entered a sequence of numbers as blue light beamed from the lens – scanning her face. The door popped free from its lock and slid sideways, revealing a huge steel room filled with piles of ore that glowed in the darkness.

Gabriel's mouth dropped as he stared into the room. Never had he seen so much ore in one place. Their colours pulsed and shimmered in the darkness. Some were as small as a shoe, others large boulders that rose to his knee. Several wall-mounted lights flickered to life as they entered the room, revealing even more pieces of ore hiding in the corners. All his mind could think of was the black ore, rooms and rooms of it. How would he ever destroy that much? It would kill him.

"This is one of the largest collections of ore in all of Europe."

She strolled through the pieces. "We've found that the blue, red, and green ores can naturally charge one another over time."

"They do?" He walked after her, twisting and turning as he found his own path through the ore.

"Well, not enough to counteract any large draw on them, so I guess it's more of a trickle." She touched a green boulder beside her. "These are all still rough cuts as we call them ..." She bent down and picked up a small piece. "See?" Pieces of stone still attached to it.

"I never realized that." The ores pulsed brighter as he navigated through the room – each stone somehow sensing the power in him.

"You have quite the gift when it comes to the ore." She watched the ore brighten around him.

"Gift or curse?" He placed his hand on a large blue shard, causing it to glow brightly. Condensed water formed on his hand. He smiled at her, shaking it dry.

She said nothing as she headed back to the vault door. She closed it and clicked off the lights along the walls. "I love how they glow."

"I see the ore doesn't bother you either." He dropped down to the floor, resting his back against the wall.

"It's peaceful to me." She made her way over to him, her dark hair gleaming in different hues as she approached. Her eyes reflected the colors around the room.

"When did you first find out?"

"I happened to find some stored in our house." She smiled, sitting down beside him.

"Sounds like a familiar story ..." He thought of Kyrie playing with a small shard as a child.

"What do you mean?"

"Just a friend who found out the same way." He smiled.

"So, your father discovered all of this." She pointed to the sea of colours in front of him.

"Yeah, he did." He sighed. "Although now I wish he hadn't ... I bet he would have wished for that too."

She frowned at him. "Why would you say that?"

"'Cause we wouldn't be here, life would have been normal …
he would still be alive." He faked a smile to hide his pain.

"I guess your life isn't so simple, is it?"

He stayed silent as he illuminated a red shard in front of them.
It cast a breath of heat towards them like a small fire.

She stretched out her hand to feel its warmth. "How did you
find out about your gift over the ore?"

"It was kinda forced on me." He pulled down his shirt collar to
reveal the tip of the white ore in his chest.

She froze. "How?"

"I had a bad day. A tornado to be exact." His lips twisted. "I
woke up the day after, with this stuck in my chest."

"I've never seen white ore." She pulled his collar down further,
running her fingertips over it, clearly amazed.

He was stunned by her boldness. Her blue eyes reflected the
glowing ore. He waited, not saying anything, holding his breath as
her fingers brushed against his skin.

"I'm sorry." She laughed and pulled her hand back quickly.

"It's alright. It's part of me, no getting rid of it!" He straightened out his collar.

He reached out again, touching a red shard for a breath of
heat. He felt at peace sitting there. He could feel the energy moving around him – flowing from shard to shard. He shut his eyes and
rested his head against the wall, absorbing the moment.

After several minutes of silence, Claire spoke. "How do you
feel about tomorrow?"

"Numb, I guess." He opened his eyes and looked at her.

"Numb?" She shook her head. "I would be so scared!"

"It has to be done. It's my purpose … my father's purpose. It's
something I have to do."

"Your father's?" She rested her head on her knees, which she
had pulled up to her chest. She looked cold.

He reached for the red shard and this time, left his hand on it. The air around them heated up quickly. "You know one of the last things he said about the ore before he died? That it needed to be destroyed."

"Destroyed? Maybe the black, but the others are so important!" Claire moved closer to the red shard.

"Are they?" He stared at her.

"Yes!" She frowned. "We don't have much energy left to keep things going in this world ... we need the ore to survive."

"Really? Do we?" He stared at her, his jaw tense. "No one will ever stop using it. No one will even try to find other solutions. Maybe if we had to change, if it was no longer an option, we might be better off."

She stared at the ground, avoiding his eyes. "My father and the church are trying to utilize the ore only for good, just like the IP is. It's a gift from God, left behind to us."

"I'm sorry but in my life the ore is a curse ... too many have died for it already." He stood up. "The ore has taken my father, my mother, and possibly my brother from me ... they are all dead. That isn't much of a gift if you ask me!" He drew a ragged breath. "A month ago I was in a cage, being treated like an experiment because of this thing in my chest ... people were being killed and beaten to discover the 'potential' of the ore. I have no home ... everything I own sits in a bag in my room, nothing but death and pain come with the ore ... it has to be destroyed!"

"I'm sorry ..." She spoke softly.

He sighed, running his hands through his hair. "No ... I'm sorry ... that isn't fair of me." He knelt back down beside her. "I was out of line. I am just so tired of how everyone treats the ore, and those who have a connection to it. I just want it all to stop."

"You don't have to be sorry." She touched his hand. "Losing someone you love is hard. But there are still those left around you that need you." She let go of his hand and stared at a piece of green ore, her fingers tracing its shape. "Patriarch Goodwin was a Bishop when he fell in love with my mother. He repented and left her. I was still young when she got sick,. She was dying. He came rushing back. He tried to treat her with a shard of green ore, hoping it would heal her. It killed her so fast. He never forgave himself. I guess as my father he was obligated to care for me but that caused problems. So, I was left alone with the nuns as an exile. His work with the ore and the church consumed him. I barely talk to him anymore. Most days I don't even know where he is."

He could feel the pain in her voice. It trembled as she kept talking. "If the ore is used properly we could save so many. The church would see the world renewed. Isn't that worth keeping it?"

Time to change the subject. "Where will you be tomorrow?"

She smiled. "Where it's safe … my father wouldn't have me involved, even if I wanted to be there."

"Will I see you again? Who knows? Maybe I will have changed my mind." He smiled at her.

"I would like that." She leaned over to him, kissing him gently on the check.

His heart stirred and he slowly turned his head, pressing his lips gently against hers. She took a deep breath, pulling away ever so slightly. He kissed her again, his body leaned into hers, his head feeling dizzy as his chest grew with heat. The ore all around him suddenly flared with light.

She rested her forehead against his. "Please, be safe tomorrow."

"Destroying a bunch of black ore. What can be safer?" He smiled.

She faked a smile and reached out for his hand. "I hope you're right."

Hand in hand, the two walked out of the peaceful room, in silence.

CHAPTER FORTY

Gabriel and Nate left Saint Petersburg in the dark morning hours of the next day. The small plane they boarded took them to a remote airstrip inside Kazakhstan. Gabriel did his best to sleep most of the trip, trying to keep calm during the bumpy flight. Upon arriving they off-loaded the plane's cargo into a waiting van and drove three hours on dirt roads to their final stop. It was a small building in the middle of the woods, miles from anywhere.

A pair of priests hustled to set up a remote command centre for Nate as Gabriel stood out of the way, not sure what to do. He watched an old clock on the wall tick minute after minute away, getting closer to the strike time later that evening. This single attack would trigger dozens around the world and slow T.E.R.A.'s expansion for sure. That was an admirable mission but not where his heart was. To him the only solution was to destroy the ore, to remove the reason behind all of this. This world would find another path – perhaps a return to simpler times. Despite his fondness for the ore in his chest, he wished it had all stayed in the ground.

He wandered into a closet-sized room that branched off from the main room of the building. It offered a quiet place he could work out his thoughts. He only had the facilities layout that Father Clarence had given him – each page a different tint, separating them by floors. His destination was on the lowest of them. Everything would be prepared for him before the strike time but sitting there, he wished for a distraction. Nothing was in the room to distract him so he went back to the layout.

It highlighted the most direct routes to stairwells, access panels, and any other route to the next floor down – he did his best to memorize it. His job was simple. Destroy as much of the black ore as possible, while remaining strong enough to escape. It was a task he was more than willing to do, but inside, he was terrified. How big would the pieces be? How much could he truly withstand? If he couldn't destroy it then the future he wanted was impossible. Maybe God had designed it that way, a final reminder to a technological world that we are not our own masters.

The premises became quieter as they got closer to the strike time. Fewer and fewer people were left. Nate constantly poked his head into the closet to give him a quick jab or grin. As long as he could hear Nate's voice, it seemed easier to be alone in the room.

"Still here?" Nate stepped into the room once more, carrying a small black duffle bag, like the one he always travelled with. He set it down on the table and leaned on the flat surface.

Gabriel sat up, pleased to see him. Being alone only left him with his fear to think about. "I've got nowhere to go. You ever think about things before all of this? No worry about being killed around the next corner?"

Nate shrugged. "I guess, when I find the time. There's nothing I can say to make what we are about to do okay … It's scary. What happens in the next 24 hours is going to play out across the world. It's our ticket home, a non-negotiable one. If we can stop T.E.R.A and keep things safer here, we get to go home. I've already spoken with Cardinal Vincent."

Gabriel smiled. Nate's words always seemed to set things on the right path. "So you're scared too?" The tension in his stomach was eating away at him.

"Me?" Nate made a face at him. "Nah, I just said that so you would feel better!"

He laughed. "I appreciate the lie."

Nate pushed the bag out of the way as he sat down on the table. "I've seen you do some amazing things. And in the end – all of the tight spots you were in – you came out, okay. Hell! Bullets bounce off your hands!"

He grabbed Gabriel's shoulder giving him a small shake, then looked into his eyes. "I'm not going to be far from you. We will be in radio contact the whole time. You just focus on blowing up as much of that black ore as you can, I'll worry about everything else. We're going to do this and get home."

"Good to know." He squeezed Nate's hand on his shoulder.

"It is good to know! This is what I do!" Nate laughed, changing the mood and grabbing the bag on the table."Okay." He unzipped the bag. "We got some gear in here for you."

He began pulling things out and tossing them on the table in front of Gabriel as he listed what they were. "Pants ... shirt ... vest ... helmet ... boots ... hell, I even put some socks and change of under- wear in here; all in black camo!" The pile of clothes made a pile of dark greys and black stripes, all blending together with one another.

"Alright ... see this vest." Nate showed him. "Radio all dialled in for you. Earpiece – works as a mic too." He began opening the pockets. "Some flares, a small light, your electronic magic key, snap lights ... there's some rations here ... first aid kit in this pouch but I don't think you will be using it much." He winked.

Gabriel grabbed the vest, opening the pockets, checking everything out. He tried it on over his shirt. An empty holster rested under the arm. He looked back to Nate. "I think you forgot something."

Nate barely smiled at the joke, looking quite serious. "No. Not this time. I don't want you in this fight. You need to just stay behind cover. Stay hidden. Let me and my team do our job, if we get into a fire fight. I don't want the other side to even know you exist ... if they don't know you're there, they won't aim for you."

He nodded. "Alright."

"Good!" Nate grabbed him by the back of the neck and pulled him in for a hug. "You just stay safe." Nate held on to him, his hand giving him a strong pat on the back. "Nothing crazy, alright?" He pulled Gabriel back, holding his face. "You're all the family I got. I'm not losing you."

Gabriel's eyes stung with tears. He grabbed onto Nate's shoulders, trying to keep his emotions inside. "I'm afraid."

Nate nodded in agreement. "I know kid ... we all are." They hugged, thumping each other on the back. "You get changed and ready. I'll be back for you in an hour. Then we move out."

Nate left the room and Gabriel changed into his gear. Everything fit, right down to the boots. He sat down on the bed, drumming on the mattress under him. The clock still showed thirty minutes until Nate would be ready to leave. He lay back on the bed, leaving his feet still touching the ground. He stared at the discoloured ceiling, eventually closing his eyes.

His thoughts drifted back to his family. His parents in each others' arms, laughing, no fear in their eyes. His dad's long dark hair hanging down over his face, his mom resting her head against his chest. Her arms wrapped around him as he kissed the top of her head. The image settled his heart. Gabriel thought of Adin. Not the Adin in a pressed black suit but a younger version – running through the fields in a raggedy T-Shirt that read "I love rocks" on the back of it. He called out to Gabriel, telling him to keep up, laughing as he ran through the endless sun and tall grass. His hair hung over his face, lifting in the wind. His face was flecked with dirt, his cheeks covered with blonde peach fuzz in the golden light. Gabriel choked on a sob at the image of his brother continuing off into the distance. He might never be found. Tears rolled down his face, as he struggled to come to terms with that image of his brother leaving him behind as he ran happily into the bright horizon.

Adin was lost. Just like his father had been to T.E.R.A. ten years earlier. Tears wet his face. He let them take their course down his face. Adin was gone. The tears slowed, finally. Mourn later – now was not the time. He sat up. The pain still fresh in his heart but his mind now focused on one purpose – destroy the ore.

CHAPTER FORTY-ONE

GABRIEL ENTERED THE MAIN ROOM OF THE BUILDING IN THE
WOODS. He found Nate giving orders, marching back and forth.
Nate's face was smeared with black paint and he looked ready for war
– a sub machine gun dangled across his overloaded vest of tricks. A
pistol was strapped to his leg. He wore the same black and grey camo.

"Once you're finished, you leave nothing behind. There must
be no trace of us left in this building … take everything with you."
Nate pointed to all the electronic equipment in the room.

The priest nodded. "Yes, Sir."

"Good." Nate looked up at the clock, then at Gabriel. He
roughly grabbed at Gabriel's vest, checking out his gear.

Gabriel smiled and allowed the inspection. "Nice makeup."
He grinned.

"Funny!" Nate smacked Gabriel in the stomach. He flinched
as Nate smeared paint across his face, leaving four sticky lines on it.

Nate spun him around and pushed him towards the doorway.
"No traces left!" Nate hollered as they left the priest alone with all
the equipment.

Gabriel stepped aside, letting Nate take the lead. He followed Nate's back in the dim light as they entered a small staircase that wound deep into the ground. Nate clicked on a light, illuminating the space in blue. The tunnel the staircase led them to smelled of rot and Gabriel felt the splash of small puddles as they continued down it. After a couple hundred yards, they stepped out into the fresh night air. It was cool as they ran up into the woods, where an unmarked jeep waited for them. No one said anything as they got in. The ride was short, only a couple of miles under the thick cover of the woods.

The jeep abruptly stopped at a large clearing surrounded with trees where a small helicopter waited for them. They jogged towards it, as the jeep disappeared back into the wooded darkness.

Gabriel climbed into the small cabin, barely big enough for the two of them. Nate hit the pilot on the shoulder signalling him to take off. The pilot powered up the machine – the blades started spinning overhead. He made sure that he was buckled in as they began to lift off the ground and pulled on a headset. The small craft rose high into the air, leaving his stomach back on the ground. As they crested the tree line, the small open craft surged forward at an alarming speed. The pilot stayed low, skilfully cutting between some of the taller trees. Gabriel stared at the ground below as it passed by in flashes and focused on keeping his stomach calm.

"Sir!" The pilot's voice came through their headsets. "Teams Alpha, Bravo, and Charlie have engaged the base at the southwest corner of the structure." He pointed out at the flashes of small explosions and streaming bright lines of bullets in the blackness several miles away.

"Good." Nate leaned forward. "Resistance?"

"Light so far, the enemy has barricaded themselves inside the walls of the facility returning fire like we expected. Standard ammunition, nothing heavy and no signs of ore being used."

"What about Delta?" Nate held on to a bar over their heads, as they began to bank towards the fighting in the distance.

"They are on the north side, completely undetected, awaiting you and Mr. Roberts."

"Get us there!" Nate commanded. He then turned to Gabriel and attached a small carabiner to the back of his vest.

"What's that?" Gabriel hollered into the mic.

"It's for when you jump out of this thing!" Nate smiled devilishly at him.

"What!" He swallowed. Hard.

The helicopter swung low into a small opening above the tree line, just outside of the fighting. Coming to a smooth hover the pilot gave them a signal. Nate motioned for Gabriel to take off the head set, put his helmet on and unbuckle his belt – leaving him very unsteady in the hovering chopper. Nate then yelled "Out you go!" and pushed him out of the open cockpit.

Gabriel's heart jumped high into his throat as he began to free fall from the chopper. He felt his chest tighten, caught by his vest. Steadily, he descended into the darkness below. Nate came zipping up to him and passed him, a huge grin on his face in the weak light. An uneasy minute passed until his feet finally met Nate's hands as he neared the ground. Nate unhooked him with a quick jerk. He fell to the ground, unsteady on his feet, waiting for his stomach to catch up. Nate knelt down beside him, snickering and patting him on the back as the chopper pulled away.

The chopper's stutter faded away, replaced by the popping noises of distant gunfire. Gabriel stood up as Nate quickly adjusted his radio, and heard Nate's breath in his ear.

"Little much." Gabriel pointed to his ear. "It's kinda loud."

Nate put a finger over his lips and said to him in a whisper that boomed in his ear. "You will need to hear me over the gunfire. Now, keep up."

Nate turned on a device attached to his arm and positioned a thin green lens over one of his eyes. He looked around at the darkness, then turned Gabriel and pushed him to march forward into the unknown. Gabriel stumbled towards a nearby bush, his eyes not fully adjusted to the lack of light. The bush he was heading towards twisted around and stared at him. He froze.

"Keep going, Gabriel." A voice echoed in his ear. He recognized Father Clarence's voice. The 'bush'.

Nate moved from behind him, quickly pushing him towards the Father and whispering, "Everyone move ... together."

The three began to creep through the woods towards the flashes of light now only several hundred yards away. They made a distinct turn away from the fire fight, using the dark woods to mask their movements. Nate soon signalled to slow their pace as they turned back in their original direction. They continued to creep through the small bushes and raised roots of the old trees around them. Nate drew his sidearm and took point. Gabriel followed the dark silhouette of Nate's back. As they continued to move ahead, a solider flanked in behind Nate, coming from out of nowhere in the darkness, parallel to him. Then another joined in line, then another eventually filling the space all around Gabriel, not missing a step towards the northern end of the structure.

As they neared the tree line, Gabriel could make out a solid wall of blackened steel. They came to a sudden halt. Tall lights burned brightly on top of the wall, illuminating the ground below.

Nate knelt down as he surveyed the area. "No guards in the area ... what's our status?"

Father Clarence kept his voice at a whisper as well. "Alpha, Bravo and Charlie have them tied up, holding their approach at the gates of the facility."

"How's the other side of the pond?" Nate stayed still.

"All marks have begun their operations, no problems yet. We took them completely by surprise." Father Clarence chuckled.

"ETA on any enemy reinforcements to our position?" Nate crawled forward.

Gabriel stared along the top of the armour plated walls of the facility, looking for any movement.

"Intercept teams are in place but the owners of this facility aren't showing their faces."

"Look alive gentlemen, we hold this exit position … I want kills all around, we do not want to draw any extra attention to ourselves," Nate commanded the soldiers around him. "Alright everyone, let's do this!" He stepped out of the safety of the woods.

CHAPTER FORTY-TWO

THE TEAM SPRINTED IN PAIRS. Gabriel stayed with Father Clarence, following his rush towards the towering wall of steel. Each pair spread out along the base of the massive wall, avoiding the shine of the lights. His hand ran across the series of bolts and heavy plates – welds running between each of the pieces to form an impressive barrier.

"Lowest density is here." One of the soldiers scanned the wall with a set of goggles over his eyes.

Gabriel moved with the group towards the spot. The soldier signalled his partner to begin their job. He pulled a hand held laser cutter from his pack. He pulled at the fuel line attached to it – giving himself room to work.

Gabriel jumped, as the laz saw popped loudly against the steel. He hoped no one heard the noise. The sound dulled as it dug into the steel, heating the surface around it with a soft glow. He stared at the cutter as it worked its way through the armoured steel – it moved slow, the soldier making adjustments for speed and cutting depth every several inches. Nate grew restless, whispering into his radio for updates and checking his wrist watch. He crept over to the soldiers working on the armoured wall.

He returned to Father Clarence and Gabriel. "The damn plating on the wall is thick. They reinforced it from the inside with something. The laz saw is having problems cutting through it. I didn't think it would take this long."

"I don't think they like uninvited guests." The Father smiled.

"Time isn't our friend. If the team at the main gate gets too aggressive and we are not inside – we could lose all the information about who's behind this place." Nate glanced at his watch again, throwing up his hands in frustration.

"Can we preheat the steel with flares or something to help the laz saw move faster?" The Father frowned at the wall.

"Heat?" Gabriel was confused.

Nate grunted as he wrapped on the wall with his knuckles. "This is armour plating. It's damn thick too. Only weakness is heat, but using flares is going to draw a lot of attention. I don't –"

Gabriel cut him off. "I can do it."

"What?" Nate stared at him.

"I can melt steel. Heating up the wall will be easy." He shrugged at Nate, not sure how to explain it any easier.

Nate grabbed him by his vest, pulling him as they went back up along the wall to where the team was trying to cut through it. He pointed at the wall then spoke over the radio, "Robins get ready to speed up."

Robins looked back at Nate, plainly confused by the order. Gabriel reached out, placing his hand against the rough steel wall. A pulse of heat filled the air as the rusted steel surface turned red and glowed. Robins quickly adjusted the laz saw and pushed it towards Gabriel's hand. His partner, Volmer, secured clamps into the thick cuts of steel, grasping the back of the plates. Gabriel remained focused, kneeling on the ground beside them. His left hand glowed against the steel plating as he kept it just in front of the saw.

Things were going well. With his help, the team was making

up for lost time. Only a couple of feet remained as the laz cut through the plating without a problem. The rest of the team stayed silent, scanning the area for any signs of discovery. Father Clarence had moved up in front of Gabriel to keep him covered.

"Simply amazing." Father Clarence commented over the radio.

Nate threw a rock at him hitting him square in the back. "Pay attention."

The Father turned away from Gabriel and looked down the wall into the darkness. Gabriel followed his stare, struggling to make anything out past the lights. The tall trees even vanished in the darkness. A single pulse of light flashed from the tree line. Followed quickly by another, just seconds after the first. Father Clarence fell back against the wall, grabbing at his shoulder as he fell.

"Sniper!" Nate hollered over the radio.

The team hit the ground and fanned out looking for cover.

Father Clarence rolled into the base of the wall beside Gabriel. "It's a small caliber round," grunted over the radio. "They're close!"

Gabriel's eyes flashed with heat, his vision warping the darkness into a silhouette of outlines. There was movement in the treeline, two figures repositioned behind a makeshift blind of branches, their rifles at the ready. He crawled over the injured Father, trying to keep his eyes focused on their attackers location.

"I can see them —"A pulse of light exploded from one of the barrels. Before he could react, it slammed into his chest, sending him toppling over backwards.

"Gabriel!" Nate's voice erupted in his ear.

He whispered back "I'm fine. The ore stopped it."

"Don't move! Everyone stay low to the ground, they've got us completely pinned." Nate ordered.

"They're in the treeline. About 200 yrds up, hiding in a blind." Gabriel stayed still, playing dead.

"Lawrence. You see them?" Nate whispered.

"The blind is my sights." The soldier replied.

"Chamber an incendiary round. Punch one through the blind." Nate paused.

"Taking the shot." Lawrence whispered.

A streak of fire blazed out across the darkness, as the round slammed into the blind. It exploded into flame. The air around Gabriel filled with muffled popping noises as the team targeted the blazing blind. A dozen streaks of light pounded into it, sending embers and shattered wood flying. The shooting ended and Robins twisted the top of a small black container, throwing it out in front of them. It erupted with thick grey smoke, covering them. The team rushed towards Gabriel, surrounding him, each scanning the area around them for more enemies.

Nate's voice came over the radio after a minute of terrifying silence. "We're clear." Gabriel breathed out and climbed to his feet with Robins' help.

Breathing heavily, he could see a faint black silhouette moving through the smoke towards them – Nate. He ran towards the priest holstering his side arm and signalled the rest of the team to flank out and cover them.

Nate ripped open Father Clarence's vest and shirt with a knife, inspecting his wounds. Gabriel joined him hoping for the best.

The Father faked a smile. "I must have forgotten to say enough prayers this morning!"

"That'll teach ya." Nate rolled him over, inspecting the exit wounds. "God still loves you though. The bullets passed straight through."

Ing dropped to his knees beside the Father, taking his pack off to reveal a field kit of medical supplies. Nate rifled through it, setting the items he needed on the ground beside him.

"This is gonna hurt," Nate warned Father Clarence as he put on some latex gloves.

The Father recited a prayer in Latin as Nate sprayed the wounds down with an aerosol can. The priest winced in pain, continuing his prayer, over and over. Nate smeared a blue paste over the wounds, front and back, his fingers digging deep inside the openings. Blood spit back at him, as his fingers came back out of the wound. They laid the Father down on his back, and put a loose stick in his mouth.

"Bite down." Nate's jaw line tense.

The blue paste steamed, as a scorched meat smell filled the air around them as the paste cauterized the wound. Nate grabbed at the father's flailing arms, fighting to keep him still. Gabriel rushed over to help hold him down, as the priest writhed in pain. Nate eye's met his gaze as he fought to hold onto the father. "Another couple of seconds! I know it hurts like hell. You won't feel a thing soon, I promise."

A minute later, the Father passed out. Nate patted Gabriel on the back. "He'll live but I have to send a man back with him for pickup, which cuts into our team. You, alright?" He pulled out a chunk of ration, tore it in half, and offered it to Gabriel.

He nodded, taking the food with shaky hands. "I'll be good."

One of the soldiers picked up the Father, hoisting him over his shoulder and sprinted toward the cover of the woods.

Nate looked around at the remaining team. "They were watching the wall, they guessed we would come in this way. We don't have a choice to turn back. We need to focus, who knows what else is going to be waiting for us but whatever it is let's hit hard and fast. Gabriel, you're going to have to go alone. Find the main vault and take out the black ore there. The rest of us will put charges in the laboratories and then we all get the hell out. Destroy as much of that ore as you can, the rest we'll bury in rubble."

"No problem." Gabriel said with his mouth full. .

"Alright." Nate looked at his watch. "We've got nine minutes until our intercept teams hit their reinforcements. That buys us, maybe, five more minutes so we gotta move fast in there but be careful."

The hole in the wall was ready, the team already making their way inside. Nate pointed for Gabriel to join them. He stepped through the steel panel to the inside of the wall, which was lined with cinder blocks. He waited as the soldiers knocked out some of the cinder blocks, creating a small space they could slide through. The small opening led to a bright white hallway, lights buzzing softly overhead. Two of the soldiers assumed flanking positions at the end of each side of the hallway, signaled it clear. Two more soldiers stayed back behind the cinder block wall, securing the heavy steel panel back in place with clamps from the inside to hide their entrance.

Nate gathered everyone up. "Okay. Robins and Lawrence will hold our exit, Ing and Grutz will take the west labs." He pulled out the layout of the building, marking it off for the soldiers to see. "Volmer and I will take the east labs" He ran his fingers along the map to the opposite side of the building. "Gabriel you know your path. Now that we are inside, the boys at the front gate are going to get loud. That should keep the halls clear in here but my guess is they know we're coming, so don't take any chances and move silently."

Nate synced his watch with everyone, including Gabriel, marking twelve minutes on a timer, then he thumbed the radio. "Alpha, Bravo, Charlie ... we are home ... I repeat we are home ... knock on the front door." A simple "roger" came back over the radio.

"I want radios on all the time in here. We need to know what everyone else does. No mistakes – let's be fast. In and out." Nate gave Gabriel a final pat on the back as they travelled down the hallway, then split into different directions.

The back of the building was abandoned just as Nate had predicted. Gabriel found his entrance to the lower levels. The maintenance hatch in front of him popped open with ease. Two stories of steel rungs hung from the wall below him, each covered in rust and slime. He took a deep breath and set his foot down on the first rung.

The dark hole felt eerie. He climbed down carefully, passing dripping pipes and electrical wires running along the walls. Keeping his focus on the slippery rungs, he made it to the bottom. Safely stepping off the last rung, he checked his watch – 8:51. He tried the door leading out, but the handle didn't move. *Locked.* He kicked the door open, the lock blowing out part of the wall as it smashed open. He bolted down the hallway to a large steel door as his map had showed him.

Staring at the keypad to the left of it, he remembered what Father Clarence had explained to him in one of their meetings. *"Melt the green and white wires together so they short, then pull out the 8 pin cable reader from the unit and plug it into this ..."*

Gabriel pulled the electronic device out of his vest and followed his instructions, prying the keypad open with a small steel tool. It sparked as the device activated, scanning for the right sequence. A small click on the chip sounded out and the steel door slid aside revealing a decontamination room, with white suits hanging on the walls. He quickly ran through the chamber and burst the door at the end of it open with another good kick.

"How's it going?" Nate's voice echoed in his ear.

"Just making my way to the vault. Not a soul here. Maybe the snipers were just lucky." He sprinted through the area, turning down another hall.

"I hope so." Nate didn't sound convinced.

Gabriel rounded two more corners, ignoring the doors on either side of them. His boots screeched as he came to a sudden halt. He stared down the hallway from where he came from, pulling out his map. He retraced his steps. *Shit.*

"Nate!" Gabriel twisted around, looking up and down the hall. "They don't match!"

"What do you mean? What doesn't match?"

"The floor plan is different." He tried not to panic.

"Shit. Do your best to find it."

CHAPTER FORTY-THREE

Nate pointed out two more places for Volmer to set up charges and looked at his watch. 5:28. He pulled out his map and opened it over a table, staring at it in the vacant dark lab. He flipped to the final floor, searching for something to help Gabriel.

A computerized voice announced over the speakers in the lab, "Decontamination Complete".

He dropped to a knee and slid behind a table, drawing his side arm. He cocked the hammer back with a click. A slow shuffling of boots echoed on the floors ahead of him. Thin red beams of laser sights rolling across the dark room.

He stayed hidden. Sharp bangs of gunfire rang out in his earpiece. Ing's voice came over the radio. "Troops inside!"

Nate glanced at his watch again keeping himself hidden from any of the unwelcome guests in the lab. 4:49. *They know we're here.* His gut tightened.

A series of pops filled the air, followed by the loud collapse of bodies on the ground.

A low voice, in a thick Russian accent, came over the earpiece. "Room cleared, east lab cleared."

He peaked out from behind his cover. Volmer was circling the room, checking the bodies for movement.

Nate sprinted to the lab's computer and stuck a small optic stick into the port and powered the computer up. The light on the small stick flickered. The artificial intelligence took over and hacked the system, sending out every bit of data it could find.

"Optics setup in the east lab ... how's west?"

"We're pinned!" Ing's voice rang out over the background noise of gun fire.

He remained calm and motioned for Volmer to check the hallway. He switched his radio to an open frequency, not caring about who was listening. "Intercept, do you copy? I repeat do you copy?" Something in their plan had gone wrong, he could feel it.

A shaky voice answered the radio. "Hello? Sir, I copy"

"What's going on out there?"

"They've broke our back, sir" The soldier's voice fluctuated. Nate could hear the panic all around him. "We don't know where they came from!"

Nate cursed under his breath and kept listening to the report.

"They have most of the front team surrounded. We are attempting to regroup but they are everyw –" The radio went dead.

3:37.

His heart pounded as he darted out of the lab at a run. "Heading to the west labs," he informed the team. At the end of the hall, he could see Volmer crouched low, signalling him to hold. He crept towards him, glancing around the corner – guards approached from down the hallway. Nate signalled to count down from five as they readied to engage them. Nodding, Volmer raised his hand opening it wide – with his fingers and thumb counting down. *Five, four, three, two, one.*

Nate erupted from his cover, skidding around the corner past Volmer, firing shots with his pistol at the team of defenders. They were in full combat gear, their faces hidden behind the sheen of their combat visors. The bolts of light found their targets but failed to penetrate the armor. Red beams of light traced after him as he sprinted for cover. He smashed through a thin glass wall of an office and scrambled behind the desk. Everything on the office wall exploded. Rounds of light blasting into the room.

He crawled towards the corner of the front of the room, staying outside of their shooting angle. He kept his back against the wall, grasping the sub machine gun hanging across his chest. Sweat dripped off his brow. Wiping it away with his arm, he gripped the weapon tightly, readying himself for a fight. As he was about to return fire around the corner, a small black metallic ball bounced along the shiny floors towards the attackers. He dropped to his knees, covering his head. A spray of marbles ejected from it, pelting the area and armored enemies with small explosions.

His ears rang from the blast in the hallway. He passed his arm through the broken glass wall that remained. He held the grip tight and squeezed the trigger. The gun vibrated in his hand, as he blindly shot it down the hall. It sent what looked like a constant beam of light towards the armoured attackers. Volmer joined in the fight, spraying more bolts of light at the guards. Nate leaned out to take better aim. The shells slammed through the weakened armour, exploding into burst of blood as the guards fell to the ground. The final casings clinked off the floor and he took a deep breath, reloading his weapon.

Volmer slid into the room on his knees. "Hallway clear."

Nate patted him on the back. "Good thinking there." His watch beeped as they ran out of time. "Shit. We need to move!"

They sprinted towards Ing and Grutz on the west side of the building. He called over the radio to try and get a response from them. "Ing ... Grutz ... do you copy?"

Robins spoke. "Exit is still good."

A garbled response followed over more gunfire. He couldn't make it out.

He knew they would reach them sooner by foot and gave up on the radio. They passed through the original hallway – two bodies lay on the floor. Two sleek black barrels poked out of the wall. Robins and Lawrence keeping their escape through the wall safe. He sprinted down the hall with Volmer, ignoring the two men.

He slowed his pace as they neared the west laboratories, his weapon ready as they moved towards the bursts of light coming from the next hallway. He tapped his trigger finger, sending several bolts of light into the backs of several armoured guards blocking the entrance to the labs.

"Clear!" Grutz yelled over the radio.

Nate burst into the lab, keeping his weapon ready. Grutz stood up waiting for them from behind a tall raised laboratory bench. The reinforced base was covered in bullet holes. Nate smiled at Grutz, lowering his weapon and moved around behind the bench. Ing was furiously working on a laptop, completely ignoring their arrival.

"What the hell are you doing!" Nate scolded him. "We're compromised. Let's go!"

Ing hit the keyboard with another fury of characters then looked up at Nate. "We're in more trouble than that … Take a look."

Nate stared at the screen, searching for the answer. Ing had a program open on the screen. A remote uplink into T.E.R.A.'s mainframe and research department.

"That doesn't make any sense."

"It might not be T.E.R.A. directly but they are all over the research." Ing jumped up on to his feet.

Nate didn't have time to debate the topic. He had to focus on getting everyone out of there alive. "Pack it up. The fight outside is lost."

CHAPTER FORTY-FOUR

GABRIEL ABANDONED HIS SET OF PLANS AND SEARCHED THE LOWER LEVELS. He forced open every door in the hallway. Nothing. He retraced his steps back to the dead end he found earlier, searching for something he might have missed.

Where is it?

His hands ran along the smooth cold surface of the wall, one side to another. He knocked his knuckle against the surface and listened. An echo. He repeated the knocking. The other side sounded hollow. He could hear the emptiness behind it. He focused, and pressed into the cold steel wall with his glowing hands. The steel turned red instantly, getting brighter and brighter until it burned white hot, lumps falling down the wall. He dug his fingers into the hot surface, breaking through to the other side, just inches away. His hands continued to melt the hole wider and wider, pressing the scorching steel closer to the floor. Several minutes of working the steel and the hole was large enough to step through.

On the other side he found a hallway – not listed on the map – lined with steel doors on each side. All double bolted shut with small panels of reinforced glass in them. He rushed to the first door, peering through the small glass window, his eyes searching the darkness.

His stomach twisted. There were people strung up along the walls, each of them barely clinging to life. His hand shook with anger as he unbolted the door and stepped inside. Machines pumped their blood through tubes into big clear containers full of ore – a brutal manner of recharging. The people's faces looked like ghosts; stripped of all their will to live but unable to die. The ore pulsed deep within, as if it was drinking the red fluid. This is what he feared. What he couldn't allow the world to become.

Gabriel's stare was broken by Ing's voice on the radio. "Troops inside." He pulled back his sleeve on his wrist. 4:48. He couldn't save them.

He turned down the flurry of activity over the radio and rushed to another door, breaking it open despite its lock. The room held more victims. Tubes plumbed into their chests – feeding another machine in obedience to the ore's need for blood. One man's eyes had lost their colour. He stared into the darkness of the ceiling. Room after room, he found the same nightmare. The same disregard for life. Men, women, children – it didn't matter. No one deserved this – their future stolen from them to feed the rest of the world. He walked over to the machine and stared at the dull ore, resting in the steel tank, bathing in blood. This was no way to live, death was the only mercy left for these people. One by one, he unplugged the lines attached to them. His anger building with each one, the ore surging in his chest for a release. His watch beeped, he was out of time. He needed to end this.

At the end of the hall lay an open room larger than the others. As he approached, it reeked of death, nearly causing him to throw up as the stench overcame him. He pressed the old copper switch on the wall, igniting a series of overhead lamps. Shadows around the room moved as the light swayed from the fight outside the base walls. A section of one of the walls offered a strange glassy reflection of himself. The rest of the room was crude – reinforced concrete walls with small chips hammered out of it, as if someone had chopped at them with a blunt axe. The source of the stench came from a grate in the middle of the room. It drained any fluids splattered on the floor and walls. Several stands stood in the room, with primitive guns mounted on them. A series of steel racks and leather straps stood across from them. A table rested against the entrance wall with ammunition all over it and several steel containers with small shards of ore. The bullets glowed as he approached. The ore tipped rounds were all different in design – he guessed they were still searching for the best results.

"Isn't fate a funny thing. Here I spent countless resources searching for you, all in the hope of bringing you here." A light flashed from beyond the glassy wall in the room. Gabriel twisted on the spot to face the voice. "And here you are, playing soldier with your friends from the Church." Cymru grinned at him and laughed. "I knew the Church would target this facility but once I heard their plan to bring you along – I couldn't miss that opportunity."

"What are you talking about?"

"Oh, Gabriel. Everyone's corruptible – even priests dream of sin. Supply that to them and well, they became an addict, trading anything for more." Cymru paced behind the wall.

"All this for me?"

"Of course. You should have listened to your brother." He chuckled. "I wouldn't have had to kill so many people."

"You better pray that the wall is strong enough to stop me." He summoned the ore down into his hands, ready to strike the surface.

"Impressive control but I doubt you are that strong. The design of this polymer is quite unique – as you can see from the room. I doubt you will be able to break through this fast enough to reach me." Cymru crossed his arms. "If you would like to try, I can give you a head start before I call my men in." He shrugged smugly.

Gabriel abandoned his plans, letting the energy dissipate from his hands. "So, this dungeon is yours."

"One of many – as governments realize they have no future without the ore. I will build even more. Filled with people like you. Your immunity to the ore makes you perfect for recharging it. We will have a lifetime after lifetime of reusable energy – and in that time the earth will renew itself. It will be a new beginning for us, a chance for generations to survive the apocalypse we created. Don't you see, you're destined to sacrifice yourselves for the greater good." Cymru waved his hands.

"There is always another way. We can change, adapt – learn to survive." He shook his head.

Cymru laughed. "Just like your father, your power over the ore blinds you to the truth. I studied your kind for years, trying to reproduce the mutation in your DNA. Hoping we could change everyone – make everyone immune to the ore. It was a such a foolish dream. I quickly realized the solution was not to make everyone like you, but to use you for what you were made for. Think of it – your life traded for a million others. Some would call that heroic."

"What's happening in these rooms is murder." Gabriel's chest swelled with energy.

"No, it's progress!" Cymru gritted his teeth. "We've done it for thousands of years and no one complained except those sacrificed to move us forward in our evolution."

He glared at Cymru, rage vibrating through his body. The ore burned with each pulse – his heart beating fast. "You're a monster."

"I beg to differ. Don't waste your life opposing me. Stand with us like your brother – the future is ours for the taking." Cymru's words pierced Gabriel. "How can you not see that?"

Gabriel stepped towards him, white heat surging from his chest. "What did you do to my brother?"

"I gave him what he wanted. I unlocked the power that rested within him. It was beautiful. The way the ore manifests within your bodies – it's truly incredible." Cymru paced in the small space. "I have augmented individuals with ore for years. For some it just destroys the body – they don't survive the operation. But those that do – the truly gifted like you and your brother – the ore makes them gods among men."

"You implanted ore in him?" Gabriel was shocked.

Cymru smirked. "You seem surprised?"

"Adin would never agree to that."

"Well, he wasn't given much of choice, but in the end I knew what was best for him. And he thanked me." Cymru smiled.

"You son of a bitch!" Gabriel rushed the clear wall and slammed a glowing fist against it. The surface barely cracked.

Cymru laughed aloud. "Gabriel, don't bother. Just surrender. Even if you don't, you're mine."

He refused to give up and slammed his fist into the impenetrable wall again. It didn't do much. He searched the table for something to break through the wall. The ammunition would be useless, there wasn't enough power in the shells to dent the surface. He popped open the steel containers, each filled with lose shards of ore. A red shard was the size of his fist. He picked it up immediately and turned around to face the wall. The whole room changed to a fiery red. He marched at the wall and slammed the shard against it. The shard melted into the surface, the energy in his chest feeding it more and more heat.

"What are you doing?" Cymru stepped back away from the wall.

"Exactly what you did to everyone else here." Gabriel gritted his teeth and pressed the ore deeper into the surface.

"Stop!" Cymru dashed to a ladder and began to climb it.

It was too late. The shard pierced the wall, Gabriel's fist forcing it through the thick polymer. The super-charged ore flooded the room with fierce energy. Cymru disappeared upward, out of Gabriel's view. It was too late, he was feeding the ore more and more power – the ruby light from the wildly energized crystal filled the small space. He knew it wouldn't take long. Cymru fell backwards on to the floor of the room, gasping for air. Gabriel dropped the stone on the ground beside him.

The old man's hand shook as he pressed the silver disc behind his ear. "Help!" He coughed as his nose began to bleed. "Someone get down here!"

Gabriel wanted to watch the man writhe in agony but he had a job to do. He didn't say anything and turned to leave the room.

"Wait!" Cymru screamed at him. "Please! I – I can save your friends at the Church! The Horsemen are there."

Gabriel wanted the man to die, to rot in that small room, but he needed to hear this. "What are you talking about?"

"Open the door! I'll tell you everything. Get me out of here!" Cymru pointed at the pin pad at the end of the wall. "9 … 8 … 2 … 6." He struggled to get the numbers out.

Gabriel punched it in and the door to the room released and slid it sideways. "Finish your story or I shut the door."

"One of the Patriarchs is not what he seems. He deals with the Horsemen, they corrupted him. He told us your plan." Cymru struggled to get to his knees and crawled towards the door. "They intend to tear the Church apart from the inside."

"Where's my brother?" Gabriel stared at him.

"I – I don't know. Adin left. He escaped." Cymru grunted as he continued towards the door.

"So he's alive." Gabriel breathed in deeply, holding back his tears.

"Yes." Cymru collapsed just feet from the exit. "I swear it. Help me, please."

"Help yourself." Gabriel grabbed the steel containers off the table and dumped them all over the floor.

"What are you doing?" Cymru recoiled, clutching himself.

"You put people through hell. I'm going to give you a taste of that. You want out … you can crawl." He shook another of the steel containers out all over the floor. Shards sparked and chipped as they hit the floor. He threw the final container down and marched out of the room, leaving Cymru screaming behind him.

He needed to find the ore. Pressing forward he continued his search of the floor. Room after room was empty, each full of the same equipment for recharging the ore. The last room held two large steel doors, towering above him, built with strength to hide their precious treasures. He pressed his hand against one of the massive steel doors – its cold touch sending a chill down his spine. Something strong lay behind it. A menacing unknown. Waiting for him.

He searched the room for a key pass but found nothing. No handle, no screen and no keyhole. The doors were completely sealed.

"Nate! You gotta leave! They know we're here," he cried out into the radio, turning up the volume.

Nate was obviously running, his voice bouncing with each step. "We're trying! Did you find the cache?"

"Yeah, I am at the doors but there is no keypad, lock or anything to open this thing."

"Stay put! We are heading to you – Volmer move!" Nate screamed. Gunfire echoed in the background of the radio.

There was no time. He couldn't wait for Nate and it sounded like he had enough trouble upstairs. Gabriel yelled angrily and slammed his fist into the centre of the doors. It glowed as he hit the surface and the steel bent from the impact. Again, he drove his other fist into the surface – aiming at the same spot. Right where the two doors met. The steel gave way to his strikes, folding deeper into itself, exposing a large crack between the two doors. He tried to muscle the doors apart, putting his leg against the one wall and pulling on the thin crack. Nothing. He tried again, his veins filling with light, desperate to pull the doors apart. The door creaked, barely separating.

It was progress. Enough to slide his hand between the steel doors. He took off his vest, freeing himself from all the equipment – including his ear piece. He stood in front of the doors and focused on strengthening his body – channelling his rage – unlocking everything the ore could give him. Beams of bright light rocketed through his muscles, his skin on fire. He plunged his fingers deep into the crater of the door, his hands glowing. They burned as they pierced the crack between the two titanic panels. The door screeched as it began to give way. Sparks rained down on him as the locks broke, sending bits of steel and parts to the floor. Gabriel opened it enough to start sliding his body into the gap, his back up against one side as he continued to fight his way through the doors.

He spilled out of the gap into a large dark room. The door sprung partially closed behind him, as more pieces of it fell to the floor. He paused, trying to catch his breath but something sucked the air from his lungs with each breath. Something in the room. It seemed completely empty and void of everything. The air didn't move. It choked him as he coughed, trying to catch his breath. He spotted a switch on wall beside him and punched down the large button with the base of his hand.

The room awoke to the glow of yellow lights, one after another in sequence around the room. There it stood. The black ore. Death in its purest form. Gabriel stopped breathing. It was not a cache of pieces like they had hoped. It was a single massive boulder. Larger than him. He stood there stunned by its presence. *How do I do this?*

His thoughts broke as Nate yelled from the hallway. He turned to look through the gap of the door, seeing Nate rush into the room.

Nate surveyed the double doors and looked at him on the other side, shaking his head., "I don't even want to know … do your thing and let's get out of here!"

"Nate …" Gabriel paused, not sure what to tell him.

"The team's at the exit. I can wait in the hall. How many pieces can you take out? Can you contain each one? Let's …" Nate stabilized himself, grabbing on to the doorway, fighting the ore's effects. "Damn …"

"Nate, look." He stepped aside, allowing Nate to peer into the large lit room.

He squinted at first, then his eyes widened with fear.

"Come on." Nate stretched his arm out in the gap of the two doors, trying to push them apart and reach Gabriel. "We are getting you out of there!"

Gabriel shook his head and stepped back. "No." He straightened. "I have to stop things here and now."

"No!" Nate yelled at him "We will find another way! We can detonate it from a distance and blow this place apart. Burying it!"

"It won't stop them!" Gabriel stamped his foot against the concrete floor. "It will never stop them. They will recover it. Make another facility. One that we won't be able to touch! It has to be this way!"

"No!" Nate slammed his hand against the steel door and rested his head on the small gap. "Please … don't. Let's go." He reached his hand through the gap towards Gabriel. "Don't do this! It'll kill you!"

"This is why I came here. I have to do this. No one else can." He grabbed Nate's hand pushing it back through the gap as he rested his head against the door just a foot away from Nate's face. He could see the tears on Nate's face.

"I'll make it. I promise." He broke into a smile as he felt tears on his own face.

Nate stared back at him. Nodding his head at Gabriel, he grabbed the small radio off the floor, handing it through the gap to him. Gabriel took it. Nate tried to smile then turned and walked away.

Gabriel's eyes burned with tears. Nate disappeared out of his sight and he turned to face the giant ore. He put the earpiece on and listened to Nate's shaking voice. "Fall back. Everyone, fall back."

Gabriel stood there, staring at the massive black boulder that was patiently waiting. Several minutes passed until he heard Nate's shaky voice: "We're clear. I'll see you on the other side, kid. I'm not going anywhere."

"Goodbye, Nate." Gabriel took off the radio and let it drop to the ground, the clatter echoing in the room.

He remembered what Cymru had said, scrambled to scoop up the radio. "Nate! Can you hear me." Nothing but static. *Damn.* They needed to know about the Horsemen and one of the Patriarchs. He had to survive.

He marched towards the ore, his skin searing as he got closer. Memories of his father, mother, and brother flowed into his mind, strengthening him. His father's words, "I *find myself in a position of a destroyer of the ore … I must find a means to safely destroy the ore rather than leave it in the hands of those who would do evil with it.*"

Other voices spoke in his head, as he continued his slow stride towards the black boulder. "*He felt responsible for all the ore and the way it was being used. It defined him, made him make decisions to try and change the ore's fate: to change all of our fate.*" Kyrie's voice rang out.

"*I would like that.*" Claire's smiling face froze in his mind. He held on to the thoughts, his skin glowing, his hands brighter than he had ever seen. He pressed them down onto the cold, black surface. Images of pain and death swallowed him. Fear flooded his mind. He desperately wanted to pull away. To run back to Nate.

He closed his eyes. His parents were smiling before him, walking in an open field of tall golden grass. Arm in arm, they strolled through it with no effort. They called for Gabriel to follow. He wanted to run towards them. Meet their arms waiting to wrap him up and tell him how much they loved him. It would have been easy to give up but he needed to survive. To live. His eyes popped open. The room filled with bright white light, as he screamed out in pain, consumed by the blinding light.

Outside Nate and his team waited on a small bluff overlooking the facility. The ground trembled all around them, as if a great earthquake had struck. Trees and broken branches came crashing down as they dived for cover. Nate struggled to keep his balance, as a wave of energy blew out across the woods, knocking him to the ground. The facility exploded in a mass of pure white light, filling the night sky like the mid-day sun. The armoured walls burst violently, sending chunks of steel and concrete flying in every direction. Enemies near the entrance of the base, scrambled to flee but were engulfed by the energy. Everyone was consumed. The blast destroyed everything it touched. The huge ball of pure energy carved a crater into the earth, swallowing it as it grew. No piece of the base was untouched. The trees around the blast toppled over like a deck of cards, tearing their great roots up from the ground.

Nate refused to look away. He held on, digging his hands into the ground. The light began to retreat, pulling back to the source. The image burned into his eyes. A small object floated in the centre of the explosion, the light pouring into it. As the last of the light disappeared, it hung there glowing for a moment then a deafening crack echoed across the woods. The glow winked out and the faint object dropped deep into the crater.

Gabriel.

Daylight was fast approaching. The team of soldiers waited, positioned by the open crater. A whistle broke through the air. Two of the soldiers rushed towards a rope tied off to a huge root ball. They grunted as they heaved on the rope, pulling something up from within.

"It's about time!" Volmer called down as he joined in hauling up the rope. The darkness had almost faded completely as the sun began to rise, exposing their position.

Nate didn't care. He was almost to the surface with his salvage. Robins lay down on the edge of the crater, his arm stretched out to him. Nate grasped it and struggled up over the steep ledge. "Call for extraction."

Ing nodded and spoke into his radio as he jogged towards the treeline.

"Careful!" Nate ordered as he removed the tight straps from around his chest. His arms burned as he passed the body to Lawrence and Robins.

There was Gabriel. His clothes half burnt away, his skin covered in black soot. The crystal in his chest was exposed – huge cracks running through its surface like an empty piece of broken glass. Nate knelt down beside him, gently pressing his fingers against Gabriel's throat.

Nothing. He refused to give up. His two fingers searched for a pulse beneath the cold skin.

"ETA is thirty minutes on a fast bird," Ing returned. "We're going to have to find cover until it arrives."

Dub. A flicker under Nate's fingers. Or was it his imagination? He closed his eyes and focused, his fingers frozen to Gabriel's throat.

"Sir, we're wide open here. Commander Reinhart!" Ing reached out and touched his shoulder.

"Wait!" He glared at Ing. "No one move!" He blocked out every sound, every sense – except his two calloused finger tips. "Come on, kid." He whispered.

Dub. Again a small pulse gently pushed back against his fingers.

Nate twisted to Ing. "Make sure that bird doesn't leave without Osho and a full medical team aboard for Gabriel. Let's move out!"

Ing smiled at him, nodding. "Yes, sir!"

ABOUT THE AUTHOR

From selling time share in Cancun to working in the not-for-profit industry, B.V. Bayly has had a myriad of jobs. Never one to conform to the traditional nine to five work model, he did whatever it took to provide for his family while still maintaining the simple life they desired. Imagine his pleasure when he discovered his passion was creating and telling stories. The life of a writer is far from the norm. He resides on Vancouver Island with his beautiful wife, two energetic sons and one lazy dog.